THE
CAMBRIDGE EDITION OF
THE LETTERS AND WORKS OF
D. H. LAWRENCE

THE WORKS OF D. H. LAWRENCE

GENERAL EDITORS
James T. Boulton
† Warren Roberts

STUDY OF THOMAS HARDY

AND OTHER ESSAYS

D. H. LAWRENCE

EDITED BY
BRUCE STEELE

CAMBRIDGE
UNIVERSITY PRESS

PUBLISHED BY THE PRESS SYNDICATE OF THE UNIVERSITY OF CAMBRIDGE
The Pitt Building, Trumpington Street, Cambridge, United Kingdom

CAMBRIDGE UNIVERSITY PRESS
The Edinburgh Building, Cambridge CB2 2RU, UK
40 West 20th Street, New York NY 10011–4211, USA
10 Stamford Road, Oakleigh, VIC 3166, Australia
Ruiz de Alarcón 13, 28014 Madrid, Spain
Dock House, The Waterfront, Cape Town 8001, South Africa

http://www.cambridge.org

Library of Congress catalogue card number: 84-19872

British Library cataloguing in publication data
Lawrence, D. H.
Study of Thomas Hardy and other essays. –
(The Cambridge edition of the letters and works of D. H. Lawrence)
1. English literature – 19th century – History and criticism.
2. English literature – 20th century – History and criticism.
I. Title II. Steele, Bruce
820.9'008 PR451

ISBN 0 521 25252 0 hardback
ISBN 0 521 27248 3 paperback

Transferred to digital printing 2002

CONTENTS

GENERAL EDITORS' PREFACE

D. H. Lawrence is one of the great writers of the twentieth century – yet the texts of his writings, whether published during his lifetime or since, are, for the most part, textually corrupt. The extent of the corruption is remarkable; it can derive from every stage of composition and publication. We know from study of his MSS that Lawrence was a careful writer, though not rigidly consistent in matters of minor convention. We know also that he revised at every possible stage. Yet he rarely if ever compared one stage with the previous one, and overlooked the errors of typists or copyists. He was forced to accept, as most authors are, the often stringent house-styling of his printers, which overrode his punctuation and even his sentence-structure and paragraphing. He sometimes overlooked plausible printing errors. More important, as a professional author living by his pen, he had to accept, with more or less good will, stringent editing by a publisher's reader in his early days, and at all times the results of his publishers' timidity. So the fear of Grundyish disapproval, or actual legal action, led to bowdlerisation or censorship from the very beginning of his career. Threats of libel suits produced other changes. Sometimes a publisher made more changes than he admitted to Lawrence. On a number of occasions in dealing with American and British publishers Lawrence produced texts for both which were not identical. Then there were extraordinary lapses like the occasion when a compositor turned over two pages of MS at once, and the result happened to make sense. This whole story can be reconstructed from the introductions to the volumes in this edition; cumulatively they will form a history of Lawrence's writing career.

The Cambridge edition aims to provide texts which are as close as can now be determined to those he would have wished to see printed. They have been established by a rigorous collation of extant manuscripts and typescripts, proofs and early printed versions; they restore the words, sentences, even whole pages omitted or falsified by editors or compositors; they are freed from printing-house conventions which were imposed on Lawrence's style; and interference on the part of frightened publishers has been eliminated. Far from doing violence to the texts Lawrence would have wished to see published, editorial intervention is essential to recover them. Though we have to accept that some cannot now be recovered in their entirety because early states have not survived, we must be glad that so much evidence remains. Paradoxical as it may seem, the outcome of this recension will be texts which differ, often radically and certainly frequently, from those seen by the author himself.

Editors have adopted the principle that the most authoritative form of the text is to be followed, even if this leads sometimes to a 'spoken' or a 'manuscript' rather than a 'printed' style. We have not wanted to strip off one house-styling in order to impose another. Editorial discretion has been allowed in order to regularise Lawrence's sometimes wayward spelling and punctuation in accordance with his most frequent practice in a particular text. A detailed record of these and other decisions on textual matters, together with the evidence on which they are based, will be found in the textual apparatus or an occasional explanatory note. These give significant deleted readings in manuscripts, typescripts and proofs; and printed variants in forms of the text published in Lawrence's lifetime. We do not record posthumous corruptions, except where first publication was posthumous.

In each volume, the editor's introduction relates the contents to Lawrence's life and to his other writings; it gives the history of composition of the text in some detail, for its intrinsic interest, and because this history is essential to the statement of editorial principles followed. It provides an account of publication and reception which will be found to contain a good deal of hitherto unknown information. Where appropriate, appendixes make available extended draft manuscript readings of significance, or important material, sometimes unpublished, associated with a particular work.

Though Lawrence is a twentieth-century writer and in many respects remains our contemporary, the idiom of his day is not invariably intelligible now, especially to the many readers who are not native speakers of British English. His use of dialect is another difficulty, and further barriers to full understanding are created by now obscure literary, historical, political or other references and allusions. On these occasions explanatory notes are supplied by the editor; it is assumed that the reader has access to a good general dictionary and that the editor need not gloss words or expressions that may be found in it. Where Lawrence's letters are quoted in editorial matter, the reader should assume that his manuscript is alone the source of eccentricities of phrase or spelling. An edition of the letters is still in course of publication: for this reason only the date and recipient of a letter will be given if it has not so far been printed in the Cambridge edition.

ACKNOWLEDGEMENTS

I would like to record my gratitude to those individuals and institutions who made their materials available to me: manuscripts of 'Rachel Annand Taylor' and 'Art and the Individual', W. H. Clarke; manuscript of 'Art and the Individual', the late John Baker; typescripts of 'Study of Thomas Hardy', 'Art and Morality', 'Morality and the Novel', 'Why the Novel Matters' and 'The Novel and the Feelings', Bancroft Library, University of California at Berkeley; typescripts of 'Study of Thomas Hardy', manuscripts and typescripts of 'Art and Morality', 'Morality and the Novel', 'Why the Novel Matters', 'The Novel and the Feelings', 'The Novel', and manuscripts of 'John Galsworthy' and 'A Britisher Has a Word With an Editor', Harry Ransom Humanities Research Center, University of Texas at Austin; manuscript and typescript of 'The Future of the Novel', Columbia University; typescripts of 'The Future of the Novel' and 'The Novel', University of Tulsa; manuscript and typescript of 'The Novel', Yale University.

The Australian Research Grants Scheme funded my research and overseas travel over three years and Monash University granted me study leave and travel assistance. I gratefully acknowledge their support.

I would like to thank James T. Boulton, Warren Roberts and Michael Black for their advice and encouragement, and Lindeth Vasey for invaluable criticism and practical advice.

Many people have given ungrudging assistance in many ways to this book, and I specially thank: Louise Annand, Carl Baron, Teresa Battaglia, A. A. C. Bierrum, the late Arthur Brown, John Carswell, Mimi Colligan, the late Helen Corke, Emile Delavenay, Doreen Dougherty, Ellen Dunlap and the staff of the Harry Ransom Humanities Research Center, Paul Eggert, David Farmer, Desmond Flower, the late David Garnett, Michael Herbert, Edwin Kennebeck and the Viking Press, Norman Lambert, George Lazarus, Magdala Lee, Harold Love, Alan McBriar, Brenda Niall, D. J. Peters, Estelle Rebec and the staff of Bancroft Library, Mary Steele, Sam Steele, E. W. Tedlock Jr, Betsy Wallace, John Worthen.

February 1984   B. S.

CHRONOLOGY

11 September 1885	Born in Eastwood, Nottinghamshire
September 1898–July 1901	Pupil at Nottingham High School
1902–1908	Pupil teacher; student at University College, Nottingham
7 December 1907	First publication: 'A Prelude', in *Nottinghamshire Guardian*
early March 1908	Writes 'Art and the Individual'
19 March 1908	Reads 'Art and the Individual' in Eastwood
13 May 1908	Undertakes to rewrite 'Art and the Individual' for Blanche Jennings
1 September 1908	New version of 'Art and the Individual' sent to Blanche Jennings
October 1908	Appointed as teacher at Davidson Road School, Croydon
November 1909	Publishes five poems in *English Review*
10? March 1910	Meets Rachel Annand Taylor
30 September 1910	Requests loan of Rachel Annand Taylor's *Poems* and *Rose and Vine*; plans paper on her poetry
15 October 1910	Visits Rachel Annand Taylor and borrows her *Poems*
17? November 1910	Presents 'Rachel Annand Taylor' to the Croydon English Association
3 December 1910	Engagement to Louie Burrows; broken off on 4 February 1912
9 December 1910	Death of his mother, Lydia Lawrence
19 January 1911	*The White Peacock* published in New York (20 January in London)
19 November 1911	Ill with pneumonia; resigns his teaching post on 28 February 1912
March 1912	Meets Frieda Weekley; they elope to Germany on 3 May
23 May 1912	*The Trespasser*
September 1912–March 1913	At Gargnano, Lago di Garda, Italy
February 1913	*Love Poems and Others*
29 May 1913	*Sons and Lovers*

Chronology

June–August 1913	In England
August 1913–June 1914	In Germany, Switzerland and Italy
24 June 1914	Arrives in England with Frieda Weekley
July 1914–December 1915	In London, Buckinghamshire and Sussex
c. 7 July 1914	Invited to write book on Thomas Hardy for James Nisbet & Co.
13 July 1914	Marries Frieda Weekley in London
15 July 1914	Asks Edward Marsh for loan of Hardy books; receives them as a gift, 17 July
31 July–8 August 1914	Walking tour in Lake district; meets S. S. Koteliansky
15? August 1914	To The Triangle, Bellingdon Lane, Chesham, Buckinghamshire
c. 5 September 1914	Begins 'Study of Thomas Hardy'
11 October 1914	Sends some revised 'Hardy' MS to Kot for typing
13 October 1914	'A third' of 'Hardy' revision completed
31 October 1914	Sends second batch of 'Hardy' MS to Kot
26 November 1914	*The Prussian Officer*
5 December 1914	Sends last of 'Hardy' MS to Kot
18 December 1914	Intends to rewrite 'Hardy' again
30 September 1915	*The Rainbow*; suppressed by court order on 13 November
June 1916	*Twilight in Italy*
July 1916	*Amores*
15 October 1917	After twenty-one months' residence in Cornwall, ordered to leave by military authorities
October 1917–November 1919	In London, Berkshire and Derbyshire
December 1917	*Look! We Have Come Through!*
October 1918	*New Poems*
November 1919–February 1922	To Italy, then Capri and Sicily
20 November 1919	*Bay*
November 1920	Private publication of *Women in Love* (New York), *The Lost Girl*
10 May 1921	*Psychoanalysis and the Unconscious* (New York)
12 December 1921	*Sea and Sardinia* (New York)
March–August 1922	In Ceylon and Australia
14 April 1922	*Aaron's Rod* (New York)
September 1922–March 1923	In New Mexico
23 October 1922	*Fantasia of the Unconscious* (New York)
24 October 1922	*England, My England* (New York)
1 February 1923	Completes 'The Future of the Novel'

March 1923	*The Ladybird, The Fox, The Captain's Doll*
March–November 1923	In Mexico and USA
April 1923	'Surgery for the Novel—or a Bomb' ('The Future of the Novel') in *Literary Digest International Book Review* (New York)
27 August 1923	*Studies in Classic American Literature* (New York)
September 1923	*Kangaroo*
9 October 1923	*Birds, Beasts and Flowers* (New York)
by 16 November 1923	Writes 'A Britisher Has a Word With an Editor'
December 1923–March 1924	In England, France and Germany
December 1923	'A Britisher' in *Palms* (Mexico)
March 1924–September 1925	In New Mexico and Mexico
August 1924	*The Boy in the Bush* (with Mollie Skinner)
10 September 1924	Death of his father, John Arthur Lawrence
14 May 1925	*St. Mawr together with The Princess*
June 1925	Writes 'Art and Morality', 'Morality and the Novel' and 'The Novel'
29 June 1925	'The Novel' (revised) sent to Centaur Press
September 1925–June 1928	In England and mainly Italy
November 1925	'Art and Morality' in *Calendar of Modern Letters*; writes 'Why the Novel Matters' and 'The Novel and the Feelings'
December 1925	'Morality and the Novel' in *Calendar of Modern Letters*
7 December 1925	'The Novel' in *Reflections on the Death of a Porcupine* (Philadelphia)
January 1926	*The Plumed Serpent*
28 February 1927	Completes 'John Galsworthy'
12 March 1927	Corrects TS of 'John Galsworthy'
June 1927	*Mornings in Mexico*
Late August 1927	Corrects proofs of 'John Galsworthy'
23 March 1928	'John Galsworthy' in *Scrutinies*
24 May 1928	*The Woman Who Rode Away and Other Stories*
June 1928–March 1930	In Switzerland and, principally, in France
July 1928	*Lady Chatterley's Lover* privately published (Florence)
September 1928	*Collected Poems*

CUE-TITLES

A. Manuscript Locations

BL	British Library
ColU	Columbia University
UCB	University of California at Berkeley
UT	University of Texas at Austin
UTul	University of Tulsa
YU	Yale University

B. Printed Works

(The place of publication is London unless otherwise stated.)

Abercrombie   Lascelles Abercrombie. *Thomas Hardy: A Critical Study*. Martin Secker, 1912.

Carswell   Catherine Carswell. *The Savage Pilgrimage: A Narrative of D. H. Lawrence*. Chatto and Windus, 1932; reprinted Cambridge: Cambridge University Press, 1981.

Delavenay   Emile Delavenay. *D. H. Lawrence: L'Homme et la Genèse de son Œuvre*. 2 volumes. Paris: Librairie C. Klincksieck, 1969.

DHL Review   James C. Cowan, ed. *The D. H. Lawrence Review*. Fayetteville: University of Arkansas, 1968–

E.T.   E.T. [Jessie Wood]. *D. H. Lawrence: A Personal Record*. Jonathan Cape, 1935; reprinted Cambridge: Cambridge University Press, 1980.

Letters, i.   James T. Boulton, ed. *The Letters of D. H. Lawrence*. Volume I. Cambridge: Cambridge University Press, 1979.

Letters, ii.   George J. Zytaruk and James T. Boulton, eds. *The Letters of D. H. Lawrence*. Volume II. Cambridge: Cambridge University Press, 1981.

Letters, iii.   James T. Boulton and Andrew Robertson, eds. *The Letters of D. H. Lawrence*. Volume III. Cambridge: Cambridge University Press, 1984.
Nehls   Edward Nehls, ed. *D. H. Lawrence: A Composite Biography*. 3 volumes. Madison: University of Wisconsin Press, 1957–9.
Phoenix   Edward D. McDonald, ed. *Phoenix: The Posthumous Papers of D. H. Lawrence*. New York: Viking Press, 1936.
Phoenix II   Warren Roberts and Harry T. Moore, eds. *Phoenix II: Uncollected, Unpublished and Other Prose Works by D. H. Lawrence*. Heinemann, 1968.
Roberts   Warren Roberts. *A Bibliography of D. H. Lawrence*. 2nd edn. Cambridge: Cambridge University Press, 1982.
Tedlock, *Lawrence MSS*   E. W. Tedlock. *The Frieda Lawrence Collection of D. H. Lawrence Manuscripts: A Descriptive Bibliography*. Albuquerque: University of New Mexico, 1948.

INTRODUCTION

INTRODUCTION

'Study of Thomas Hardy'

On 24 June 1914, D. H. Lawrence returned to England with Frieda Weekley after almost nine months at Fiascherino near Lerici on the Golfo della Spezia in Italy.[1] They stayed for a time with Gordon Campbell, an Irish barrister practising in London, whom they had met the previous summer on holiday in Kent. Campbell's wife, Beatrice, was spending the summer of 1914 in Ireland, where he and the Lawrences planned to visit her in August.

Lawrence had returned to London with, as he thought, *The Rainbow* completed.[2] His immediate task was to provide his previous publisher, Duckworth, with a collection of short stories to replace *The Rainbow* which he had promised to Methuen. Within a fortnight, and while still at work on the stories, Lawrence was personally approached by another publisher with an invitation to write a short book on Thomas Hardy. On 8 July he explained the position to his agent, J. B. Pinker:

> The man in Nisbet's, Bertram Christian, has been asking me would I do a little book for him – a sort of interpretative essay on Thomas Hardy, of about 15,000 words. It will be published at 1/- net. My payment is to be 1½d. per copy, £15 advance on royalties, half profits in America. It isn't very much, but then the work won't be very much. I think it is all right don't you? When the agreement comes I will send it on to you, and we need not make any trouble over it.[3]

The publishing firm of James Nisbet and Co. had recently launched a series entitled 'Writers of the Day' edited by Bertram Christian, one of the directors, and it is most likely that he envisaged Lawrence's book on Hardy as

---

[1] Frieda left her husband, Ernest Weekley, and children in May 1912 to elope with DHL; they lived in Europe, mostly in Italy. The divorce became absolute in May 1914; DHL and Frieda's return to England in June was in part prompted by the wish to be married as soon as possible and in England.

[2] This was the penultimate version of the novel, known until May 1914 as 'The Wedding Ring'. See *Letters*, ii. 173, and *The Rainbow*, ed. by Mark Kinkead-Weekes (to be published by Cambridge University Press).

[3] *Letters*, ii. 193.

xix

one of that series. Nothing further is known for certain of Lawrence's dealings with Christian.[4]

At first he seemed keen to write the book. An extended literary study of a living established writer, and one for whom he had some affinity as well as admiration, was an agreeable challenge and would mark a quite new direction in his writing. 'I am going to do a little book of about 15000 words on Thomas Hardy', he wrote to his old friend and former teaching colleague at Croydon, Arthur McLeod. 'What do you think of that. Later on I shall ask you to lend me some Hardy books.'[5] But his personal circumstances and political events in Europe combined to change both his plans for writing the book and, to some extent, the nature of it.

On 13 July 1914 Lawrence married Frieda at the Kensington Registry Office. Three days before, he had written to Edward Marsh, another friend he had made the previous summer, and a generous patron of writers, inviting him to be a witness at the ceremony. Business at the Admiralty, where he was Private Secretary to Winston Churchill, made it impossible for Marsh to attend. Both he and Lawrence were disappointed; but only two days after the wedding, Lawrence, perhaps unwittingly, allowed Marsh to make tangible expression of his regret. He wrote not to McLeod but to Marsh asking for the loan of Hardy books for his new work:

Have you got Lascelles Abercrombie's book on Thomas Hardy; and if so, could you lend it me for the space of, say, six weeks; and if so, do you mind if I scribble notes in it? And if you've got any of those little pocket edition Hardy's, will you lend me those too ... I am going to write a little book on Hardy's people. I think it will interest me. We are going to Ireland at the end of this month. I shall do it there ... We had Campbell and Murry as witnesses at the marriage. I wish you'd been there.[6]

Marsh responded with characteristic generosity: as a belated wedding gift he sent Lawrence the complete works of Hardy and also Abercrombie's *Thomas Hardy: A Critical Study* (1912). Lawrence wrote to Marsh straight away expressing his embarrassed jubilation, adding: 'If my book – a tiny book – on Hardy comes off and pleases me, and you would like it, I dedicate it to you with a fanfare of trumpets. Thank you a million times.'[7] The materials he needed for his 'tiny book' were thus easily assembled and in accordance with his plan Lawrence must have begun his reading at once.

4 Information from A. A. C. Bierrum, a director of James Nisbet & Co. Nisbet's records were destroyed during the Second World War.
5 *Letters*, ii. 194. McLeod constantly lent and gave books to DHL.   6 Ibid., ii. 198.
7 Ibid., ii. 199–200. DHL's copy of Abercrombie, with autograph annotations, is at UT. The edition of Hardy's works is not known, but would probably be a set of the 1912 Wessex edition. See Christopher Hassall, *Edward Marsh* (1959), p. 288.

His request for Abercrombie's critical study suggests that he held that book in particular regard. It is the only book about Hardy that he is known to have read in preparing his own. He had read it first more than a year before, and later had met Abercrombie when he visited Fiascherino. '[He] *is* sharp', Lawrence wrote of him, 'he is much more *intellectual* than I had imagined: keener, more sharp-minded. I shall enjoy talking to him.'[8] Lawrence, while often in disagreement, nevertheless found a stimulus in Abercrombie's 'intellectual' reading of Hardy, and the book seems to have acted as a spring-board for his own intuitive interpretation. Meanwhile, (apart from a good deal of work on the proofs in October) Lawrence had for the moment completed his collection of stories which was to appear in November as *The Prussian Officer and Other Stories.* He sent the last story to Edward Garnett, his old friend and mentor at Duckworth's on 17 July, and in his letter he mentioned the Hardy commission: 'I *wonder* what sort of a mess I shall make of it. However it doesn't very much matter.'[9] In this apparently light-hearted spirit Lawrence embarked on his re-reading of Hardy and Abercrombie.

In less than three weeks, however, Britain was at war. On 8 August Lawrence returned to London to find that his visit to Ireland could not take place, and, more seriously, his return to Italy before the winter was now totally out of the question. A further blow came when Methuen returned the manuscript of *The Rainbow*, refusing to publish it at present: they were postponing new publications, but may also have expressed concern to Pinker about some scenes in Lawrence's novel (which Pinker would later have passed on).[10] To his agent, Pinker, on 10 August, Lawrence lamented his impecunious state: 'I am wondering how I am going to get on. We can't go back to Italy as things stand, and I must look for somewhere to live.'[11]

The Lawrences left the Campbells' house in South Kensington, and by 16 August were installed in a farm-labourer's cottage, 'The Triangle', near Chesham in Buckinghamshire. With bleak financial prospects before them they settled in.[12] In these changed circumstances Lawrence continued his reading of Hardy. The little book for Nisbet and the forthcoming volume of short stories for Duckworth now seemed his only literary and financial hopes;[13]

8 *Letters*, ii. 120.   9 Ibid., ii. 199.
10 Methuen later stated that their objection was on grounds of indecency, but most publishers returned unedited manuscripts at the start of the war.
11 *Letters*, ii. 206–7.   12 See ibid., ii. 208–10.
13 He had an article 'With the Guns' published in the *Manchester Guardian*, 18 August 1914 (reprinted *Encounter*, August 1969, 5–6) and received gifts from friends like Marsh (see *Letters*, ii. 211). In October he received a grant for £50 from the Royal Literary Fund (see ibid., ii. 223–4).

he does not appear to have contemplated immediate revision of *The Rainbow*.

On 5 September, after a further complaint to Pinker about money – 'I can last out here only another month – then I don't know where to raise a penny, for nobody will pay me' – in a sudden outburst, he wrote: 'What a miserable world. What colossal idiocy, this war. Out of sheer rage I've begun my book about Thomas Hardy. It will be about anything but Thomas Hardy I am afraid – queer stuff – but not bad.'[14] Throughout September Lawrence seems to have devoted himself exclusively to writing the first draft. He makes no reference to any other creative work. On 15 September he asked Pinker: 'If I am very badly off will you type it for me?'[15] In the event Lawrence's new friend S. S. Koteliansky offered to do it himself free.

On a walking tour of the Lake district at the end of July, Lawrence had met Samuel Solomonovich Koteliansky ('Kot'), a Russian-Jewish emigré about three years his senior. Kot had come to England as a student of economics, and, because of Russian secret police interest in him, had decided to stay on in London, where he now worked as a secretary and translator in the Russian Law Bureau in High Holborn. He took to Lawrence immediately and became a devoted and life-long friend.[16]

It was at the beginning of October 1914 that Koteliansky made his offer to type Lawrence's manuscript. Lawrence took up the offer enthusiastically, writing on 5 October:

Will you really type-write me my book – which is supposed to be about Thomas Hardy, but which seems to be about anything else in the world but that. I have done about 50 pages – re-written them. I must get it typed somehow or other. Don't do it if it is any trouble – or if it is much trouble, for it is sure to be some. I should like a duplicate copy also.[17]

Kot must have agreed at once. He visited the Lawrences on the following Sunday, 11 October, and probably took the first batch of manuscript back to London with him the same day.[18]

Thus Lawrence had written a first draft and then rewritten some fifty pages of it in the space of little more than a month. Despite his assessment of its contents as 'queer' or 'rum stuff' and not very much about Hardy, he still appeared optimistic about submitting it to Nisbet for he wrote to Garnett in mid-October: 'I have been writing my book more or less – very much

---

[14] *Letters*, ii. 212.   [15] Ibid., ii. 216.

[16] Koteliansky was to make a modest literary reputation as a translator of Russian writers – among them, Chekhov, Tolstoy and Dostoievsky. He worked always with collaborators, including DHL himself and Katherine Mansfield.

[17] *Letters*, ii. 220.   [18] Ibid., ii. 221.

less – about Thomas Hardy. I have done a third of it. When this much is typed I shall send it to Bertram Christian.'[19] But in fact he had already signalled to himself the altered nature of the book by entitling his manuscript not 'Thomas Hardy' but 'Le Gai Savaire'.[20] On 31 October he sent a further parcel of manuscript to Kot for typing, but whether he sent the first part of the typescript either to Pinker, as he had at first promised, or to Christian as he later intended, is not known but both seem unlikely.[21] During November, as the work was nearing completion, Lawrence confided in Amy Lowell, the American poet and writer whom he had met in London on the eve of the war: 'I am just finishing a book, supposed to be on Thomas Hardy, but in reality a sort of Confessions of my Heart. I wonder if ever it will come out – and what you'd say to it.'[22] From this it might be inferred that Christian or Pinker had seen part of the work and been discouraging. On the other hand, on 3 December he urged Koteliansky: 'Do please get my typing done. If I can send it in, I may get a little money for it.'[23] It remains uncertain at what point the Nisbet proposal was abandoned, and whether Pinker was inclined to try other publishers. Catherine Carswell, one of Lawrence's early biographers, states clearly that the book represented a commission that failed to please, and adds, but without supporting evidence, that the book was 'everywhere rejected at the time'.[24]

On 5 December, Lawrence despatched 'the last of the MS' for typing.[25] By this time he had already advanced 'the first hundred or so pages' into a rewriting of *The Rainbow* and sent them to Pinker.[26] This was no mere revision to meet Methuen's scruples, but a reconsideration and a thorough rewriting of the novel. With the experience of extensive revisions to the stories for *The Prussian Officer* volume[27] and of the 'Hardy' book, he approached the task with new insight and an extraordinary release of creative energy. 'It is a beautiful piece of work, really. It will be, when I have finished it: the body of it is so now', he told Pinker. He was working '*frightfully* hard' at it, and it would occupy him almost exclusively until March 1915.[28]

It was the working out of his philosophy, nourished by, and also stimulating his imaginative reading of Hardy, which gave Lawrence not only the impetus he needed to rework *The Rainbow*, but a clearer metaphysical structure which would 'subserve the artistic purpose'. In the conclusion of 'Hardy' Lawrence

[19] Ibid., ii. 212, 216, 222.
[20] DHL's French: 'The Gay Science'. See below 'The Title' and Explanatory note on 7:2.
[21] *Letters*, ii. 228, 216, 222.   [22] Ibid., ii. 235. See note 30 below.
[23] Ibid., ii. 239.   [24] In the *Spectator* (27 November 1936), 960 and Carswell 27.
[25] *Letters*, ii. 239.   [26] Ibid., ii. 240.
[27] See *The Prussian Officer and Other Stories*, ed. John Worthen (Cambridge, 1983), pp. xxx–xxxii.
[28] *Letters*, ii. 240, 239.

is virtually challenging himself to produce a novel in which the spirit of his knowledge and the body of his artistic purpose are reconciled: 'equal, two-in-one, complete. This is the supreme art, which yet remains to be done. Some men have attempted it . . . But it remains to be fully done.'[29]

But in giving his principal attention to *The Rainbow* in December 1914 he neither abandoned nor forgot his 'Hardy'. Even while Kot was typing the final pages, and although possible publication seemed more and more remote, Lawrence wrote again to Amy Lowell on 18 December: 'My wife and I we type away at my book on Thomas Hardy, which has turned out as a sort of *Story of My Heart*: or a Confessio Fidei: which I must write again, still another time'.[30] But this effort, like his attempt to type his revision of *The Rainbow*, was probably short-lived.[31] In any case it was over three months before he was free enough to concentrate on the rewriting, and by then he had abandoned altogether the idea of it as a book on Hardy. If he called the existing state of the book a 'confessio fidei', and referred to it as 'mostly philosophicalish, slightly about Hardy',[32] the new version was to be unambiguously 'my "philosophy"'.[33] Lawrence's attempts to rewrite this philosophy into a definitive form were to occupy him from time to time for more than three years.

Lawrence's Philosophy

Lawrence's first attempt to set down his distinctive philosophy had been made nearly two years before 'Hardy'. In January 1913, on completion of *Sons and Lovers*, he wrote a 'Foreword' for the novel, insisting that it was a personal exercise – like 'Hardy' a 'confessio fidei' – and not for publication.[34] In it he set down his intuitive philosophy of the relation between Male and Female, man and woman in the act of creation. As its original sub-title – 'Of the Trinity, the Three-in-One' – suggests, the philosophy is worked out through Lawrence's heterodox versions of the Christian theology of Creation, Incarnation and Trinity. These, familiar to the reader of 'Hardy', offer

---

[29] See 91:37–8, 128:12–15.
[30] *Letters*, ii. 243. DHL's reference to Richard Jefferies' *Story of My Heart* (1883) is probably more general than specific. Cf. Explanatory note on 114:19. For DHL's view of Jefferies' book see *Letters*, i. 337, 353. The reference to typing may have been to indicate to Amy Lowell that her gift of a typewriter was being put to use. Whatever he and Frieda typed of this rewritten version no longer survives.
[31] *Letters*, ii. 240. (DHL typed only the first seven pages of his revised *Rainbow*.)
[32] Ibid., ii. 292.   [33] Ibid., ii. 309; see also p. 307.
[34] See ibid., i. 507. The 'Foreword' is inaccurately printed in *The Letters of D. H. Lawrence*, ed. Aldous Huxley (1932), pp. 95–102. The quotations which follow are from DHL's MS (Roberts E373.1; UT).

probably the most strikingly idiosyncratic feature of his philosophy in this period, 1913–15.

The 'Foreword' opens, for instance, with a text from St John 'the beloved disciple': 'The Word was made Flesh', but the orthodoxy is immediately reversed: 'The Flesh was made Word'. God the Father, Lawrence asserts, is the Flesh, and we know the flesh as Woman; Woman, the Flesh, gives birth to Man, who in due time utters the Word. Woman or Flesh is the source of our instinctive or blood-knowledge. The Son, Man, constantly moves out, like a bee, from the Queen, Woman, to his work of conscious or intellectual endeavour, and back to her again for renewal.

God expels forth to waste himself in utterance, in work, which is only God the Father realising himself in a moment of forgetfulness ... For every petalled flower, which alone is a Flower, is a waste of productiveness. It is a moment of joy, of saying 'I am I.' And every table or chair a man makes is a self same waste of his life, a fixing into stiffness and deadness of a moment of himself, for the sake of the glad cry 'This is I – I am I!' And this glad cry when we know, is the Holy Ghost the Comforter.

This central perception is extensively developed in 'Hardy', twenty months later. Its fundamental tenet that human life is properly seen as of the same order as nature, imaged in the flower, governs the parable of the poppy from which the philosophy of 'Hardy' emerges. It is related to that 'inhuman' quality in human life – the quality of being, rather than knowing – which Lawrence emphasized in letters to Edward Garnett and to Ernest Collings in 1913 and 1914.

To Collings, an artist and illustrator, he wrote of his conception of the body as a flame, the intellect being the light shed on surrounding things:

I am not so much concerned with the things around ... but with the mystery of the flame forever flowing ... and being *itself* ... We have got so ridiculously mindful, that we never know that we ourselves are anything ... We cannot *be*. 'To be or not to be' – it is the question with us now, by Jove. And nearly every Englishman says 'Not to be.' So he goes in for Humanitarianism and such like forms of not-being. The real way of living is to answer to one's wants ... Instead of that, all these wants ... are utterly ignored, and we talk about some sort of ideas.[35]

His 'theology', especially when transposed into these secular terms, gave Lawrence a basis for social and literary criticism which he developed far in 'Hardy'. At the same time to see human life in terms of non-human 'life' was what Lawrence was attempting in his own art: 'that which is physic – non-human, in humanity, is more interesting to me than the old-fashioned human element – which causes one to conceive a character in a certain moral scheme and make him consistent'.[36] In this famous letter of June 1914 to Edward Garnett in which he defended *The Rainbow*, Lawrence shows the immediate influence of his recent critical reading of the Italian Futurists – Marinetti, Buzzi and Soffici.[37] For Lawrence the Futurists were instinctively right in breaking with stultifying traditions and an outworn civilisation in order to make 'modern life' the stuff of their art. But they went too far. The art of the Futurists, he said, betrays their over-insistence on intellect (the Word, the Son, the male line); it is scientific, dehumanised. Indeed, their works are diagrams and mechanisms, not art. Only when the intellect, the male, is properly balanced with the flesh, the female, is there truly living and incorporated art, he asserted.

This conception of marriage between Flesh and Word, Woman and Man, was to Lawrence both symbol and fact. It gave him a doctrine with which to interpret and criticise art – his own and others' – and on which to base his own writing. At the same time it was inseparable from the central fact in his life. Thus he records, sometimes to the mystification of his readers, two aspects of his experience: the struggle to 'get right' his art and his relationship, finally his marriage, with Frieda. To McLeod he confessed:

I think the only re-sourcing of art, re-vivifying it, is to make it more the joint work of man and woman. I think *the* one thing to do, is for men to have courage to draw nearer to women, expose themselves to them, and be altered by them: and for women to accept and admit men. That is the only way for art and civilisation to get a new life, a new start – by bringing themselves together, men and women – revealing themselves each to the other, gaining great blind knowledge and suffering and joy, which it will take a big further lapse of civilisation to exploit and work out. Because the source of all

---

[36] Ibid., ii. 182; see pp. 182–3.
[37] Filippo Tommaso Marinetti (1876–1944), Italian writer and critic, launched Futurism in his 'Manifeste du futurisme' in *Le Figaro* (Paris, February 1909). Paolo Buzzi (1874–1956), Italian poet and editor of *I Poeti Futuristi* (Milan, 1912) which DHL read. It contained essays by Marinetti and Buzzi as well as poems in Italian and French. Ardengo Soffici (1879–1964), an Italian painter, author of *Cubismo e Futurismo* (Florence, 1914) which DHL read also. See *Letters*, ii. 180–3, and Paul Eggert, 'Identification of Lawrence's Futurist Reading', *Notes and Queries* (August 1982), 342–4.
      Futurism announced a revolutionary break with the past and with artistic tradition. It asserted that 'modern life is the only source of inspiration for a modern artist', especially its characteristics of energy, speed and mechanical power. Art must therefore be dynamic. It must be free from tradition and from the dead weight of academicism; artistic emotion must be taken 'back to its physical and spontaneous source – *Nature* – from which anything philosophical or intellectual would tend to alienate it.' A work of art cannot be static, its subject isolated; it must be dynamic and reach outwards in widening circles or spheres towards an expression of the 'universal dynamism'. See *Futurist Manifestos*, ed. Umbro Apollonio (1973), pp. 110, 122.

life and knowledge is in man and woman, and the source of all living is in the interchange and the meeting and mingling of these two: man-life and woman-life, man knowledge and woman-knowledge, man-being and woman-being.[38]

The letters to Garnett and McLeod were written just as he finished the version of *The Rainbow* which Methuen was to reject, and just before he began work on the final form of his *Prussian Officer* stories. Despite his spirited defence of his novel against Garnett's criticism that 'the psychology is wrong', there is a suggestion that the criticism and his own developing philosophy together confirmed a barely recognised sense that the 'hitherto unachieved' utterance in the novel was not yet achieved. Instead, he became involved, apparently tangentially, with his 'little book' on Hardy, which in the outcome necessarily contained more of his own philosophy than criticism of Hardy. The rejection of the novel and the challenge of the Futurists and others, seem to have confirmed his instinctive sense that his philosophy must be clear before his novel could be got right.

His typically personal readings of the novels of Thomas Hardy helped greatly. The interpretations of the characters and relationships particularly in the great novels, *The Return of the Native, Tess of the D'Urbervilles* and *Jude the Obscure*, recorded in the Hardy book, while always either exciting or infuriating for the reader of Hardy, are most remarkable in the end as demonstrations of Lawrence's own approach to characterisation and the relationships between men and women. This appears to have been his aim: to lay down a philosophy of character and relationships in terms of the fundamental, opposed and opposing forces which, he asserted, underlie all life; a philosophy which had been growing steadily from his 'Foreword to *Sons and Lovers*'.

But Lawrence was also concerned with a more specific problem: the proper relation between an artist's metaphysic or philosophy and its embodiment in the work of art itself, a problem exemplified by the imbalance which, he asserted, marred both Tolstoy's and Hardy's novels. One immediate spur to his thought in this direction must have been Abercrombie's *Thomas Hardy* where the argument centred on that very question. He wrote:

The highest art must have a metaphysic; the final satisfaction of man's creative desire is only to be found in aesthetic formation of some credible correspondence between perceived existence and a conceived absoluteness of reality. Only in such art will the desire be employed to the uttermost; only in such art, therefore, will conscious mastery seem complete. And Thomas Hardy, by deliberately putting the art of his fiction under the control of a metaphysic, has thereby made the novel capable of the highest service to man's consciousness . . .

---

[38] *Letters*, ii. 181.

For if the metaphysic be there at all, it must be altogether in control ... The metaphysic will be something (as it is in Hardy's work) which can only be expressed by the *whole* of the art which contains it ... There are no novels like Thomas Hardy's for perfection of form; and this is the sign of the inward perfection ... Mr. Hardy's metaphysic is ... tragical ... for who knows better than he how the senseless process of the world for ever contradicts the human will?[39]

When Lawrence first read this in 1913, he considered Abercrombie's claim that Hardy put his art 'under the control of a metaphysic', 'beautifully said'.[40] On re-reading he had found much to disagree with: he found Hardy deficient as a metaphysician. Hardy's conscious metaphysic, he said, 'is almost silly', and when he allows it to assume control, when he forces events into line with it, 'his form is execrable in the extreme'.[41] Abercrombie had found the highest statement of Hardy's tragic metaphysic in *The Dynasts*, and made large claims for that work as 'one of the most momentous achievements of modern literature'.[42] Lawrence read his chapter on *The Dynasts* with attention, as his notes on the end papers of his copy testify;[43] but he vigorously rejected Hardy's 'sense of the purposelessness in the scheme of things', the 'habit of the immanent Will', just as he rejected 'a good deal of the *Dynasts* conception' itself as 'sheer rubbish, fatuity'.[44]

Lawrence even called in question the tragic status of Hardy's work, if by tragedy was meant the vision of an Aeschylus or Euripides. Hardy's characters, he asserted, do not struggle against the great ordinances of life and fate: they are merely at odds with the laws and opinions of a society to which, in the end, they submit.

In his reaction, Lawrence stressed in his own way an element which Abercrombie had considered secondary: Hardy showed a greater and deeper feeling, instinct, and sensuous understanding than 'that perhaps of any other English novelist'. What Lawrence concluded from his reading of Hardy and his study of Abercrombie was that Hardy's tragic metaphysic was pessimistic, perverse and untrue because it was at odds with the affirmation of his

---

[39] Abercrombie 19–20, 22, 20–1.   [40] *Letters*, i. 544.
[41] See 93:4–13.   [42] Abercrombie 225.
[43] The most connected notes are the last four which refer to passages in the chapter on *The Dynasts* concerned with Hardy's metaphysic. DHL wrote:

p. 200 the sense of purposelessness in the scheme of things

p. 202 – man's enjoyment of that which goes counter to his idea of rightness.

p. 209 The habit of the immanent Will is all that remains – so the habit in the human soul – break the habit and the Will is free 'rapt aesthetic rote'
That feeling is something apart from the Will

213 The human intelligence sees itself separate from the Will, raptly magnipotent – it would have a separate will

[44] See 93:6–7.

'sensuous understanding'.[45] Consequently the art which that metaphysic controlled was deeply flawed. Abercrombie nevertheless had thrown him back to the problem which he knew only too well from his own recent experience he must solve if his own art was to succeed. He ruefully reflected:

> It is the novelists and dramatists who have the hardest task in reconciling their metaphysic, their theory of being and knowing, with their living sense of being. Because a novel is a microcosm, and because man in viewing the universe must view it in the light of a theory, therefore every novel must have the background or the structural skeleton of some theory of being, some metaphysic. But the metaphysic must always subserve the artistic purpose beyond the artist's conscious aim. Otherwise the novel becomes a treatise.[46]

And, he might have added, the resulting form of the novel will appear imposed or contrived, rather than a natural flowering.

This disagreement with Abercrombie and Hardy may well have been the starting point for Lawrence's 'Hardy', even though it is expressed overtly only in chapter IX. But the overriding consideration was to set down his 'confessio fidei': his rejected novel, a world at war and bleak prospects even for subsistence made this only more pressing if his art and therefore his life as a writer were to progress. He must ascertain his own 'theory of being and knowing' and reconcile it with his 'living sense of being'.[47] Hardy had been important in this process, but could be pushed almost to the periphery of the work, certainly away from the centre. Lawrence soon signified this change of intention by his new title 'Le Gai Savaire' – at the head of the copy Kot was to type.

Hardy had therefore been the catalyst for Lawrence's philosophy. His diagnosis of Hardy gave him confidence in the power and the truth of his doctrine of the Law and Love, of Flesh and Word, of Being and Knowing. In his reading of Hardy it was as if he allowed Hardy to read him in turn, and he emerged from the experience with his earlier insights strengthened and clarified to the point where he could see how *The Rainbow* 'missed being itself' and what that true self must be. His joyful philosophy provided the 'structural skeleton' he needed; and in December 1914 he could say with joy of *The Rainbow*: 'It is a beautiful piece of work'. But to the extent that it was still 'slightly about Hardy', the philosophy needed to be written over again.[48]

The final rewriting of *The Rainbow* was not completed until the beginning of March 1915; but Lawrence already was planning the new version of his philosophy. He had begun rethinking it even in December 1914. Early in

---

[45] See 93:14–16.   [46] See 91:31–9.
[47] Ibid.   [48] *Letters*, ii. 146, 240, 292; see 91:35–7.

1915 he set down a new proposal which shows the influence of his 'pet scheme' for an ideal community to be called Rananim:[49]

The book I wrote – mostly philosophicalish, slightly about Hardy – I want to re-write and publish in pamphlets. We must create an idea of a new, freer life, where men and women can really meet on natural terms, instead of being barred within so many barriers. And if the money spirit is killed, and eating and sleeping is free, then most of the barriers will collapse. Something must be done, and we must begin soon.[50]

Nothing of this proposed new version of his philosophy survives, so that it is impossible to do more than guess at its content. What is fundamentally different is the purpose of the work. No longer a criticism of Hardy, an artist's metaphysic or a personal 'story of my heart', nor even some amalgam of these, it is conceived as a fervent public call to 'new life', born out of a sense that 'something must be done', that a revolution must take place.

Throughout 1915 Lawrence made several frustrated attempts to rewrite 'Le Gai Savaire'. Nothing substantial of these attempts survives, but it is clear that towards mid-1915 he abandoned for the time being his 'Christian' theology: 'I shall write all my philosophy again. Last time I came out of the Christian Camp.'[51] One reason for this change was the influence of Bertrand Russell whom he had first met in February and with whom later he proposed to give public lectures – 'he on Ethics, I on Immortality'.[52] By October 1915 he had written the six essays of 'The Crown'. Three of them were published in a little magazine *The Signature* devised and produced by himself and Middleton Murry, with Koteliansky as business manager,[53] but this public call to a new life in the midst of the horror of the First World War itself foundered for lack of support. Wise after the event, Lawrence reflected on this failure when he revised 'The Crown' for publication in a later work in 1925:

I knew then, and I know now, it is no use trying to do anything – I speak only for myself – publicly. It is no use trying merely to modify present forms. The whole great form of

[49] See *Letters*, ii. 259. For the name see ibid., ii. 252 and n. 3.   [50] Ibid., ii. 292–3.

[51] Ibid., ii. 367. Some of this rewriting may have found its way into *Twilight in Italy*. See P. R. Eggert, 'The Subjective Art of D. H. Lawrence: *Twilight in Italy*' (unpublished Ph.D thesis, University of Kent at Canterbury, 1981).

[52] *Letters*, ii. 359. DHL's lectures were never given and probably not written as such. Russell's revised lectures were given in January–March 1916 (published as *Principles of Social Reconstruction*). Russell suggested that DHL read John Burnet's *Early Greek Philosophy* (Edinburgh, 1892) and this changed the direction of his philosophy.

[53] Three issues of *Signature* appeared (4 and 18 October and 1 November 1915) with an essay from 'The Crown' in each. The public (only about fifty subscribers) was baffled by DHL's philosophy, Murry and Mansfield withdrew their support and DHL's attempt at 'action' was at an end.

our era will have to go. And nothing will really send it down but the new shoots of life
springing up and slowly bursting the foundations.[54]

As the last sentence, so close to the heart of Lawrence's philosophy, suggests,
public failure was not the end of his personal endeavour. In January 1916, he
began his philosophy for the fifth time: 'It's come at last. I am satisfied, and as
sure as a lark in the sky.'[55] But this version entitled 'Goats and Compasses'
was abandoned during 1916, and the manuscript destroyed.[56] By September
1917 yet another version was complete entitled 'At the Gates', and this time
the manuscript was sent to Pinker in whose hands it remained until 1920.[57] It
has since disappeared, so that the final definitive version of a work which
began with the book on Hardy is unknown. It would be a book of about 140
pages, he told Pinker, 'based upon the more superficial "Reality of Peace"'.[58]
Four of the essays from the 'Reality of Peace' series were written, published
by the *English Review*, in 1917, and are the last surviving testimony to this
phase of Lawrence's philosophy.[59] At what was for the moment the end of his
long struggle with his metaphysics, he recalled Koteliansky's help and advice
at the beginning in 1914:

I have written into its final form that philosophy which you once painfully and
laboriously typed out, when we were in Bucks, and you were in the Bureau. I always
remember you said 'Yes, but you will write it again'. – I have written it four times since
then. Now it is done: even it is in the hands of my friend Pinker. But I have no fear that
anybody will publish it.[60]

The text and its transmission

Neither Lawrence's first draft nor his rewritten manuscript, from which
Koteliansky typed 'Hardy', has survived. Of the three typescript versions
extant, two – designated TS (Roberts E384a) and TCC (Roberts E384b) – are
relevant to this edition. The third is an agent's copy in duplicate of TCC.[61]

---

54 Note to revised version of 'The Crown' in *Reflections on the Death of a Porcupine* (Philadelphia,
   1925); reprinted in *Phoenix II* 364.
55 *Letters*, ii. 504.
56 For accounts of this phase of the philosophy see Emile Delavenay, *D. H. Lawrence: The Man
   and His Work: The Formative Years, 1885–1919* (1972), pp. 388, 450ff., and Paul Delany, *D. H.
   Lawrence's Nightmare* (Hassocks, Sussex: 1979), chaps. v and vii.
57 *Letters*, iii. 163, 453 and 472 n. 2.   58 Ibid., iii. 152, 155.
59 May, June, July and August 1917 (reprinted in *Phoenix* 669–694).   60 *Letters*, iii. 163.
61 This typescript appears to have been made hastily by two typists. Corrections and page
   references confirm that it is a copy of TCC, not an independent version of TS. English
   watermarks on the paper show that it was made in London. When copies were needed for
   London and New York publishers, Curtis Brown presumably had these additional copies
   made. The carbon copy is uncorrected. Both copies are at UT (Roberts E384c and d).

TS is Kot's typing of Lawrence's manuscript. Since it is the only source for the work, some account of its nature and history is appropriate. It is entitled simply 'Le Gai Savaire' with no reference to Hardy. It contains 186 pages, of which the first 88 are on cartridge paper, the remainder on lightweight paper watermarked Silver Linen; there are no corrections in Lawrence's hand. Pages 1–86 are carbon copy, 87–186 are ribbon copy. Lawrence required Kot to type his manuscript in duplicate, and some months later, when asking him to type a later version of his philosophy (now lost), he specifically requested Silver Linen paper.[62] This, together with the amateur quality of the typing, is the primary evidence for TS being Kot's work: it is clearly not Lawrence's or Frieda's typing (see footnote 30). What became of the second composite copy of TS is not known: Lawrence probably destroyed it.

TS has survived, despite Lawrence's failure to find a publisher and his several attempts to rewrite the book in different form, because he gave it to John Middleton Murry 'for safe keeping' at some time during the war years.[63] On Lawrence's death in March 1930 Murry handed the typescript along with others in his possession to Laurence Pollinger of Curtis Brown, Lawrence's agent in London.[64] Pollinger had it copied in duplicate and then deposited TS in a bank. After Frieda's legal entitlement to Lawrence's manuscripts was established, TS passed to her.[65]

There is further evidence to support the authenticity of TS. Lawrence's letters to Kot indicate that he sent the manuscript for typing in three batches. The despatch dates and the estimated size of the batches of manuscript can be related to significant breaks in the typescript: pages 1–50 (manuscript sent 11 October); '50 *bis*'–86 (sent 31 October); 87–186 (sent 5 December).[66] Page 50 breaks off after 20 lines, page 86 after only 4 lines of type.

Kot was not a trained typist: 'I cannot type, and never could,' he told a correspondent in 1948.[67] The typescript contains a large number of errors; there are omissions, gaps and obvious misreadings of Lawrence's manuscript. On the other hand, since the manuscript itself may have contained heavy

[62] *Letters*, ii. 317. The letter, in BL, is on Silver Linen.   [63] See 'Publication' below.
[64] Letters from Laurence Pollinger to Frieda Lawrence and Field, Roscoe, 6 April 1933 in Curtis Brown archives; UT.
[65] After Frieda's death it was sold to UCB in 1957; documents relating to the sale are also in UCB. TS was exhibited in the Los Angeles Public Library in 1937: see Lawrence Clark Powell, *The Manuscripts of D. H. Lawrence: A Descriptive Catalogue* (Los Angeles, 1937), item 86. (It was not, however, included in Tedlock, *Lawrence MSS*, when Tedlock catalogued the manuscripts in Frieda's possession 1944–8.)
[66] There are two pages numbered 50; on the second, the pencilled word *bis* follows the numeral. Pages 87–186 have the typed numbers 95–194 but are renumbered in pencil. Mispagination and pencilled emendations are discussed below.
[67] Letter to Lucy O'Brien, 11 February 1948; BL.

revisions and corrections, it is not surprising that Kot occasionally became confused; in seven places a space is left either because of a lacuna in the manuscript or because a word was illegible. Two larger breaks in the typescript more seriously affect the transmission of Lawrence's text. Page 57 is missing which means that a passage of more than 300 words is lacking in chapter V. On page 181, in chapter X, there is a gap of five lines between '"Thou shalt love thy enemy"' and 'Therefore, since by the law ...' (see 124:39–40), and the latter is not indented. The considerable sense break in the text and the lack of indentation together suggest some missing manuscript, possibly a whole page.

Some light is shed on the evolution of the work from the chapter divisions and numberings in TS. While the chapters are in the same order as in the printed text, TS numbers them as follows: I (in two sections, only the second of which is numbered), II, III, III, V, V, IV, VIII, IX (in two sections, only the second of which is numbered), XII. In the seventh chapter (numbered IV), a misnumbering of pages begins: 87, the beginning of the third batch of typing, is numbered 95, and this misnumbering continues to the end. Since it can be assumed that Kot copied Lawrence's manuscript accurately, something of the original plan for the book can be inferred.

Lawrence said in October 1914 that he had already rewritten the first quarter of the book, and it was 'less – very much less' about Thomas Hardy. The chapter numbering of TS suggests that this early part of the first draft may have been even less about Hardy than the revised manuscript. Since the final chapter bore the number XII when Kot typed it, it is possible that the first draft contained twelve chapters, or, at least, that twelve were planned.[68] It seems that the sequence of chapters was different in the draft, and that the revision involved rearrangement (as well as rewriting and new material). Lawrence records no details of his rewriting, so the following account is based on evidence in TS.

He probably began with four chapters – here called 1–4 – where 1 and 2 represented something like the present chapters I and II, and 3 was the present IV (which, with whatever revisions Lawrence had made, reached Kot with its number unchanged, hence the second 'III' in TS) together with most of the present very brief chapter VI. The close connections in the argument between chapters II and IV, and IV and VI, are evident. The principal alteration in revision would then have been the inclusion of the present chapter III (the first 'III' in TS) between the existing 2 and 3. This chapter, 'Containing Six Novels and the Real Tragedy', can be read as an interpolation in the

---

[68] If the two sections of chaps. I and IX are counted, there are twelve.

otherwise continuing argument of the neighbouring chapters. It opens with a reminder that 'This is supposed to be a book about the people in Thomas Hardy's novels.'[69]

The fourth chapter, consisting of the first part of the old chapter 3 and still so numbered, was now followed by a 'new' chapter 5 (the first 'v' in TS) mostly about Hardy as the inserted III had been. This chapter was more carefully bonded into the argument – in this case about work and the freedom to live: the transition to Hardy's 'heroes' is less abrupt. The second part of the old chapter 3, picking up the argument about four hours a day spent in work, became the new chapter VI (though wrongly numbered v).

It seems likely that the present chapter IX with its two sections – on *Tess* and on *Jude* – is the conflation of two earlier chapters (10 and 11). As it now stands, separated from the earlier chapters on Hardy by the 'philosophy' of chapters VI to VIII, chapter IX was ironically entitled 'A Nos Moutons'. There can be little doubt that chapter X (originally 12) was the conclusion to the book, although it is untitled.

There are a number of handwritten markings in TS – deletions, additions and alterations – all made in the same heavy pencil. These were made by Frieda's third husband, Angelo Ravagli, when preparing the manuscript for sale in the 1950s.[70] Three small corrections to the text are in ink but are unlikely to be Lawrence's, and are probably Kot's.[71] The general pattern indicates that Ravagli first tried to order the pagination and the chapter numbering and then, sporadically, to make TS agree with the *Phoenix* text. (In doing so he unwittingly introduced errors made by the intermediary typist of TCC.) The 'corrections' are both sparse and random: more errors are allowed to stand than are corrected. The lack of any authorial correction may simply mean that in rewriting the work Lawrence was using either his manuscript or the other copy of TS.

TS, incomplete and uncorrected authorially, is thus the sole surviving text of Lawrence's 'Hardy' book. The author may have laid it aside as representing merely an unsuccessful commission or a stage in the writing out of his philosophy, but there is nothing to suggest that it is an 'unfinished study' as Murry and Pollinger believed.[72] It is the base-text for this edition.

---

[69] Its virtual completeness in itself made it easy to extrapolate for serial publication in the *Book Collector's Quarterly* in 1932.

[70] Powell listed TS as having 194 pages, showing that the repagination to 87–186 had not yet been done. Two erased pencilled notes, on p. 50 *bis* and p. 178, were both initialled by Ravagli.

[71] For these ink corrections see Explanatory note on 91:34. For two other ink corrections probably by Frieda see Explanatory note on 37:27.

[72] See 'Reception' below.

In July 1930 Curtis Brown had duplicate copies made of TS.[73] Of these, the carbon copy (TCC) survives. During the early 1930s while negotiations to publish the work either separately or in a collection proceeded, the two copies circulated, one on each side of the Atlantic. TCC eventually reached Edward McDonald when he agreed to edit *Phoenix* late in 1935.[74] Hence it was the basis for the only complete edition of 'Hardy'. The heading of the text reads 'Le Gai Savaire', but a title page has been added which reads: Study of Thomas Hardy | By | D. H. Lawrence. Pencilled cancellings, now faded, have been made through the words 'Study of', and a similar cancellation appears in the title on the agent's cardboard folder into which the typescript is clipped. The text has ten chapters and rationalises the confused numbering of TS.

There are corrections of two kinds: those made by the typist, and those made later by McDonald in his own hand. The typist attempted to 'tidy up' Kot's version. Unconventional punctuation (whether Lawrence's or Kot's cannot always be determined) is occasionally normalised; a nonsensical or anomalous word in TS is replaced by one the sense seems to require; rhetorical questions ending with a full stop are given question marks. Despite these 'corrections', new errors were introduced and remained uncorrected. McDonald left them since he had no knowledge of TS, and so they appear in the *Phoenix* text. In particular the seven lacunae noted in the discussion of TS remain, as do the two longer omissions in chapters V and X, and there were four sizeable omissions, due to the typist's eye-skip.[75]

McDonald's own corrections to the typescript are easily identifiable: they are all in pencil, and most are of punctuation. The corrections are neither internally consistent nor exhaustive, being heavier in the earlier chapters than in the later. Together they represent McDonald's preliminary marking for the Viking Press printer, and reflect his policy as editor of *Phoenix*: 'editing as such was almost wholly restricted to technical details in order that a reasonable typographical consistency might be achieved'.[76]

Since TCC transmitted Lawrence's text to its first publication as 'Study of Thomas Hardy', its variants are recorded: for the recovery of Lawrence's text it has no value.

73 Expenses recorded include on 22 July 1930 for the cost of typing 'Hardy': '52,000 words 2 copies £5-4.-.'; UT.
74 See 'Publication' below.
75 See Textual apparatus entries for 46:4, 60:36, 74:26 and 85:27.   76 *Phoenix* xi.

The Title

The title of TS appears in a letter Lawrence wrote to Bertrand Russell on 24 February 1915 in which he expresses his intention to rewrite the book: 'I used to call it *Le Gai Savaire*.'[77] Despite Lawrence's spelling 'Savaire', which is neither modern French 'savoir' nor a medieval dialect of French 'savair', the meaning – The Gay Science (or Skill) – is clear.[78]

The first appearance of the title 'Study of Thomas Hardy' is on the cover page of the 1930 typescript TCC. In records and correspondence relating to its posthumous publication, Curtis Brown's staff used a variety of titles, all of them containing some reference to Hardy.[79] As late as 1946 Frieda still referred to the work as 'that essay on Thomas Hardy'.[80] It was probably Laurence Pollinger in consultation with Frieda (and Murry) who authorised the title for TCC. When McDonald prepared the typescript for the printer of *Phoenix*, he marked Lawrence's own title for deletion and retained 'Study of Thomas Hardy'.

The linguistic oddity of Lawrence's own title is insufficient reason for suppressing it. Yet the grounds for retaining the editorial title of 1930 as well, are strong: it is the familiar title of the work, and has been cited countless times. Both titles are given in this edition.

Publication

The first publication of any part of 'Hardy' was in the *Book Collector's Quarterly* in 1932 where chapter III appeared under the title 'Six Novels of Thomas Hardy and the Real Tragedy'. It was prefaced by an editorial note:

This chapter, complete in itself . . . forms part of a larger unfinished study, which was written shortly before the War, during the *Sons and Lovers* period. Lawrence gave it for safe keeping to Mr J. Middleton Murry, in whose hands it lay, forgotten by both of them until to-day – this being the first time that any portion of it has been published.[81]

Publication had been suggested to the editor of the *Quarterly*, Desmond Flower, by Laurence Pollinger who provided the account of its history.[82]

---

77 *Letters*, ii. 295.
78 DHL also gives it as 'Le Gai Saver' in *Letters*, ii. 300; see Explanatory note on 7:2.
79 Papers in Curtis Brown archives (UT) variously have *Thomas Hardy, Essay on Hardy*, etc.
80 Letter from Frieda to Ernest W. Tedlock, 15 December 1946; E. W. Tedlock, ed., *Frieda Lawrence: The Memoirs and Correspondence* (1961), p. 284.
81 January–March 1932, pp. 44–61.
82 Dr Flower in conversation with the editor, February 1981. The *Quarterly* was facing a difficult period, and Dr Flower wanted something unusual for this number in order to attract subscribers and help sales. He consulted Pollinger who offered him the extract from 'Hardy'. Curtis Brown's records note a payment of £9-9-0 for the serial rights; UT.

Although edited in accordance with the style of the journal, the text derives directly from TS.[83]

Attempts to publish the complete 'Hardy' either separately or as part of a larger collection, were spread over a period of more than six years from July 1930. At first legal problems relating to the Lawrence estate combined with uncertainty about the market for such a work were largely responsible for Secker in England and the Viking Press in New York changing and delaying plans for publication. By the end of 1933 Viking had decided on a Lawrence 'omnibus' volume, but another year passed before their proposed collection 'A World of Men and Women: Last Essays by D. H. Lawrence' began to take shape. The contents of this volume were for the most part those which eventually appeared in *Phoenix*. Secker, never really happy about separate publication of the 'Essay on Thomas Hardy', asked that it be included.[84] Secker and Pollinger consulted Frieda about an editor, and in October 1934 Edward Garnett agreed to undertake the task; he too supported the inclusion of 'Hardy' in the new volume.

In September 1935 Viking appointed McDonald, who had been Lawrence's bibliographer, as co-editor, and by December 1935 he became sole editor with Garnett's agreement. McDonald took no particular interest in 'Hardy', and used the only available text TCC.[85] The title of the volume was changed to *Phoenix* in May 1936 at Viking's suggestion, and the book was published in New York on 19 October. The English edition was published by Heinemann in November from plates supplied by the Viking Press.[86] This text was used for subsequent reprintings.[87]

Reception

Confronted with *Phoenix* – a large and varied collection of 850 pages – reviewers limited themselves to generalities: few made any reference at all to 'Hardy'. Most American reviewers were content to let Lawrence's reputation rest on his poems and stories and saw his criticism and philosophy as

---

[83] See Textual apparatus for chap. III. *John O'London's Weekly* reproduced the *Quarterly*'s text in two parts, on 12 and 19 March 1932.

[84] The sources of information in this and the following paragraph are: Curtis Brown archives, UT; correspondence between Garnett and McDonald, UT; correspondence and files of Viking Press.

[85] McDonald learned of the existence of TS, then in Frieda's possession, more than a year later.

[86] Heinemann purchased Martin Secker's DHL interest on 11 January 1935.

[87] Excerpts from 'Hardy' appeared in Anthony Beal's *D. H. Lawrence: Selected Literary Criticism* (Heinemann, 1956; Mercury Books, 1961). The *Phoenix* text was reproduced with one or two minor corrections in *Lawrence on Hardy and Painting* (Heinemann Educational Books, 1973).

objectionable, even dangerous. Setting the general tone in a prepublication review for the *New Yorker*, Clifton Fadiman found little of the 'spontaneously creative' Lawrence in *Phoenix*. 'The rest is, for the most part, Lawrence "thinking", preaching, arguing. And it is dull. It is tiresome. It is dated.'[88] Of those who referred specifically to 'Hardy', few were any more sympathetic and most were vague and general. Kerker Quinn in the *Yale Review* saw it as 'provocative'.[89] Harry T. Moore noted that, while the work 'is really more about Lawrence than about Hardy, it nevertheless tells a good deal about the older writer, from a fresh line of approach, and about literature itself'.[90] Other American reviewers were dismissive.[91] Almost alone among them was Theodore Spencer: 'Even when he is off the track, as in the long essay on Hardy . . . he is worth listening to', and 'it is a reproach to our decade that we can say it has left Lawrence to one side.'[92]

On the other side of the Atlantic, reviewing began with a lively and affectionate memoir-review by David Garnett who confessed: 'The long study of Thomas Hardy I haven't read.'[93] The same day, however, *The Times Literary Supplement* devoted a quarter of its long review to 'Hardy'. After summarising Lawrence's general view in chapter III, the reviewer continued: 'The analysis of Hardy's noblest novels in terms of the . . . struggle of intuition against intellectual judgment is a characteristic and remarkable piece of writing. Some of the seeming-digressions may be harder to follow, but . . . they have all an eventual relevance to the main theme, and are worth the effort they demand.'[94]

Catherine Carswell, defensive in her review of *Phoenix* for the *Spectator*, mentioned the origin of 'Hardy' in a 'commission which failed to please', but said nothing of its substance.[95] In the *Observer*, C. Henry Warren suggested that of the whole collection, most attention would probably be paid to 'Hardy', since 'as a piece of extended criticism it must surely be unique'.[96] Edward Garnett was less convinced. In a long review – in fact his rejected introduction to *Phoenix*, slightly revised – he referred to the philosophy of the central chapters of 'Hardy' as 'magnificent rant most of it, and sown with

[88] 17 October 1936, pp. 82–3.   [89] June 1937, pp. 847–8.
[90] *Nation* (24 October 1936), 492–3.
[91] *Living Age* (December 1936), 370; *New Republic* (28 October 1936), 358–9; *New York Times Book Review* (29 November 1936), 29.
[92] *Saturday Review of Literature* (31 October 1936), 13. Other American reviewers of *Phoenix* were Lorine Pruette in *New York Tribune Books* (1 November 1936), 16; Fanny Butcher in *Chicago Tribune* (24 October 1936), 10; S. C. Chew in *Christian Science Monitor* (4 November 1936), 11; W. E. Harris in *Boston Evening Transcript* (28 November 1936), p.2.
[93] *New Statesman and Nation* (21 November 1936), 812, 814.
[94] 21 November 1936, p. 956.   [95] 27 November 1936, pp. 959–60.
[96] 13 December 1936, p. 19.

pregnant things'. Garnett saw 'Hardy' as clearly showing the 'two interlacing strands' in Lawrence's genius – 'his religious spirit' and his 'artist's instinct "for utterance . . ."': 'From the interaction of these two elements sprang his characteristic attitude, his special position, and his appeal as an iconoclast to the younger generation, 1911–30, and also the confused dogmatism of much of his writings. The purest expression of Lawrence's artistic genius found vent in *The Prussian Officer and Other Stories*, 1914.'[97] Two long and influential reviews appeared the following year – in June and December 1937 – by Desmond Hawkins in the *Criterion* and by F. R. Leavis in *Scrutiny*. Of 'Hardy', Leavis wrote:

> It is an early work, and hasn't much to do with Hardy. Lawrence frankly admits that he is using Hardy as an occasion and a means, and that his real purpose is to explore, refine and develop certain ideas and intuitions of his own. I found the study difficult to read through; it is diffuse and repetitive, and Lawrence has dealt with the same matters better elsewhere . . .
>
> If Lawrence's criticism is sound that seems to me to be because of the measure in which his criteria are sound, and because they and their application represent . . . an extraordinarily penetrating, persistent and vital kind of thinking.[98]

Alone among all the reviewers Desmond Hawkins saw a connection between 'Hardy' and Lawrence's novels which was to be fruitfully explored by a later generation of critics.[99] In regretting that publication of 'Hardy' had been so long delayed he wrote: 'Lawrence's major period as a novelist, from about 1913 to about 1921, produced two essays which propound a general argument on which the novels are based. One is *The Crown*, the other is this long study of Hardy.' Hawkins concluded his review with a forecast:

> The *Study of Thomas Hardy* attempts a full statement, theoretically and in application . . . This transposition of the work of one artist into the categories of another seems to me to be always a potentially fruitful sort of criticism . . . In particular, the detailed commentary on *Jude the Obscure* is criticism of the very highest order, a piece of sustained and uncanny insight which leaves nothing further to be said. We must now expect a whittling down of Lawrence's prodigious output to a body of writing representative of his specific genius. Much of *Phoenix* will not survive this process, but the volume will be indispensable so long as it contains this Study of Hardy . . .

97 *London Mercury* (December 1936), 152–60. Garnett's corrected draft Introduction is at UT.
98 December 1937, pp. 352–8.
99 See especially Mark Kinkead-Weekes: 'The Marble and the Statue: The Exploratory Imagination of D. H. Lawrence' in *Imagined Worlds*, ed. Ian Gregor and Maynard Mack (1968), pp. 371–418.
    Phoenix II (1968) was accompanied by a re-issue of *Phoenix*: several reviewers, recalling the earlier volume, emphasised the importance of 'Hardy' in DHL's work.

[Lawrence's] method is perfectly expounded in his own analysis of the one English novelist he seems always to have respected.[100]

[100] *Criterion* (June 1937), 748–52. There is an important review (in French) by Emile Delavenay in *Etudes Anglaises* (March 1937), 157–9.

Literary Essays, 1908–27

'Art and the Individual' (1908)

For the first half of 1908 Lawrence, aged 22, was a student at the Nottingham University College where he took the final examination for the Board of Education Teacher's Certificate in July.[1] Blanche Jennings, a postmistress in Liverpool, a socialist and suffragist, had met him when she visited her friend Alice Dax in Eastwood early in 1908. Subsequently, he wrote to her at some length on his novel, the second version of *The White Peacock*; his life; and his embryonic philosophy. In the second week of May 1908, Blanche Jennings asked if she might read a paper of his on 'Art and the Individual'. She had probably heard of it from Alice Dax who was present when Lawrence read it on Thursday 19 March at a meeting of the Eastwood 'Debating Society'. The *Eastwood & Kimberley Advertiser* reported: 'A highly interesting paper on "Art and the Individual" was read before the members of the society on March 19, when the attendance reached its maximum since the formation of the society. The same subject (with illustrations of standard works of art) will be discussed at the next meeting on April 2nd.'[2]

His closest friend at this time, Jessie Chambers, wrote down her memory of the occasion nearly thirty years later. Although she was at fault about the date of the meeting, her recollection was vivid: Lawrence read his essay to a little gathering of the Eastwood intelligentsia at the house of a friend, where he sprawled at full length on the hearth-rug, shy at reading his own work. She also recalled that the paper was given 'at the house of W. E. Hopkin; Mr. and Mrs. Dax were there, my brother and I, and another couple who were strangers to me and whose names I don't remember, and Mr. and Mrs. Hopkin of course'.[3]

Blanche Jennings was curious to read the paper. Lawrence replied: 'You may certainly read that paper on "Art and the Individual" – better "Art and Individual Development" – when I have written it out again. In its present scrappy condition you would not enjoy it; most likely you never would, for that matter.'[4]

Work for his Certificate examinations was more pressing, and the paper remained unrevised: Lawrence was 'unable to remit . . . that vapouring . . . on

---

[1] Delavenay 667; for details of DHL's course and examinations see ibid. 657–61.
[2] 27 March 1908, p. 2.
[3] 'The Collected Letters of Jessie Chambers', ed. George Zytaruk, *DHL Review*, xii (1979), 82.
[4] *Letters*, i. 53.

"Art"' when he wrote a month later.[5] While he may have rewritten it, even in part, by mid-July, it was not until 1 September that he finally despatched a fair copy to Blanche Jennings asking her opinion of it.[6] She had, in the meantime, read and commented in some detail on Lawrence's novel. She expressed her approval of the essay, and Lawrence replied two days before his departure from Eastwood to take up his teaching post in Croydon:

> Pray do not trouble about that paper on Art; I did not want *it*, I wanted your acknowledgment. I'm glad you like it – I had much rather you found it to your taste than that your friend 'J' should. She is a Ruskinite; well, *all* Ruskinites are not fools . . .
> As for the paper, keep it as long as you like, give it to whom you like, and do you think I could do anything with it?[7]

But there is no record of any attempt being made to publish the essay.

'Art and the Individual' makes considerable use of quotation, reference and allusion, and shows Lawrence's capacity for turning things at hand to immediate use in his writing (as can be seen in Explanatory notes 136:32, 140:25). Yet when its sources and influences have been identified, the paper remains most distinctively Lawrence's own. It is important as his first, youthful attempt to set down a philosophy of art – one of the continuing endeavours of his life.

Of the two manuscripts of the essay, the first entitled simply 'Art and The Individual' (Roberts E24.3a) is the version from which Lawrence delivered his talk in 1908. Lawrence's reference to its 'scrappy condition' is apt. It is reproduced in Appendix I. It was published by Ada Lawrence and Stuart Gelder in *Young Lorenzo* (Florence) in January 1932, and was reprinted with slight editorial corrections (not from the manuscript) in *Phoenix II*.

The second manuscript (Roberts E24.3b), a neat and carefully written fair copy bearing the subtitle 'A Paper for Socialists', is the final version which Lawrence sent to Blanche Jennings. It is published here for the first time.

'Rachel Annand Taylor' (1910)

In the spring of 1910, probably on 10 March, Ford Madox Hueffer took Lawrence, now in his second year as a teacher at Croydon, to a poets' supper party at the home of Ernest Rhys in Hampstead.[8] Lawrence met there the

---

[5] Ibid., i. 55.   [6] Ibid., i. 63, 72.   [7] Ibid., i. 80–1.

[8] Nehls, i. 129–32 and *Letters*, i. 156, 180. If these three reports refer to the same occasion, DHL met Rachel Annand Taylor on 10 March.

Scottish poetess Rachel Annand Taylor whose poems he had admired in the *English Review*, edited by Hueffer.[9] His accurate sketch of her recorded in his essay shows that he was as impressed by her personally as he was by her poems: she was 'all that a poetess should be'.[10]

Born in 1876, Rachel Annand had married in 1901 Alexander Taylor, a classics master at Dundee High School. By 1910, her husband's mental illness had led to their separation, and she was living alone in Chelsea, making a modest living from reviewing and writing. She had published *Poems* in 1904 and *Rose and Vine* in 1909, and in September 1910 her latest volume *The Hours of Fiammetta: a sonnet sequence* appeared. Lawrence had just read this sequence when the Croydon branch of the English Association invited him 'to give a paper on "A Living Poet". "I will give you . . . Rachel Annand Taylor."' he replied.[11]

At this time, he had read the three poems in the *English Review* and *The Hours of Fiammetta*, so he wrote to Rachel Annand Taylor on 30 September recalling their meeting and asking about her two earlier volumes. In return she invited him to meet her on Saturday 15 October. There he gathered the personal material for his paper: he also borrowed her volume of *Poems*. The same evening he met Adrian Berrington, a young architect and close friend of Rachel Annand Taylor's, who agreed to lend Lawrence his copy of *Rose and Vine*.[12]

The paper 'Rachel Annand Taylor' was delivered in Croydon in mid-November – probably on Thursday 17. It 'went very well. Croydonians seem to find the poetry highly provocative, if no more. They raved at me for bringing them this fantastic decadent stuff: but they were caught in the spell of it, and I laughed.'[13]

Although Lawrence's attitude towards Rachel Annand Taylor and her poetry was ironic to a degree which angered her when she eventually read the paper in 1932, he found a fascination both in her and her extravagant verse. She was one in whom he could confide: 'he told me all his story when he came to tea', she recalled, and his letters to her continue the story.[14] In her

9 Rachel Annand Taylor's 'Three Poems' appeared in the *English Review*, iii (October 1909), 378–9. See *Letters*, i. 141.
10 The accuracy of DHL's sketch of Rachel Annand Taylor is confirmed by her niece, Louise Annand.
11 *Letters*, i. 179.   12 Ibid., i. 182, 185, 189.
13 Ibid., i. 189. DHL reports the success of his talk in this letter dated Friday 18 November. If the letter to Rachel Annand Taylor (p. 187) is correctly dated 15 November, the paper had not been given by then. Assuming that DHL returned Berrington's book the day after the talk, Thursday 17 November seems the most likely date.
14 Richard Aldington, *Portrait of a Genius, But . . .* (1950), p. 94. The seven letters to Rachel Annand Taylor are in *Letters*, i. 179–91.

Fiammetta he encountered the idea of the Dreaming Woman which was to
influence his conception of Helena when he came to revise *The Trespasser* a
year later. Rachel Annand Taylor's Preface to *Fiammetta* contains a distinction between 'two great traditions of womanhood. One presents the Madonna
brooding over the mystery of motherhood: the other, more confusedly, tells of
the acolyte, the priestess, the clairvoyante of the unknown gods.'[15] In this
Lawrence found a confirmatory statement of his own intuitions and these
conceptions are pervasive in his work from *The Trespasser* on.[16]

Lawrence's autograph manuscript (Roberts E330.5) with considerable
correction, is extant. There appears to have been no attempt on Lawrence's
part to publish it, and it was preserved with other papers by his sister Ada.
'Rachel Annand Taylor' was first published in edited form by Ada Lawrence
and Stuart Gelder in *Young Lorenzo: Early Life of D. H. Lawrence*; it was
reprinted in *Phoenix II*. Under threat of an action by Rachel Annand Taylor, it
was omitted from Secker's English edition of *Early Life of D. H. Lawrence*
(November 1932).[17]

'The Future of the Novel' (1923)
'[Surgery for the Novel – Or a Bomb]'

On his 37th birthday, 11 September 1922, Lawrence arrived in Taos, New
Mexico after a seven-month journey from Europe by way of Ceylon, Australia
and San Francisco. He stayed in Taos barely three months before escaping
from the oppressive presence of his hostess, Mabel Dodge Luhan, to the Del
Monte ranch.[18] The three months spent there before his first journey down to
old Mexico were happy if not enormously productive. Indeed his first six
months in the USA produced no major new work at all: a projected novel
based on the life of Mabel Luhan was soon abandoned[19] and he confined
himself to the revision of existing work,[20] and the writing of a handful of
reviews and articles – among them 'The Future of the Novel'.
    This essay and its title seem likely to have had their origins some six

---

[15] P. 5.
[16] See *The Trespasser*, ed. Elizabeth Mansfield (Cambridge, 1981), p. 64 and 'Hardy' 121–2.
[17] The story 'Adolf' replaced it. Correspondence of June 1932 in Curtis Brown archives, UT;
    letter from Ada Clarke to Koteliansky, 6 November 1932, BL.
[18] She was instrumental in bringing DHL to Taos; see her *Lorenzo in Taos* (New York, 1932).
    See letter to Catherine Carswell, 17 December 1922.
[19] See *St. Mawr and Other Stories*, ed. Brian Finney (Cambridge, 1983), p. xviii.
[20] *Kangaroo, Studies in Classic American Literature, Little Novels of Sicily* and *Birds, Beasts and
    Flowers*.

months or more earlier. On 20 July 1922, the day Lawrence posted the manuscript of *Kangaroo* to his agent from Australia, the Sydney *Bulletin* published a lengthy account of Meredith Starr's interviews with sixty English writers concerning 'the future of the novel'.[21] The article summarised the views of more than half the participants, among them Louis Golding who claimed Lawrence was 'the greatest of his generation' and that it was in his hands that 'the future of the novel rests'. As a keen reader of the *Bulletin* Lawrence must certainly have read the report. Had he been able to read Starr's book *The Future of the Novel* (1921) (as he may have later) he would have seen that among all the discussion of contemporary novels and novelists Golding's reference to him – as 'author of "Sons and Lovers"' – was the only one.[22] He had not even been asked for an interview.

At this time several passages in *Kangaroo*, written only weeks before, show Lawrence acutely conscious of the problem of the contemporary novel, its conventional limitations and its new directions.[23] Thus on his arrival at Taos he was eager to keep abreast of developments, and asked his publisher Thomas Seltzer, to send him a copy of James Joyce's *Ulysses*: 'I read it is the last thing in novels: I'd best look at it.'[24] The book arrived on 6 November, but he returned it a fortnight later with the comment: '*Ulysses* wearied me: so like a schoolmaster with dirt and stuff in his head: sometimes good, though: but too mental.'[25]

Seltzer evidently saw a possibility in Lawrence's comments and suggested publication. Lawrence replied on 5 December: 'Do you really want to publish my James Joyce remarks? No, I don't think it's quite fair to him.' Instead, he returned to the general topic of the novel and its future, and by 1 February 1923 was able to write again to Seltzer: 'I got your telegram about an article this morning. Have just finished enclosed. If they don't want it, burn it.'

The 'they' of the letter were the publishers of the *Literary Digest International Book Review* where in April 1923 the essay appeared, considerably edited, and under the publisher's title 'Surgery for the Novel – Or a Bomb'. Their invitation to Lawrence may well have been related to the prosecution of Seltzer's trade edition of *Women in Love* brought by the New York Society for the Suppression of Vice in the summer of 1922. The prosecution was unsuccessful, but had its effect on the success of Lawrence's

---

[21] The interviews were originally published in the *Pall Mall Gazette* and were collected in book form. The *Bulletin* review (p. 25) is by Adrian Lawlor. (DHL had met Starr and his wife when they were neighbours in Cornwall: 'I don't like them very much', *Letters*, iii. 154.)
[22] P. 181. Golding had published an essay on DHL in *Voices*, January 1919. DHL commented: 'The essay praises me too much' (*Letters*, iii. 342 and n. 3).
[23] See chaps. XIV and XV.   [24] 22 September 1922.
[25] Letter to Thomas Seltzer, 21 November 1922.

novel.[26] Since prosecuting agencies were active at this time, publishers were much preoccupied with censorship. If the *Literary Digest* expected a contribution to the current debate from Lawrence who was achieving fame, or notoriety, in this respect, the essay they got ignored the question.

On receipt of Lawrence's manuscript (Roberts E385.5a), Seltzer had it typed with two carbon copies. One carbon copy no longer exists, and was probably the one from which the *Digest* printed the essay; the two surviving copies are Roberts E385.5b and c. Lawrence made two small corrections to all the typescript copies, but allowed other obvious errors to pass – e.g. 'Come' for 'Some' (152:33). The *Digest* editor supplied the new title and made cuts, insertions and changes to the paragraphing and punctuation. Even here there is evidence of censorship, most notably the removal of the passages making reference to the Gospels as novels. Two changes were made to accommodate the illustrations in the double-column format of the paper.[27]

The text reprinted in *Phoenix* was taken from the *Digest* version with no reference to either the manuscript or the typescripts. The base-text for this edition is Lawrence's manuscript; his unexpurgated text is printed for the first time. The published title is retained as a sub-title because of its familiarity.

'A Britisher Has a Word With an Editor' (1923)

For the month 16 October to 16 November 1923 Lawrence was staying at the Hotel Garcia in Guadalajara on his second visit to Mexico. He renewed his acquaintance with Dr George Purnell, United States Consul in Guadalajara, and with his daughter Idella.[28] She had graduated from the University of California the previous year, having been deeply influenced by Witter Bynner's poetry course.[29] On her return to Guadalajara, she founded and edited a little poetry magazine, *Palms*, which appeared monthly from April 1923. Lawrence had first met Idella Purnell in April 1923, when he had shown an encouraging interest in *Palms*. He contributed several poems, and designed covers for one or two numbers.[30]

---

[26] See G. Thomas Tanselle, 'The Thomas Seltzer Imprint', *Papers of the Bibliographical Society of America*, lviii (1964), 394–401.

[27] Three line cartoons illustrating passages from DHL's text were contributed by J. Norman Lynd.

[28] Idella Purnell (later Mrs Stone) was born 1901 in Guadalajara, Mexico; in 1923 she was a secretary in the American Consulate there.

[29] Witter Bynner (1881–1968), American poet; Associate Editor of *Palms* for a time. His association with DHL is recorded in *Journey with Genius* (New York, 1951).

[30] DHL's designs have not been positively identified. One water-colour (of a negro climbing a palm-tree) is at UT.

Anticipating his return to Mexico in October, he wrote to Dr Purnell: 'Tell Idella we will talk *Palms* and everything when I come.'[31] During this visit he actually worked with her on *Palms*, especially on the Christmas issue, for which he rewrote her draft advertisement 'A Year of Christmas', and contributed an anonymous rejoinder to the editor of *Poetry* entitled 'A Britisher has a Word with Harriett Monroe':[32] Harriet Monroe had visited England and France in the summer of 1923, and on her return had written an editorial article of which the concluding paragraphs stirred patriotic ire in Lawrence.[33]

Lawrence's manuscript (Roberts E57.5) was scarcely altered in the published version. Because of his editorial involvement with this number it can be assumed that he approved the change to the title in which 'An Editor' replaced MS 'Harriett Monroe'. The text in *Palms* was printed from MS, and reprinted in *Phoenix II*.

'Art and Morality', 'Morality and the Novel' and 'The Novel' (1925)

Much of the summer of 1925 Lawrence spent on his New Mexico ranch, recuperating after the almost fatal malaria he contracted on his third visit to Mexico. During that illness, in March, his tubercular condition was first definitely diagnosed. In April he was still very weak: 'I was awfully sick: malaria, typhoid condition inside, and chest going wrong. Am much better – but must be careful all summer – lie down a great deal.'[34] Yet by 7 May he had completed his new play *David*, and two months later had revised *The Plumed Serpent*.[35] While this might seem enough for a convalescent it was not all: at some time between 7 May and the end of June, probably during and after the novel revisions, Lawrence wrote three essays on the value and the 'morality' of the modern novel.

The order of composition, established from their position in a notebook, the pages of which were mechanically numbered, was 'Art and Morality I', 'Morality and the Novel I', 'Art and Morality II', 'Morality and the Novel II' and 'The Modern Novel' (published as 'The Novel'). Together with an abandoned start to the first, these essays occupied pages 101–131.[36] Each of the first two essays exists in two separate manuscript versions here numbered

---

[31] 5 October 1923.
[32] The texts with facsimiles appear in Nehls, ii. 268–70 and facing p. 139.
[33] See Explanatory note on 159:2.   [34] Letter to Emily King, 21 April 1925.
[35] Letter to Curtis Brown, 23 June 1925.
[36] See Tedlock, *Lawrence MSS* 162–7. The versions are respectively Roberts E24b, E244a, E24e, E244d and E280a. E24a records a false start to 'Art and Morality I'.

I and II. Lawrence wrote the first versions of each essay and began at once to revise them: each has heavy correction and interlinear revision. Dissatisfied with them, he proceeded to write both essays again. These second versions, comparatively lightly corrected, were then typed for him and forwarded to Curtis Brown's New York office early in July.[37]

Lawrence had been meditating for some time upon a new approach to criticism of the novel by way of painting. Writing on 11 July 1925 to Stuart Sherman, book section editor of the New York *Tribune*, Lawrence outlined his purpose:

> I have thought many times it would be good to review a novel from the standpoint of what I call morality: what I feel to be essentially moral. Now and then review a book plainly. – I will do it for your paper if you like.
>
> To pave the way – and have some stones to pull up and throw at the reader's head – I did two little articles: 'Art and Morality' and 'Morality and the Novel'. If you care to ask my agent, Curtis Brown, for them, you can have them if you like.
>
> The point was easier to see in painting, to start with. But it wouldn't be so very out of the way, in a literary paper.

Sherman, however, did not take up this offer.

The two essays first appeared in 1925 in the November and December numbers respectively of the *Calendar of Modern Letters*. On 3 October Nancy Pearn of Curtis Brown's London office notified Lawrence: 'I am not sure whether you heard when in New York [in September], that we had sold "Art and Morality" and "Morality and the Novel" to the "Calendar", who will pay at their rate of three guineas a thousand.'[38]

The *Calendar* followed the typescripts closely in wording, but made alterations to the punctuation. However, Lawrence had made some small substantive corrections to the carbon copy typescripts in his possession, which did not appear in the *Calendar* texts.[39] Both essays were reprinted in *Phoenix* in 1936. For this collection Curtis Brown provided new typescripts not from Lawrence's revised typescripts but from his manuscripts. Errors introduced into these typescripts were left uncorrected and so appear in the *Phoenix* text.

The present edition takes the manuscript of the second version of each essay as base-text and incorporates Lawrence's minor corrections to his

---

37 The typescripts (Roberts E24f and E244e) are not Dorothy Brett's work. It seems that DHL sent his manuscripts away from the ranch for typing at this time; see Nehls, ii. 406.

38 UT.

39 The *Living Age* (New York), 26 December 1925, pp. 681–5, reprinted 'Art and Morality' from the *Calendar*, introducing errors and a different house-styling. 'Morality and the Novel' was reprinted in the *Golden Book* (New York), 13 February 1926, pp. 248–50; considerable editorial changes were made, including the omission of the last paragraph.

carbon copy typescripts. The earlier versions are reproduced from the manuscripts in Appendixes II and III.

The third essay of this group, 'The Novel', while following the manuscript sequence, may have been drafted and certainly was revised a little later than the other two. Its history is more complicated. As early as April 1925, Harold T. Mason of the Centaur Press in Philadelphia had suggested publication of a 'book of uncollected essays' to Lawrence.[40] Some time later Mr Jester, of the same firm, proposed that Lawrence include an essay on the novel, and on 29 June Lawrence complied: 'I am sending you here a little article on "The Novel", as you asked me, for the small book of essays. Let me know if it is too antiseptic for you. I think it's amusing.' In reporting this to Edward McDonald, Lawrence added: 'my wife says [it] is too much. But it's what I genuinely feel, and *how* I feel, so what's the odds. Anyhow it can be altered if necessary.'[41]

It appears that Lawrence slightly revised his manuscript draft and had it typed in duplicate by Dorothy Brett (Roberts E280b). He then made revisions and corrections to the whole of the ribbon copy, changing the title from 'The Modern Novel'. Perhaps it was at this stage that Jester's suggestion arrived, for Lawrence carefully corrected the first five pages of the carbon copy (Roberts E280c) but abandoned the last two pages; these he replaced with seven tightly-written autograph pages of largely new material, beginning at 183:30. Jester probably received the work in this form since the essay next appears in a completely new typescript, TS (Roberts E340.6), of the whole volume (not by Brett) to which Lawrence made corrections and some short additions. What is noticeable in TS is the toning down of the language in the last two pages. Either Lawrence agreed in the end with Frieda that it was 'too much', or Jester, having seen the essay, decided that it was 'too antiseptic'. There is no indication that these changes are in any way different from other corrections to TS, nor is there evidence that Lawrence was requested to make the changes, which are therefore accepted in this edition.[42] TS is the base-text: it is substantially the text published in *Reflections on the Death of a Porcupine and Other Essays*.

It is unlikely that Lawrence saw proofs. The corrected typescript of the whole volume was delivered to Centaur in mid-August.[43] Towards the end of October Lawrence, now in London, wondered whether Centaur had

---

[40] Letter to Harold Mason, 17 April 1925.
[41] Letters to Mr Jester and Edward McDonald, 29 June 1925.
[42] See Explanatory note on 189:11.
[43] See letter to Jester, 12 August 1925: 'I will send you the complete thing in a few days', and letter to Secker, 25 August 1925: 'I sent them the prepared MS. last week'.

abandoned the project, and a fortnight later he learned that Curtis Brown's New York office had arranged the publication details with Mason.[44] 'The Novel' is the second essay in the *Porcupine* volume, published in Philadelphia on 7 December 1925. The first English edition, by Martin Secker, did not appear until February 1934. The collection was reprinted in *Phoenix II*.

'Why the Novel Matters' and 'The Novel and the Feelings' (1925)

Lawrence wrote two more essays on the novel in 1925. 'Why the Novel Matters' and 'The Novel and the Feelings' were written together and in that order since the manuscript pages were torn from the same notebook and the pattern of tearing indicates the page order. The notebook was not the one used for the three earlier essays, but another containing writings from later in 1925. The dating of these two essays is conjectural: they were neither typed nor published in Lawrence's lifetime, are not mentioned in his letters, and there is no record of their having been offered to his agent. It has been assumed from the similarity of subject that they belong, with the three 'ranch' essays, to the summer of 1925.[45] But there is evidence to suggest a date nearer the end of the year, probably after Lawrence had left America in late September. His offer in July of a review to Sherman for the New York *Herald Tribune Books*[46] was not taken up until November, and then was not of a novel but *The Origins of Prohibition* by J. A. Krout. The review was completed on 21 November and sent with a covering note to Nancy Pearn of Curtis Brown: both review and letter are on leaves torn from the same notebook as these two essays.[47] It is probably not coincidence that one essay refers to 'prohibition beer' and spirits and the other to wine.[48]

The two manuscripts were among those lodged with Curtis Brown by Frieda shortly after Lawrence's death. Typescripts were made early in 1930, and these were held, like 'Hardy', for publication in a projected collection of essays and articles.[49] The typescripts were used as setting-copy for publication in *Phoenix*. The manuscripts (Roberts E281a and E432a) are base-texts for this edition.

[44] Letters to McDonald and Mason 26 October and 2 November 1925.
[45] Tedlock, *Lawrence MSS* 168–9; Keith Sagar, *D. H. Lawrence: A Calendar of His Works* (Manchester, 1979), p. 145.
[46] See p. xlviii above.
[47] The letter begins on p. 7 of DHL's review and continues overleaf.
[48] See 201:30–1. and 193:4.
[49] In 1933 Curtis Brown offered them to A. Richards for publication by his White Owl Press, but the project came to nothing; UT. These typescripts are Roberts E432d ('Why the Novel Matters') and Roberts E281b and one copy of E281c ('The Novel and the Feelings').

'John Galsworthy' (1927)

Lawrence was a contributor to the *Calendar of Modern Letters* throughout its three years of publication. His story, 'The Princess', was serialised in the first three monthly numbers, while 'Art and Morality' and 'Morality and the Novel' appeared at the end of 1925. After the monthly became a quarterly in 1926, he continued to contribute poems and book reviews.[50]

A significant feature of the *Calendar* was its occasional series of critical essays entitled 'Scrutinies' in which critics examined 'the reputations of certain writers who are the object of somewhat indiscriminate admiration'.[51] Although by the end of July 1927, when the last number appeared, only seven of these scrutinies had been published, the editor Edgell Rickword, perhaps in anticipation of the journal's collapse, had conceived a plan to collect and extend the series in a separate volume. He was keen to have Lawrence as a 'scrutineer', but exactly when he invited him to write on Galsworthy is not known. If, as seems reasonable, it was late in 1926, his intention may originally have been to include the essay in the *Calendar* itself. But by the time Lawrence sent off his manuscript on 28 February 1927 Rickword intended it (as Lawrence knew) for his volume *Scrutinies By Various Writers*.

For Lawrence himself, the completion of the Galsworthy essay brought to an end three months of intensive work during which he had written the second version of *Lady Chatterley's Lover*[52] and five book reviews, and completed several paintings. Settled at the Villa Mirenda near Florence through the winter of 1926–7, reading and writing and painting at this extraordinary rate, Lawrence on several occasions complained: 'I seem to be losing my will-to-write altogether . . . Painting is more fun than writing, much more of a game, and costs the soul far, far less.'[53] The writing he did appears to have been in intermittent bursts of great concentration – 'sudden intense whacks' as he described them.[54]

The Galsworthy project was evidently done in a number of such 'whacks'. Lawrence re-read Galsworthy – or 'most of him, for all is too much' – at the same time making notes on the books and recording his reactions.[55]

In February 1927, having decided to let his own novel lie for a while, he began work on the Galsworthy essay itself.[56] The first untitled draft (Roberts E172a) he discarded after five pages, just as Galsworthy made his sudden entry. It is likely that he abandoned the first attempt because it was turning

50 Subsequent contributions were two poems and five reviews.
51 *Calendar*, i (March 1925).   52 Published as *John Thomas and Lady Jane* (1972).
53 Letter to Else Jaffe, 10 January 1927.   54 Letter to Koteliansky, 20 January 1927.
55 210:6. One page of notes survives at UT; extracts are quoted in the Explanatory notes.
56 Letter to Nancy Pearn, 25 February 1927.

into 'philosophy' rather than criticism. In any case it was becoming lengthy for an introduction, and Galsworthy, as he admitted, arrived with 'a bump'.[57] Indeed, the editor of *Phoenix* took this draft to be an independent unfinished essay, and published it under the editorial title 'The Individual Conscious- ness v. The Social Consciousness'.[58] (The draft is printed in Appendix V.) Nevertheless, although Lawrence discarded this opening, he retained its distinction between individual beings and social beings for his criticism of Galsworthy's characters.

One reason why this draft tended towards philosophy may be found in Lawrence's renewed contact with the American psychoanalyst Trigant Burrow.[59] On Christmas Day 1926 Lawrence enthusiastically acknowledged receipt of Burrow's paper 'Psychoanalysis in Theory and in Life', and Burrow sent him another article in February 1927 as he was about to begin 'Galsworthy'.[60] The marked concomitance of ideas – even of phrasing – while it endorses the sense of a kindred spirit each felt in the other's work, also suggests that Burrow had deflected Lawrence from his main task.

So Lawrence began his essay again, this time giving in blander and less lively style an account of his view of criticism and the qualities of a good critic. There is a sense of restraint in this occasioned perhaps by the sense of contributing to a planned volume – 'a book of "scrutinies" ... by that *Calendar* young man Edgell Rickword'.[61] Lawrence may even have had doubts about the undertaking: he was unwilling to do another scrutiny when invited three months later.[62] Once launched on 'Galsworthy', he wrote rapidly and proceeded to rewrite and correct copiously. The result was an untidy manuscript which, when he sent it to his agent, he felt needed an apology: 'I am sending a "scrutiny" on John Galsworthy, for a book of "scrutinies" by the younger writers on the elder ... Will you please have it typed for me – I am ashamed of the scribbled MS: and will you please send me the typescript again, so I can go over it.'[63]

Neither typescripts nor proofs survive, yet Lawrence saw both (he returned

---

57 See 251:30.   58 Pp. 761–4.

59 Trigant Burrow (1881–1950), also pioneer of group therapy. DHL had received copies of some of his papers as early as 1920. For their correspondence see Nehls, iii. 678–85 and DHL's letters of 6 June 1925, 25 December 1926, 13 July and 3 August 1927 and 15 March 1928. DHL reviewed Burrow's *The Social Basis of Consciousness* (1927) in the *Bookman* (November 1927; reprinted *Phoenix* 377–82).

60 Published in *Journal of Nervous and Mental Disease*, lxiv (September 1926), 209–24, and later used as chap. 1 of *The Social Basis*. Burrow records sending 'The Reabsorbed Affect and Its Elimination' to DHL on 7 February 1927; see Nehls, iii. 681.

61 Letter to Nancy Pearn, 28 February 1927.

62 On Bernard Shaw (letter to Koteliansky, 27 May 1927).

63 Letter to Nancy Pearn, 28 February 1927.

the typescript to Nancy Pearn on 12 March, and proofs were sent to him on 22 August),[64] and there are some twelve substantive changes between manuscript and printed text which were made at one or the other stage. Lawrence's manuscript (Roberts E181.3b) emended from the *Scrutinies* text, is taken as the base-text for this edition.

Scrutinies By Various Writers edited by Edgell Rickword was published in London on 23 March 1928. For his contribution Lawrence received '£20 advance on publication on account of 1% royalty'.[65] When returning the corrected typescript to his agent Lawrence raised the possibility of American magazine publication, but nothing came of the proposal.[66] The essay was reprinted in *Phoenix*.

Reception

Scrutinies elicited more abuse than praise from reviewers. The *Spectator* called it 'a foolish symposium' and supposed 'we must try to take as serious Mr D. H. Lawrence's remarks about Mr Galsworthy'. It found the essay 'revolting in taste and indecent in expression' and suggested that it might be 'the crowning joke of a ludicrous volume'.[67] *The Times Literary Supplement* in a brief notice also objected to the bad taste shown in the 'predominant metaphor' of Lawrence's 'attack'.[68] Herbert Read, in a long review for the *Nation and Athenæum*, took exception to Lawrence's making 'anti-criticism' into a doctrine. He recognised Lawrence's 'acute perception of how Mr Galsworthy just missed being a social satirist of the first order'; and he, too, concluded that the essay is 'rather disgusting with its superfluity of similes drawn from the sexual life of the dog world'.[69]

R. Ellis Roberts in the *Bookman* found Lawrence's essay 'a more serious affair' than most of the others in *Scrutinies*. He too disliked the style but found his criticism of Galsworthy's 'creed of Beauty' contained some 'shrewd hitting'.[70] The *New Statesman* pointed to Lawrence's 'formidable indictment' of the Forsytes: 'more perhaps to the discredit of the Forsytes and their counterparts in real life ... But Mr Lawrence shows, more vividly than any other critic has shown, where Mr Galsworthy's gentlemanliness has stopped him short from rising to the front rank of English novelists.' Lawrence stood

---

64 Letters to Nancy Pearn and from Curtis Brown to DHL; UT.

65 Note dated 23 March 1927 in Curtis Brown archives; UT.

66 Letter to Nancy Pearn, 12 March 1927: 'a new magazine *Larus* – published in Boston or somewhere in Mass. – asked me for anything whatsoever that other papers weren't likely to want.'

67 31 March 1928, p. 502.   68 10 May 1928, p. 362.

69 12 May 1928, p. 180.   70 May 1928, pp. 124, 126.

out sharply from the other scrutineers because he himself had the 'force and complexity' he demanded of a critic.[71]

Geoffrey West reached the same conclusion in the *Outlook*: 'Mr Lawrence has earned his right to speak thus frankly to a fellow-craftsman.'[72]

---

[71] 12 May 1928, pp. 162, 164.
[72] 7 April 1928, pp. 442–3. *Scrutinies* was also noticed in the *Observer* (25 March 1928), 8 and the *Daily Herald* (9 April 1928), 7.

STUDY OF THOMAS HARDY
AND OTHER ESSAYS

STUDY OF THOMAS HARDY
[LE GAI SAVAIRE]

Note on the text

The base-text for this edition is the composite ribbon and carbon copy typescript (TS) entitled 'Le Gai Savaire', located at UCB. S. S. Koteliansky typed TS from DHL's manuscript (unlocated), but DHL did not correct it.

The apparatus records all textual variants between TS and the first publication of chap. III in the *Book Collector's Quarterly*, No. 5 (January–March 1932), 44–61 (Per); the posthumous carbon copy typescript (TCC), located at UT, which was made from TS and used as the setting-copy for *Phoenix*; and the first complete publication in *Phoenix* (1936), pp. 398–516 (A1).

Inconsistencies of punctuation arise from either DHL's idiosyncrasies or Kot's mistyping in TS or from both. DHL's practice has been checked against the manuscripts of his 'Foreword to *Sons and Lovers*' (1913) and essays IV to VI of 'The Crown' (1915), particularly in the matter of punctuation and capitalisation of the first word in a quotation. The text has been lightly emended in this respect; all emendations are recorded.

Square brackets in the text are used for words that have been provided editorially (i) to fill a blank space left in TS, (ii) to supply an omitted word required by the sense or the grammar or (iii) to substitute for a probable misreading in TS. In most cases an Explanatory note supplements the evidence of the Textual apparatus.

The apparatus records all textual variants, except for the following silent emendations:

1 TS contains numerous mistypings. In cases where these have given rise to later misreadings – 'decr ee' becomes 'door' in TCC (32:17) – or in cases where the identification of a mistyping might be disputed – 'improductive' for 'unproductive' (120:16) – the full information is recorded; otherwise they have been silently emended.

2 Incomplete quotation marks and missing full stops at the ends of sentences have been supplied.

3 'Dr.' and 'Mrs.' in TS are normalised to the majority usage, 'Dr' and 'Mrs'; TCC and A1 have the full stop.

4 Obvious spelling errors are corrected, e.g. 'utterly' for 'uterly'.

5 The preferred forms are 'judgement' in TS and Per (for 'judgment' in TCC and A1); 'mediaeval' (for 'medieval' in A1); 'Tolstoi' (for 'Tolstoy' in Per); 'Michel Angelo' in TS (for 'Michelangelo' in A1); 'Nirvana', the majority practice in TS (for 'nirvana'); 'Dürer' in A1 (for 'Durer' in TS and TCC); the rejected forms are not recorded.

6 The spelling 'Shakespeare', which appears only once among several variants in TS, is adopted throughout. Hyphens in the following compound terms are majority usage in TS and have been added where TS omits them: 'Will-to-Motion', 'Will-to-Inertia', 'Two-in-One' and 'two-in-one', 'God-Idea' and 'God-idea'. 'Colour', 'honour', 'labour', etc. are preferred to occasional 'color', 'honor', 'labor' in TS.

4

7 The titles of Hardy's novels are italicised. In TS these are underlined, put in inverted commas or, frequently, not signalled. The titles of paintings, sculptures, poems and plays are placed within inverted commas, following the practice of TS, where it gives any indication at all. Later states of the text italicise all titles.

8 'D'Urberville', 'De Stancey' (unless they occur at the beginning of a sentence) and 'Philtotson' in TS are corrected to 'd'Urberville', 'de Stancy', 'Phillotson'.

9 TCC presents chapter numbers and titles on one line with a colon separating them; A1 printed them on two lines with the titles in italics; TS's form has been restored.

Study of Thomas Hardy
[Le Gai Savaire]*

Chapter I.

Of Poppies and Phoenixes and the Beginning of the Argument.

5

- I -*

Man has made such a mighty struggle to feel at home on the face of the earth, without even yet succeeding. Ever since he first discovered himself exposed naked betwixt sky and land, belonging to neither, he has gone on fighting for more food, more clothing, more shelter, and   10 though he has roofed-in the world with houses and though the ground has heaved up massive abundance and excess of nutriment to his hand, still he cannot be appeased, satisfied. He goes on and on. In his anxiety he has evolved nations and tremendous governments to protect his person and his property, his strenuous purpose, unremitting, has   15 brought to pass the whole frantic turmoil of modern industry, that he may have enough, enough to eat and wear, that he may be safe. Even his religion has for the systole of its heart-beat,* propitiation of the Unknown God who controls death and the sources of nourishment.

But for the diastole of the heart-beat, there is something more,   20 something else, thank heaven, than this unappeased rage of self-preservation.* Even the passion to be rich is not merely the greedy wish to be secured within triple walls of brass, along with huge barns of plenty.* And the history of mankind is not altogether the history of an effort at self-preservation which has at length become over-blown   25 and extravagant.

Working in contradiction to the will of self-preservation, from the very first man wasted himself begetting children, colouring himself and dancing and howling and sticking feathers in his hair, in scratching pictures on the walls of his cave, and making graven images of his   30 unutterable feelings. So he went on, wildly and with gorgeousness taking no thought for the morrow, but, at evening, considering the ruddy lily.*

In his sleep, however, it must have come to him early that the lily is a wise and housewifely flower, considerate of herself, laying up secretly   35

7

her little storehouse and barn, well under the ground, well tucked with supplies. And this providence on the part of the lily, man laid to heart. He went out anxiously at dawn to kill the largest mammoth, so that he should have a huge hill of meat, that he could never eat his way
5   through.

And the old man at the door of the cave, afraid of the coming winter with its scant supplies, watching the young man go forth, told impressive tales to the children of the ant and the grasshopper;* and praised the thrift and husbandry of that little red squirrel, and drew
10 a moral from the gaudy, fleeting poppy.

"Don't, my dear children," continued the ancient palaeolithic man as he sat at the door of his cave, "don't behave like that reckless, shameless scarlet flower. Ah, my dears, you little know the amount of labour, the careful architecture, all the [physics]* and chemistry,
15 the weaving and the casting of energy, the business of day after day and night after night, yon gaudy wreck has squandered. Pfff!—and it is gone, and the place thereof shall know it no more.* Now, my dear children, don't be like that."

Nevertheless, the old man watched the last poppy coming out, the
20 red flame licking into sight; watched the blaze at the top clinging around a little tender dust, and he wept, thinking of his youth. Till the red flag fell before him, lay in rags on the earth. Then he did not know whether to pay homage to the void, or to preach.

So he compromised, and made a Story about a phoenix.* "Yes,
25 my dears, in the waste desert, I know the green and graceful tree where the phoenix has her nest. And there I have seen the eternal phoenix escape away into flame, leaving life behind in her ashes. Suddenly she went up into red flame, and was gone, leaving life to rise from her ashes."
30 "And did it?"

"Oh yes, it rose up."

"What did it do then?"

"It grew up, and burst into flame again."

And the flame was all the story and all triumph. The old [man] knew
35 this. It was this he praised, the red outburst at the top of the poppy, in his innermost heart* that had no fear of winter. Even the latent seeds were secondary, within the fire. No red; and there were just a herb, without name or sign of poppy. But he had seen the flower in all its evanescence and its being.
40 When his educated grandson told him that the red was there to bring

the bees and the flies, he knew well enough that more bees and flies and wasps would come to a sticky smear round his grandson's mouth, than to yards of poppy red.

Therefore his grandson began to talk about the excess which always accompanies reproduction. And the old man died during this talk, and 5 was put away. But his soul was uneasy, and come back from the shades to have the last word, muttering inaudibly in the cave door. "If there is *always** excess accompanying reproduction, how can you call it excess? When your mother makes a pie, and has too much paste, then that is excess. So she carves a paste rose with her surplus, and sticks it 10 on the top of the pie. That is the flowering of the excess. And children, if they are young enough, clap their hands at this blossom of pastry. And if the pie bloom not too often with the rose of excess, they eat the paste blossom-shaped lump with reverence. But soon they become sophisticated, and know that the rose is no rose, but only excess, 15 surplus, a counterfeit, a lump, unedifying and unattractive and they say 'No thank you mother: no rose.'

"Wherefore, if you mean to tell me that the red of my shed poppy was no more than the rose of the paste on the pie, you are a fool. You mean to say, that young blood had more stuff than he knew what to do 20 with. He knocked his structure of leaves and stalks together, hammered the poppy-knob safe on top, sieved and bolted the essential seeds, shut them up tight, and then said 'Ah!' And whilst he was dusting his hands, he saw a lot of poppy-stuff to spare. 'Must do something with it—must do something with it—mustn't be wasted!' So he just rolled it out into 25 red flakes, and dabbed it round the knobby seed-box, and said 'There, the simple creatures will take it in, and I've got rid of it.'

"My dear child, that is the history of the poppy and of the excess which accompanied his reproduction, is it? That's all you can say of him, when he makes his red splash in the world?—that he had a bit left 30 over from his pie with the five and twenty blackbirds in, so he put a red frill round? My child, it is good you are young, for you are a fool."

So the shade of the ancient man passed back again, to foregather with all the shades. And it shook its head as it went, muttering "Conceit, conceit of self-preservation and of race-preservation, con- 35 ceit!" But he had seen the heart of his grandson, with the wasteful red peeping out, like a poppy bud. So he chuckled.

- 2 -

Why, when we are away for our holidays, do we exclaim with such
rapture "What a splendid field of poppies!" or "Isn't the poppy sweet, a
red dot among the camomile flowers!",—only to go back on it all, and
5   when the troubles come in, and we walk forth in heaviness, taking
ourselves seriously, later on, to cry, in a harsh and bitter voice: "Ah, the
gaudy treason of those red weeds in the corn"; or when children come
up with nosegays: "Nasty red flowers, poison, darling, make baby go to
sleep," or when we see the scarlet flutter in the wind: "Vanity and
10 flaunting vanity,"* and with gusto watch the red bits disappear into
nothingness, saying: "It is well such scarlet vanity be cast to nought."

   Why are we so rarely away on our holidays? Why do we persist in
taking ourselves seriously, in counting our money and our goods and
our virtue? We are down in the end. We rot and tumble away. And that
15 without ever bursting the bud, the tight economical bud of caution and
thrift and self-preservation.

   The phoenix grows up to maturity and fulness of wisdom, it attains to
fatness and wealth and all things desirable, only to burst into flame and
expire in ash. And the flame and the ash are the be-all and the end-all,
20 and the fatness and wisdom and wealth are but the fuel spent. It is a
wasteful ordering of things, indeed, to be sure:—but so it is, and what
must be must be.

   But we are very cunning. If we cannot carry our goods and our
fatness, at least our goodness can be stored up like coin. And if we are
25 not sure of the credit of the bank, we form ourselves into an unlimited
liability company to run the future. We must have an obvious eternal
deposit in which to bank our effort. And because the red of the poppy
and the fire of the phoenix are contributed to no store, but are spent
with the day and disappear, we talk of vanity and foolish mortality.

30   The phoenix goes gadding off into flame, and leaves the future
behind, unprovided* for, in its ashes. There is no prodigal poppy
left to return home in repentance, after the red is squandered in a day.
Vanity, and vanity, and pathetic [transience]* of mortality. All that
is left us to call eternal is the tick-tack of birth and death, monotonous
35 as time. The vain blaze flapped away into space and is gone, and what is
left but the tick-tack of time, of birth and death.

   But I will chase that flamy phoenix that gadded off into nothingness.
Whoop and halloo and away we go into nothingness, in hot pursuit.

Say, where are the flowers of yesteryear? Où sont les neiges de l'antan?* Where's Hippolita, where's Thais, each one loveliest among women? Who knows? Where are the snows of yesteryear.

That is all very well, but they must be somewhere. They may not be in any bank or deposit, but they are not lost for ever. The virtue of them 5 is still blowing about in nothingness and in somethingness. I cannot walk up and say "How do you do, Dido?" as Aeneas* did in the shades. But Dido—Dido!—the robin cocks a scornful tail and goes off, disgusted with the noise. You might as well look for your own soul as to look for Dido. "Didon dina dit-on du dos d'un dodu dindon",* 10 comes rapidly into my mind, and a few frayed scraps of Virgil, and [a] vision of fair, round, half globe breasts and blue eyes with tears in them; and a tightness comes into my heart: all forces rushing into me through my consciousness. But what of Dido my unconsciousness has, I could not tell you. Something, I am sure, and something that has 15 come to me without my knowledge, something that flew away in the flames long ago, something that flew away from that pillar of fire,* which was her body, day after day whilst she lived, flocking into nothingness to make a difference there. The reckoning of her money and her mortal assets may be discoverable in print. But what she is in 20 the roomy space of somethingness, called nothingness, is all that matters to me.

She is something, I declare, even if she were utterly forgotten. How could any new thing be born unless it had a new nothingness to breathe. A new creature breathing old air, or even renewed air: it is 25 terrible to think of. A new creature must have new air, absolutely bran-new air to breathe. Otherwise, there is no new creature, and birth and death are a tick-tack.

What was Dido was new, absolutely new. It had never been before, and in Dido it *was*. In its own degree, the prickly sow-thistle I have just 30 pulled up *is*, for the first time in all time. It is itself, a new thing. And most vividly it is itself in its yellow little disc of a flower: most vividly. In its flower it is. In its flower it issues something to the world that never was issued before. Its like has been before, its exact equivalent never. And this richness of new being is richest in the flowering yellow disc of 35 my plant.

What then of this excess that accompanies reproduction? The excess is the thing itself at its maximum of being. If it had stopped short of this excess, it would not have been at all. If this excess were missing, darkness would cover the face of the earth. In this excess, the plant is 40 transfigured into flower, it achieves at last itself. The aim, the culmination of all is the red of the poppy, this flame of the phoenix, this extravagant being of Dido, even her so-called waste.

But no, we dare not. We dare not fulfil the last part of our
5 programme. We linger into inactivity at the vegetable, self-preserving stage. As if we preserved ourselves merely for the sake of remaining as we are. Yet there we remain, like the regulation cabbage, hide-bound, a bunch of leaves that may not go any farther for fear of losing market value.* A cabbage seen straddling up into weakly fiery flower is a
10 piteous, almost an indecent sight to us. Better be a weed, and noxious. So we remain tight shut, a bunch of leaves, full of greenness and substance.

But the rising flower thrusts and pushes at the heart of us, strives and wrestles, while the static will holds us immovable. And neither will
15 relent. But the flower, if it cannot beat its way through into being, will thrash destruction about itself. So the bound-up cabbage is beaten rotten at the heart.

Yet we call the poppy "vanity", and we write it down a weed. It is humiliating to think, that when we are taking ourselves seriously, we are
20 considering our own self-preservation, or the greater scheme for the preservation of mankind. What is it that really matters? For the poppy, that the poppy disclose its red: for the cabbage, that it run up into weakly fiery flower: for Dido, that she *be* Dido, that she become herself, and die as fate will have it. Seed and fruit and produce, these are only a
25 minor aim: children and good works are a minor aim. Work, in its ordinary meaning, and all effort for the public good, these are labour of self-preservation, they are only means to the end. The final aim is the flower, the fluttering singing nucleus which is a bird in spring, the magical spurt of being which is a hare all explosive with fulness of self,
30 in the moonlight; the real passage of a man down the road, no sham, no shadow, no counterfeit, whose eyes shine blue with his own reality, as he moves amongst things free as they are, a being; the flitting under the lamp of a woman [incontrovertible],* distinct from everything and from everybody, as one who is herself, of whom Christ said "to them
35 that have shall be given."*

The final aim of every living thing, creature, or being is the full achievement of itself. This accomplished, it will produce what it will produce, it will bear the fruit of its nature. Not the fruit, however, but the flower is the culmination and climax, the degree to be striven for.
40 Not the work I shall produce, but the real Me I shall achieve, that is the

consideration; of the complete Me will come the complete fruit of me, the work, the children.

And I know that the common wild poppy has achieved so far its complete poppy-self, unquestionable. It has uncovered its red. Its light, its self, has risen and shone out, has run on the winds for a moment. It is splendid. The world is a world because of the poppy's red. Otherwise it would be a lump of clay. And I am I as well, since the disclosure. What it is, I breathe it and snuff it up, it is about me and upon me and of me. And I can tell that I do not know it all yet. There is more to disclose. What more, I do not know. I tremble at the inchoate infinity of life when I think of that which the poppy has to reveal, and has not as yet had time to bring forth. I make a jest of it. I say to the flower, "Come, you've played that red card long enough. Let's see what else you have got up your sleeve." But I am premature and impertinent. My impertinence makes me ashamed. He has not played his red card long enough to have outsatisfied me.

Yet we must always hold that life is the great struggle for self-preservation, that this struggle for the means of life is the essence and whole of life. As if it would be anything so futile, so ingestive. Yet we ding-dong at it, always hammering out the same phrase, about the struggle for existence, the right to work, the right to the vote, the right to this and the right to that, all in the struggle for existence, as if any external power could give us the right to ourselves. That we have within ourselves. And [if] we have it not, then the remainder that we do possess will be taken away from us. "To them that have shall be given, and from them that have not shall be taken away even that which they have."

Chapter II.

Still introductory: about Women's Suffrage,* and Laws, and the War, and the Poor, with some Fancyful Moralising.

5 It is so sad, that the earnest people of to-day serve at the old, second-rate altar of self-preservation. The women suffragists, who are certainly the bravest, and, in the old sense, most heroic party amongst us, even they are content to fight the old battles on the old ground, to fight an old system of self-preservation to obtain a more advanced system of
10 preservation. The vote is only a means, they admit. A means to what?—a means to making better laws, laws which shall protect the unprotected girl from a vicious male, which shall protect the sweated woman-labourer from the unscrupulous greed of the capitalist, which shall protect the interest of woman in the State. And surely this is
15 worthy and admirable.

Yet it is like protecting the well-being of a cabbage in the cabbage-patch, while the cabbage is rotting at the heart for lack of power to run out into blossom. Could you make any law in any land, empowering the poppy to flower? You might make a law refusing it liberty to bloom. But
20 that is another thing. Could any law put into being something which did not before exist? It could not. Law can only modify the conditions, for better or worse, of that which already exists.

But law is a very, very clumsy and mechanical instrument, and we people are very, very delicate and subtle beings. Therefore I only ask
25 that the law shall leave me alone as much as possible. I insist that no law shall have immediate power over me, either for my good or for my ill. And I would wish that many laws be unmade, and no more laws made. Let there be a parliament of men and women for the careful and gradual unmaking of laws.
30 If it were for this purpose that women wanted the vote, I should be glad, and the opposition would be vital and intense, instead of just flippantly or exasperatedly static. Because then the woman's movement would be a living human movement. But even so, the claiming of a vote for the purpose of unmaking the laws would be rather like taking a
35 malady in order to achieve a cure.

The women, however, want the vote in order to make more laws. That is the most lamentable and pathetic fact. They will take this clumsy machinery to make right the body politic. And pray, what is the sickness of the body politic? Is it that some men are sex-mad or sex-degraded, and that some, or many employers, are money-degraded? And if so, will you by making laws for putting in prison the sex-degraded, and putting out of power the money-degraded, thereby make whole and clean the State? Wherever you put them, will not the degradation exist, and continue? And is the State, then, merely an instrument for weeding the public of destructive members? And is this, then, the crying necessity for more thorough weeding?

Whence does the degradation or perversion arise? Is there any great sickness in the body politic? Then where and what is it? Am I, or you suffragist woman or you voting man sex-whole and money-healthy, are we sound human beings? Have we achieved to true individuality and to a sufficient completeness in ourselves? Because if not,—then physician, heal thyself.

That is no taunt, but the finest and most damning criticism ever passed: "Physician, heal thyself."* No amount of pity can blind us to the inexorable reality of the challenge.

Where is the source of all money-sickness, and the origin of all the sex-perversion? That is the question to answer. And no cause shall come to life unless it contain an answer to this question. Laws, and all State machinery, these only regulate the sick, separate the sick and the whole, clumsily, oh, so clumsily that it is worse than futile. Who is there who searches out the origin of the sickness, with a hope to quench the malady at its source?

It lies in the heart of man, and not in the conditions—that is obvious, yet always forgotten. It is not a malaria° which blows in through the window and attacks us when we are healthy. We are each one of us a swamp, we are like the hide-bound cabbage going rotten at the heart. And for the same reason that, instead of producing our flower, instead of continuing our activity, satisfying our true desire, climbing and clambering till, like the poppy, we lean on the sill of all the unknown, and run our flag out there in the colour and shine of being, having surpassed that which has been before, we hang back, we dare not even peep forth, but, safely shut up in bud, safely and darkly and snugly enclosed, like the regulation cabbage, we remain secure till our hearts go rotten, saying all the while how safe we are.

No wonder there is a war. No wonder there is a great waste and squandering of life. Anything, anything to prove that we are not altogether sealed in our own self-preservation as dying chrysalides. Better the light be blown out, wilfully, recklessly, in the wildest wind, than remain secure under the bushel,* saved from every draught.

5   So we go to war to show that we can throw our lives away. Indeed, they have become of so little value to us. We cannot live, we cannot *be*. Then let us tip-cat* with death, let us rush throwing our lives away. Then at any rate we shall have a sensation—and "perhaps", after all, the value of life is in death.

10   What does the law matter? What does money, power, or public approval matter? All that matters is that each human being shall *be* in his own fulness. If something obstruct us we break it or put it aside, as the shoots of the trees break even through the London pavements. That is, if life is strong enough in us. If not, we are glad to fight with

15   death. Does not the war show us how little, under all our carefulness, we count human life and human suffering, how little we value ourselves at bottom, how we hate our own security. We have many hospitals and many laws and charities for the poor. And at the same time we send ourselves to be killed and torn and tortured, we spread grief and

20   desolation, and then, only then, we are somewhat satisfied. For have we not proved that we can transcend our own self-preservation, that we do not care so much for ourselves after all. Indeed, we almost hate ourselves.

Indeed, well may we talk about a just and righteous war [not]*

25   against Germany, but against ourselves, our own self-love and caution. It is no war for the freedom of man from militarism or the Prussian yoke: it is a war for freedom of the bonds of our own cowardice and sluggish greed of security and well-being: it is a fight to regain ourselves out of the grip of our own caution.

30   Tell me no more we care about human life and suffering. We are, every one of us, revelling at this moment in the squandering of human life as if it were something we needed. And it is shameful. And all because that, to *live*, we are afraid to [be]* ourselves. We can only die.

35   Let there be an end then of all this welter of pity, which is only self-pity reflected on to some obvious surface. And let there be an end of this German hatred. We ought to be grateful to Germany that she still has the power to burst the bound hide of the cabbage. Where do I meet a man or a woman who does not draw deep and thorough satisfaction

40   from this war? Because of pure shame that we should have seemed

such poltroons, living safe and atrophied, not daring to take one step to life. And this is the only good that can result from the "world disaster":* that we realise once more that self-preservation is not the final goal of life; that we realise that we can still squander life and property and inflict suffering wholesale. That will free us, perhaps, from the bushel we cower under, from the paucity of our lives, from the cowardice that will not let us *be*, which will only let us exist in security, unflowering, unreal, fat, under the cosy jam-pot of the State, under the shelter of the social frame.

And we must be prepared to fight, after the war, a renewed rage of activity for greater self-preservation, a renewed outcry for a stronger bushel to shelter our light. We must also undertake the incubus of crippled souls that will come home, and of crippled souls that will be left behind: men in whom the violence of war shall have shaken the life-flow and broken or perverted the course, women who will cease to live henceforth, yet will remain existing in the land, fixed at some lower point of fear or brutality.*

Yet if we are left maimed and halt, if you die or I die, it will not matter, so long as there is alive in the land some new sense of what is and what is not, some new courage to let go the securities, and to *be*, to risk ourselves in a forward venture of life, as we are willing to risk ourselves in a rush of death.

Nothing will matter so long as life shall sprout up again strong after this winter of cowardice and well-being, sprout into the unknown. Let us only have had enough of pity: pity, that stands before the glass and weeps for ever over the sight of its own tears. This is what we have made of Christ's Commandment:* "Thou shalt love thy neighbour as thyself"—a mirror for the tears of self-pity. How do we love our neighbour? By taking to heart his poverty, his small wage, and the attendant evils thereof. And is that how we love our neighbour as *ourselves*? Do I then think of myself as [a] moneyed thing enjoying advantages, or a non-moneyed thing suffering from disadvantages? Evidently I do. Then why the tears? They must rise from the inborn knowledge that neither money or non-money, advantages or disadvantages, matter supremely: what matters is the light under the bushel, the flower fighting under the safeguard of the leaves. I am weeping over my denied self. And I am very sorry for myself, held in the grip of some stronger force. Where can I find an image of myself?—ah, in the poor, in my poor neighbour labouring in the grip of an unjust system of capitalism. Let me look at him, let my heart be wrung, let me give

myself to his service. Poor fellow, poor image, he is so badly off. Alas
and alas, I do love my neighbour as myself: I am as anxious about his
pecuniary welfare as I am about my own. I am so sorry for him, the poor
X. He is a man like me. So I lie to myself and to him. For I do not care
5 about him and his poverty: I care about my own unsatisfied soul. But I
side-track to him, my poor neighbour, to [vent] on him my self-pity.

It is as if a poppy, when he is grown taller than his neighbours, but
has not come to flower, should look down and because he can get no
further, say: "Alas for those poor dwindlers down there: they don't get
10 half as much rain as I do." He grows no more, and his non-growing
makes him sad, and he tries to crouch down so as not to be any taller
than his neighbour, thinking his sorrow is for his neighbour, and his
neighbour struggles weakly into flower, after his fight for the sunshine.
But the rich poppy crouches gazing down, nor even once lifts up his
15 head to blossom. He is so afraid of giving himself forth, he cannot move
on to expose his new nakedness, up there to confront the horrific space
of the void,* he is afraid of giving himself away to the unknown. He
stays within his shell.

Which is the parable of the rich poppy. The *truth* about him is, he
20 grows as fast as he can, though he devours no man's substance, because
he has neither storehouse nor barn to devour them with, and neither a
poppy nor a man can devour much through his own mouth. He grows
as fast as he can, and from his innermost self he shuttles the red fire
out, bit by bit, a little further, till he has brought it together and up to
25 bud. There he hangs his head, hesitates, halts, reflects a moment,
shrinking from the great climax when he lets off his fire. He ought to
perceive now his neighbours, and to stand arrested, crying "Alas those
poor dwindlers." But his fire breaks out of him, and he lifts his head,
slowly, subtly, tense in an ecstasy of fear overwhelmed by joy, submits
30 to the issuing of his flame and his fire, and there it hangs at the brink of
the void, scarlet and radiant for a little while, imminent on the
unknown, a signal, an out-post, an advance-guard, a forlorn, splendid
flag, quivering from the brink of the unfathomed void, into which it
flutters silently, satisfied, whilst a little ash, a little dusty seed remains
35 behind on the solid ledge of the earth.

And the day is richer for a poppy, the flame of another phoenix is
filled in to the universe, something is, which was not.

That is the whole point: something is which was not. And I wish it
were true of us. I wish we were all like kindled bonfires on the edge of
40 space, marking out the advance-posts. What is the aim of self-

preservation, but to carry us right out to the firing line, where what *is* is in contact with what is not. If many lives be lost by the way, it cannot be helped, nor if much suffering be entailed. I do not go out to war in the intention of avoiding all danger or discomfort: I go to fight for myself. Every step I move forward into being brings a newer, juster proportion 5 into the world, gives me less need of storehouse and barn, allows me to leave all, and to take what I want by the way, sure that it will always be there; allows me in the end to fly the flag of myself, at the extreme tip of life.

He who would save his life must lose it. But why should he go on and 10 waste it? Certainly let him cast it upon the waters.° Whence and how and whither it will return is no matter, in terms of values. But like a poppy that has come to bud, when he reaches the shore, when he has traversed his known and come to the beach to meet the unknown, he must strip himself naked and plunge in, and pass out: if he dare. And 15 the rest of his life he will be a stirring at the unknown, cast out upon the waters. But if he dare not plunge in, if he dare not take off his clothes and give himself naked to the flood, then let him prowl in rotten safety weeping for pity of those he imagines worse off than himself. He dare not weep aloud for his own cowardice. And weep he must. So he will 20 find him objects of pity.

Chapter III.

Containing Six Novels and the Real Tragedy.

This is supposed to be a book about the people in Thomas Hardy's novels. But if one wrote everything they give rise to it would fill the Judgement Book.*

One thing about them is that none of the heroes and heroines care very much for money, or immediate self-preservation, and all of them are struggling hard to come into being. What exactly the struggle into being consists in, is the question. But most obviously, from the Wessex novels, the first and chiefest factor is the struggle into love and the struggle with love: by love meaning the love of a man for a woman and a woman for a man. The via media to being, for man or woman, is love, and love alone. Having achieved and accomplished love, then the man passes into the unknown. He has become himself, his tale is told. Of anything that is complete there is no more tale to tell. The tale is about becoming complete, or about the failure to become complete.

It is urged against Thomas Hardy's characters that they do unreasonable things—quite, quite unreasonable things. They are always going off unexpectedly and doing something that nobody would do. That is quite true, and the charge is amusing. These people of Wessex are always bursting suddenly out of bud and taking a wild flight into flower, always shooting something out of a tight convention, a tight, hide-bound cabbage state into something quite madly personal. It would be amusing to count the number of special marriage licences taken out in Hardy's books. Nowhere, except perhaps in Jude, is there the slightest development of personal action in the characters: it is all explosive. Jude, however, does see more or less what he is doing, and act from choice. He is more consecutive. The rest explode out of the convention. They are people each with a real, vital, potential self, even the apparently wishy-washy heroines of the earlier books, and this self suddenly bursts the shell of manner and convention and commonplace opinion, and acts independently, absurdly, without mental knowledge or acquiescence.

And from such an outburst the tragedy usually develops. For there does exist, after all, the great self-preservation system, and in it we must all live. How to live in it after bursting out of it was the problem these Wessex people found themselves faced with. And they never solved the problem, none of them except the comically-, insufficiently-, treated Ethelberta.

This because they must subscribe to the system in themselves. From the more immediate claims of self-preservation, they could free themselves: from money, from ambition for social success. None of the heroes or heroines of Hardy cared much for these things. But there is the greater idea of self-preservation, which is formulated in the State, in the whole modelling of the Community. And from this idea, the heroes and heroines of Wessex, like the heroes and heroines of almost anywhere else, could not free themselves. In the long run, the State, the Community, the established form of life remained, remained intact and impregnable, the individual, trying to break forth from it, died of fear, of exhaustion, or of exposure to attacks from all sides, like men who have left the walled city to live outside in the precarious open.

This is the tragedy of Hardy, always the same: the tragedy of those who, more or less pioneers, have died in the wilderness whither they had escaped for free action, after having left the walled security, and the comparative imprisonment, of the established convention. This is the theme of novel after novel: remain quite within the convention, and you are good, safe, and happy in the long run, though you never have the vivid pang of sympathy on your side: or, on the other hand, be passionate, individual, wilful, you will find the security of the convention a walled prison, you will escape, and you will die, either of your own lack of strength to bear the isolation and the exposure, or by direct revenge from the community, or from both. This is the tragedy, and only this: it is nothing more metaphysical than the division of a man against himself in such a way: first, that he is a member of the community, and must, upon his honour, in no way move to disintegrate the community either in its moral or its practical form; second, that the convention of the community is a prison to his natural, individual desire, a desire that compels him, whether he feel justified or not, to break the bounds of the community, lands him outside the pale, there to stand alone, and say: "I was right, my desire was real and inevitable; if I was to be myself I must fulfil it, convention or no convention", or else, there to stand alone, doubting, and saying: "Was I right, was I wrong? If I was wrong, oh, let me die"—in which case he courts death.

The growth and the development of this tragedy, the deeper and
deeper realisation of this division and this problem, the coming towards
some conclusion, is the one theme of the Wessex novels.

And therefore the books must be taken chronologically,* to
5 reveal the development and to advance towards the conclusion.

    1. *Desperate Remedies.*

Springrove, the dull hero, fast within the convention, dare not tell
Cytherea that he is already engaged, and thus prepares the complica-
tion. Manston, represented as fleshly passionate, breaks the convention
10 and commits murder, which is very extreme, under compulsion of his
desire for Cytherea. He is aided by the darkly passionate, lawless Miss
Aldclyffe. He and Miss Aldclyffe meet death and Cytherea and
Springrove are united to happiness and success.

    2. *Under the Greenwood Tree.*

15 After a brief excursion from the beaten track in the pursuit of social
ambition and satisfaction of the imagination, figured by the Clergyman,
Fancy, the little school-mistress, returns to Dick, renounces imagination, and settles down to steady, solid, physically satisfactory married
life, and all is as it should be. But Fancy will carry in her heart all her
20 life many unopened buds that will die unflowered; and Dick will
probably have a bad time of it.

    3. *A Pair of Blue Eyes.*

Elfride breaks down in her attempt to jump the first little hedge of
convention, when she comes back after running away with Stephen.
25 She cannot stand even a little alone. Knight, his conventional idea
backed up by selfish instinct cannot endure Elfride when he thinks she
is not virgin, though now she loves him beyond bounds. She submits to
him, and owns the conventional idea entirely right, even whilst she is
innocent. An aristocrat walks off with her whilst the two men hesitate,
30 and she, poor innocent victim of passion not vital enough to overthrow
the most banal conventional ideas, lies in a bright coffin, while the three
confirmed lovers mourn, and say how great the tragedy is.

    4. *Far from the Madding Crowd.*

The unruly Bathsheba, though almost pledged to Farmer Boldwood,
35 a ravingly passionate, middle-aged bachelor pretendant, who has
suddenly started in mad pursuit of some unreal conception of woman,
personified in Bathsheba, lightly runs off and marries Sergeant Troy,
an illegitimate aristocrat, unscrupulous and yet sensitive in taking his
pleasures. She loves Troy, he does not love her. All the time she is
40 loved faithfully and persistently by the good Gabriel, who is like a dog

that watches the bone and bides the time. [Sergeant] Troy° treats Bathsheba badly, never loves her, though he is the only man in the book who knows anything about her. Her pride helps her to recover. Troy is killed by Boldwood, exit the unscrupulous, but discriminative, almost cynical young soldier and the mad, middle-aged pursuer of the Fata Morgana, enter the good steady Gabriel, who marries Bathsheba because he will make her a good husband, and the flower of imaginative fine love is dead for her with Troy's scorn of her.

5. *The Hand of Ethelberta.*

Ethelberta, a woman of character and of brilliant parts, sets out in pursuit of social success, finds that Julian, the only man she is inclined to love, is too small for her, hands him over to the good little Picotee, and she herself, sacrificing almost cynically what is called her heart, marries the old scoundrelly Lord Mountclere, runs him and his estates and governs well, a sound strong pillar of established society, now she has nipped off the bud of her heart. Moral, it is easier for a butler's daughter to marry a Lord than to find a husband with her love, if she be an exceptional woman.

The Hand of Ethelberta is the one almost cynical comedy. It marks the zenith of a certain feeling in the Wessex novels, the zenith of the feeling that the best thing to do is to kick out the craving for "Love", and substitute common-sense, leaving sentiment to the minor characters.

This novel is a shrug of the shoulders and a last taunt to hope, it is the end of the happy endings, except where sanity and a little cynicism again appear in *The Trumpet-Major*, to bless where they despise. It is the hard resistant, ironical announcement of personal failure, resistant and half grinning. It gives way to violent, angry passions and real tragedy, real killing of beloved people, self-killing. Till now, only Elfride among the beloved has been killed, the good men have always come out on top.

6. *The Return of the Native.*

This is the first tragic and important novel. Eustacia, dark, wild, passionate, quite conscious of her desires and inheriting no tradition which would make her ashamed of them, since she is of a novelistic Italian birth, loves first the unstable Wildeve, who does not satisfy her, then casts him aside for the newly returned Clym, whom she marries. What does she want? She does not know, but it is evidently some form of self-realisation; she wants to be herself, to attain herself. But she does not know how, by what means, so romantic imagination says Paris and the beau monde. As if that would stay her unsatisfaction.

Clym has found out the vanity of Paris and the beau monde. What then does he want? He does not know, his imagination tells him he wants to serve the moral system of the community, since the material system is despicable. He wants to teach little Egdon boys in school. There is [as]
5 much vanity in this, easily, as in Eustacia's Paris. For what is the moral system but the ratified form of the material system? What is Clym's altruism but a deep very subtle cowardice, that makes him shirk his own being whilst apparently acting nobly; which makes him choose to improve mankind rather than to struggle at the quick of himself into
10 being. He is not able to undertake his own soul, so he will take a commission for society to enlighten the souls of others. It is a subtle equivocation. Thus both Eustacia and he side-track from themselves, and each leaves the other unconvinced, unsatisfied, unrealised. Eustacia because she moves outside the convention, must die, Clym because he
15 identified himself with the community, is transferred from Paris to preaching. He had never become an integral man, because when faced with the demand to produce himself, he remained under cover of the community and excused by his altruism.

His remorse over his mother is adulterated with sentiment, it is
20 exaggerated by the push of tradition behind it. Even in this he does not ring true. He is always according to pattern, producing his feelings more or less on demand, according to the accepted standard. Practically never is he able to act or even feel in his original self: he is always according to the convention. His punishment is his final loss of all his original self: he
25 is left preaching, out of sheer emptiness.

Thomasin and Venn have nothing in them turbulent enough to push them to the bounds of the convention. There is always room for them inside. They are genuine people, and they get the prize within the walls.

Wildeve, shifty and unhappy, attracted always from outside and never
30 driven from within, can neither stand with or without the established system. He cares nothing for it, because he is unstable, has no positive being. He is an eternal assumption.

The other victim, Clym's mother, is the crashing down of one of the old, rigid pillars of the system. The pressure on her is too great. She is
35 weakened from the inside also, for her nature is non-conventional, it cannot own the bounds.

So, in this book, all the exceptional people, those with strong feelings and unusual characters, are reduced, only those remain who are steady and genuine, if commonplace. Let a man will for himself, and he is
40 destroyed. He must will according to the established system.

The real sense of tragedy is got from the setting. What is the great, tragic power in the book?—it is Egdon Heath. And who are the real spirits of the Heath?—first Eustacia, then Clym's mother, then Wildeve. The natives have little or nothing in common with the place.

What is the real stuff of tragedy in the book? It is the Heath.* It is the primitive, primal earth, where the instinctive life heaves up. There, in the deep, rude stirring of the instincts, there was the reality that worked the tragedy. Close to the body of things, there can be heard the stir that makes us and destroys us. The [earth]* heaved with raw instinct, Egdon whose dark soil was strong and crude and organic as the body of a beast. Out of the body of this crude earth are born Eustacia, Wildeve, Mistress Yeobright, Clym, and all the others. They are one year's accidental crop. What matter* if some are drowned or dead, and others preaching or married: what matter, any more than the withering heath, the reddening berries, the seedy furze and the dead fern of one autumn of Egdon. The Heath persists. Its body is strong and fecund, it will bear many more crops beside this. Here is the sombre, latent power that will go on producing, no matter what happen to the product. Here is the deep, black source from whence all these little contents of lives are drawn. And the contents of the small lives are spilled and wasted. There is savage satisfaction in it: for so much more remains to come, such a black, powerful fecundity is working there that what does it matter!

Three people die and are taken back into the Heath, they mingle their strong earth again with its powerful soil, having been broken off at their stem. It is very good. Not Egdon is futile, sending forth life on the powerful heave of passion. It cannot be futile, for it is eternal. What is futile is the purpose of man.

Man has a purpose which he has divorced from the passionate purpose that issued him out of the earth, into being. The Heath threw forth its shaggy heather and furze and fern, clean into being. It threw forth Eustacia and Wildeve and Mistress Yeobright and Clym, but to what purpose? Eustacia thought she wanted the hats and bonnets of Paris. Perhaps she was right. The heavy, strong soil of Egdon, breeding original native beings, is under Paris as well as under Wessex, and Eustacia sought herself in the gay city. She thought life there, in Paris, would be tropical, and all her energy and passion out of Egdon would there come into handsome flower. And if Paris real had been Paris as she imagined it, no doubt she was right, and her instinct was soundly expressed. But Paris real was not Eustacia's imagined Paris. Where was her imagined Paris, the place where her powerful nature could come to blossom? Beside some strong-passioned, unconfined man, her mate.

Which mate Clym might have been. He was born out of passionate Egdon to live as a passionate being whose strong feelings moved him
5 ever further into being. But quite early his life became narrowed down to a small purpose: he must of necessity go into business, and submit his whole being, body and soul as well as mind, to the business and to the greater system it represented. His feelings, that should have produced the man, were suppressed and contained, he worked accord-
10 ing to a system imposed from without. The dark struggle of Egdon, a struggle into being as the furze struggles into flower, went on in him, but could not burst the enclosure of the idea, the system which contained him. Impotent to *be*, he must transform himself, and live in an abstraction, in a generalisation, he must identify himself with the
15 system. He must live as Man or Humanity, or as the Community, or as Society, or as Civilisation. "An inner strenuousness was preying on his outer symmetry, and they rated his look as singular———His counte-nance was overlaid with legible meanings. Without being thought-worn, he yet had certain marks derived from a perception of his
20 surroundings, such as are not unfrequently found on men at the end of the four or five years of endeavour which follow the close of placid pupilage. He already showed that thought is a disease of flesh, and indirectly bore evidence that ideal physical beauty is incompatible with emotional development and a full recognition of the coil of things.
25 Mental luminousness must be fed with the oil of life, even if there is already a physical need for it; and the pitiful sight of two demands on one supply was just showing itself here."*

But did the face of Clym show that thought is a disease of flesh, or merely that in his case a dis-ease, an un-ease of flesh produced
30 thought. One does not catch thought like a fever: one produces it. If it be in any way a disease of flesh, it is rather the rash that indicates the disease, than the disease itself. The "inner strenuousness" of Clym's nature was not fighting against his physical symmetry, but against the limits imposed on his physical movement. By nature, as a passionate,
35 violent product of Egdon, he should have loved and suffered in flesh and in soul from love, long before this age. He should have lived and moved and had his being,* whereas he had only his business, and afterwards his inactivity. His years of pupilage were past, "he was one of whom something original was expected",* yet he continued in
40 pupilage. For he produced nothing original in being or in act, and

certainly no original thought. None of his ideas were original. Even he himself was not original. He was over-taught, had become an echo. His life had been arrested, and his activity turned into repetition. [Far] from being emotionally developed, he was emotionally undeveloped, almost entirely. Only his mental faculties were developed. And his emotions* were obliged to work according to the label he put upon them: a ready-made label.

Yet he remained for all that an original, the force of life was in him, however much he frustrated and suppressed its natural movement. "As is usual with bright natures, the deity that lies ignominiously chained within an ephemeral human carcase shone out of him like a ray."* But was the deity chained within his ephemeral human carcase, or within his limited human consciousness? Was it his blood, which rose dark and potent out of Egdon, which hampered and confined the deity, or was it his mind, that house built of extraneous knowledge and guarded by his will, which formed the prison.

He came back to Egdon—what for? To re-unite himself with the strong, free flow of life that rose out of Egdon as from a source? No—"to preach to the Egdon eremites that they might rise to a serene comprehensiveness without going through the process of enriching themselves."* As if the Egdon eremites had not already far more serene comprehensiveness than ever he had himself, rooted as they were in the soil of all things, and living from the root. What did it matter how they enriched themselves, so long as [they] kept this strong, deep root in the primal soil, so long as their instincts moved out to action and to expression. The system was big enough for them, and had not power over their instincts. They should have taught him rather than he them.

And Egdon made him marry Eustacia. Here was action and life, here was a move into being on his part. But as soon as he got her, she became an idea to him, she had to fit in his system of ideas. According to his way of living, he knew her already, she was labelled and classed and fixed down. He had got into this way of living, and he could not get out of it. He had identified himself with the system, and he could not extricate himself. He did not know that Eustacia had her being beyond him. He did not know that she existed untouched by his system and his mind, where no system had sway and where no consciousness had risen to the surface. He did not know that she was Egdon, the powerful, eternal origin seething with production. He thought he knew. Egdon to him was the tract of common land, producing familiar rough herbage, and having some few unenlightened inhabitants. So he skated over heaven and hell, and having made a map of the surface, thought he knew all. But underneath and among his mapped world, the eternal powerful fecundity worked on heedless of him and his arrogance. His preaching, his superficiality made no difference. What did it matter if he had calculated a moral chart from the surface of life? Could that affect life, any more than a chart of the heavens affects the stars, affects the whole stellar universe which exists beyond our knowledge? Could the sound of his words affect the working of the body of Egdon, where in the unfathomable womb was begot and conceived all that would ever come forth. Did not his own heart beat far removed and immune from his thinking and talking. Had he been able to put even his own heart's mysterious resonance upon his map, from which he charted the course of lives in his moral system? And how much more completely, then, had he left out in utter ignorance, the dark, powerful source whence all things rise into being, whence they will always continue to rise, to struggle forward to further being. A little of the static surface he could see, and map out. Then he thought his map was the thing itself. How blind he was, how utterly blind to the tremendous movement carrying and producing the surface. He did not know that the greater part of every life is underground, like roots in the dark in contact with the beyond. He preached thinking lives could be moved like hen-houses from here to there. His blindness indeed brought on the calamity. But what matter if Eustacia or Wildeve or Mrs Yeobright died: what matter if he himself became a mere rattle of repetitive words—what did it matter? It was regrettable, no more. Egdon, the primal impulsive body would go on producing all that was to be produced, eternally, though the will of man should destroy the blossom yet in bud, over and over again. At last he must learn what it is to be at one, in his mind and will, with the primal impulses that rise in him. Till then let him perish or preach. The great reality on which the little tragedies enact themselves cannot be detracted from. The will and words which militate against it are the only vanity.

This is a constant revelation in Hardy's novels: that there exists a great background, vital and vivid, which matters more than the people who move upon it. Against the background of dark, passionate Egdon, of the leafy, sappy passion and sentiment of the woodlands, of the unfathomed stars, is drawn the lesser scheme of lives: *The Return of the Native*, *The Woodlanders*, or *Two on a Tower*. Upon the vast, incomprehensible pattern of some primal morality greater than ever the human

mind can grasp, is drawn the little, pathetic pattern of man's moral life
and struggle, pathetic almost ridiculous. The little fold of law and
order, the little walled city within which man has to defend himself
from the waste enormity of nature becomes always too small, and the
pioneers venturing out with the code of the walled city upon them, die 5
[confined]* in the bonds of that code, free and yet unfree,
preaching the walled city and looking to the waste.

This is the wonder of Hardy's novels, and gives them their beauty.
The vast, unexplored morality of life itself, what we call the immorality
of nature, surrounds us in its eternal incomprehensibility, and in its 10
midst goes on the little human morality play, with its queer frame of
morality and its mechanised movement; seriously, portentously, till
some one of the protagonists chance to look out of the charmed circle,
weary of the stage, to look into the wilderness raging round. Then he is
lost, his little drama falls to pieces, or becomes mere repetition, but the 15
stupendous theatre outside goes on enacting its own incomprehensible
drama, untouched. There is this quality in almost all Hardy's work, and
this is the magnificent irony it all contains, the challenge, the contempt.
Not the deliberate ironies, little tales of widows* or widowers,
contain the irony of human life as we live it in our self-aggrandised 20
gravity, but the big novels, *The Return of the Native*, and the others.

And this is the quality Hardy shares with the great writers,
Shakespeare or Sophocles or Tolstoi, this setting behind the small
action of his protagonists the terrific action of unfathomed nature,
setting a smaller system of morality, the one grasped and formulated by 25
the human consciousness within the vast, uncomprehended and
incomprehensible morality of nature or of life itself, surpassing human
consciousness. The difference is, that whereas in Shakespeare or
Sophocles the greater, uncomprehended morality, or fate, is actively
transgressed and gives active punishment, in Hardy and Tolstoi the 30
lesser, human morality, the mechanical system is actively transgressed,
and holds, and punishes the protagonist, whilst the greater morality is
only passively, negatively transgressed, it is represented merely as being
present in background, in scenery, not taking any active part, having no
direct connection with the protagonist. Oedipus, Hamlet, Macbeth set 35
themselves up against, or find themselves set up against the
unfathomed moral forces of nature, and out of this unfathomed force
comes their death. Whereas Anna Karenin,* Eustacia, Tess, Sue
and Jude find themselves up against the established system of human
government and morality, they cannot detach themselves, and are 40

brought down. Their real tragedy is that they are unfaithful to the greater unwritten morality, which would have bidden Anna Karenin be patient and wait until she, by virtue of greater right, could take what she needed from society; would have bidden Vronsky detach himself from
5 the system, become an individual, creating a new colony of morality with Anna; would have bidden Eustacia fight Clym for his own soul, and Tess take and claim her Angel, since she had the greater light; would have bidden Jude and Sue endure for very honour's sake, since one must bide by the best that one has known, and not succumb to the
10 lesser good.

Had Oedipus, Hamlet, Macbeth been weaker, less full of real, potent life, they would have made no tragedy: they would have compromised and contrived some arrangement of their affairs, sheltering in the human morality from the great stress and attack of the
15 unknown morality. But, being as they are, men to the fullest capacity, when they [find] themselves daggers drawn with the very forces of life itself, they can only fight till they themselves are killed, since the morality of life, the greater morality, is eternally unalterable and invincible. It can be dodged for some time, but not opposed. On the
20 other hand, Anna, Eustacia, Tess or Sue—what was there in their position that was necessarily tragic? Necessarily painful it was, but they were not at war with God, only with Society. Yet they were all cowed by the mere judgement of man upon them, and all the while by their own souls they were right. And the judgement of man killed them, not the
25 judgement of their own souls, or the judgement of eternal God.

Which is the weakness of modern tragedy, where transgression against the social code is made to bring destruction, as though the social code worked our irrevocable fate. Like Clym, the map appears to us more real than the land. Short sighted almost to blindness, we [pore]
30 over the chart, map out journeys and confirm them: and we cannot see life itself giving us the lie the whole time.

Chapter IV.

An Attack on Work and the Money Appetite and on the State.

There is always excess, the biologists say,* a brimming over. For they have made the measure, and the supply must be made to fit. They have charted the course, and if at the end of it there is a jump beyond the bounds into nothingness: well, there is always excess, for they have charted the journey aright.

There is always excess, a brimming over. At spring-time a bird brims over with blue and yellow, a glow worm brims over with a drop of green moonshine, a lark flies up like heady wine, with song, an errand boy whistles down the road, and scents brim over the measure of the flower. Then we say, it is spring.

When is a glow worm a glow worm? When she's got a light on her tail. What is she when she hasn't got a light on her tail? Then she's a mere worm, an insect.

When is a man a man? When he is alight with life. Call it excess? If it is missing, there is no man, only a creature, a clod, undistinguished.

With man, it is always spring—or it may be; with him every day is a blossoming day, if he will. He is a plant eternally in flower, he is an animal eternally in rut, he is a bird eternally in song. He has his excess constantly on his hands, almost every day. It is not with him a case of seasons, spring and autumn and winter. And happy man if his excess come out in blue and gold and singing, if it be not like the paste rose on the pie, a burden, at last a very sickness.

The wild creatures are like fountains whose sources gather their waters until spring-time, when they leap their highest. But man is a fountain that is always playing, leaping, ebbing, sinking, and springing up. It is not for him to gather his waters till spring-time, when his fountain, rising higher, can at last flow out flower-wise in mid-air, teeming awhile with excess, before it falls spent again.

His rhythm is not so simple. A pleasant little stream of life is a bud at autumn and winter, fluttering in flocks over the stubble, the fallow, rustling along. Till spring, when many waters rush in to the sources, and each bird is a fountain playing.

31

Man, fortunate or unfortunate, is rarely like an autumn bird, to enjoy his pleasant stream of life flowing at ease. Some men are like that, fortunate and delightful. But those men or women will not read this book. Why should they?

5   The sources of man's life are overfull, they receive more than they give out. And why? Because a man is a well-head built over a strong, perennial spring and enclosing it in, a well-head whence the water may be drawn at will, and under which the water may be held back indefinitely. Sometimes, and in certain ways, according to certain rules,
10 the source may bubble and spring out, but only at certain times, always under control. And the fountain cannot always bide for the permission, the suppressed waters strain at the well-head, and hence so much sadness without cause. Weltschmerz* and other unlocalised pains where the source presses for utterance.

15 And how is it given utterance? In sheer play of being free? That cannot be. It shall be given utterance in work, the conscious mind has unanimously decreed. And the decree is held holy. My life is to be utilised for work, first and foremost,—and this in spite of Mary of Bethany.*

20 Only, or very largely in the work I do, must I live, must my life take movement. And why do I work? To eat,—is the original answer. When I have earned enough to eat, what then? Work for more, to provide for the future. And when I have provided for the future? Work for more to provide for the poor. And when I have worked to provide for the poor,
25 what then? Keep on working, the poor are never provided for, the poor have ye always with you.*

That is the best that man has been able to do.

But what a ghastly programme! I do not want to work.—You must,—comes the answer. But nobody wants to work, originally.—Yet
30 everybody works, because he must,—it is repeated. And what when he is not working?—Let him rest and amuse himself, and get ready for tomorrow morning.

Oh my God, work is the great body of life, and sleep and amusement, like two wings, beat* only to carry it along. Is this then
35 all?

And Carlyle gets up and says, it is all,* and mankind goes on in grim, serious approval, more than acquiescent, approving, thinking itself religiously right.

But let us pull the tail out of the mouth of this serpent.* Eternity
40 is not a process of eternal self-inglutination. We must work to eat, and

eat to work—that is how it is given out. But the real problem is quite different. "We must work to eat, and eat to—what?" Don't say "work", it is so unoriginal.

In Nottingham, we boys began learning German by learning proverbs. "Man muss essen um zu leben, aber man muss nicht leben 5 um zu essen", was the first. "One must eat to live, but one must not live to eat": a good German proverb according to the lesson book.* Starting a step further back, it might be written "one must work to eat, but one must not eat to work". Surely that is just, because the second [proverb]* says "one must eat to live". 10

"One must work to eat, and eat to live", is the result.

Take this vague and almost uninterpretable word "living". To how great a degree are "to work" and "to live" synonymous? That is the question to answer, when the highest flight that our thought can take, for the sake of living, is to say that we must return to the mediaeval 15 system of handicrafts, and that each man must become a labouring artist, producing a complete article.

Work is, simply, the activity necessary for the production of a sufficient supply of food and shelter: nothing more holy than that. It is the producing of the means of self-preservation. Therefore it is obvious 20 that it is not the be-all and the end-all of existence. We work to provide means of subsistence, and when we have made provision, we proceed to live. But all work is only the making provision for that which is to follow.

It may be argued that work has a fuller meaning, that man lives most 25 intensely when he works. That may be, for some few men, for some few artists whose lives are otherwise empty. But for the mass, for the 99.9 per cent of mankind, work is a form of non-living, of non-existence, of submergence.

It is necessary to produce food and clothing. Then, under necessity 30 the thing must be done as quickly as possible. Is not the highest recommendation for a labourer the fact that he is quick? And how does any man become quick, save through finding the shortest way to his end, and by repeating one set of actions? A man who can repeat certain movements accurately, is an expert, if his movements are those which 35 produce the required result.

And these movements are the calculative or scientific movements of a machine. When a man is working perfectly, he is the perfect machine. Aware of certain forces, he moves accurately along the line of their resultant. The perfect machine does the same. 40

All work is like this, the approximation to a perfect mechanism, more
or less intricate and adjustable. The doctor, the teacher, the lawyer, just
as much as the farm-labourer or the mechanic, when working most
perfectly is working with the utmost of mechanical, scientific precision,
along a line calculated from known fact, calculated instantaneously.

In this work, man has a certain definite, keen satisfaction. When he is
utterly impersonal, when he is merely the node where certain mechanical forces meet to find their resultant, then a man is something perfect,
the perfect instrument, the perfect machine.

It is a state which, in his own line, every man strives and longs for. It
is a state which satisfies his moral craving, almost the deepest craving
within him. It is a state when he lies in line with the great force of
gravity, partakes perfectly of its subtlest movement and motion, even to
psychic vibration.

But it is a state which every man hopes for release from. The dream
of every man, is that in the end he shall have to work no more. The joy
of every man, is when he is released from his labour, having done his
share for the time being.

What does he want to be released from, and what does he want to be
released unto? A man is not a machine: when he has finished work, he
is not motionless, inert. He begins a new activity. And what?

It seems to me as if a man, in his normal state, were like a palpitating
leading-shoot of life, where the unknown, all unresolved, beats and
pulses, containing the quick of all experience, as yet unrevealed, not
singled out. But when he thinks, when he moves, he is retracing some
proved experience. He is as the leading-shoot which, for the moment,
remembers only that which is behind, the fixed wood, the cells
conducting towards their undifferentiated tissue of life. He moves as it
were in the trunk of the tree, in the channels long since built, where the
sap must flow as in a canal. He takes knowledge of all this past
experience upon which the new tip rides quivering, he becomes again
the old life, which has built itself out in the fixed tissue, he lies in line
with the old movement, unconscious of where it breaks, at the growing
plasm, into something new, unknown. He is happy, all is known, all is
finite, all is established, and knowledge can be perfect, here in the
trunk of the tree, which life built up and climbed beyond.

Such is a man at work, safe within the proven, deposited experience,
thrilling as he traverses the fixed channels and courses of life, he is only
matter of some of the open ways which life laid down for its own
passage, he has only made himself one with what has been, travelling

the old, fixed courses, through which life still passes, but which are not in themselves living.

And in the end, this is always a prison to him, this proven, deposited experience which he must explore, this past of life. For is he not in himself a growing tip, is not his own body a quivering plasm of what will be, and has never yet been. Is not his own soul a fighting line, where what is and what will be separates itself off from what has been. Is not this his purest joy of movement, the indistinguishable, complex movement of being. And is not this his deepest desire, to be himself, to be this quivering bud of growing tissue which he is. He may find knowledge by retracing the old courses, he may satisfy his moral sense by working within the known, certain of what he is doing. But for real, utter satisfaction, he must give himself up to complete quivering uncertainty, to sentient non-knowledge.

And this [is] why man is always crying out for freedom, to be free. He wants to be free to be himself. For this reason, he has always made a heaven where no work need be done, where to *be* is all, where to *be* comprises all that has been done, in perfect knowledge, and where that which will be done is so swift as to be a sleep, a Nirvana, an absorption.

So there is this deepest craving of all, to be free from the necessity to work. It is obvious in all mankind. "Must I become one with the old, habitual movements?" says man. "I must, to satisfy myself that the new is new and the old is old, that all is one like a tree, though I am no more than the tiniest cell in the tree." So he becomes one with the old, habitual movement: he is the perfect machine, the perfect instrument: he works. But, satisfied for the time being of that which has been and remains now finite, he wearies for his own, limitless being, for the unresolved, quivering, infinitely complex and indefinite movement of new living, he wants to be free.

And ever, as his knowledge of what is past becomes greater, he wants more and more liberty to be himself. There is the necessity for self-preservation, the necessity to submerge himself in the utter mechanical movement. But why so much: why repeat so often the mechanical movement? Let me not have so much of this work to do, let me not be consumed overmuch in my own self-preservation, let me not be imprisoned in this proven, finite experience all my days.

This has been the cry of humanity since the world began. This is the glamour of kings, the glamour of men who had opportunity to *be*, who were not under compulsion to do, to serve. This is why kings were chosen heroes, because they were the beings, the producers of new life, not servants of necessity, repeating old experience.

And humanity has laboured to make work shorter, so we may all be kings. True, we have the necessity to work, more or less, according as 5 we are near the growing tip or further away. Some men are far from the growing tip. They have little for growth in them, only the power for repeating old movement. They will always find their own level. But let those that have life live.

So there has been produced machinery, to take the place of the 10 human machine. And the inventor of the labour saving machine has been hailed as a public benefactor, and we have rejoiced over his discovery. Now there is a railing against the machine, as if it were an evil thing. And the thinkers talk about the return to the mediaeval system of handicrafts. Which is absurd.

15 As I look round this room, at the bed, at the counterpane, at the books and chairs and the little bottles, and think that machines made them, I am glad. I am very glad of the bedstead, of the white enamelled iron with brass rail. As it stands, I rejoice over its essential simplicity. I would not wish it different. Its lines are straight and parallel, or at right 20 angles, giving a sense of static motionlessness. Only that which is necessary is there, whittled down to the minimum. There is nothing to hurt me or to hinder me; my wish for something to serve my purpose is perfectly fulfilled.

Which is what a machine can do. It can provide me with the perfect 25 mechanical instrument, a thing mathematically and scientifically correct. Which is what I want. I like the books, on the whole, I can scarcely imagine them more convenient to me, I like the common green-glass smelling salts, and the machine turned feet of the common chest of drawers. I hate the machine carving on a chair, and the stamped pattern 30 on a rug. But I have no business to ask a machine to make beautiful things for me. I can ask it for perfect accommodating utensils or articles of use, and I shall get them.

Wherefore I do honour to the machine and to its inventor. It will produce what we want, and save us the necessity of much labour. 35 Which is what it was invented for.

But to what pitiable misuse is it put! Do we use the machine to produce goods for our need, or is it used as a muck-rake for raking together heaps of money? Why, when man, in his godly effort has produced a means to freedom, do we make it a means to more slavery? 40 Why?—because the heart of man is crude and greedy. Why is a labourer willing to work ten hours a day for a mere pittance? Because he is serving a system for the enrichment of the individual, a system to which he subscribes, because he might himself be that individual, and, since his one ideal is to be rich, he owes his allegiance to the system established for the raking of riches into heaps, a system that satisfies his imagination. Why try to alter the present industrial system on behalf of the working man, when his imagination is satisfied only by such a system?

The poor man and the rich, they are the head and tail of the same penny. Stand them naked side by side, and which is better than the other? The rich man, probably, for he is likely to be the sadder and the wiser.

The universal ideal, the one conscious ideal of the poor people, is riches. The only hope lies in those people who, in fact or imagination, have experienced wealth, and have appetites accordingly.

It is not true, that, before we can get over our absorbing passion to be rich, we must each one of us know wealth. There are sufficient people with sound imagination and normal appetite to put away the whole money tyranny of England today.

There is no evil in money. If there were a million pounds under my bed, and I did [not] know of it, it would make no difference to me. If there were a million pounds under my bed, and I did know of it, it would make a difference, perhaps, to the form of my life, but to the living me, and to my individual purpose, it could make no difference, since I depend neither on riches nor on poverty for my being.

Neither poverty nor riches obsesses me. I would not be like a begging friar to forswear all [owning]* and having. For I would not admit myself so weak, that either I must abstain totally from wealth, or succumb to the passion for possessions.

Have I not a normal money appetite, as I have a normal appetite for food? Do I want to kill a hundred bison, to satisfy the imaginative need of my stomach, as the Red Indian did? Then why should I want a thousand pounds, when ten are enough? "Thy eyes are bigger than thy belly," says the mother of the child who takes more than he can eat. "Your pocket is bigger than your breeches," one could say to a man greedy to get rich.

It is only greediness. But it is very wearisome. There are plenty of people who are not greedy, who have normal money appetites. They need a certain amount, and they know they need it. It is no honour to be a pauper. It is only decent that every man should have enough and a little to spare, and every self-respecting man will see he gets it. But why can't we really grow up, and become adult with regard to money as with regard to food. Why can't we know when we have enough, as we know when we have had enough to eat?

5 We could, of course, if we had any real sense of values. It is all very well to leave, as Christianity tries to leave the dinner to be devoured by the glutton, whilst the Christian draws off in disgust, and fasts. But we each have our place at the board, as we well know, and it is indecent to withdraw before the glutton, leaving the earth to be devoured.

10 Can we not stay at the board? We must eat to live. And living is not simply not-dying. It is the only real thing, it is the aim and end of all life. Work is only a means to subsistence. The work done, the living earned, how then to go on to enjoy it, to fulfil it, that is the question. How shall a man live? What do we mean by living?

15 Let every man answer for himself. We only know, we want the freedom to live, the freedom of leisure and means. But there are ample means, there is half an eternity of pure leisure for mankind to take if he would, if he did not think, at the back of his mind, that riches are the means of freedom. Riches would be the means of freedom, if there were no poor, if there were equal riches everywhere. Till then, riches and poverty alike are bonds and prisons, for every man must live in the ring of his own defences, to defend his property. And this ring is the surest of prisons.

So cannot we see, rich and poor alike, how we have circumscribed, 25 hampered, imprisoned ourselves within the limits of our poor-and-rich system, till our life is utterly pot-bound. It is not that some of us want more money and some of us less. It is that our money is like walls between us, we are immured in gold, and we die of starvation or etiolation.

30 A plant has strength to burst its pot. The shoots of London trees have force to burst through the London pavements. Is there not life enough in us to break out of this system? Let every man take his own, and go his own way, regardless of system and State, when his hour comes. Which is greater, the State or myself? Myself, unquestionably, 35 since the State is only an arrangement made for my convenience. If it is not convenient for me, I must depart from it. There is no need to break laws. The only need is to be a law unto oneself.

And if sufficient people came out of the walled defences, and pitched in the open, then very soon the walled city would be a mere dependent 40 on the free tents of the wilderness. Why should we care about bursting the city walls? We can walk through the gates into the open world. These states and nations with their ideals, their armaments of aggression and defence, what are they to me? They must fight out their own fates. As for me, I would say to every decent man whose heart is straining at the enclosure, "Come away from the crowd and the community, come away and be separate in your own soul, and live. Your business is to produce your own real life, no matter what the nations do. The nations are made up of individual men, each man will know at length that he must single himself out, nor remain any longer embedded in the matrix of his nation, or community, or class. Our time has come, let us draw apart. Let the physician heal himself."*

And outside what will it matter save that a man is a man, is himself? If he must work, let him work a few hours a day, a very few, whether it be at wheeling bricks, or shovelling coal into a furnace or tending a machine. Let him do his work, according to his kind, for some three or four hours a day. That will produce supplies in ample sufficiency. Then let him have twenty hours for being himself, for producing himself.

Chapter V.

Work and the Angel* and the Unbegotten Hero.

It is an inherent passion, this will to work, it is a craving to produce, to create, to be as God. Man turns his back on the unknown, on that
5 which is yet to be, he turns his face towards that which has been, and he sees, he re-discovers, he becomes again that which has been before. But this time he is conscious, he knows what he is doing. He can at will reproduce the movement life made in its initial passage, the movement life still makes, and will continue to make, as a habit,* the
10 movement already made so unthinkably often that rather than a movement it has become a state, a condition of all life; it has become matter, or the force of gravity, or cohesion, or heat, or light. These old, old habits of life man rejoices to rediscover in all their detail.

Long, long ago life first rolled itself into seed, and fell to [earth], and
15 covered itself up with soil, slowly. And long, long ago man discovered the process, joyfully, and, in this wise as God, repeated it. He found out how soil is shifted. Proud as a needy God, he dug the ground, and threw the little, silent fragments of life under the dust. And was he not doing what life itself had initiated, was he not, in this particular, even
20 greater than life, more definite?

Still further back, in an unthinkable period long before chaos, life formed the habit we call gravitation. This was almost before any differentiation, before all those later, lesser habits, which we call matter or such a thing as centrifugal force, were formed. It was a habit of the
25 great mass of life, not of any part in particular. Therefore it took man's consciousness much longer to apprehend, and even now we have only some indications of it, from various parts. But we rejoice in that which we know. Long long ago, one surface of matter learned to roll on a rolling motion across another surface, as the tide rolls up the land. And
30 long ago man saw this motion, and learned a secret, and made the wheel, and rejoiced.

So, facing both ways, like Janus, face forward, in the quivering, glimmering fringe of the unresolved, facing the unknown, and looking backward over the vast rolling tract of life which follows and
35 [repeats]* the initial movement, man is given up to his dual

40

business, of being, in blindness and wonder and pure godliness, the living stuff of life itself, unrevealed; and of knowing, with unwearying labour and unceasing success, the manner of that which has been, which is revealed.

And work is the repetition of some one of those re-discovered 5 movements, the enacting of some part imitated from life, the attaining of a similar result as life attained. And this, even if it be only shovelling coal on to a fire, or hammering nails into a shoe-sole, or making accounts in ledgers, is what work is and in this lies the initial satisfaction of labour. The motive of labour, that of obtaining wages, is 10 only the overcoming of inertia. It is not the real driving force. When necessity alone compels man, from moment to moment, to work, then man rebels and dies. The driving force is the pleasure in doing something, the living will to work.

And man must always struggle against the *necessity* to work, though 15 the necessity to work is one of the inevitable conditions of man's existence. And no man can continue in any place of work, out of sheer necessity, devoid of any essential pleasure in that work.

It seems as if the great aim and purpose in human life were to bring all life into the human consciousness. And this is the final meaning of 20 work: the extension of human consciousness. The lesser meaning of work is the achieving of self-preservation. From this lesser, immediate necessity man always struggles to be free. From the other, greater necessity, of extending the human consciousness, man does not struggle to be free. 25

And to the immediate necessity for self-preservation man must concede, but always having in mind the other, greater necessity, to which he would hasten.

But the bringing of life into human consciousness is not an aim in itself, it is only a necessary condition of the progress of life itself. Man 30 is himself the vivid body of life, rolling glimmering against the void. In his fullest living he does not know what he does, his mind, his consciousness, unacquaint,* hovers behind, full of extraneous gleams and glances, and altogether devoid of knowledge. Altogether devoid of knowledge and conscious motive is he when he is heaving 35 into uncreated space, when he is actually living, becoming himself.

And yet, that he may go on, may proceed with his living, it is necessary that his mind, his consciousness, should extend behind him. The mind itself is one of life's later developed habits. *To know* is a force, like any other force. Knowledge is only one of the conditions of 40

this force, as combustion is one of the conditions of heat. *To will* is only
a manifestation of the same force, as expansion may be a manifestation
of heat. And this *knowing* is a now inevitable habit of life's developed
late, it is a force active in the immediate rear of life, and the greater its
5   activity, the greater the forward, unknown movement ahead of it.

It seems as though one of the conditions of life is, that life shall
continually and progressively differentiate itself, almost as though this
differentiation were a Purpose. Life starts crude and unspecified, a
great Mass. And it proceeds to evolve out of that mass ever more
10 distinct and definite particular forms, an ever-multiplying number of
separate species and orders, as if it were working always to the
production of the infinite number of perfect individuals, the individual
so thorough that he should have nothing in common with any other
individual. It is as if all coagulation must be loosened, as if the elements
15 must work themselves free and pure from the compound.

Man's consciousness, that is, his mind, his knowing, is his grosser
manifestation of individuality. With his consciousness he can perceive
and know that which is not himself. The further he goes, the more
extended his consciousness, the more he realises the things that are not
20 himself. Everything he perceives, everything he knows, everything he
feels, is something extraneous to him, is not himself, and his perception
of it is like a cell wall, or more, a real space separating him. I see a
flower, because it is not me. I know a melody, because it is not me. I
feel cold, because it is not me. I feel joy when I kiss, because it is not
25 me, the kiss, but rather one of the bounds or limits where I end. But the
kiss is a closer division of me from the mass, than a sense of cold or
heat. It whittles [me]* the more keenly naked from the gross.

And the more that I am driven from admixture, the more I am
singled out into utter individuality, the more this intrinsic me rejoices.
30 For I am as yet a gross impurity, I partake of everything. I am still
rudimentary, part of a great, unquickened lump.

In the origin life must have been uniform, a great unmoved, utterly
homogeneous infinity, a great not-being, at once a positive and negative
infinity: the whole universe, the whole infinity, one motionless
35 homogeneity, a something, a nothing. And yet it can never have been
utterly homogeneous: mathematically, yes; actually, no. There must
always have been some reaction, infinitesimally faint, stirring somehow
through the vast, homogeneous inertia.

And since the beginning, the reaction has become extended and
40 intensified, what was one great mass of individual constituency has

stirred and resolved itself into many smaller, characteristic parts, what was an utter, infinite neutrality has become evolved into still rudimentary, but positive, orders and species. So on and on till we get to naked jelly, and from naked jelly to enclosed and separated jelly, from homogeneous tissue to organic tissue, on and on, from invertebrates to mammals, from mammals to man, from man to tribesman, from tribesman to me: and on and on, till, in the future, wonderful, distinct individuals, like angels, move about, each one being himself, perfect as a complete melody or a pure colour.

How one craves that his life should be more individual, that I and you and my neighbour should each be distinct in clarity from each other, perfectly distinct from the general mass. Then it would be a melody if I walked down the road, if I stood with my neighbour it would be a pure harmony.

Could I then, being my perfect self, be selfish? A selfish person is an impure person, one who wants that which is not himself. Selfishness implies admixture, grossness, unclarity of being. How can I, a pure person incapable of being anything but myself, detract from my neighbour? That which is mine is singled out to me from the mass, and to each man is left his own. And what can any man want for, except that which is his own, if he be himself? If he have that which is not his own, it is a burden, he is not himself. And how can I help my neighbour,* except by being utterly myself? That gives him into himself: which is the greatest gift a man can receive.

And necessarily accompanying this more perfect being of myself is the more extended knowledge of that which is not myself. That is, the finer, more distinct the individual, the more finely and distinctly is he aware of all other individuality. It needs a delicate, pure soul to distinguish between the souls of others, it needs a thing which is purely itself to see other things in their purity, or their impurity.

Yet in life, so often, one feels that a man who is, by nature, intrinsically an individual, is by practice and knowledge an impurity, almost a nonentity. To each individuality belongs, by nature, its own knowledge. It would seem as if each soul, detaching itself from the mass, the matrix, should achieve its own knowledge. Yet this is not so. Many a soul which we feel should have detached itself and become distinct, remains embedded, and struggles with knowledge that does not pertain to it. It reached a point of distinctness and a degree of personal knowledge, and then became confused, lost itself.

And then, it sought for its whole being in work. By re-enacting some old movement of life's, a struggling soul seeks to detach itself, to become pure. By gathering all the knowledge possible, it seems to receive the stimulus which shall help it to continue to distinguish itself.

"Ye must be born again,"* it is said to us. Once we are born,
5 detached from the flesh and blood of our parents, issued separate, as distinct creatures. And later on, the incomplete germ which is a young soul must be fertilised, the parent womb which encloses the incomplete individuality must conceive, and we must be brought forth to ourselves, distinct. This is at the age of twenty or thirty.

10 And we, who imagine we live by knowledge, imagine that the impetus for our second birth must come from knowledge, that the germ, the sperm impulse, can come out of some utterance only. So, when I am young, at eighteen, twenty, twenty three, when the anguish of desire comes upon me, as I lie in the womb of my times, to receive
15 the quickening, the impetus, I send forth all my calls and call hither and thither, asking for the Word, the Word which is the [spermatazoon] which shall come and fertilise me and set me free. And it may be the word, the idea exists which shall bring me forth, give me birth. But it may also be that the word, the idea, has never yet been uttered.

20 Shall I then be able, with all the knowledge in the world, to produce my being, if the knowledge be not extant? I shall not.

And yet we believe that only the Uttered Word can come into us and give us the impetus to our second birth. Give us a religion, give us something to believe in, cries the unsatisfied soul embedded in the
25 womb of our times. Speak the quickening word, it cries, that will deliver us into our own being.

So it searches out the Spoken Word, and finds it, or finds it not. Possibly it is not yet uttered. But all that will be uttered lies potent in life. The fools do not know this. They think the fruit of knowledge is
30 found only in shops. They will go anywhere to find it, save to the Tree.* For the Tree is so obvious, and seems so played out.

Therefore the unsatisfied soul remains unsatisfied, and chooses Work, maybe Good Works, for its incomplete action. It thinks that in work it has being, in knowledge it has gained its distinct self.

35 Whereas all amount of clumsy distinguishing ourselves from some other things will not make us thus become ourselves, and all amount of repeating even the most complex motions of life will [not] produce one new motion.

We start the wrong way round: thinking, by learning what we are not,
40 to know what we as individuals are: whereas the whole of the human

consciousness contains, as we know, not a tithe of what *is*, and therefore it is hopeless to proceed by a method of elimination; and thinking, by discovering the motion life has made, to be able therefrom to produce the motion it will make: whereas we know that, in life, the new motion is not the resultant of the old, but something quite new, quite other, according to our perception.

So we struggle mechanically, unformed, unbegotten, unborn, repeating some old process of life, unable to become ourselves, unable to produce anything new.

Looking over the Hardy novels, it is interesting to see which of the heroes one would call a distinct individuality, more or less achieved, which an unaccomplished potential individuality, and which an impure, unindividualised life embedded in the matrix, either achieving its own lower degree of distinction, or not achieving it.

In *Desperate Remedies* there are scarcely any people at all, particularly when the plot is working. The tiresome part about Hardy is that, so often, he will neither write a morality-play nor a novel. The people of the first book, as far as the plot is concerned, are not people: they are the heroine, faultless and white; the hero, with a small spot on his whiteness; the villainess, red and black, but more red than black; the villain, black and red; the Murderer, aided by the Adulteress, obtains power over the Virgin, who, rescued at the last moment by the Virgin Knight, evades the evil clutch. Then the Murderer, overtaken by vengeance, is put to death, whilst Divine Justice descends upon the Adulteress. Then the Virgin unites with the Virgin Knight, and receives Divine Blessing.

That is a morality-play, and if the morality were vigorous and original, all well and good. But, between whiles, we see that the Virgin is being played by a nice, rather ordinary girl, who is all the while [   ]*

A Laodicean, there is all the way through a "prédilection d'artiste"* for the aristocrat, and all the way through a moral condemnation of him, a substituting the middle or lower class personage with bourgeois virtues into his place. This was the root of Hardy's pessimism. Not until he comes to Tess and Jude does he [ever]* sympathise with the aristocrat—unless it be in *The Mayor of Casterbridge*, and then he sympathises only to slay. He always, always represents them the same, as having some vital weakness, some radical ineffectuality. From first to last it is the same.

Miss Aldclyffe and Manston, Elfride and the sickly lord she married,

Troy and Farmer Boldwood, Eustacia Vye and Wildeve, de Stancy in *A Laodicean*, Lady Constantine in *Two on a Tower*, the Mayor of Casterbridge and Lucetta, Mrs Charmond and Dr Fitzpiers in *The Woodlanders*, Tess and Alec d'Urberville, and Jude, they are all in the
5 same spirit. There is the dark, passionate, arrogant lady, Miss Aldclyffe, Eustacia, Lucetta, Mrs Charmond, all of them essentially aristocratic, or at least, wealthy. There is the fair, passionate, submissive lady, always of blue blood: Elfride, Lady Constantine, Tess. There is the dark, passionate, arrogant man: Manston, Farmer Boldwood, de
10 Stancy, the Mayor of Casterbridge, Dr Fitzpiers, Alec d'Urberville, and, though different, Jude. There is also the blond, passionate, yielding man: Sergeant Troy, Wildeve, and, in spirit, Jude.

These are all, in their way, the aristocrat-characters of Hardy. They must every one die, every single one.

15 Why has Hardy this *prédilection d'artiste* for the aristocrat, and why, at the same time, this moral antagonism to him?

It is fairly obvious in *A Laodicean*, a book where, the spirit being small, the complaint is narrow. The heroine, the daughter of a famous railway engineer, lives in the castle of the old de Stancys. She sighs,
20 wishing she were of the de Stancy line: the tombs and portraits have a spell over her. "But," says the hero to her, "have you forgotten your father's line of ancestry: Archimedes, Newcomen, Watt, Telford, Stephenson?"—"But I have a prédilection d'artiste for ancestors of the other sort," sighs Paula. And the hero despairs of impressing her with
25 the list of his architect ancestors: Pheidias, Ictinus and Callicrates, Chersiphron, Vitruvius, Wilars of Cambray, William of Wykeham. He deplores her marked preference for an "animal pedigree".*

But what is this "animal pedigree"? If a family pedigree of her ancestors, working men and burghers, had been kept, Paula would not
30 have gloried in it, animal though it were. Hers was a prédilection d'artiste.

And this because the aristocrat alone has occupied a position where he could afford to *be*, to be himself, to create himself, to live as himself. That is his eternal fascination. This is why the preference for him is a
35 prédilection d'artiste. The preference for the architect line would be a prédilection de savant, the preference for the engineer pedigree would be a prédilection d'economiste.*

The prédilection d'artiste—Hardy has it strongly, and it is rooted deeply in every imaginative human being. The glory of mankind has
40 been to produce lives, to produce vivid, independent, individual men,

not buildings or engineering works or even art, nor even the public good. The glory of mankind is not in a host of secure, comfortable, law abiding citizens, but in the few or more fine, clear lives, beings, individuals, distinct, detached, single as may be from the public.

And these the artist of all time has chosen. Why then, must the aristocrat always be condemned to death, in Hardy? Has the community come to consciousness in him, as in the French Revolutionaries, determined to destroy all that is [not] the average? Certainly in the Wessex novels, all but the average people die. But why? Is there the germ of death in these more single, distinguished people, or has the artist himself a bourgeois taint, a jealous vindictiveness that will now take revenge, now that the community, the average, has gained power over the aristocrat, the exception?

It is evident that both is true. Starting with the bourgeois morality, Hardy makes every exceptional person a villain, all exceptional or strong individual traits he holds up as weaknesses or wicked faults. So in *Desperate Remedies, Under the Greenwood Tree, Far from the Madding Crowd, The Hand of Ethelberta, The Return of the Native,* (but in *The Trumpet-Major* there is an ironical dig in the ribs to this civic, communal morality), *A Laodicean, Two on a Tower, The Mayor of Casterbridge,* and *Tess,* in steadily weakening degree. The blackest villain is Manston, the next, perhaps, Troy, the next Eustacia and Wildeve, always becoming less villainous and more human. The first show of real sympathy, nearly conquering the bourgeois or [communal] morality,* is for Eustacia, whilst the dark villain is becoming merely a weak, pitiable person in Dr Fitzpiers. In *The Mayor of Casterbridge,* the dark villain is already almost the hero. There is a lapse in the maudlin, weak but not wicked Dr Fitzpiers, duly [condemned],* Alec D'Urberville is not unlikeable, and Jude is a complete tragic hero, at once the old Virgin Knight and Dark Villain. The condemnation gradually shifts over from the dark villain to the blond bourgeois virgin hero, from Alec d'Urberville to Angel Clare, till in Jude they are united and loved, though the preponderance is of dark villain, now dark, beloved, passionate hero. The condemnation shifts over at last from the dark villainess to the white virgin, the bourgeois in soul: from Arabella to Sue. Infinitely more subtle and sad is the condemnation at the end, but there it is: the virgin knight is hated with intensity, yet still loved; the white virgin, the beloved, is the arch-sinner against life at last, and the last note of hatred is against her.

It is a complete and devastating shift over, it is a complete volte-face of moralities. Black does not become white, but it takes white's place as good; white remains white, but it is found bad. The old, communal morality is like a leprosy, a white sickness:* the old, anti-social individualist morality is alone on the side of life and health.

5   But yet, the aristocrat must die, all the way through: even Jude. *Was the germ of death in him at the start?* Or was he merely at outs with his times, the times of the Average in triumph? Would Manston, Troy, Farmer Boldwood, Eustacia, de Stancy, Henchard, Alec d'Urberville, Jude, have been real heroes in heroic times, without tragedy. It seems
10   as if Manston, Boldwood, Eustacia, Henchard, Alec d'Urberville, and almost Jude, might have been. In an heroic age they might have lived and more or less triumphed. But Troy, Wildeve, de Stancy, Fitzpiers, and Jude have something fatal in them. There is a rottenness at the core of them. The failure, the misfortune, or the tragedy, whichever it
15   may be, was inherent in them: as it was in Elfride, Lady Constantine, Marty South in *The Woodlanders*, and Tess. They have all passionate natures, and in them all failure is inherent.

So that we have, of men, the noble Lord in *A Pair of Blue Eyes*, Sergeant Troy, Wildeve, de Stancy, Fitzpiers, and Jude, all passionate,
20   aristocratic males, doomed by their very being, to tragedy, or to misfortune in the end.

Of the same class among women are: Elfride, Lady Constantine, Marty South, and Tess, all aristocratic, passionate, yet necessarily unfortunate females.

25   We have also, of men, Manston, Farmer Boldwood, Henchard, Alec d'Urberville, and perhaps Jude, all passionate, aristocratic males, who fell before the weight of the average, the lawful crowd, but who, in more primitive times, would have formed romantic rather than tragic figures.

30   Of women in the same class are Miss Aldclyffe, Eustacia, Lucetta, Mrs Charmond.

The third class, of bourgeois or average hero, whose purpose is to live and have his being in the community, contains the successful hero of *Desperate Remedies*, the unsuccessful but not very much injured two
35   heroes of *A Pair of Blue Eyes*, the successful Gabriel Oak, the unsuccessful, left-preaching Clym, the unsuccessful but not very much injured astronomer of *Two on a Tower*, the successful Scotchman of Casterbridge, the unsuccessful and expired Giles Winterborne of *The Woodlanders*, the arch-type, Angel Clare, and perhaps a little of
40   Jude.

The companion women to these men are, the heroine of *Desperate Remedies*, Bathsheba, Thomasin, Paula, Henchard's daughter, Grace in *The Woodlanders*, and Sue.

This, then, is the moral conclusion drawn from the novels:

1. The physical individualist is in the end an inferior thing which must fall before the community: Manston, Henchard etc.

2. The physical and spiritual individualist is a fine thing which must fall because of its own isolation, because it is a sport, not in the true line of life: Jude, Tess, Lady Constantine.

3. The physical individualist and spiritual bourgeois or communist* is a thing, finally, of ugly, undeveloped, non-distinguished or perverted physical instinct, and must fall physically: Sue, Angel Clare, Clym, Knight. It remains, however, fitted into the community.

4. The undistinguished, bourgeois or average being with average or civic virtues usually succeeds in the end. If he fails, he is left practically uninjured. If he expire during probation, he has flowers on his grave.

By individualist is meant, not a selfish or greedy person anxious to satisfy appetites, but a man of distinct being, who must act in his own particular way to fulfil his own individual nature. He is a man who, being beyond the average, chooses to rule his own life to his own completion, and as such is an aristocrat.

The artist always has a predilection for him. But Hardy, like Tolstoi, is forced in the issue always to stand with the community in condemnation of the aristocrat. He cannot help himself, but must stand with the average against the exception, he must, in his ultimate judgement represent the interests of humanity, or the community as a whole, and rule out the individual interest.

To do this, however, he must go against himself. His private sympathy is always with the individual, against the community: as is the case with every artist. Therefore he will create a more or less blameless individual and, making him seek his own fulfilment, his highest aim, will show him destroyed by the community, or by that in himself which represents the community, or by some close embodiment of the civic idea. Hence the pessimism.* To do this, however, he must select his individual with a definite weakness, a certain oldness of temper,* inelastic, a certain inevitable and inconquerable adhesion to the community.

This is obvious in Troy, Clym, Tess, and Jude. They have naturally

distinct individuality, but, as it were, a weak life-flow, so that they cannot break away from the old adhesion, they cannot separate themselves from the mass which bore them, they cannot detach themselves from the common. Therefore they are pathetic rather than
5 tragic figures.° They have not the necessary strength: the question of their unfortunate end is begged in the beginning.

Whereas Oedipus or Agamemnon or Clytemnestra or Orestes, or Macbeth or Hamlet or Lear, these are destroyed by their own conflicting passions. Out of greed for adventure, a desire to be off,
10 Agamemnon sacrifices Iphigenia: moreover he has his love-affairs outside Troy: and this brings on him death from the mother of his daughter, and from his pledged wife. Which is the working of the natural law. Hamlet, a later Orestes, is commanded by the Erinyes of his father° to kill his mother and his uncle: but his maternal filial
15 feeling tears him. It is almost the same tragedy as Orestes, without any Goddess or God to grant peace.

In these plays, conventional morality is transcended. The action is between the great, single, individual forces in the nature of Man, not between the dictates of the community and the original passion. The
20 Commandment says: "Thou shalt not kill."° But doubtless Macbeth had killed many a man who was in his way. Certainly Hamlet suffered no qualms about killing the old man behind the curtain. Why should he. But when Macbeth killed Duncan, he divided himself in twain, into two hostile parts. It was all in his own soul and blood: it was
25 nothing outside himself: as it was, really, with Clym, Troy, Tess, Jude. Troy would probably have been faithful to his little unfortunate person, had she been a lady, and had he not felt himself cut off from society in his very being, whilst all the time he cleaved to it. Tess allowed herself to be condemned, and asked for punishment from Angel Clare.
30 Why?—She had done nothing particularly, or at least irrevocably unnatural, were her life young and strong. But she sided with the community's condemnation of her. And almost the bitterest, most pathetic, deepest part of Jude's misfortune was his failure to obtain admission to Oxford, his failure to gain his place and standing in the
35 world's knowledge, in the world's work.

There is a lack of sternness, there is a hesitating betwixt life and public opinion, which diminishes the Wessex novels from the rank of pure tragedy.° It is not so much the eternal, immutable laws of being which are transgressed, it is not that vital life-forces are set in
40 conflict with each other, bringing almost inevitable tragedy—yet not

necessarily death, as we see in the most splendid Aeschylus. It is, in Wessex, that the individual succumbs to what is in its shallowest, public opinion, in its deepest, the human compact by which we live together, to form a community.

Chapter VI.

The Axle and the Wheel of Eternity.

It is agreed, then, that we will do a little work—two or three hours a day—labouring for the community, to produce the ample necessities of life. Then we will be free.

Free for what? The terror of the ordinary man is lest leisure should come upon him. His eternal, divine instinct is to free himself from the labour of providing what we call the necessities of life, in the common sense. And his personal horror is of finding himself with nothing to do.

What does a flower do? It provides itself with the necessities of life, it propagates itself in its seeds, and it has its fling all in one. Out from the crest and summit comes the fiery self, the flower, gorgeously.

This is the fall into the future, like a waterfall that tumbles over the edge of the known world into the unknown. The little, individualised river of life issues out of its source, its little seed, its well-head, flows on and on, making its course as it goes, establishing a bed of green tissue and stalks, flows on and draws near the edge where all things disappear. Then the stream divides. Part hangs back, recovers itself, and lies quiescent, in seed. The rest flows over, the red dips into the unknown, and is gone.

The same with man. He has to build his own tissue and form, serving the community for the means wherewithal, and then he comes to the climax. And at the climax, simultaneously, he begins to roll to the edge of the unknown, and in the same moment, lays down his seed for security's sake. That is the secret of love: it contains the lesser motions in the greater. In love, a man, a woman, flows on, to the very furthest edge of known feeling, being, and out beyond the furthest edge: and taking the superb and supreme risk, deposits a security of life in the womb.

Am I here to deposit security, continuance of life in the flesh? Or is that only a minor function in me? Is it not merely a preservative measure, procreation. It is the same for me as for any man or woman. That she bear children is not a woman's significance. But that she bear herself, that is her supreme and risky fate: that she drive on to the edge of the unknown, and beyond. She may leave children behind, for security. It is arranged so.

It is so arranged that the very act which carries us out into the unknown, shall probably deposit seed for security to be left behind. But the act, called the sexual act, is not for the depositing of seed. It is for leaping off into the unknown, as from a cliff's edge, like Sappho into the sea.°　　　　5

It is so plain in my plant, my poppy. Out of the living river, a fine silver stream detaches itself, and flows through a green bed which it makes for itself. It flows on and on, till it [reaches] the crest beyond which is ethereal space. Then, in tiny, concentrated pools, a little hangs back, in reservoirs that shall later seal themselves up as quick but silent　10 sources. But the whole, almost the whole, splashes splendidly over, is seen in red just as it [dips]° into darkness, and disappears.

So with a man in the act of love. A little of him, a very little, flows into the tiny quick pool to start another source. But the whole spills over in waste to the beyond.　　　　15

And only at high flood should the little hollows fill to make a new source. Only when the whole rises to pour in a great [wave]° over the edge of all that has been, should the little seed-wells run full. In the woman lie the reservoirs. And when there comes the flood-tide, then the dual stream of woman and man, as the whole two waves meet and　20 break to foam, bursting into the unknown, these wells and fountain heads are filled.

Thus man and woman pass beyond this Has-been and this is when the two waves meet in flood and heave over and out of Time, leaving their dole to Time deposited. It is for this man needs liberty, and to　25 prepare him for this he must use his leisure.

Always so that the wave of his being shall meet the other wave, that the two shall make flood which shall flow beyond the face of the earth, must a man live. Always the dual wave. Where does my poppy spill over in red, but there where the two streams have flowed and [clashed]°　30 together, where the pollen stream clashes into the pistil stream, where the male clashes into the female, and the two heave out in utterance. There, in the seethe of male and female, seeds are filled as the flood rises to pour out in a red fall. There, only there where the male seethes against the female, comes the transcendent flame and the filling of　35 seeds.

In plants where the male stream and the female stream flow separately, as in dogs-mercury or in the oak-tree,° where is the flame? It is not. But in my poppy, where at the summit the two streams, which till now have run deviously, scattered down many ways, at length　40 flow concentrated together, and the pure male stream meets the pure female stream in a heave and an overflowing, there there is the flower indeed.

And this is happiness: that my poppy gather his material and build his tissue till he has led the stream of life in him on and on to the end, to the whirlpool at the summit, where the male seethes and whirls in incredible speed upon the pivot of the female, where the two are one, as axle and wheel are one, and the motion travels out to infinity. There, where he is a complete full stream, travelling with and upon the other complete female stream, the twain make a flood over the face of all the earth, which shall pass away from the earth.

And since I am a man with a body of flesh, I shall contain the need to make sure this continuing of life in this body of flesh, I shall contain the need for the woman of flesh in whom to beget my children.

But this is an incorporate need: it is really no separate or distinct need. The clear, full inevitable need in me is that I, the male, meet the female stream which shall carry mine so that the two run to fullest flood, to furthest motion. It is no primary need of the begetting of children. It is the arriving at my highest mark of activity, of being; it is her arrival at her intensest self.

Why do we consider the male stream, and the female stream, as being only in the flesh: it is something other than physical. The physical, what we call in its narrowest meaning, the sex, is only a definite indication of the great male and female duality and unity. It is that part which is settled into an almost mechanised system of detaining some of the life which otherwise sweeps on and is lost in the full adventure.

There is female apart from Woman, as we know, and male apart from Man. There is male and female in my poppy plant, and this is neither man nor woman. It is part of the great twin river, eternally each branch resistant to the other, eternally running each to meet the other.

It may be said that male and female are terms relative only to physical sex. But this [is] the consistent indication of the greater meaning. Do we for a moment believe that a man is a man and a woman a woman, merely according to, and for the purpose of, the begetting of children? If there were organic reproduction of children, would there be no distinction between man and woman? Should we all be asexual?

We know that our view is partial. Man is man, and woman is woman, whether no children be born any more for ever. As long as time lasts, man is man. In eternity, where infinite motion becomes rest, the two may be one. But until eternity man is man. Until eternity, there shall be this separateness, this interaction of man upon woman, male upon female, this suffering, this delight, this imperfection. In eternity, maybe, the action may be perfect. In infinity, the spinning of the wheel upon the hub may be a frictionless whole, complete, an unbroken sleep 5 that is infinite, motion that is utter rest, a duality that is sheerly one.

But except in infinity, everything of life is male or female, distinct. But the consciousness, that is of both: and the flower, that is of both. Every impulse that stirs in life, every single impulse, [is] either male or female, distinct, except the being of the complete flower, of the 10 completed consciousness, which is two in one, fused. These are infinite and eternal. The consciousness, what we call the truth, is eternal, beyond change or motion, beyond time or limit.

But that which is not conscious, which is Time, and Life, that is our field. 15

Chapter VII.

Of Being and Not-Being.*

In life, then, no new thing has ever arisen, or can arise, save out of the impulse of the male upon the female, the female upon the male. The interaction of the male and female spirit begot the wheel, the plough, and the first utterance that was made on the face of the earth.

As in my flower, the pistil, female, is the centre and swivel, the stamens, male, are close clasping the hub, and the blossom is the great motion outwards into the unknown, so in a man's life, the female is the swivel and centre on which he turns closely, producing his movement. And the female to a man is the obvious form, a woman. And normally, the centre, the turning pivot of a man's life is his sex life, the centre and swivel of his being in the sexual act. Upon this turns the whole rest of his life, from this emanates every motion he betrays. And that this should be so, every man makes his effort. The supreme effort each man makes, for himself, is the effort to clasp as a hub the woman who shall be the axle, compelling him to true motion, without aberration. The supreme desire of every man is for mating with a woman, such that the sexual act be the closest, most concentrated motion in his life, closest upon the axle, the prime movement of himself, of which all the rest of his motion is a continuance in the same kind. And the vital desire of every woman is that she shall be clasped as axle to the hub of the man, that his motion shall portray her motionlessness, convey her static being into movement, complete and radiating out into infinity, starting from her stable eternality, and reaching eternity again, after having covered the whole of time.

This is complete movement: man upon woman, woman within man. This is the desire, the achieving of which, frictionless, is impossible, yet for which every man will try, with greater or less intensity, achieving more or less success.

This is the desire of every man, that his movement, the manner of his walk, and the supremest effort of his mind, shall be the pulsation outwards from stimulus received in the sex, in the sexual act, that the woman of his body shall be the begetter of his whole life, that she, in her female spirit, shall beget in him his idea, his motion, himself. When

56

a man shall look at the work of his hands, that has succeeded, and shall know that it was begotten in him by the woman of his body, then he shall know what fundamental happiness is. Just as when a woman shall look at her child, that was begotten in her by the man of her spirit, she shall know what it is to be happy, fundamentally. But when a woman   5
looks at her children that were begotten in her by a strange man, not the man of her spirit, she must know what it is to be happy with anguish, and to love with pain. So with a man who looks'at his work which was not begotten in him by the woman of his body. He rejoices, trembles, and suffers an agony like death which contains resurrection.   10

For while, ideally, the soul of the woman possesses the soul of the man, procreates it and makes it big with new idea, motion, in the sexual act, yet, most commonly, it is not so. Usually, sex is only functional, a matter of relief or sensation, equivalent to eating or drinking or passing of excrement.   15

Then, if a man must produce work, he must produce it to some other than the woman of his body: as, in the same case, if a woman produce children, it must be to some other than the man of her desire.

In this case, a man must seek elsewhere than in woman for the female to possess his soul, to fertilise him and make him [big]*   20
with increase. And the female exists in much more than his woman. And the finding of it for himself gives a man his vision, his God.

And since no man and no woman can get a perfect mate, nor obtain complete satisfaction at all times, each man according to his need must have a God, an idea, that shall compel him to the movement of his own   25
being. And then, when he lies with his woman, the man may concurrently be with God, and so get increase of his soul. Or he may have communion with his God apart and averse from the woman.

Every man seeks in woman, for that which is stable, eternal. And if, under his motion, this break down in her, in the particular woman, so   30
that she be no axle for his hub, but be driven away from herself, then he must seek elsewhere for his stability, for the centre to himself.

Then either he must seek another woman, or he must seek to make conscious his desire to find a symbol, to create and define in his consciousness the object of his desire, so that he may have it at will, for   35
his own complete satisfaction.

In doing this latter, he seeks with his desire the female elsewhere than in the particular woman. Since everything that is, is either male or female or both, whether it be clouds or sunshine or hills or trees or a fallen feather from a bird, therefore in other things and in such things   40 man seeks for his complement. And he must at last always call God the unutterable and the inexpressible, the unknowable, because it is his unrealised complement.

But all Gods have some attributes in common. They are the
5 unexpressed Absolute: eternal, infinite, unchanging. Eternal, Infinite, Unchanging: the High God of all Humanity is this.

Yet man, the male, is essentially a thing of movement and time and' change. Until he is stirred into thought, he is complete in movement and change. But once he thinks, he must have the Absolute, the
10 Eternal, Infinite, Unchanging.

And man is stirred into thought by dissatisfaction, or unsatisfaction, as heat is born of friction. Consciousness is the same effort in male and female to obtain perfect frictionless interaction, perfect as Nirvana. It is the reflex both of male and female from defect in their dual motion.
15 Being reflex from the dual motion, consciousness contains the two in one, and is therefore in itself Absolute.

And desire is the admitting of deficiency. And the embodiment of the object of desire reveals the original defect or the defaulture. So that the attributes of God will reveal that which man lacked and yearned for
20 in his living. And these attributes are always, in their essence, Eternality, Infinity, Immutability.

And [these]° are the qualities man feels in woman, as a principle. Let a man walk alone on the face of the earth, and he feels himself like a loose speck blown at random. Let him have a woman to
25 whom he belongs, and he will feel as though he had a wall to back up against, even though the woman be mentally a fool. No man can endure the sense of space, of chaos, on four sides of him. It drives him mad. He must be able to put his back to the wall. And this wall is his woman.

From her he has a sense of stability. She supplies him with the
30 feeling of Immutability, Permanence, Eternality. He himself is a raging activity, change potent within [change]. He dare not even conceive of himself, save when he is sure of the woman permanent beneath him, beside him. He dare not leap into the unknown save from the sure stability of the unyielding female. Like a wheel, if he turn without an
35 axle, [his] motion is wandering neutrality.

So always, the fear of a man is that he shall find no axle for his motion, that no woman can centralise his activity. And always, the fear of a woman is that she can find no hub for her stability, no man to convey into motion her full stability. Either the particular woman
40 breaks down before the stress of the man, becomes erratic herself, no

stay, no centre, or else the man is insufficiently active to carry out the static principle of his female, of his woman.

So life consists in the dual form of the Will-to-Motion and the Will-to-Inertia, and everything we see and know and are is the resultant of these two Wills. But the One Will, of which they are dual forms, that is   5
as yet unthinkable.

And according as the Will-to-Motion predominates in [a] race,° or the Will-to-Inertia, so must that race's conception of the One Will enlarge the attributes which are lacking or deficient in the race.

Since there is never to be found a perfect balance or accord of the two   10
Wills, but always one triumphs over the other, in life, according to our knowledge, so must the human effort be always to recover balance, to symbolise and so to possess that which is missing. Which is the religious effort of Man.°

There seems to be a fundamental, insuperable division, difference,   15
between man's artistic effort and his religious effort. The two efforts are mixed with each other, as they are revealed, but all the while they remain two, not one, all the while they are separate, single, never compounded.

The religious effort is to conceive, to symbolise that which the human soul, or the soul of the race, lacks, that which it is not, and which it   20
requires, yearns for. It is the portrayal of that complement to the race-life which is known only as a desire: it is the symbolising of a great desire, the statement of the desire in terms which have no meaning apart from the desire.

Whereas the artistic effort is the effort of utterance, the supreme effort   25
of expressing knowledge, that which has been for once, that which was enacted, where the two wills met and interacted and left their result, complete for the moment. The artistic effort is the portraying of a moment of union between the two wills, according to knowledge. The religious effort is the portrayal or symbolising of the eternal union of the   30
two wills, according to aspiration. But in this eternal union, the features of one or the other Will are always salient.

The dual Will we call the Will-to-Motion and the Will-to-Inertia. These cause the whole of life, from the ebb and flow of a wave, to the stable equilibrium of the whole universe, from birth and being and   35
knowledge to death and decay and forgetfulness. And the Will-to-Motion we call the male will or spirit, the Will-to-Inertia the female. This will to inertia is not negative, and the other positive. Rather, according to some conception, is Motion negative and Inertia, the static, geometric idea, positive. That is according to the point of view.   40

According to the race-conception of God, we can see whether in that race the male or the female element triumphs, becomes predominant.

But it must first be seen that the division into male and female is arbitrary, for the purpose of thought. The rapid motion of the rim of a
5 wheel is the same as the perfect rest at the centre of the wheel. How can one divide them? Motion and rest are the same, when seen completely. Motion is only true of things outside oneself. When I am in a moving train, strictly, the land moves under me, I [and] the train are still. If I were both land and train, if I were large enough, there would
10 be no motion. And if I were very very small, every fibre of the train would be in motion for me, the point of rest would be infinitely reduced.

How can one say, there is motion and rest? If all things move together in one infinite motion, that is rest. Rest and motion are only
15 two degrees of motion, or two degrees of rest. Infinite motion and infinite rest are the same thing. It is obvious. Since, if motion were infinite, there would be no standing ground from which to regard it as motion. And the same with rest.

It is easier to conceive that there is no such thing as rest. For a thing
20 to us at rest is only a thing travelling at our own rate of motion: or, from another point of view, it is a thing moving at the lowest rate of motion we can recognise. But this table on which I write, which I call at rest, I know is really in motion.

So there is no such thing as rest. There is only infinite motion. But
25 infinite motion must contain every degree of rest. So that motion and rest are the same thing. Rest is the lowest speed of motion which I recognise under normal conditions.

So how can one speak of a Will-to-Motion or a Will-to-Inertia when there is no such thing as rest or motion. And yet starting from any given
30 degree of motion, and travelling forward in ever-increasing degree, one comes to a state of speed which covers the whole of space instantaneously, and is therefore rest, utter rest. And starting from the same speed and reducing the motion infinitely, one reaches the same condition of utter rest. And the direction or method of approach to this
35 infinite rest is different to our conception. And only travelling upon the slower, does the swifter reach the infinite rest of speed. And only by travelling upon the swifter does the slower reach the infinite rest of inertia: which is the same as the infinite rest of speed, the two things having united to surpass our comprehension.
40 So we may speak of Male and Female, of the Will-to-Motion and of

the Will-to-Inertia. And so, looking at a race, we can say whether the Will-to-Inertia or the Will-to-Motion has gained the ascendancy, and in which direction this race tends to disappear.

For it is as if life were a double cycle, of men and of women, facing opposite ways, travelling opposite ways, revolving upon each other, man 5 reaching forward with outstretched hand, woman reaching forward with outstretched hand, and neither able to move till their hands have grasped each other, when they draw towards each other from opposite directions, draw nearer and nearer, each travelling in his separate cycle, till the two are abreast, and side by side, until [eventually]* they 10 pass on again, away from each other, travelling their opposite ways to the same infinite goal.

Each travelling to the same goal of infinity, but entering it from the opposite ends of space. And man, remembering what lies behind him, how the hands met and grasped and tore apart, utters his tragic art. 15 Then moreover, facing the other way into the unknown, conscious of the tug of the goal at his heart, he hails the woman coming from the place whither he is travelling, searches in her for signs, and makes his God from the suggestion he receives, as she advances.

Then she draws near, and he is full of delight. She is so close, that 20 they touch, and then there is a joyful utterance of religious art. They are torn apart, and he gives the cry of tragedy, and goes on remembering, till the dance slows down and breaks, and there is only a crowd.

It is as if this cycle dance where the female makes the chain with the male became ever wider, ever more extended, and the further they get 25 from the source, from the infinity, the more distinct and individual do the dancers become. At first they are only figures. In the Jewish cycle, David,* with his hand stretched forth, cannot recognise the woman, the female. He can only recognise some likeness of himself. For both he and she have not danced very far from the source and 30 origin where they were both one. Though she is in the gross utterly other than he, yet she is not very distinct from him. And he hails her Father, Almighty, God, Beloved, Strength, hails her in his own image. And with hand outstretched, fearful and passionate, he reaches to her. But it is Solomon who touches her hand, with rapture and joy, and cries 35 out his gladness in the Song of Songs. Who is the Shulamite,* but God come close, for a moment into physical contact? The Song may be a drama: it is still religious art. It is the development of the Psalms. It is utterly different from the Book of Job, which is remembrance.

Always the threefold utterance: the declaring of the God seen 40 approaching, the rapture of contact, the anguished joy of remembrance, when the meeting has passed into separation. Such is religion, religious art, and tragic art.

But the chain is not broken by the letting-go of hands. It is broken by
5 the overbearing of one cycle by the other. David, when he lay with a woman, lay also with God. Solomon, when he lay with a woman, knew God and possessed him and was possessed by him. For in Solomon and in the Woman, the male clasped hands with the female.

But in the terrible moment, when they should break free again, the
10 male in the Jew was too weak, the female overbore him. He remained in the grip of the female. The force of inertia overpowered him, and he remained remembering. But very true had been David's vision, and very real Solomon's contact. So that the living thing was conserved, kept always alive and powerful, but restrained, restricted, partial.

15 For centuries, the Jew knew God as David had perceived him, as Solomon had known him. It was the God of the body, the rudimentary God of physical laws and physical functions. The Jew lived on in physical contact with God. Each of his physical functions he shared with God, he kept his body always like the body of a bride ready to
20 serve the bridegroom. He had become the servant of his God, the female, passive. The female in him predominated, held him passive; set utter bounds to his movement, to his roving, kept his mind as a slave to guard intact the state of sensation wherein he found himself. Which persisted century after century, the secret, scrupulous voluptuousness
25 of the Jew, become almost self-voluptuousness, engaged in the consciousness of his own physique, or in the extracted existence of his own physique. His own physique included the woman, naturally, since the man's body included the woman's, the woman's the man's. His religion had become a physical morality, deep and fundamental, but entirely of
30 one sort. Its living element was this scrupulous physical voluptuousness, wonderful and satisfying in a large measure.

Its conscious element was a resistance to the male or active principle. Being female, occupied in self-feeling, in realisation of the ego, in submission to sensation, the Jewish temper was antagonistic to the
35 active male principle, which would deny the ego and refuse sensation, seeking ever to make transformation, desiring to be an instrument of change, to register relationships. So this race recognised only male sins: it conceived only sins of commission, sins of change, of transformation. In the whole of the ten commandments, it is the female who
40 speaks. It is natural to the male to make the male God a God of

benevolence and mercy, susceptible to pity. Such is the male conception of God. It was the female spirit which conceived the saying: "For I, the Lord thy God, am a jealous God, visiting the iniquities of the fathers upon the children unto the third and fourth generation of them that hate me, and showing mercy unto thousands of them that love 5 me."*

It was a female conception. For is not man the child of woman. Does she not see in him her body, even more vividly than in her own. Man is more her body to her, even than her own body. For the whole of flesh is hers. Woman knows that she is the fountain of all flesh. And her pride 10 is that the body of man is of her issue. She can see the man as the One Being, for she knows he is of her issue.

It were a male conception to see God with a manifold Being, even though he be One God. For man is ever keenly aware of the multiplicity of things, and their diversity. But woman issuing from the 15 other end of infinity, coming forth as the flesh, manifest in sensation, is obsessed by the one-ness of things, the One Being, undifferentiated. Man, on the other hand, coming forth as the desire to single out one thing from another, to reduce each thing to its intrinsic self by process of elimination, cannot but be possessed by the infinite diversity and 20 contrariety in life, by a passionate sense of isolation, and a poignant yearning to be at one.

That is the fundamental of female conception: that there is but One Being: this Being necessarily female. Whereas man conceives a manifold Being, the supreme of which is male. And owing to the 25 complete Monism* of the female, which is essentially static, self-sufficient, the expression of God has been left always to the male, so that the supreme God is forever He.

Nevertheless, in the God of the Ancient Jew, the female has triumphed. That which was born of Woman, that is indeed the God of 30 the Old Testament. So utterly is he born of Woman, that he scarcely needs to consider Woman: she is there unuttered.

And the Jewish race continued in this Monism, stable, circumscribed, utterly unadventurous, utterly self-preservative, yet very deeply living, until the present century. 35

But Christ rose from the suppressed male spirit of Judea, and uttered a new commandment: thou shalt love thy neighbour as thyself. He repudiated woman: "Who is my mother?"* He lived the male life utterly apart from woman.

"Thou shalt love thy neighbour as thyself"—that is the great 40

utterance against Monism, and the compromise with Monism. It does
not say "Thou shalt love thy neighbour because he is thyself", as the
ancient Jew would have said. It commands "Thou shalt recognise thy
neighbour's distinction from thyself, and allow his separate being,
5 because he also is of God, even though he be almost a contradiction to
thyself."

Such is the cry of anguish of Christianity: that man is separate from
his brother, separate, maybe even, in his measure, inimical to him. This
the Jew had to learn. The old Jewish creed of identity, that Eve was
10 identical with Adam, and all men children of one single parent, and
therefore, in the absolute, identical, this must be destroyed.

Cunning and according to female suggestion is the story of the
Creation: that Eve was born from the single body of Adam, without
intervention of sex, both issuing from one flesh, as a child at birth
15 seems to issue from one flesh of its mother. And the birth of Jesus is the
retaliation of this: a child is born, not to the flesh, but to the spirit: and
you, woman, shall conceive, not to the body but to the Word. "In the
beginning was the Word," says the New Testament.*

The great assertion of the Male, was the New Testament, and, in its
20 beauty, the Union of Male and Female. Christ was born of Woman,
begotten by the Holy Spirit. This was why Christ should be called the
Son of Man. For he was born of Woman. He was born to the Spirit, the
Word, the Man, the Male.

And the assertion entailed the sacrifice of the Son of Woman. The
25 body of Christ must be destroyed, that of him which was Woman must
be put to death, to testify that he was Spirit, that he was Male, that he
was Man, without any womanly part.

So the other great camp was made. In the creation, Man was driven
forth from Paradise to labour for his body and for the woman. All was
30 lost for the knowledge of the flesh. Out of the innocence and Nirvana
of Paradise came, with the Fall, the consciousness of the flesh, the body
of man and woman came into very being.

This was the first great movement of Man: the movement into the
conscious possession of a body. And this consciousness of the body
35 came through woman. And this knowledge, this possession, this
enjoyment, was jealously guarded. In spite of all criticism and attack,
Job remained true to this knowledge, to the utter belief in his body, in
the God of his body. Though the Woman herself turned tempter, he
remained true to it.*

40 The senses, sensation, sensuousness, these things which are incon-

trovertibly Me, these are my God, these belong to God, said Job. And
he persisted and he was right. They issue from God on the female
side.

But Christ came with his contradiction: that which is Not-Me, that is
God. All is God, except that which I know immediately as Myself. First 5
I must lose Myself, then I find God. [Ye] must be born again.

Unto what must man be born again? Unto knowledge of his own
separate existence, as in Woman he is conscious of his own incorporate
existence. Man must be born unto knowledge of his own distinct
identity, as in woman he was born to knowledge of his identification 10
with the Whole. Man must be born to the knowledge, that in the whole
being he is nothing, as he was born to know that in the whole being he
was all. He must be born to the knowledge that other things exist
beside himself, and utterly apart from all, and before he can exist
himself as a separate identity, he must allow and recognise their distinct 15
existence. Whereas previously, on the more female Jewish side, it had
been said: "All that exists, is as Me. We are all one family, out of one
God, having one being."

With Christ ended the Monism of the Jew. God, the One God,
became a Trinity, three-fold. He was the Father, the All-containing; he 20
was the Son, the Word, the Changer, the Separator, and he was the
Spirit, the Comforter, the Reconciliator between the Two.

And according to its conditions, Christianity has, since Christ,
worshipped the Father or the Son, the one more than the other. Out of
an over-female race came the male utterance of Christ. Throughout 25
Europe, the suppressed, inadequate male desire, both in men and
women, stretched to the idea of Christ, as a woman should stretch her
hands out to a man. But Greece, in whom the female was overriden and
neglected, became silent. So through the Middle Ages went on in
Europe this fight against the body, against the senses, against this 30
continual triumph of the senses. The worship of Europe, predomi-
nantly female, all through the mediaeval period was to the male, to the
incorporeal Christ, as a bridegroom, whilst the art produced was the
collective, stupendous emotional gesture of the Cathedrals, where a
blind, collective impulse rose into concrete form. It was the profound, 35
sensuous desire and gratitude which produced an art of architecture,
whose essence is in utter stability, of movement resolved and central-
ised, of absolute movement, that has no relationship with any other
form, that admits the existence of no other form, but is conclusive,
propounding in its sum, the One Being of All. 40

There was, however, in the Cathedrals, already the denial of the
Monism which the Whole uttered. All the little figures, the gargoyles,
the imps, the human faces, whilst subordinated within the Great
Conclusion of the Whole, still, from their obscurity, jeered their
5   mockery of the Absolute,* and declared for multiplicity, polygeny.
But all mediaeval art has the static, architectural, absolute quality, in
the main, even whilst in detail it is differentiated and distinct. Such is
Dürer,* for example.' When his art succeeds, it conveys the sense
of Absolute Movement, movement proper only to the given form, and
10 not relative to other movements. It portrays the Object, with its
Movement [contained],* and not the movement which contains in
one of its moments, the Object.

It is only when the Greek stimulus is received, with its addition of
male influence, its addition of relative movement, its revelation of
15 movement driving the object, the highest revelation which had yet been
made, that Mediaeval art became complete Renaissance Art, that there
was the Union and fusion of the male and female spirits, creating a
perfect expression for the time being.

During the mediaeval times, the God had been Christ on the Cross,
20 the Body Crucified, the flesh destroyed, the Virgin, Chastity combating
Desire. Such had been the God of the Aspiration. But the God of
Knowledge, of that which they acknowledged as themselves, had been
the Father, the God of the Ancient Jew.

But now, with the Renaissance, the God of Aspiration became in
25 accord with the God of Knowledge, and there was a great outburst of
joy, and the theme was not Christ Crucified, but Christ born of
Woman, the Infant Saviour and the Virgin; or of the Annunciation, the
Spirit embracing the flesh in pure embrace.

This was the perfect union of male and female, in this the hands met
30 and clasped and never was such a manifestation of Joy. This Joy
reached its highest utterance perhaps in Botticelli, as in his "Nativity of
the Saviour" in our National Gallery.° Still there is the architectural composition, but what an outburst of movement from the source
of motion. The Infant Christ is a centre, a radiating spark of movement,
35 the Virgin is bowed in Absolute Movement, the earthly father, Joseph,
is folded up, like a clod or a boulder, obliterated, whilst the Angels fly
round in ecstasy, embracing and linking hands.

The bodily father is almost obliterated. As balance to the Virgin
Mother, he is there, presented, but silenced, only the movement of his
40 loin conveyed. He is not the male. The male is the radiant infant, over

which the mother leans. They two are the ecstatic centre, the complete origin, the force is both centrifugal and centripetal.

This is the joyous utterance of the Renaissance, to which we listen forever. Perhaps there is a melancholy in Botticelli, a pain of Woman mated to the Spirit, a nakedness of the Aphrodite issued exposed to the 5 clear elements,* to the fleshlessness of the male. But still it is joy transparent over pain. It is the utterance of complete, perfect religious art, unwilling perhaps, when the true male and the female meet. In the Song of Solomon, the female was preponderant, the male was impure, not single. But here the heart is satisfied for the moment, there is a 10 moment of perfect being.

And it seems to be so in other religions: the most perfect moment centres round the mother and the male child, whilst the physical male is deified separately, as a bull, perhaps.

After Botticelli came Correggio.* In him the development from 15 gesture to articulate expression was continued, unconsciously, the movement from the symbolic to the representation went on in him, from the object to the animate creature. The Virgin and Child are no longer symbolic, in Correggio: they no longer belong to religious art, but are distinctly secular. The effort is to render the living person, the 20 individual perceived, and not the great aspiration, or an idea. Art now passes from the naive, intuitive stage, to the state of knowledge. The female impulse, to feel and to live in feeling, is now embraced by the male impulse—to know, and almost carried off by knowledge. But not yet. Still Correggio is unconscious, in his art, he is in that state of 25 elation which represents the marriage of male and female, with the pride of the male perhaps predominant. In the "Madonna with the Basket" of the National Gallery, the Madonna is most thoroughly a wife, the child is most triumphantly a man's child. The Father is the origin. He is seen labouring in the distance, the true support of this 30 mother and child. There is no Virgin worship, none of the mystery of woman. The artist has reached to a sufficiency of knowledge. He knows his woman. What he is now concerned with, is not her great female mystery, but her individual character. The picture has become almost lyrical—it is the woman as known by the man, it is the woman as 35 he has experienced her. But still she is also unknown, also she is the mystery. But Correggio's chief business is to portray the woman of his own experience and knowledge, rather than the woman of his aspiration and fear. The artist is now concerned with his own experience, rather than with his own desire. The female is now more or less within 40

the power and reach of the male. But still she is there, to centralise and control his movement, still the two react and are not resolved. But for the man, the woman is henceforth part of a stream of movement, she is herself a stream of movement, carried along with himself. He sees
5 everything as motion, retarded perhaps by the flesh, or by the stable being of this life in the body. But still man is held and pivoted by the object, even if he tend to wear down the pivot to a nothingness.

Thus Correggio leads on to the whole of modern art, where the male still wrestles with the female, in unconscious struggle, but where he
10 gains ever gradually over her, reducing her to nothing. Ever there is more and more vibration, movement, and less and less stability, centralisation. Ever man is more and more occupied with his own experience, with his own overpowering of resistance, ever less and less aware of any resistance in the object, less and less aware of any stability,
15 less and less aware of anything unknown, more and more preoccupied with that which he knows, till his knowledge tends to become an abstraction, because it is limited by no unknown.

It is the contradiction of Dürer, as the Parthenon Frieze* was the contradiction of Babylon and Egypt. To Dürer woman did not exist,
20 even as to a child at the breast, woman does not exist separately. She is the overwhelming condition of life. She was to Dürer that which possessed him, and not that which he possessed. Her being overpowered his, he could only see in her terms, in terms of stability and of stable, incontrovertible being. He is overpowered by the vast assurance
25 at whose breasts he is suckled, and as if astounded, he grasps at the unknown. He knows that he rests within some great stability, and marvelling at his own power for movement, touches the objects of this stability, becomes familiar with them. It is a question of the starting point. Dürer starts with a sense of that which he does not know and
30 would discover, Correggio with the sense of that which he has known, and would re-create.

And in the Renaissance, after Botticelli, the motion begins to divide in these two directions. The hands no longer clasp in perfect union, but one clasp overbears the other. Botticelli develops to Correggio and to
35 Andrea del Sarto, develops forward to Rembrandt, and Rembrandt to the Impressionists,* to the male extreme of motion. But Botticelli on the other hand becomes Raphael, Raphael and Michael Angelo.

In Raphael we see the stable, architectural developing out further, and becoming the geometric: the denial or refusal of all movement. In
40 the "Madonna degli Ansidei" the child is drooping [motionless,]*

the mother stereotyped, the picture geometric, static, abstract. When there is any union of male and female, there is no goal of abstraction: the abstract is used in place, as a means of a real union. The goal of the male impulse is the announcement of motion, endless motion, endless diversity, endless change. The goal of the female impulse is the announcement of infinite oneness, of infinite stability. When the two are working in combination, as they must in life, there is, as it were, a dual motion, centrifugal for the male, fleeing abroad, away from the centre, outward to infinite vibration, and centripetal for the female, fleeing in to the eternal centre of rest. A combination of the two movements produces a sum of motion and stability at once, satisfying. But in life there tends always to be more of one than the other. The Cathedrals, Fra Angelico, frighten us or [bore] us* with their final annunciation of centrality and stability. We want to escape. The influence is too female for us.

In Botticelli, the architecture remains, but there is the wonderful movement outwards, the joyous if still clumsy, escape from the centre. His religious pictures tend to be stereotyped, resigned. The Primavera* herself is static, melancholy, a stability become almost a negation. It is as if the female, instead of being the great, unknown Positive, towards which all must flow, became the great Negative, the centre which denied all motion. And the Aphrodite stands there not as a force, to draw all things unto her, but as the naked, almost unwilling pivot, as the keystone which endured all thrust and remained static. But still there is the joy, the great motion around her, sky and sea, all the elements and living, joyful forces.

Raphael, however, seeks and finds nothing there. He goes to the centre to ask: "What is this mystery we are all pivoted upon?" To Fra Angelico it was the unknown Omnipotent. It was a goal, to which man travelled inevitably. It was the desired, the end of the long horizontal journey. But to Raphael it was the negation. Still he is a seeker, an aspirant, still his art is religious art. But the Virgin, the essential female, was to him a negation, a neutrality. Such must have been his vivid experience. But still he seeks her. Still he desires the stability, the positive keystone which grasps the arch together, not the negative keystone neutralising the thrust, itself a neutrality. And reacting upon his own desire, the male reacting upon itself, he creates the Abstraction, the geometric conception of life. The fundament of all, is the geometry of all. Which is Plato's conception. And the desire is to formulate the complete geometry.

So Raphael, knowing that his desire reaches out beyond the range of possible experience, sensible that he will not find satisfaction in any one woman, sensible that the female impulse does not, or cannot unite in him with the male impulse sufficiently to create a stability, an eternal
5 moment of truth for him, of realisation, closes his eyes and his mind upon experience, and abstracting himself, reacting upon himself, produces the geometric conception of the fundamental truth, departs from religion, from any God-idea, and becomes philosophic.

Raphael is the real end of [the] Renaissance in Italy; almost, he is the
10 real end of Italy, as Plato was the real end of Greece. When the God-idea passes into the philosophic or geometric-idea, then there is a sign that the male impulse has thrown the female impulse, and has recoiled upon itself, has become abstract, asexual.

Michael Angelo, however, too physically passionate, containing too
15 much of the female in his body ever to reach the geometric abstraction, unable to abstract himself, and at the same time, like Raphael, unable to find any woman, who in her being should resist him and reserve still some unknown from him, strives to obtain his own physical satisfaction in his art. He is obsessed by the desire of the body. And he must react
20 upon himself to produce his own bodily satisfaction, aware that he can never obtain it through woman. He must seek the moment, the consummation, the keystone, the pivot, in his own flesh. For his own body is both male and female.

Raphael and Michael Angelo are men of different nature placed in
25 the same position and resolving the same question in their several ways. Socrates and Plato are a parallel pair, and, in another degree, Tolstoi and Turgenev, and perhaps, St. Paul and St. John the Evangelist, and perhaps, Shakespeare and Shelley.

The body it is which attaches us directly to the female. Sex, as we
30 call it, is only the point where the dual stream begins to divide, where it is nearly together, almost one. An infant is of no very determinate sex: that is, it is of both. Only at adolescence is there a real differentiation, the one is singled out to predominate. In what we call happy natures, in the lazy, contented, people, there is a fairly equable balance of sex.
35 There is sufficient of the female in the body of such a man as to leave him fairly free. He does not suffer the torture of desire of a more male being. It is obvious even from the physique of such a man, that in him there is a proper proportion between male and female, so that he can be easy, balanced, and without excess. The Greek sculptors of the "best"
40 period, Phidias and [Myron],* then Sophocles, Alcibiades, then

Horace, must have been fairly well-balanced men, not passionate to
any excess, tending to voluptuousness rather than to passion. So also
Victor Hugo and Schiller and Tennyson. The real voluptuary is a man
who is female as well as male, and who lives according to the female
side of his nature, like Lord Byron. 5

The pure male is himself almost an abstraction, almost bodyless, like
Shelley or Edmund Spenser. But, as we know humanity, this condition
comes of an omission of some vital part. In the ordinary sense, Shelley
never lived. He transcended life. But we do not want to transcend life,
since we are of life. 10

Why should Shelley say of the skylark:

"Hail to thee, blithe spirit, bird thou never wert—"*

Why should he insist on the bodylessness of beauty, when we cannot
know of any save embodied beauty. Who would wish that the skylark
were not a bird, but a spirit? If the whistling skylark were a spirit, then 15
we should all wish to be spirits. Which were impious and flippant.

I can think of no being in the world so transcendently male as
Shelley. He is phenomenal. The rest of us have bodies which contain
the male and the female. If we were so singled out as Shelley, we
should not belong to life, as he did not belong to life. But it were 20
impious to wish to be like the angels. So long as mankind exists it must
exist in the body, and so long must each body pertain both to the male
and the female.

In the degree of pure maleness below Shelley are Plato and Raphael
and Wordsworth, then Goethe and Milton and Dante, then Michael 25
Angelo, then Shakespeare, then Tolstoi, then St. Paul.

A man who is well balanced between male and female, in his own
nature, is as a rule, happy, easy to mate, easy to satisfy, and content to
exist. It is only a disproportion, or a dissatisfaction, which makes the
man struggle into articulation. And the articulation is of two sorts, the 30
cry of desire or the cry of realisation, the cry of satisfaction, the effort to
prolong the sense of satisfaction, to prolong the moment of consummation.

A bird in spring sings with the dawn, ringing out, out from the
moment of consummation in wider and wider circles. Dürer, Fra 35
Angelico, Botticelli all sing of the moment of consummation, some of
them still marvelling and lost in the wonder at the other being,
Botticelli poignant with distinct memory. Raphael too sings of the

moment of consummation. But he was not lost in the moment, only sufficiently lost to know what it was. In the moment, he was not completely consummated. He must strive to complete his satisfaction from himself. So, whilst making his great acknowledgement to the
5   Woman, he must add to her to make her whole, he must give her his completion. So he rings her round with pure geometry, till she becomes herself almost part of the geometric figure, an abstraction. The picture becomes a great ellipse crossed by a dark column. This is the "Madonna degli Ansidei". The Madonna herself is almost insigni-
10 ficant. She and the child are contained within the shaft thrust across the ellipse.

This column must always stand for the male aspiration, the arch or ellipse for the female completeness containing this aspiration. And the whole picture is a geometric symbol of the consummation of life.
15 What we call the Truth is, in actual experience, that momentary state in living [when]* the union between the male and the female is consummated. This consummation may be also physical, between the male body and the female body. But it may be only spiritual, between the male and female spirit.
20 And the symbol by which Raphael expresses this moment of consummation is by a dark, strong shaft or column leaping up into, and almost transgressing a faint, radiant, inclusive ellipse.

To express the same moment Botticelli uses no symbol, but builds up a complicated system of circles, of movements wheeling in their
25 horizontal plane about their fixed centres, the whole builded up dome-shape, and then the dome surpassed by another singing cycle in the open air above.

This is Botticelli always: different cycles of joy, different moments of embrace, different forms of dancing round, all contained in one
30 picture, without solution. He has not solved it yet.

And Raphael, in reaching the pure symbolic solution, has surpassed art and become almost mathematics. Since the business of art is never to solve, but only to declare.

There is no such thing as solution. Nietzsche talks about the Ewige
35 Wiederkehr.* It is like Botticelli singing cycles. But each cycle is different. There is no real recurrence.

And to single out one cycle, one moment, and to exclude from this moment all context, and to make this moment timeless, is what Raphael does, and what Plato does. So that their absolute Truth, their
40 geometric Truth, is only true in timelessness.

Michael Angelo, on the other hand, seeks for no absolute Truth. His desire is to realise in his body, in his feeling, the moment-consummation which is for Man the perfect truth-experience. But he knows of no embrace. For him, personally, woman does not exist. For Botticelli she existed as the Virgin-Mother, and as the Primavera, and as Aphrodite. 5 She existed as the pure origin of life on the female side, as the bringer of light and delight, and as the passionately Desired of every man, as the Known and Unknown in one. To Raphael she existed either as a minor part of his experience, having nothing to do with his aspiration, or else his aspiration merely used her as a statement included within 10 the Great Abstraction.

To Michael Angelo the female scarcely existed outside his own physique. There he knew of her and knew the desire of her. But Raphael, in his passion to be self-complete, roused his desire for consummation to a white-hot pitch, so that he became incandescent, 15 re-acting on himself, consuming his own flesh and his own bodily life, to reach the pitch of perfect abstraction, the resisting body holding back the raging stream of outward force, till the two formed a stable incandescence, a luminous geometric conception of permanence and inviolability. Meanwhile his body burned away, overpowered, in this 20 state of incandescence.

Michael Angelo's will was different. The body in him, that which knew of the female and therefore was the female, was stronger and more insistent. His desire for consummation was desire for the satisfying moment when the male and female spirits touch in closest 25 embrace, vivifying each other, not one destroying the other, but still are two. He knew that for Man, consummation is a temporal state. The pure male spirit must ever conceive of timelessness, the pure female—of the moment. And Michael Angelo, more mixed than Raphael, must always rage within the limits of time and of temporal 30 form. So he re-acted upon himself, sought the female in himself, aggrandised it, and so reached a wonderful momentary stability, of flesh exaggerated till it became tenuous, but filled and balanced by the outward-pressing force. And he reached his consummation in that way, reached the perfect moment, when he realised and revealed his figures 35 in all their marvellous equilibrium. The Jewish tradition with its great physical God, source of male and female, attracted him. By turning towards the female goal, of utter stability and permanence in Time, he arrived at his consummation. But only by re-acting on himself, by withdrawing his own mobility. Thus he made his great figures, the 40

Moses, static and looming, announcing, like the Jewish God, the magnificence and eternality of the physical law; the David, young, but with too much body for a young figure, the physique exaggerated, the clear, outward-leaping, essential spirit of the young man smothered
5   over, the real maleness cloaked, so that the statue is almost a falsity. Then the Slaves, heaving in body, fastened in bondage, that refuses them movement; the motionless Madonna, no Virgin, but Woman in the flesh, not the pure female conception, but the spouse of man, the mother of bodily children. The men are not male, nor the women
10   female, to any degree.

The Adam can scarcely stir into life. That large body of almost transparent, tenuous texture is not established enough for motion. It is not that it is too ponderous: it is too unsubstantial, unreal. It is not motion, life, he craves, but body. Give him but a firm, concentrated
15   physique. That is the cry of all Michael Angelo's pictures.*

But, powerful male as he was, he satisfies his desire by insisting upon and exaggerating the body in him, he reaches the point of consummation in the most marvellous equilibrium which his figures show. To attain this equilibrium he must exaggerate and exaggerate and exagger-
20   ate the flesh, make it ever more tenuous, keeping it really in true ratio. And then comes the moment, the perfect stable poise, the perfect balance between object and movement, the perfect combination of male and female in one figure.

It is wonderful, and peaceful, this equilibrium, once reached. But it
25   is reached through anguish and self-battle and self-repression, there-fore it is sad. Always, Michael Angelo's pictures are full of the effects of self-repression, as Raphael's pictures are full of joy, of self-acceptance and self-proclamation. Michael Angelo fought and arrested the mobile male in him, Raphael was proud in the male he was, and gave himself
30   utter liberty, at the female expense.

And it seems as though Italy had ever since the Renaissance been possessed by the Raphaelesque conception of the ultimate geometric basis of life, the geometric essentiality of all things. There is in the Italian, at the very bottom of all, the fundamental, geometric concep-
35   tion of absolute static combination. There is the shaft enclosed in the ellipse, as a permanent symbol. There exists no shaft, no ellipse separately, but only the whole complete thing; there is neither male nor female, but an absolute interlocking of the two in one, an absolute combination, so that each is gone in the complete identity. There is
40   only the geometric abstraction of the moment of consummation, a

moment made timeless. And this conception of a long, clinched,
timeless embrace, this overwhelming conception of timeless consummation, of which there is no beginning nor end, from which there is no
escape, has arrested the Italian race for three centuries. It is the source
of its indifference and its fatalism and its positive abandon, and of its   5
utter incapacity to be sceptical, in the Russian sense.*

This conception contains also, naturally, as part of the same idea,
Aphrodite-worship and Phallic-worship. But these are subordinate,
and belong to a sort of initiatory period. The real conception, for the
individual, is Marriage, inviolable marriage, which always was and   10
always has been, no matter what apparent aberrations there may or may
not be. And the manifestation of divinity is the child. In marriage, in
utter, interlocked marriage, man and woman cease to be two beings and
become one, one and one only, not two in one as with us, but absolute
One, a geometric absolute, timeless, the Absolute, the Divine. And the   15
child, as issue of this divine and timeless state, is hailed with love and
joy.

But the Italian is now beginning to withdraw from his clinched and
timeless embrace, from his geometric abstraction, into the northern
conception of himself and the woman as two separate identities, which   20
meet, combine, but always must withdraw again.

So that the Futurist Boccioni now makes his sculpture "Development of a Bottle through Space",* try to express the withdrawal,
and at the same time he must adhere to the conception of this same
interlocked state of marriage between centripetal and centrifugal   25
forces, the geometric abstraction of the bottle. But he can neither do
one thing nor the other. He wants to re-state the real abstraction. And
at the same time he has an unsatisfied desire to satisfy. He must insist
on the centrifugal force, and so destroy at once his abstraction. He
must insist on the male spirit of motion outwards, because, during   30
three static centuries, there has necessarily come to pass a preponderance of the female in the race, so that the Italian is rather more female
than male, now, as is the whole Latin race rather voluptuous than
passionate, too much aware of their utter lockedness male with female,
and too hopeless, as males, to act, to be passionate. So that when I look   35
at Boccioni's sculpture, and see him trying to state the timeless,
abstract being of a bottle, the pure geometric abstraction of the bottle, I
am fascinated. But then, when I see him driven by his desire for the
male complement into portraying motion, simple motion, trying to give
expression to the bottle in terms of mechanics, I am confused. It is for   40

science to explain the bottle in terms of force and motion. Geometry, pure mathematics, is very near to art, and the vivid attempt to render the bottle as a pure geometric abstraction, might give rise to a work of art, because of the resistance of the medium, the stone. But a
5　representation in stone of the lines of force which create that state of rest called a bottle, that is a model in mechanics.

And the two representations require two different states of mind in the appreciator, so that the result is almost nothingness, mere confusion. And the portraying of a state of mind is impossible. There can
10　only be made scientific diagrams of states of mind. A state of mind is a resultant between an attack and a resistance. And how can one produce a resultant without first causing the collision of the originating forces?

The attitude of the Futurists is the scientific attitude, as the attitude of Italy is mainly scientific. It is the forgetting of the old, perfect
15　Abstraction, it is the departure of the male from the female, it is the act of withdrawal: the denying of consummation and the starting afresh, the learning of the alphabet.

Chapter VIII.

"The Light of the World."*

The climax that was reached in Italy with Raphael has never been reached in like manner in England. There has never been, in England, the great embrace, the surprising consummation, which Botticelli recorded and which Raphael fixed in a perfect Abstraction.

Correggio, Andrea del Sarto, both men of less force than those other supreme three,* continued the direct line of development, turning no curve. They still found women whom they could not exhaust: in them, the male still [reacted] upon the incontrovertible female. But ever there was a tendency to greater movement, to a closer characterisation, a tendency to individualise the human being, and to represent him as being embedded in some common, divine matrix.

Till after the Renaissance, supreme God had always been God the Father. The Church moved and had its being in Almighty God, Christ was only the distant, incandescent gleam towards which humanity aspired, but which it did not know.

Raphael and Michael Angelo were both servants of the Father, of the Eternal Law, of the Prime Being. Raphael, faced with the question of Not-Being, when it was forced upon him that he would never accomplish his own being in the flesh, that he would never know completeness, the momentary consummation, in the body, accomplished the Geometric Abstraction, which is the abstraction from the Law, which is the Father.

There was, however, Christ's great assertion of Not-Being, of [Non]-Consummation, of life after death, to reckon with. It was after the Renaissance, Christianity began to exist. It had not existed before.

In God the Father we are all one body, one flesh. But in Christ we abjure the flesh, there is no flesh. A man must lose his life to save it. All the natural desires of the body, these a man must be able to deny, before he can live. And then, when he lives, he shall live in the knowledge that he is himself, so that he can always say: "I am I."

In the Father we are one flesh, in Christ we are crucified, and rise again, and are One with Him in Spirit. It is the difference between Law and Love. Each man shall live according to the Law, which changeth

77

not, says the old religion. Each man shall live according to Love, which
shall save us from death and from the Law, says the new religion.

But what is Love? What is the deepest desire Man has yet known? It
is always for this consummation, this momentary contact or union of
5   male with female, of spirit with spirit and flesh with flesh, when each is
complete in itself and rejoices in its own being, when each is in himself
or in herself complete and single and essential. And love is the great
aspiration towards this complete consummation and this joy; it is the
aspiration of each man that all men, that all life, shall know it and
10 rejoice. Since, until all men shall know it, no man shall fully know it.
Since, by the Law, we are all one flesh. So that Love is only a closer
vision of the Law, a more comprehensive interpretation: "Think not I
come to destroy the Law, or the prophets: I come not to destroy, but to
fulfil! For verily I say unto you, till heaven and earth pass, one jot or one
15 tittle shall in no wise pass from the Law, till all be fulfilled."*

In Christ, I must save my soul through love, I must lose my life, and
thereby find it. The Law bids me preserve my life to the Glory of God.
But Love bids me lose my life to the Glory of God. In Christ, when I
shall have overcome every desire I know in myself, so that I adhere to
20 nothing, but am loosed and set free and single, then, being without
fear, and having nothing that I can lose, I shall know what I am, I,
transcendent, intrinsic, eternal.

The Christian commandment "Thou shalt love thy neighbour as
thyself" is a more indirect and moving, a more emotional form of the
25 Greek commandment "Know thyself."* This is what Christianity
says, indirectly: "Know thyself, and each man shall thereby know
himself."

Now in the Law, no man shall know himself, save in the Law. And
the Law is the immediate law of the body. And the necessity of each
30 man to know himself, to achieve his own consummation, shall be
satisfied and fulfilled in the body. God, Almighty God, is the father,
and in fatherhood man draws nearest to him. In the act of love, in the
act of begetting, Man is with God and of God. Such is the Law. And
there shall be no other God devised. That is the great obstructive
35 commandment.

This is the old religious leap down, absolutely, even if not in direct
statement. It is the Law. But through Christ it was at last declared that
in the physical act of love, in the begetting of children, man does not
necessarily know himself, nor become Godlike, nor satisfy his deep,
40 innate desire to *BE*. The physical act of love may be a complete

disappointment, a nothing, and fatherhood may be the least significant attribute to a man. And physical love may fail utterly, may prove a sterility, a nothingness. Is a man then duped, and is his deepest desire a joke played on him?

There is a law, beyond the known law, there is a new Commandment. 5
There is love. A man shall find his consummation in the crucifixion of the body and the resurrection of the spirit.

Christ, the Bridegroom, or the Bride, as may be, awaits the desiring soul that shall seek Him, and in Him shall all men find their consummation, after their new birth. It is the New Law, the Old Law is 10 revoked.

"This is my body, take, and eat," says Christ, in the communion,* the ritual representing the Consummation. "Come unto me all ye that labour and are heavy laden, and I will give you rest."*

For each man, there is the bride, for each woman the bridegroom, for 15 all, the Mystic Marriage. It is the New Law. In the mystic embrace of Christ each man shall find fulfilment and relief, each man shall become himself, a male individual, tried, proved, completed, and satisfied. In the mystic embrace of Christ each man shall say "I am myself, and Christ is Christ." Each woman shall be proud and satisfied, saying "It is enough." 20

So, by the New Law, man shall satisfy this his deepest desire. "In the body ye must die, even as I died, on the cross," says Christ,* "that ye may have everlasting life." But this is a real contradiction of the Old Law, which says "In the life of the body we are one with the Father." The Old Law bids us live: it is the old, original commandment, that we shall live in 25 the Law, and not die. So that the new Christian preaching of Christ Crucified is indeed against the Law. "And when ye are dead in the body, ye shall be one with the spirit, ye shall know the Bride, and be consummate in Her Embrace, in the Spirit," continues the Christian Commandment. 30

It is a larger interpretation of the Law, but also, it is a breach of the Law. For by the Law, Man shall in no wise injure or deny or desecrate his living body of flesh, which is of the Father. Therefore, though Christ gave the Holy Ghost, the Comforter; though he bowed before the Father, though he said, that no man should be forgiven the denial of the 35 Holy Spirit, the Reconciler between the Father and the Son; yet did the Son deny the Father, must he deny the Father?

"Ye are My Spirit, in the Spirit ye know Me, and in marriage of the Spirit I am fulfilled of you," said the Son.

And it is the Unforgivable Sin to declare that these two are 40 contradictions one of the other, though contradictions they are. Between them is linked the Holy Spirit, as a reconciliation, and whoso shall speak hurtfully against the Holy Spirit shall find no forgiveness.°

5   So Christ, up in arms against the Father, exculpated himself and bowed to the Father. Yet man must insist either on one or on the other, either he must adhere to the Son or to the Father. And since the Renaissance, disappointed in the flesh, the northern races have sought the consummation through Love; and they have denied the Father.

10   The greatest and deepest human desire, for consummation, for Self-Knowledge, has sought a different satisfaction. In Love, in the act of love, that which is mixed in me becomes pure, that which is female in me is given to the female, that which is male in her draws into me, I am complete, I am pure male, she is pure female, we rejoice in contact

15   perfect and naked and clear, singled out unto ourselves, and given the surpassing freedom. No longer we see through a glass, darkly.° For she is she and I am I, and, clasped together with her, I know how perfectly she is not me, how perfectly I am not her, how utterly we are two, the light and the darkness, and how infinitely and eternally

20   not-to-be-comprehended by either of us, is the surpassing One we make. Yet of this One, this incomprehensible, we have an inkling that satisfies us.

And through Christ Jesus, I know that I shall find my Bride, when I have overcome the impurity of the flesh. When the flesh in me is put

25   away, I shall embrace the Bride, and I shall know as I am known.

But why the Schism? Why shall the Father say "Thou shalt have no other God before me"? Why is the Lord Our God a jealous God?° Why, when the body fails me, must I still adhere to the Law, and give It praise as the perfect Abstraction, like Raphael, announce It as the

30   Absolute? Why must I be imprisoned within the flesh, like Michael Angelo, till I must stop the voice of my crying out, and be satisfied with a little where I wanted completeness?

And why, on the other hand, must I lose my life to save it? Why must I die, before I can be born again? Can I not be born again, save out of

35   my own ashes, save in resurrection from the dead? Why must I deny the Father, to love the Son? Why are they not One God to me, as we always protest they are?

It is time that the schism ended, that man ceased to oppose the Father to the Son, the Son to the Father. It is time that the Protestant

40   Church, the Church of the Son, should be one again with the Roman

Catholic Church, the Church of the Father. It is time that man shall cease, first to live in the flesh, with joy, and then, unsatisfied, to renounce and to mortify the flesh, declaring that the Spirit alone exists, that Christ he is God.

If a man find incomplete satisfaction in the body, why therefore shall he renounce the body and say, it is of the devil? And why, at the start, shall a man say, "The body, that is all, and the consummation, that is complete in the flesh, for me."

Must it always be, that a man set out with a worship of passion and a blindness to love, and that he end with a stern commandment to love and a renunciation of passion?

Does not a youth now know that he desires the body as the via media, that consummation is consummation of body and spirit, both?

How can a man say "I am this body", when he will desire beyond the body tomorrow? And how can a man say "I am this spirit", when his own mouth gives lie to the words it forms?

Why is a race, like the Italian race, fundamentally melancholy, save that it has circumscribed its consummation within the body? And the Jewish race for the same reason has become now almost hollow with a pit of emptiness and misery in their eyes.

And why is the English race neutral, indifferent, like a thing that eschews life, save that it has said so insistently: "I am this spirit. This body, it is not me, it is unworthy." The body at last begins to wilt and become corrupt. But before it submits, half the life of the English race must be a lie. The life of the body, denied by the professed adherence to the spirit, must be something disowned, corrupt, ugly.

Why should the worship of the Son entail the denial of the Father?

Since the Renaissance, northern humanity has sought for consummation in the spirit, it has sought for the female apart from woman. "I am I, and the Spirit is the Spirit, in the Spirit I am myself", and this has been the utterance of our art since Raphael.

There has been the ever-developing dissolution of form, the dissolving of the solid body within the spirit. He began to break the clear outline of the object, to seek for further marriage, not only between body and body, not the perfect, stable union of body with body, not the utter completeness and accomplishment of architectural form, with its recurrent cycles, but the marriage between body and spirit, or between spirit and spirit.

It is no longer the Catholic exultation "God is God", but the Christian annunciation "Light is come into the world."* No longer

has a man only to obey, but he has to die and be born again, he has to
close his eyes upon his own immediate desires, and in the darkness
receive the perfect light. He has to know himself in the spirit, he has to
follow Christ to the Cross, and rise again in the light of life.°

5   And, in this light of life, he will see his Bride, he will embrace his
complement and his fulfilment, and achieve his consummation. "It is
the spirit that quickeneth; the flesh [profiteth] nothing; the words I
speak unto you, they are the spirit, and they are life."°

And though in the Gospel, according to John particularly, Jesus
10   constantly asserts that the Father has sent him, and that he is of the
Father, yet there is always the spirit of antagonism to the Father.

"And it came to pass, as he spake these things, a certain woman of
the company lifted up her voice and said unto him, 'Blessed is the
womb that bare thee, and the paps thou hast sucked.'

15   "But he said, 'Yea, rather, blessed are they that hear the word of
God, and keep it.'"°

And the woman who heard this, knew that she was denied of the
honour of her womb, and that the blessing of her breasts was taken
away.

20   Again he said: "And there be those that were born eunuchs; and
there be those that were made eunuchs by men, and there be eunuchs
which have made themselves eunuchs for the kingdom of heaven's
sake. He that is able to receive it, let him receive it."° But before
the Father a eunuch is blemished, even a childless man is without
25   honour.

So that the spirit of Jesus is antagonistic to the spirit of the Father.
And St. John enhances this antagonism. But in St. John, there is the
constant insistence on the Oneness of Father and Son, and on the Holy
Spirit.

30   Since the Renaissance there has been the striving for the Light, and
the escape from the Flesh, from the Body, the Object. And sometimes
there has been the antagonism to the Father, sometimes reconciliation
with Him. In painting, the Spirit, the Word, the Love, all that was
represented by John, has appeared as light. Light is the constant
35   symbol of Christ in the New Testament. It is light, actual sunlight or
the luminous quality of day which has infused more and more into the
defined body, fusing away the outline, absolving the concrete reality,
making a marriage, an embrace between the two things, light and
object.

40   In Rembrandt there is the first great evidence of this, the new

exposition of the commandment "Know thyself." It is more than the "Hail, holy Light!" of Milton.* It is the declaration that light is our medium of existence, that where the light falls upon our darkness, there we *are*: that I am but the point where light and darkness meet, and break upon one another.

There is now a new conception of life, an utterly new conception, of duality, of two-fold existence, light and darkness, object and spirit two-fold, and almost inimical.

The old desire, for movement about a centre of rest, for stability, is gone, and in its place rises the desire for pure ambience, pure spirit of change, free from all laws and conditions of being.

Henceforward there are two things, and not one. But there is journeying towards the one thing again. There is no longer the One God who contains us all, and in whom we live and move and have our being, and to whom belongs each one of our movements. I am no longer a child of the Father, brother of all men. I am no longer part of the great body of God, as all men are part of it. I am no longer consummate in the body of God, identified with it and divine in the act of marriage.

The conception has utterly changed. There is the Spirit, and there is Myself. I exist in contact with the Spirit, but I am not the Spirit. I am other, I am Myself. Now I am become a man, I am no more a child of the Father. I am a man. And there are many men. And the Father has lost his importance. We are multiple, manyfold men, we own only one Hope, one Desire, one Bride, one Spirit.

At last man insists upon his own separate Self, insists that he has a distinct, inconquerable being which stands apart even from Spirit, which exists other than the Spirit, and which seeks marriage with the Spirit.

And he must study himself and marvel over himself in the light of the Spirit, he must become lyrical: but he must glorify the Spirit, above all. Since that is the Bride. So Rembrandt paints his own portrait again and again,* sees it again and again within the light.

He has no hatred of the flesh. That he was not completed in the flesh, even in the marriage of the body, is inevitable. But he is married in the flesh, and his wife is with him in the body, he loves his body, which she gave him complete, and he loves her body, which is not himself, but which he has known. He has known and rejoiced in the earthly bride, he will adhere to her always. But there is the Spirit beyond her: there is his desire which transcends her, there is the Bride still he craves for and courts. And he knows, this is the Spirit, it is not the body. And he paints it as the light. And he paints himself within the light. For he has a deep desire to know himself in the embrace of the Spirit. For he does not know himself, he is never consummated.

5   The Old Law, fulfilled in him, he is not appeased, he must transcend the Law. The Woman is embraced, caught up, and carried forward, the male spirit, passing on half satisfied, must seek a new bride, a further consummation. For there is no bride on earth for him.

To Dürer, the whole earth was as a bride, unknown and unaccom-
10 plished, offering [inexhaustible]° satisfaction to him. And he sought out the earth endlessly, as a man seeks to know a bride who surpasses him. It was all: the Bride.

But to Rembrandt, the bride was not to be found, he must re-act upon himself, he must seek in himself for his own consummation.
15 There was the Light, the Spirit, the Bridegroom. But when Rembrandt sought the complete Bride, sought for his own consummation, he knew it was not to be found, he knew she did not exist in the concrete. He knew, as Michael Angelo knew, that there was not on the earth a woman to satisfy him, to be his mate. He must seek for the Bride
20 beyond the physical woman, he must seek for the great female principle in an abstraction.

But the abstraction was not the geometric abstraction, created from knowledge, a state of Absolute Remembering, making Absolute of the Consummation which had been, as in Raphael. It was the desired
25 Unknown, the goodly Unknown, the Spirit, the Light. And with this Light Rembrandt must seek even the marriage of the body. Everything he did approximates to the Consummation, but never can realise it. He paints always faith, belief, hope, never Raphael's terrible, dead certainty.

30 To Dürer, every moment of his existence was occupied. He existed within the embrace of the Bride, which embrace he could never fathom nor exhaust.

Raphael knew and outraged the Bride, but he harked back, obsessed by the consummation which had been.

35 To Rembrandt, woman was only the first acquaintance with the Bride. Of woman he obtained and expected no complete satisfaction. He knew he must go on, beyond the woman. But though the flesh could not find its consummation, still he did not deny the flesh. He was an artist, and in his art no artist ever could blaspheme the Holy Spirit,
40 the Reconciler. Only a dogmatist could do that. Rembrandt did not

deny the flesh, as so many artists try to do. He went on from her to the fuller knowledge of the Bride, in true progression. Which makes the wonderful beauty of Rembrandt.

But, like Michael Angelo, owning the flesh, and, a northern Christian being bent on personal salvation, personal consummation, consummation in the flesh, such as a Christian feels with us when he receives the Sacrament and hears the words "This is my Body, take, and eat", Rembrandt craved to marry the flesh and the Spirit, to achieve consummation in the flesh through marriage with the Spirit.

Which is the great northern confusion.* For the flesh is of the flesh, and the Spirit of the Spirit, and they are two, even as the Father and the Son are two, and not One.

Raphael conceived the two as One, thereby revoking Time. Michael Angelo would have created the bridal Flesh, to satisfy himself. Rembrandt would have married his own flesh to the Spirit, taken the consummate Kiss of the Light upon his fleshly face.

Which is a confusion. For the Father cannot know the Son, nor the Son the Father. So in Rembrandt the marriage is always imperfect, the embrace is never close nor consummate, as it is in Botticelli or in Raphael or in Michael Angelo. There is an eternal non-marriage betwixt flesh and spirit. They are two, they are never Two-in-One. So that in Rembrandt, there is never complete marriage betwixt the Light and the Body. They are contiguous, never [consummate.]*

This has been the confusion and the error of the northern countries, but particularly of Germany, this desire to have the spirit mate with the flesh, the flesh with the spirit. Spirit can mate with spirit, and flesh with flesh, and the two matings can take place in one, but they are always Two-in-One. Or the two matings can take place separately, flesh with flesh, or spirit with spirit. But to try to mate flesh with spirit makes confusion.

The bride I mate with my body may or may not be the Bride in whom I find my consummation. It may be that, at times, the great female principle does not abide abundantly in woman: that, at certain periods, woman, in the body, is not the supreme representative of the Bride. It may be the Bride is hidden from Man, as the Light, or as the Darkness, which he can never know in the flesh.

It may be, in the same way, that the great male principle is only weakly evidenced in man during certain periods, that the Bridegroom be hidden away from woman, for a century or centuries, and that she can only find Him as the voice, or the Wind.* So I think it was with her during the mediaeval period; that the greatest women of the period knew that the Bridegroom did not exist for them in the body, but as the Christ, the Spirit.

And, in times of the absence of the bridegroom from the body, then
5 woman in the body must either die in the body, or, mating in the body, she must mate with the Bridegroom in the Spirit, in a separate marriage. She cannot mate her body with the Spirit, nor mate her spirit with the Body. That is confusion. Let her mate the man in body, and her spirit with the Spirit, in a separate marriage. But let her not try to
10 mate her spirit with the body of the man, that does not mate her Spirit.

The effort to mate spirit with body, body with spirit, is the crying confusion and pain of our times.

Rembrandt made the first effort. But art has developed to a clarity since then. It reached its climax in our own Turner.° He did not
15 seek to mate body with spirit. He mated his body easily, he did not deny it. But what he sought was the mating of the Spirit. Ever, he sought the consummation in the Spirit, and he reached it at last. Ever, he sought the Light, to make the light transfuse the body, till the body was carried away, a mere bloodstain, became a ruddy stain of red sunlight within
20 white sunlight. This was perfect consummation in Turner, when, the body gone, the ruddy light meets the crystal light in a perfect fusion, the utter dawn, the utter golden sunset, the extreme of all life, where all is One, One-Being, a perfect glowing One-ness.

Like Raphael, it becomes an abstraction. But this, in Turner, is the
25 abstraction from the spiritual marriage and consummation, the final transcending of all the Law, the achieving of what is to us almost a nullity. If Turner had ever painted his last picture, it would have been a white, incandescent surface, the same whiteness when he finished as when he began, proceeding from nullity to nullity, through all the range
30 of colour.

Turner is perfect. Such a picture as his "Norham Castle, Sunrise",° where only the [faintest] shadow of life stains the light, is the last word that can be uttered, before the blazing and timeless silence.

35 He sought, and he found, perfect marriage in the spirit. It was apart from woman. His Bride was the Light. Or he was the bride himself, and the Light—the Bridegroom. Be that as it may, he became one and consummate with the Light, and gave us the consummate revelation.

Corot also, nearer to the Latin tradition of utter consummation in
40 the body, made a wonderful marriage in the spirit between light and

darkness, just tinctured with life.* But he contained more of the
two consummations together, the marriage in the body, represented in
geometric form, and the marriage in the spirit, represented by shim-
mering transfusion and infusion of light through darkness.

But Turner is the crisis in this effort: he achieves pure light, pure 5
and singing. In him the consummation is perfect, the perfect marriage
in the spirit.

In the body his marriage was other. He never attempted to mingle
the two. The marriage in the body, with the woman, was apart from,
completed away from the marriage in the Spirit, with the Bride, the 10
Light.

But I cannot look at a later Turner picture without abstracting
myself, without denying that I have limbs, knees and thighs and breast.
If I look at the "Norham Castle", and remember my own knees and my
own breast, then the picture is a nothing to me. I must not know. And if 15
I look at Raphael's "Madonna degli Ansidei", I am cut off from my
future, from aspiration. The gate is shut upon me, I can go no further.
The thought of Turner's Sunrise becomes magic and fascinating, it
gives the lie to this completed symbol. I know I am the other thing as
well. 20

So that, whenever art or any expression becomes perfect, it becomes
a lie. For it is only perfect by reason of abstraction from that context by
which and in which it exists as truth.

So Turner is a lie, and Raphael is a lie, and the marriage in the spirit
is a lie, and the marriage in the body is a lie, each is a lie without the 25
other. Since each excludes the other in these instances, they are both
lies. If they were brought together, and reconciled, then there were a
jubilee. But where is the Holy Spirit that shall reconcile Raphael and
Turner?

There must be marriage of body in body, and of spirit in spirit, and 30
Two-in-One. And the marriage in the body must not deny the
marriage in the spirit, for that is blasphemy against the Holy Ghost; and
the marriage in the spirit shall not deny the marriage in the body, for
that is blasphemy against the Holy Ghost. But the two must be forever
reconciled, even if they must exist on occasions apart one from the 35
other.

For in Botticelli the dual marriage is perfect, or almost perfect, body
and spirit reconciled, or almost reconciled, in a perfect dual consummation. And in all art, there is testimony to the wonderful dual
marriage, the true consummation. But in Raphael, the marriage in the 40

spirit is left out so much that it is almost denied, so that the picture is almost a lie, almost a blasphemy. And in Turner, the marriage in the body is almost denied in the same way, so that his picture is almost a blasphemy. But neither in Raphael nor in Turner is the denial positive:

5 it is only an over-affirmation of the one at the expense of the other.

But in some men, in some small men, like bishops, the denial of marriage in the body is positive and blasphemous, a sin against the Holy Ghost. And in some men, like Prussian army officers, the denial of marriage in the spirit is an equal blasphemy.* But which of the

10 two is a greater sinner, working better for the destruction of his fellow man, that is for the One God to judge.

Chapter IX.

A nos Moutons.*

- I -

Most fascinating in all artists is this antinomy between the Law and
Love, between the Flesh and the Spirit, between the Father and the Son. 5
For the moralist it is easy. He can insist on that aspect of the Law or
Love, which is in the immediate line of development for his age, and he
can sternly and severely exclude or suppress all the rest.

So that all morality is of temporary value, useful to its times. But Art
must give a deeper satisfaction. It must give fair play all round. 10

Yet every work of art adheres to some system of morality. But if it be
really a work of art, it must contain the essential criticism on the morality
to which it adheres. And hence the antinomy, hence the conflict
necessary to every tragic conception.

The degree to which the system of morality, or the metaphysic, of any 15
work of art is submitted to criticism within the work of art makes the
lasting value and satisfaction of that work. Aeschylus, having caught the
oriental idea of Love, correcting the tremendous Greek conception of
the Law with this new idea, produces the intoxicating satisfaction of the
Orestean trilogy. The Law, and Love, they are here the Two-in-One in 20
all their magnificence. But Euripides, with his aspiration towards Love,
Love the supreme, and his almost hatred of the Law, Law the
Triumphant but Base Closer of Doom,* is less satisfactory, because
of the very fact that he holds Love always Supreme, and yet must endure
the chagrin of seeing Love perpetually transgressed and overthrown. So 25
he makes his tragedy: the higher thing eternally pulled down by the
lower. And this unfairness in the use of terms, higher and lower, but
above all, the unfairness of showing Love always violated and suffering,
never supreme and triumphant, makes us disbelieve Euripides in the
end. For we have to bring in pity, we must admit that Love is at a 30
fundamental disadvantage before the Law, and cannot therefore ever
hold its own. Which is weak philosophy.

If Aeschylus have a metaphysic to his art, this metaphysic is that Love
and Law are Two eternally in conflict, and eternally being reconciled.
This is the tragic significance of Aeschylus. 35

89

But the metaphysic of Euripides is that the Law and Love are two eternally in conflict, and unequally matched, so that Love must always be borne down. In Love a man shall only suffer. There is also a Reconciliation, otherwise Euripides were not so great. But there is always the unfair matching, this disposition insisted on, which at last leaves one cold and unbelieving.

The moments of pure satisfaction come in the choruses, in the pure lyrics, when Love is put into true relations with the Law, apart from knowledge, transcending knowledge, transcending the metaphysic, where the aspiration to Love meets the acknowledgement of the Law in a consummate marriage, for the moment.

Where Euripides adheres to his metaphysic, he is unsatisfactory. Where he transcends his metaphysic, he gives that supreme equilibrium wherein we know satisfaction.

The adherence to a metaphysic does not necessarily give artistic form. Indeed the overstrong adherence to a metaphysic usually destroys any possibility of artistic form. Artistic form is a revelation of the two principles of Love and the Law in a state of conflict and yet reconciled: pure motion struggling against and yet reconciled with the Spirit: active force meeting and overcoming and yet not overcoming inertia. It is the conjunction of the two which makes form. And since the two must always meet under fresh conditions, form must always be different. Each work of art has its own form, which has no relation to any other form. When a young painter studies an old master, he studies, not the form, that is an abstraction, which does not exist: he studies maybe the method of the old great artist: but he studies chiefly to understand how the old great artist suffered in himself the conflict of Love and Law, and brought them to a reconciliation. Apart from artistic method, it is not Art that the young man is studying, but the State of Soul of the great old artist, so that he, the young artist, may understand his own soul and gain a reconciliation between the aspiration and the resistant.

It is most wonderful in poetry, this sense of conflict contained within a reconciliation:

> "Hail to thee, blithe spirit,
> Bird thou never wert
> That from heaven, or near it,
> Pourest forth thy heart
> In profusest strains of unpremeditated lay."*

Shelley wishes to say, the skylark is a pure, untrammelled spirit, a pure motion. But the very "Bird thou never wert", admits that the skylark *is* in very fact a bird, a concrete, momentary thing. If the line ran, "Bird thou never art", that would spoil it all. Shelley wishes to say, the song is poured out of heaven: but "or near it", he admits. There is the perfect relation between heaven and earth. And the last line is the tumbling sound of a lark's singing, the real Two-in-One.

The very adherence to rhyme and regular rhythm is a concession to the Law, a concession to the body, to the being and requirements of the body. They are an admission of the living, positive inertia which is the other half of life, other than the pure will-to-motion. In this consummation, they are the resistance and response of the Bride in the arms of the Bridegroom. And according as the Bride and Bridegroom come closer together, so is the response and resistance more fine, indistinguishable, so much the more, in this act of consummation, is the movement that of Two-in-One, indistinguishable each from the other, and not the movement of two brought together clumsily.

So that in Swinburne, where almost all is concession to the body, so that the poetry becomes almost a sensation and not an experience or a consummation, justifying Spinoza's "Amor est titillatio, concomitante idea causae externae",* we find continual adherence to the body, to the Rose, to the Flesh, the physical in everything, in the Sea, in the marshes; there is an overbalance in the favour of Supreme Law; Love is not Love, but passion, part of the Law; there is no Love, there is only Supreme Law. And the poet sings the Supreme Law to gain rebalance in himself, for he hovers always on the edge of death, of Not-Being, he is always out of reach of the Law, bodiless, in the faintness of Love that has triumphed and denied the Law, in the dread of an overdeveloped, oversensitive soul which exists always on the point of dissolution from the body.

But he is not divided against himself. It is the novelists and dramatists who have the hardest task in reconciling their metaphysic, their theory of being and knowing, with their living sense of being. Because a novel is a microcosm, and because man in* viewing the universe must view it in the light of a theory, therefore every novel must have the background or the structural skeleton of some theory of being, some metaphysic. But the metaphysic must always subserve the artistic purpose beyond the artist's conscious aim. Otherwise the novel becomes a treatise.

And the danger is, that a man shall make himself a metaphysic to excuse or cover his own faults or failure. Indeed, a sense of fault or failure is the usual cause of a man's making himself a metaphysic, to justify himself.

Then, having made himself a metaphysic of self-justification, or a
5 metaphysic of self-denial, the novelist proceeds to apply the world to this, instead of applying this to the world.

Tolstoi is a flagrant example of this. Probably because of profligacy in his youth, because he had disgusted himself in his own flesh, by excess or by prostitution, therefore Tolstoi, in his metaphysic, renoun-
10 ced the flesh altogether, later on, when he had tried and had failed to achieve complete marriage in the flesh. But above all things, Tolstoi was a child of the Law, he belonged to the Father. He had a marvellous sensuous understanding, and very little clarity of mind.

So that, in his metaphysic, he had to deny himself, his own being, in
15 order to escape his own disgust of what he had done to himself, and to escape admission of his own failure.

Which made all the later part of his life a crying falsity and shame. Reading the reminiscences of Tolstoi, one can only feel shame at the way Tolstoi denied all that was great in him, with vehement cowardice.
20 He degraded himself infinitely, he perjured himself far more than did Peter when he denied Christ. For Peter repented.* But Tolstoi denied the Father, and propagated a great system of his recusancy, elaborating his own weakness, blaspheming his own strength. "What difficulty is there in writing about how an officer fell in love with a
25 married woman?" he used to say of his Anna Karenin, "there's no difficulty in it, and, above all, no good in it."*

Because he was mouthpiece to the Father, in uttering the law of passion, he said there was no difficulty in it, because it came naturally to him. Christ might just [as] easily have said, there was no difficulty in
30 the Parable of the Sower,* and no good in it either, because it flowed out of him without effort.

And Thomas Hardy's metaphysic is something like Tolstoi's. "There is no reconciliation between Love and the Law," says Hardy. "The spirit of Love must always succumb before the blind, stupid, but
35 overwhelming power of the Law."

Already as early as *The Return of the Native*, he has come to this theory, in order to explain his own sense of failure. But before that time, from the very start, he has had an overweening theoretic antagonism to the Law. "That which is physical, of the body, is weak,
40 despicable, bad," he said at the very start. He represented his [fleshly]

heroes as villains, but very weak and maundering villains. At its worst, the
Law is a weak, craven sensuality: at its best, it is a passive inertia. It is the
gap in the armour, it is the hole in the foundation.

Such a metaphysic is almost silly. If it were not [that]* the man is
much stronger in feeling than in thought, the Wessex novels would be   5
sheer rubbish, as they are already in parts. *The Well-Beloved* is sheer
rubbish, fatuity, as is a good deal of the *Dynasts* conception.

But it is not [as] a metaphysician that one must consider Hardy. He
makes a poor show there. For nothing in his work is so pitiable as his
clumsy efforts to push events into line with his theory of being, and to   10
make calamity fall on those who represent the principle of Love. He does
it exceedingly badly, and owing to this effort his form is execrable in the
extreme.*

His feeling, his instinct, his sensuous understanding is, however, apart
from his metaphysic, very great and deep, deeper than that perhaps of   15
any other English novelist. Putting aside his metaphysic, which must
always obtrude when he thinks of people, and turning to the earth, to
landscape, then he is true to himself.

Always he must start from the earth, from the great source of the Law,
and his people move in his landscape almost insignificantly, somewhat   20
like tame animals wandering in the wild. The earth is the manifestation
of the Father, of the Creator, Who made us in the Law. God still speaks
aloud in His Works, as to Job, so to Hardy, surpassing human conception
and the human law. "Dost thou know the balancings of the clouds, the
wondrous works of him which is perfect in knowledge?—How thy   25
garments are warm, when he quieteth the earth by the south wind?—
Hast thou with him spread out the sky, which is strong?—"

This is the true attitude of Hardy—"with God is terrible majesty".
The theory of knowledge, the metaphysic of the man, is much smaller
than the man himself. So with Tolstoi.   30

"Knowest thou the time when the wild goats of the rock bring forth?
Or canst thou mark when the hinds do calve?—Canst thou number the
months that they fulfil? Or knowest thou the time when they bring
forth?—They bow themselves, they bring forth their young ones, they
cast out their sorrows.—Their young ones are good in liking, they grow   35
up with corn; they go forth, and return not unto them."*

There is a good deal of this in Hardy. But in Hardy there is more than
the conceipt* of Job, protesting his integrity. Job says in the end:
"Therefore have I uttered that I understood not; things too wonderful
for me, which I knew not.   40

"I have heard of thee by hearing of the ear; but now mine eye seeth thee.

"Wherefore I abhor myself, and repent in dust and ashes."*

But Jude ends where Job began, cursing the day and the services of
5 his birth, and in so much cursing the act of the Lord, "who made him in the womb."*

It is the same cry all through Hardy, this curse upon the birth in the flesh, and this unconscious adherence to the flesh. The instincts, the bodily passions are strong and sudden in all Hardy's men. They are too
10 strong and sudden. They fling Jude into the arms of Arabella, years after he has known Sue, and against his own will.

For every man comprises male and female in his being, the male always struggling for predominance. A woman likewise consists in male, and female, with female predominant.

15 And a man who is strongly male tends to deny, to refute the female in him. A real "man" takes no heed for his body, which is the more female part of him. He considers himself only as an instrument, to be used in the service of some idea.

The true female, on the other hand, will eternally hold her body
20 superior to any idea, will hold full life in the body to be the real happiness. The male exists in doing, the female in being. The male lives in the satisfaction of some purpose achieved, the female in the satisfaction of some purpose contained.

In Aeschylus, in the "Eumenides", there is Apollo, Loxias, the Sun
25 God, Love, the prophet, the male: there are the Erinyes, daughters of primeval Mother Night, representing here the female risen in retribution for some crime against the flesh; and there is Pallas, unbegotten daughter of Zeus, who is as the Holy Spirit in the Christian religion, the spirit of wisdom.

30 Orestes is bidden by the male god, Apollo, to avenge the murder of his father, Agamemnon, by his mother: that is, the male, murdered by the female, must be avenged by the male. But Orestes is child of his mother. He is in himself female. So that in himself the conscience, the madness, the violated part of his own self, his own body, drives him to
35 the Furies. On the male side, he is right; on the female, wrong. But peace is given at last by Pallas, the Arbitrator, the Spirit of wisdom.

And although Aeschylus in his consciousness makes the Furies hideous, and Apollo supreme, yet, in his own self and in very fact, he makes the Furies wonderful and noble, with their tremendous hymns,
40 and makes Apollo a trivial, sixth-form braggard and ranter. Clytemnes-

tra also, wherever she appears, is wonderful and noble. Her sin is the
sin of pride: she was the first to be injured. Agamemnon is a feeble
thing beside her.

So Aeschylus adheres still to the Law, to Right, to the Creator who
created man in His Own Image, and in his Law. What he has learned of 5
Love, he does not yet quite believe.

Hardy has the same belief in the Law, but in concept of his own
understanding, which cannot understand the Law, he says that the Law
is nothing, a blind confusion.

And in concept of understanding, he deprecates and destroys both 10
women and men who would represent the old primeval Law, the great
Law of the Womb, the primeval Female principle. The Female shall
not exist. Where it appears, it is a criminal tendency, to be stamped out.

This in Manston, Troy, Boldwood, Eustacia, Wildeve, Henchard,
Tess, Jude, everybody. The women approved of are not Female in any 15
real sense. They are passive subjects to the male, the re-echo from the
male. As in the Christian religion, the Virgin worship is no real Female
worship, but worship of the Female as she is passive and subjected to
the male. Hence the sadness of Botticelli's Virgins.

Thus Tess sets out, not as any positive thing, containing all purpose, 20
but as the acquiescent complement to the male. The female in her has
become inert. Then Alec d'Urberville comes along, and possesses her.
From the man who takes her, Tess expects her own consummation, the
singling out of herself, the addition of the male complement. She is of
an old line, and has the aristocratic quality of respect for the other 25
being. She does not see the other person as an extension of herself,
existing in a universe of which she is the centre and pivot. She knows
that other people are outside her. Therein she is an aristocrat. And out
of this attitude to the other person came her passivity. It is not the same
as the passive quality in the other little heroines, such as the girl in *The* 30
Woodlanders,° who is passive because she is small.

Tess is passive out of self-acceptance, a true aristocratic quality,
amounting almost to self-indifference. She knows she is herself
incontrovertibly, and she knows that other people are not herself. This
is a very rare quality, even in a woman. And in a civilisation so unequal, 35
it is almost a weakness.

Tess never tries to alter or to change anybody, neither to alter nor to
change nor to divert. What another person decides, that is his decision.
She respects utterly the other's right to be. She is herself always.

But the others do not respect her right to be. Alec d'Urberville sees 40 her as the embodied fulfilment of his own desire: something, that is, belonging to him. She cannot, in his conception, exist apart from him nor have any being apart from his being. For she is the embodiment of his desire.

5   This is very natural and common in men, this attitude to the world. But in Alec d'Urberville it applies only to the woman of his desire. He cares only for her. Such a man adheres to the female like a parasite.

It is a male quality to resolve a purpose to its fulfilment. It is the male quality, to seek the motive power in the female, and to convey this to a 10 fulfilment: to receive some impulse into his senses, and to transmit it into expression.

Alec d'Urberville does not do this. He is male enough, in his way: but only physically male. He is constitutionally an enemy of the principle of self-subordination, which principle is inherent in every 15 man. It is this principle which makes a man, a true male, see his job through, at no matter what cost. A man is strictly only himself when he is fulfilling some purpose he has conceived: so that the principle is not of self-subordination, but of continuity, of development. Only when insisted on, as in Christianity, does it become self-sacrifice. And this 20 resistance to self-sacrifice on Alec d'Urberville's part does not make him an individualist, an egoist, but rather a non-individual, an incomplete, almost a fragmentary thing.

There seems to be in d'Urberville an inherent antagonism to any progression in himself. Yet he seeks with all his power for the source of 25 stimulus in woman. He takes the deep impulse from the female. In this he is exceptional. No ordinary man could really have betrayed Tess. Even if she had had an illegitimate child to another man, to Angel Clare, for example, it would not have shattered her as did her connection with Alec d'Urberville. For Alec d'Urberville could reach 30 some of the real sources of the female in a woman, and draw from them. Troy* could also do this. And, as a woman instinctively knows, such men are rare. Therefore they have a power over a woman. They draw from the depth of her being.

And what they draw, they betray. With a natural male, what he draws 35 from the source of the female, the impulse he receives from the source he transmits through his own being into utterance, motion, action, expression. But Troy and Alec d'Urberville, what they received they knew only as gratification in the senses, some perverse will prevented them from submitting to it, from becoming instrumental to it.

40   Which was why Tess was shattered by Alec d'Urberville, and why she murdered him in the end. The murder is badly done, altogether the

book is botched, owing to the way of thinking in the author, owing to the weak yet obstinate theory of being. Nevertheless, the murder is true, the whole book is true, in its conception.

Angel Clare has the very opposite qualities to those of Alec d'Urberville. To the latter, the female in himself is the only part of himself he will acknowledge: the body, the senses, that which he shares with the female, which the female shares with him. To Angel Clare, the female in himself is detestable, the body, the senses, that which he will share with a woman, is held degraded. What he wants really is to receive the female impulse other than through the body. But his thinking has made him criticise Christianity, his deeper instinct has forbidden him to deny his body any further, a deadlock in his own being, which denies him any purpose, so that he must take to [hard] labour* out of sheer impotence to resolve himself, drives him unwillingly to woman. But he must see her only as the Female Principle, he cannot bear to see her as the Woman in the Body. Her he thinks degraded. To marry her, to have a physical marriage with her, he must overcome all his ascetic revulsion, he must, in his own mind, put off his own divinity, his pure maleness, his singleness, his pure completeness, and descend to the heated welter of the flesh. It is objectionable to him. Yet his body, his life, is too strong for him.

Who is he, that he shall be pure male, and deny the existence of the female? This is the question the Creator asks of him. Is then the male the exclusive whole of life?—is he even the higher or supreme part of life? Angel Clare thinks so: as Christ thought.

Yet it is not so, as even Angel Clare must find out. Life, that is Two-in-One, Male and Female. Nor is either part greater than the other.

It is not Angel Clare's fault that he cannot come to Tess when he finds that she has, in his words, been defiled. It is the result of generations of ultra-Christian training, which had left in him an inherent aversion to the female, and to all in himself which pertained to the female. What he, in his Christian sense, conceived of as Woman, was only the servant and attendant and administering spirit to the male. He had no idea that there was such a thing as positive Woman, as the Female, another great living Principle counterbalancing his own male principle. He conceived of the world as consisting of the One, the Male Principle.

Which conception was already gendered in Botticelli, whence the melancholy of the Virgin. Which conception reached its fullest in

Turner's pictures, which were utterly bodiless: and also in the great
scientists or thinkers of the last generation, even Darwin and Spencer
and Huxley. For these last conceived of evolution, of one spirit or
principle starting at the far end of time, and lonelily traversing Time.
5   But there is not one principle, there are two, travelling always to meet,
each step of each one lessening the distance between the two of them.
And Space, which so frightened* Herbert Spencer, is as a Bride to
us. And the cry of Man does not ring out into the Void. It rings out to
Woman, whom we know not.
10   This Tess knew, unconsciously. An aristocrat she was, developed
through generations to the belief in her own self-establishment. She
could help, but she could not be helped. She could give, but she could
not receive. She could attend to the wants of the other person, but no
other person, save another aristocrat,—and there is scarcely such a
15   thing as another aristocrat,—could attend to her wants, her deepest
wants.

So it is the aristocrat alone, who has any real and vital sense of the
"neighbour", of the other person; who has the habit of submerging
himself, putting himself entirely away before the other person: because
20   he expects to receive nothing from the other person. So that now, he
has lost much of his initiative force, and exists almost isolated,
detached, and without the surging ego of the ordinary man, because he
has controlled his nature according to the other man, to exclude him.

And Tess, despising herself in the flesh, despising the deep Female
25   she was, because Alec d'Urberville had betrayed her very sources,
loved Angel Clare, who also despised and hated the flesh. She did not
hate d'Urberville. What a man did, he did, and if he did it to her, it was
her look-out. She did not conceive of him as having any human duty
towards her.
30   The same with Angel Clare as with Alec d'Urberville. She was very
grateful to him for saving her from her despair of contamination, and
from her bewildered isolation. But when he accused her, she could not
plead or answer. For she had no right to his goodness. She stood alone.

The female was strong in her. She was herself. But she was out of
35   place, utterly out of her elements and her times. Hence her utter
bewilderment. This is the reason why she was so overcome. She was
outwearied from the start, in her spirit. For it is only by receiving from
all our fellows, that we are kept fresh and vital. Tess was herself,
female, intrinsically a woman.
40   The female in her was indomitable, unchangeable, she was utterly

constant to herself. But she was, by long breeding, intact from
mankind. Though Alec d'Urberville was of no kin to her, yet, in the
book, he has always a quality of kinship. It was as if only a kinsman, an
aristocrat, could approach her. And this to her undoing. Angel Clare
would never have reached her. She would have abandoned herself to   5
him, but he would never have reached her. It needed a physical
aristocrat. She would have lived with her husband, Clare, in a state of
abandon to him, like a coma. Alec d'Urberville forced her to realise
him, and to realise herself. He came close to her, as Clare could never
have done. So she murdered him. For she was herself.   10
    And just as the aristocratic principle had isolated Tess, it had
isolated Alec d'Urberville. For though Hardy consciously made the
young betrayer a plebeian and an impostor, unconsciously, with the
supreme justice of the artist, he made him the same as de Stancy, a true
aristocrat, or as Fitzpiers, or Troy. He did not give him the tiredness, 15
the touch of exhaustion necessary, in Hardy's mind, to an aristocrat.
But he gave him the intrinsic qualities.
    With the men as with the women of old descent: they have nothing to
do with mankind in general, they are exceedingly personal. For many
generations they have been accustomed to regard their own desires as   20
their own supreme laws. They have not been bound by the conventional morality: this they have transcended, being a code unto themselves.
The other person has been always present to their imagination, in the
spectacular sense. He has always existed to them. But he has always
existed as something other than themselves.   25
    Hence the inevitable isolation, detachment of the aristocrat. His one
aim, during centuries, has been to keep himself detached. At last he
finds himself, by his very nature, cut off.
    Then either he must go his own way, or he must struggle towards
re-union with the mass of mankind. Either he must be an incomplete   30
individualist, like de Stancy, or like the famous Russian nobles,*
he must become a wild humanitarian and reformer.
    For as all the governing power has gradually been taken from the
nobleman, and as, by tradition, by inherent inclination, he does not
occupy himself with profession other than government, how shall he   35
use that power which is in him and which comes in to him.
    He is, by virtue of breed and long training, a perfect instrument. He
knows, as every pure-bred thing knows, that his root and source is in
his female. He seeks the motive power in the woman. And, having
taken it, has nothing to do with it, can find, in this democratic plebeian 40

age, no means by which to transfer it into action, expression, utterance. So there is a continual gnawing of unsatisfaction, a constant
seeking of another woman, still another woman. For each time the
impulse comes fresh, everything seems all right.

5   It may be, also, that in the aristocrat a certain weariness makes him
purposeless, vicious, like a form of death. But that is not necessary.
One feels that in Manston, and Troy, and Fitzpiers, and Alec
d'Urberville there is good stuff gone wrong. Just as in Angel Clare,
there is good stuff gone wrong in the other direction.

10   There can never be one extreme of wrong, without the other
extreme. If there had never been the extravagant Puritan idea, that the
Female Principle was to be denied, cast out by man from his soul, that
only the Male Principle, of Abstraction, of Good, of Public Good, of
the Community, embodied in "thou shalt love thy neighbour as
15   thyself", really existed, there would never have been produced the
extreme Cavalier type, which says that only the Female Principle
endures in man, that all the Abstraction, the Good, the Public
Elevation, the Community, was a grovelling cowardice, and that man
lived by enjoyment, through his senses, enjoyment which ended in his
20   senses. Or perhaps better, if the extreme Cavalier type had never
been produced, we should not have had the Puritan, the extreme
correction.

The one extreme produces the other. It is inevitable for Angel
Clare and for Alec d'Urberville mutually to destroy the woman they
25   both loved. Each does her the extreme of wrong, so she is destroyed.

The book is handled with very uncertain skill, botched and bung-
led. But it contains the elements of the greatest tragedy: Alec
d'Urberville, who has killed the male in himself, as Clytemnestra
symbolically for Orestes, killed Agamemnon; Angel Clare, who has
30   killed the female in himself, as Orestes killed Clytemnestra: and Tess,
the Woman, the Life, destroyed by a mechanical fate, in the communal law.

There is no reconciliation. Tess, Angel Clare, Alec d'Urberville,
they are all as good as dead. For Angel Clare, though still apparently
35   alive, is in reality no more than a mouth, a piece of paper, like Clym
left preaching.

There is no reconciliation, only death. And so Hardy really states
his case, which is not his consciously stated metaphysic, by any
means, but a statement how man has gone wrong, and brought death
40   on himself: how man has violated the Law, how he has supererogated

himself, gone so far in his male conceit as to supersede the Creator, and win death as a reward. Indeed the works of supererogation of our male assiduity help us to a better salvation.*

- 2 -

Jude is only Tess turned round about. Instead of the heroine contain- 5 ing the two principles, male and female, at strife within her one being, it is Jude who contains them both, whilst the two women with him take the place of the two men to Tess. Arabella is Alec d'Urberville, Sue is Angel Clare. These represent the same pair of principles.

But first, let it be said again that Hardy is a bad artist. Because he 10 must condemn Alec d'Urberville, according to his own personal creed, therefore he shows him a vulgar intriguer of coarse lasses, and as ridiculous convert to evangelism. But Alec d'Urberville, by the artist's account, is neither of these. It is, in actual life, a rare man who seeks and seeks among women for one of such character and intrinsic female 15 being as Tess. The ordinary sensualist avoids such characters. They implicate him too deeply. An ordinary sensualist would have been much too common, much too afraid, to turn to Tess. In a way, d'Urberville was her mate. And his subsequent passion for her is in its way noble enough. But whatever his passion, as a male, he must be a 20 betrayer, even if [he] had been the most faithful husband on earth. He betrayed the female in a woman, by taking her, and by responding with no male impulse from himself. He roused her, but never satisfied her. He could never satisfy her. It was like a soul-disease in him: he was, in the strict, though not the technical sense, impotent. But he must have 25 wanted, later on, not to be so. But he could not help himself. He was spiritually impotent in love.

Arabella was the same. She, like d'Urberville, was converted by an evangelical preacher. It is significant in both of them. They were not just shallow, as Hardy would have made them out. 30

He is, however, more contemptuous in his personal attitude to the woman than to the man. He insists that she is a pig-killer's daughter; he insists that she drag Jude into pig-killing: he lays stress on her false tail of hair. That is not the point at all. This is only Hardy's bad art. He himself, as an artist, manages in the whole picture of Arabella almost to 35 make insignificant in her these pig-sticking false hair crudities. But he must have his personal revenge on her, for her coarseness, which offends him, because he is something of an Angel Clare.

The pig-sticking and so-forth are not so important in the real picture. As for the false tail of hair, few women dared have been so open and natural about it. Few women, indeed, dared have made Jude marry them. It may have been a case with Arabella of "fools rush
5　in".* But she was not such a fool. And her motives [are] explained in the book. Life is not, in the actual, such a simple affair of getting a fellow and getting married. It is, even for Arabella, an affair on which she places her all. No barmaid marries anybody, the first man she can lay her hands on. She cannot. It must be a personal thing to her. And
10　no ordinary woman would want Jude. Moreover, no ordinary woman could have laid her hands on Jude.

It is an absurd fallacy this, that a small man wants a woman bigger and finer than he is himself. A man is as big as his real desires. Let a man, seeing with his eyes a woman of force and being, want her for his
15　own, then that man is intrinsically an equal of that woman. And the same with a woman.

A coarse, shallow woman does not want to marry a sensitive, deep-feeling man. She feels no desire for him, she is not drawn to him, but repelled, knowing he will contemn* her. She wants a man to
20　correspond to herself: that is, if she is a young woman looking for a mate, as Arabella was.

What an old, jaded, yet still unsatisfied woman or man wants, is another matter. Yet not even one of these will take a young creature of real character, superior in force. Instinct and fear prevent it.
25　Arabella was, under all her disguise of pig-fat and false hair, and vulgar speech, in character somewhere an aristocrat. She was, like Eustacia, amazingly lawless, even splendidly so. She believed in herself and she was not altered by any outside opinion of herself. Her fault was pride. She thought herself the centre of life, that all which existed,
30　belonged to her in so far as she wanted it.

In this she was something like Job. His attitude was "I am strong and rich, and also, I am a good man."* He gave out of his own sense of bounty, and felt no indebtedness. Arabella was almost the same. She felt also strong and abundant, arrogant in her hold on life. She needed
35　a complement: and the nearest thing to her satisfaction was Jude. For as she, intrinsically, was a strong female, by far overpowering her Annies and her friends, so was he a strong male.

The difference between them was not so much a difference of quality, or degree, as a difference of form. Jude, like Tess, wanted full
40　consummation. Arabella, like Alec d'Urberville, had that in her which

resisted full consummation, wanted only to enjoy herself in contact with
the male. She would have no transmission.

There are two attitudes to love. A man in love with a woman says
either: "I, the man, the male, am the supreme, I am the one, and the
woman is administered unto me, and this is her highest function, to be   5
administered unto me." This was the conscious attitude of the Greeks.
But their unconscious attitude was the reverse: they were in truth afraid
of the female principle, their vaunt was empty, they went in deep, inner
dread of her. So did the Jews, so do the Italians. But after the
Renaissance, there was a change. Then began conscious Woman-   10
reverence, and a lack of instinctive reverence, rather only an instinctive
pity. It is according to the balance between the Male and Female
Principles.

The other attitude of a man in love, besides this of "she is
administered unto my maleness", is: "she is the unknown, the undis-   15
covered, into which I plunge to discovery, losing myself".

And what we call real love has always this latter attitude.

The first attitude which belongs to passion, makes a man feel proud,
splendid. It is a powerful stimulant to him, the female administered to
him. He feels full of blood, he walks the earth like a Lord. And it is to   20
this state Nietzsche aspires in his "Wille zur Macht".* It is this the
passionate nations crave.

And under all this, there is, naturally, the sense of fear,
[transition],* and the sadness of mortality. For, the female being
herself an independent force, may she not withdraw, and leave a man   25
empty, like ash, as one sees a Jew or an Italian so often.

This first attitude, too, of male pride receiving the female administration may, and often does, contain the corresponding intense fear and
reverence of the female, as of the unknown. So that, starting from the
male assertion, there came in the old days the full consummation; as   30
often there comes the full consummation now.

But not always. The man may retain all the while of possession the
sense of himself, the primary male, receiving gratification. This constant
reaction upon himself at length dulls his senses and his sensibility, and
makes him mechanical, automatic. He grows gradually incapable of   35
receiving any gratification from the female, and becomes a roué,*
only automatically alive, and frantic with the knowledge thereof.

It is unfortunately* the tendency of the Parisian—or has
been—to take this attitude to love, and to intercourse. The woman
knows herself all the while as the primary female receiving administra-   40

tion of the male. So she becomes hard and external, and inwardly jaded, tired out. It is the tendency of English women to take this attitude also. And it is this attitude of love, more than anything else, which devitalises a race, and makes it barren.

5   It is an attitude natural enough to start with. Every young man must think that it is the highest honour he can do to a woman, to receive from her her female administration to his male being, whilst he meanwhile gives her the gratification of himself. But intimacy usually corrects this, love, or use, or marriage: a married man ceases to think of

10   himself as the primary male: hence often his dulness. Unfortunately, he also fails in the many cases to realise the gladness of a man in contact with the unknown in the female, which gives him a sense of richness and oneness with all life, as if, by being part of life, he were infinitely rich. Which is different from the sense of power, of dominating life.

15   The Wille zur Macht is a spurious feeling.

For a man who dares to look upon, and to venture within the unknown of the female, losing himself, like a man who gives himself to the sea, or a man who enters a primeval, virgin forest, feels, when he returns, the utmost gladness of singing. This is certainly the gladness of

20   a male bird in his singing, the amazing joy of return from the adventure into the unknown, rich with addition to his soul, rich with the knowledge of the utterly illimitable depth and breadth of the unknown; the ever yielding extent of the unacquired, the unattained; the inexhaustible riches lain under unknown skies over unknown seas, all the

25   magnificence that *is*, and yet which is unknown to any of us. And the knowledge of the reality with which it awaits me, the male, the knowledge of the calling and struggling of all the unknown, illimitable Female towards me, unembraced as yet, towards those men who will endlessly follow me, who will endlessly struggle after me, beyond me,

30   further into this calling, unrealised vastness, nearer to the outstretched, eager, advancing unknown in the woman.

It is for this sense of All the magnificence that is unknown to me, of All that which stretches forth arms and breast to the Inexhaustible Embrace of all the ages, towards me, whose arms are outstretched,°

35   for this moment's embrace which gives me the inkling of the Inexhaustible Embrace, that every man must and does yearn. And whether he be a roué, and vicious, or young and virgin, this is the bottom of every man's desire, for the embrace, for the advancing into the unknown, for the landing on the shore of the undiscovered half of the world, where

40   the wealth of the female lies before us.

What is true of men is so of women. If we turn our faces west, towards nightfall and the unknown within the dark embrace of a wife, they turn their faces east, towards the sunrise and the brilliant, bewildering, active embrace of a husband. And as we are dazed with the unknown in her, so is she dazed with the unknown in us. It is so. 5 And we throw up our joy to heaven like towers and spires and fountains and leaping flowers, so glad we are.

But always, we are divided within ourselves. Is it not that I am wonderful. Is it not a gratification for me when a stranger shall land on my shores and enjoy what he finds there. Shall I not also enjoy it? Shall 10 I not enjoy the strange motion of the stranger, like a pleasant sensation of silk and warmth against me, stirring unknown fibres? Shall I not take this enjoyment without venturing out in dangerous waters, losing myself, perhaps destroying myself seeking the unknown. Shall I not stay at home, and by feeling the swift, soft airs blow out of the unknown 15 upon my body, shall I not have rich pleasure of myself.

And, because they were afraid of the unknown, and because they wanted to retain the full-veined gratification of self-pleasure, men have kept their women tightly in bondage. But when the men were no longer afraid of the unknown, when they deemed it exhausted, they said, 20 "There are no women, there are only daughters of men"*—as we say now, as the Greeks tried to say. Hence the "Virgin" conception of woman, the passionless, passive conception, progressing from Fielding's "Amelia" to Dickens' "Agnes",* and on to Hardy's Sue.

Whereas Arabella in *Jude the Obscure* has what one might call the 25 selfish instinct for love, Jude himself has the other, the unselfish. She sees in him a male who can gratify her. She takes him, and is gratified by him. Which makes a man of him. He becomes a grown, independent man in the arms of Arabella, conscious of having met, and satisfied, the female demand in him. This makes a man of any youth. He is proven 30 unto himself as a male being, initiated into the freedom of life.

But Arabella refused his purpose. She refused to combine with him in one purpose. Just like Alec d'Urberville, she had from the outset an antagonism to the submission to any change in herself, to any development. She had the will to remain where she was, static, and to 35 receive and exhaust all impulse she received from the male, in her senses. Whereas in a normal woman, impulse received from the male drives her on to a sense of joy and wonder and glad freedom in touch with the unknown of which she is made aware, so that she exists on the edge of the unknown half in rapture. Which is the state the writers wish 40 to portray in "Amelia", and "Agnes", but particularly in the former; which Reynolds* wishes to portray in his pictures of women.

To all this Arabella was antagonistic. It seems like a perversion in her, as if she played havoc with the stuff she was made of, as Alec
5 d'Urberville did. Nevertheless she remained always unswerving female, she never truckled to the male idea, but was self-responsible, without fear. It is easier to imagine such a woman, out of one's desires, than to find her in real life. For, where a half criminal type, a reckless daredevil type resembling her may be found on the outskirts of society,
10 yet these are not Arabella. Which criminal type, or reckless, low woman, would want to marry Jude? Arabella wanted Jude. And it is evident she was not too coarse for him, since she made no show of refinement from the first. The female in her, reckless and unconstrained, was strong enough to draw him after her, as her male, right to
15 the end. Which other woman could have done this? At least let acknowledgement be made to her great female force of character. Her coarseness seems to me exaggerated to make the moralist's case good against her.

Jude could never hate her. She did a great deal for the true making of
20 him, for making him a grown man. She gave him to himself.

And there was danger at the outset that he should never become a man, but that he should remain incorporeal, smothered out under his idea of learning. He was somewhat in Angel Clare's position. Not that generations of particular training had made him almost rigid and
25 paralysed to the female: but that his whole passion was concentrated away from woman to re-inforce in him the male impulse towards extending the consciousness. His family was a difficult family to marry. And this because, that whilst the men were physically vital, with a passion towards the female from which no moral training had res-
30 trained them, like a plant tied to a stick and diverted, they had at the same time, an inherent complete contempt of the female, valuing only that which was male. So that they were strongly divided against themselves, with no external hold, such as a moral system, to grip to.

It would have been possible for Jude, monkish, passionate, mediae-
35 val, belonging to woman yet striving away from her, refusing to know her, to have gone on denying one side of his nature, adhering to his idea of learning, till he had stultified the physical impulse of his being and perverted it entirely. Arabella brought him to himself, gave him himself, made him free, sound as a physical male.
40 That she would not, or could not, combine her life with him for the

fulfilment of a purpose was their misfortune. But at any rate, his purpose of becoming an Oxford Don, was a cut and dried purpose which had no connection with his living body, and for which probably no woman could have united with him.

No doubt Arabella hated his books, and hated his whole attitude to study. What had he, a passionate, emotional nature, to do with learning for learning's sake, with mere academics. Any woman must know it was ridiculous. But he persisted with the tenacity of all [pervertedness]. And she, in this something of an aristocrat, like Tess, feeling that she had no right to him, no right to receive anything from him, except his sex, in which she felt she gave and did not receive, for she conceived of herself as the primary female, as that which, in taking the male, conferred on him his greatest boon, she left him alone. Her attitude was, that he would find all [he] desired in coming to her. She was occupied with herself. It was not that she wanted *him*. She wanted to have the sensation of herself in contact with him. His being she refused. She allowed only her own being.

Therefore she scarcely troubled him, when he earned little money and took no notice of her. He did not refuse to take notice of her because he hated her, or was deceived by her, or disappointed in her. He was not. He refused to consider her seriously because he adhered with all his pertinacity to the idea of study, from which he excluded her.

Which she saw and knew, and allowed. She would not force him to notice her, or to consider her seriously. She would compel him to nothing. She had had a certain satisfaction of him, which would be no more if she stayed for ever. For she was non-developing. When she knew him in her senses she knew the end of him, as far as she was concerned. That was all.

So she just went her way. He did not blame her. He scarcely missed her. He returned to his books.

Really, he had lost nothing by his marriage with Arabella: neither innocence nor belief nor hope. He had indeed gained his manhood. She left him the stronger and completer.

And now he would concentrate all on his male idea, of arresting himself, of becoming himself a non-developing quality, an academic mechanism. That was his obsession. That was his craving: to have nothing to do with his own life. This was the same as Tess when she turned to Angel Clare. She wanted life merely in the secondary, outside form, in the consciousness.

It was another form of the disease, or decay of old family, which

possessed Alec d'Urberville; a different form, but closely related. D'Urberville wanted to arrest all his activity in his senses, Jude Fawley wanted to arrest all his activity in his mind. Each of them wanted to become an impersonal force working automatically. Each of them
5 wanted to deny, or escape the responsibility and trouble of living as a complete person, a full individual.

And neither was able to bring it off. Jude's real desire was, not to live in the body. He wanted to exist only in his mentality. He was as if bored, or blasé, in the body, just like Tess. This seems to be the result
10 of coming of an old family, that had been long conscious, long self-conscious, specialised, separate, exhausted.

This drove him to Sue. She was his kinswoman, as d'Urberville was kinsman to Tess.* She was like himself in her being and her desire; like Jude, she wanted to live partially, in the consciousness, in
15 the mind only. She wanted no experience in the senses, she wished only to know.

She belonged with Tess, to the old woman-type of witch or prophetess, which adhered to the male principle, and destroyed the female. But in the true prophetess, in Cassandra,* for example, the
20 denial of the female cost a strong and almost maddening effort. But in Sue, it was done before she was born.

She was born with the vital female atrophied in her: she was almost male. Her *will* was male. It was wrong for Jude to take her physically, it was a violation of her. She was not the Virgin type, but the witch type,
25 which has no sex. Why should she be forced into intercourse that was not natural to her?

It was not natural for her to have children. It is inevitable that her children die. It is not natural for Tess nor for Angel Clare to have children, nor for Arabella nor for Alec d'Urberville. Because none of
30 these wished to give of themselves to the lover, none of them wished to mate: they only wanted their own experience. For Jude alone it was natural to have children, and this in spite of himself.

Sue wished to identify herself utterly with the male principle. That which was female in her she wanted to consume within the male force,
35 to consume it in the fire of understanding, of giving utterance. Whereas an ordinary woman knows that she *contains* all understanding, that she is the unutterable which man must for ever continue to try to utter, Sue felt that all must be uttered, must be given to the male, that in truth, only Male existed, that everything was the Word, and the Word was
40 everything.

Sue is the production of the long selection by man of the woman in whom the female is subordinated to the male principle. A long line of Amelias and Agneses, those women who submitted to the man-idea, flattered the man, and bored him, the Gretchens and the Turgenev heroines,* those who have betrayed the female and who therefore 5 only seem to exist to be betrayed by their men, these have produced at length a Sue, the pure thing. And as soon as she is produced she is execrated.

What Cassandra and Aspasia became to the Greeks, Sue has become to the northern civilisation. But the Greeks never pitied Woman. They 10 did not show her that highest impertinence—not even Euripides.

But Sue is scarcely a woman at all, though she is feminine enough. Cassandra submitted to Apollo, and gave him the Word of affiance, brought forth prophecy to him, not children. She received the embrace of the spirit, He breathed His Grace upon her: and she conceived and 15 brought forth a prophecy. It was still a marriage. Not the marriage of the Virgin with the Spirit, but the marriage of the female spirit with the male spirit, bodiless.

With Sue, however, the marriage was no marriage, but a submission, a service, a slavery. Her female spirit did not wed with the male spirit: she 20 could not prophesy. Her spirit submitted to the male spirit, owned the priority of the male spirit, wished to become the male spirit. That which was female in her, resistant, gave her only her critical faculty. When she sought out the physical quality in the Greeks,* that was her effort to make even the unknowable physique a part of knowledge, to contain the 25 body within the mind.

One of the supremest products of our civilisation is Sue, and a product that well frightens us. It is quite natural, that with all her mental alertness, she married Phillotson without ever considering the physical quality of marriage. Deep instinct made her avoid the consideration. And the 30 duality of her nature made her extremely liable to self-destruction. The suppressed, atrophied female in her, like a potent fury, was always there, suggesting her to make the fatal mistake. She contained always the rarest, most deadly anarchy in her own being.

It needed that she should have some place in society where the clarity 35 of her mental being, which was in itself a form of death, could shine out without attracting any desire for her body. She needed a refinement on Angel Clare. For she herself was a more specialised, more highly civilised product on the female side, than Angel Clare on the male. Yet the atrophied female in her would still want the bodily male. 40

She attracted to herself Jude. His experience with Arabella had for the time being diverted his attention altogether from the female. His attitude was that of service to the pure male spirit. But the physical male in him, that which knew and belonged to the female, was potent,

5 and roused the female in Sue as much as she wanted it rousing, so much that it was a stimulant to her, making her mind the brighter.

It was a cruelly difficult position. She must, by the constitution of her nature, remain quite physically intact, for the female was atrophied in her, to the enlargement of the male activity. Yet she wanted some

10 quickening for this atrophied female. She wanted even kisses. That the new rousing might give her a sense of life. But she could only *live* in the mind.

Then, where could she find a man who would be able to feed her with his male vitality, through kisses, proximity, without demanding the

15 female return. For she was such that she could only receive quickening from a strong male, for she was herself no small thing. Could she then find a man, a strong, passionate male, who would devote himself entirely to the production of the mind in her, to the production of male activity, or of female activity critical to the male.

20 She could only receive the highest stimulus, which she must inevitably seek, from a man who put her in constant jeopardy. Her essentiality rested upon her remaining intact. Any suggestion of the physical was utter confusion to her. Her principle was the ultra-Christian principle—of living entirely according to the Spirit, to the

25 One, male spirit, which knows, and utters, and shines, but exists beyond feeling, beyond joy or sorrow, or pain, exists only in Knowing. In tune with this, she was herself. Let her, however, be turned under the influence of the other dark, silent, strong principle, of the female, and she would break like a fine instrument under discord.

30 Yet, to live at all in tune with the male spirit, she must receive the male stimulus from a man. Otherwise she was as an instrument without a player. She must feel the hands of a man upon her, she must be infused with his male vitality, or she was not alive.

Here then was her difficulty: to find a man whose vitality could

35 infuse her and make her live, and who would not, at the same time, demand of her a return, the return of the female impulse into him. What man could receive this drainage,* receiving nothing back again. He must either die, or revolt.

One man had died.* She knew it well enough. She knew her

40 own fatality. She knew she drained the vital, male stimulus out of a

man, producing in him only knowledge of the mind, only mental clarity:
which man must always strive to attain, but which is not life in him,
rather the product of life.

Just as Alec d'Urberville, on the other hand, drained the female
vitality out of a woman, and gave her only sensation, only experience in   5
the senses, a sense of herself, nothing to the soul or spirit, thereby
exhausting her.

Now Jude, after Arabella, and following his own idée fixe,
[hunted]* this mental clarity, this knowing, above all. What he
contained in himself, of male and female impulse, he wanted to bring   10
forth, to draw into his mind, to resolve into understanding, as a plant
resolves that which it contains into flower.

This Sue could do for him. By creating a vacuum, she could cause
the vivid flow which clarified him. By rousing him, by drawing from
him his turgid vitality, made thick and heavy and physical with Arabella,   15
she could bring into consciousness that which he contained. For he was
heavy and full of unrealised life, clogged with untransmuted knowledge, with accretion of his senses. His whole life had been till now an
indrawing, ingestion. Arabella had been a vital experience for him,
received into his blood. And how was he to bring out all this fulness   20
into knowledge, or utterance. For all the time, he was being roused to
new physical desire, new life-experience, new sense-enriching, and
he could not perform his male function of transmitting this into
expression, or action. The particular form his flowering should take, he
could not find. So he hunted and studied, to find the call, the appeal   25
which should call out of him that which was in him.

And great was his transport when the appeal came from Sue. She
wanted, at first, only his words. That of him which could come to her
through speech, through his consciousness, her mind, like a bottomless
gulf, cried out for. She wanted satisfaction through the mind, and cried   30
out for him to satisfy her through the mind.

Great then was his joy at giving himself out to her. He gave, for it was
more blessed then to give than to receive. He gave, and she received
some satisfaction. But where she was not satisfied, there he must try
still to satisfy her. He struggled to bring it all forth. She was as himself 35
asking himself what he was. And he strove to answer, in a transport.

And he answered in a great measure. He singled himself out from
the old matrix of the accepted idea, he produced an individual flower of
his own.

It was for this he loved Sue. She did for him quickly what he would   40

have done for himself slowly, through study. By patient, diligent study, he would have used up the surplus of that turgid energy in him, and would, by long contact with old truth, have arrived at the form of truth which was in him. What he indeed wanted to get from study, was not a
5 store of learning, nor the vanity of education, a sort of superiority of educational wealth, though this also gave him pleasure. He wanted, through familiarity with the true thinkers and poets, particularly with the classic and theological thinkers, because of their comparative sensuousness, to find conscious expression for that which he held in his
10 blood. And to do this, it was necessary for him to resolve and to reduce his blood, to overcome the female sensuousness in himself, to transmute his sensuous being into another state, a state of clarity, of consciousness. Slowly, laboriously, struggling with the Greek and the Latin, he would have burned down his thick blood as fuel, and have
15 come to the true light of himself.

This Sue did for him. In marriage, each party fulfils a dual function with regard to the other: exhaustive and enrichening. The female at the same time exhausts and invigorates the male, the male at the same time exhausts and invigorates the female. The exhaustion and invigoration
20 are both temporary and relative. The male, making the effort to penetrate into the female, exhausts himself and invigorates her. But that which, at the end, he discovers and carries off from her, some seed of being, enrichens him and exhausts her. Arabella, in taking Jude, accepted very little from him. She absorbed very little of his strength
25 and virility into herself. For she only wanted to be aware of herself in contact with him, she did not want him to penetrate into her very being, till he moved her to her very depths, till she loosened to him some of her very self, for his enrichening. She was intrinsically impotent, as was Alec d'Urberville.
30 So that in her, Jude went very little further in Knowledge, or in Self-Knowledge. He took only the first step: of knowing himself sexually, as a sexual male. That is only the first, the first, necessary, but rudimentary step.

When he came to Sue, he found her physically impotent, but
35 spiritually potent. That was what he wanted. Of Knowledge in the blood he had a rich enough store: more than he knew what to do with. He wished for the further step, of reduction, of essentialising into Knowledge. Which Sue gave to him.

So that his experience with Arabella plus his first experience of
40 trembling intimacy and incandescent realisation with Sue made one

complete marriage: that is, the two women added together made One Bride.

When Jude had exhausted his surplus self, in spiritual intimacy with Sue, when he had gained through her all the wonderful understanding she could evoke in him, when he was clarified to himself, then his marriage with Sue was over. Jude's marriage with Sue was over before he knew her physically. She had, physically, nothing to give him.

Which in her deepest instinct, she knew. She made no mistake in marrying Phillotson. She acted according to the pure logic of her nature. Phillotson was a man who wanted no marriage whatsoever with the female. Sexually, he wanted her as an instrument through which he obtained relief, and some gratification: but really, relief. Spiritually, he wanted her as a thing to be wondered over and delighted in, but quite separately from himself. He knew quite well he could never marry her. He was a human being as near to mechanical functioning as a human being can be. The whole process of digestion, masticating, swallowing, digesting, excretion, is a sort of super-mechanical process. And Phillotson was like this. He was an organ, a function-fulfilling organ, he had no separate existence. He could not create a single new movement or thought or expression. Everything he did was a repetition of what had been. All his study was a study of what had been. It was a mechanical functional process. He was a true, if small, form of the "Savant". He could understand only the functional laws of living, but these he understood honestly. He was true to himself, he was not overcome by any cant or sentimentalising. So that in this he was splendid. But it is a cruel thing for a complete, or a spiritual individuality to be submitted to a functional organism.

The Widow Edlin said that there are some men no woman of any feeling could touch, and Phillotson was one of them.* If the Widow knew this, why was Sue's instinct so short.

But Mrs Edlin was a full human being, creating life in a new form through her personality. She must have known Sue's deficiency. It was natural for Sue to read and to turn again to:

"Thou hast conquered, O pale Galilean:
The world has grown grey from thy breath."*

In her, the pale Galilean had indeed triumphed. Her body was as insentient as hoar-frost. She knew well enough that she was not alive in the ordinary human sense. She did not, like an ordinary woman, receive all she knew through her senses, her instincts, but through her consciousness. The pale Galilean had a pure disciple in her: in her He was fulfilled. For the senses, the body, did not exist to her, she existed as a consciousness. And this so much so, that she was almost an Apostate.

5 She turned to look at Venus and Apollo. As if she could know either Venus or Apollo, save as ideas. Nor Venus nor Aphrodite had anything to do with her, but only Pallas and Christ.*

She was unhappy every moment of her life, poor Sue, with the knowledge of her own non-existence within life. She felt all the time the

10 ghastly sickness of dissolution upon her, she was as a void unto herself.

So she married Phillotson, the only man she could, in reality, marry. To him she could be a wife: she could give him the sexual relief he wanted of her, and supply him with the transcendence which was a pleasure to him; it was hers to seal him with the seal which made an

15 honourable human being of him. For he felt, deep within himself, something a reptile feels. And she was his guarantee, his crown.

Why does a snake horrify us, or even a newt? Why was Phillotson like a newt? What is it, in our life or in our feeling, to which a newt corresponds?* Is it that life has the two sides, of growth and of decay,

20 symbolised most acutely in our bodies by the semen and the excreta? Is it that the newt, the reptile, belong to the putrescent activity of life, the bird, the fish to the growth activity? Is it that the newt and the reptile are suggested to us through those sensations connected with excretion? And was Phillotson more or less connected with the decay activity of life? Was

25 it his function to reorganise the life-excreta of the ages? At any rate, one can honour him, for he was true to himself.

Sue married Phillotson according to her true instinct. But, being almost pure Christian, in the sense of having no physical life, she had turned to the Greeks, and with her mind was an Aphrodite-worshipper.

30 In craving for the highest form of that which she lacked, she worshipped Aphrodite. There are two sets of Aphrodite-worshippers: daughters of Aphrodite and the almost neutral daughters of Mary of Bethany. Sue was, oh, cruelly far from being a daughter of Aphrodite. She was the furthest alien from Aphrodite. She might excuse herself through her

35 Venus Urania*—but it was hopeless.

Therefore, when she left Phillotson, in whose marriage she consummated her own crucifixion, to go to Jude, she was deserting the God of her being for the God of her hopeless want. How much could she become a living, physical woman? But she would get away from

40 Phillotson.

She went to Jude to continue the spiritual marriage, bodiless. That
was all very well, if he had been satisfied. If he had been satisfied, they
might have lived in this spiritual intimacy, without physical contact, for
the rest of their lives, so strong was her true instinct for herself.

He, however, was not satisfied. He reached the point where he was   5
clarified, where he had reduced from his blood into his consciousness
all that was uncompounded before. He had become himself as far as he
could, he had fulfilled himself. All that he had gathered in his youth, all
that he had gathered from Arabella, was assimilated now, fused and
transformed into one clear Jude.   10

Now he wants that which is necessary for him if he is to go on. He
wants, at its lowest, the physical, sexual relief. For continually balked
sexual desire, or necessity, makes a man unable to live freely, scotches
him, stultifies him. And where a man is roused to the fullest pitch, as
Jude was roused by Sue, then the principal connection becomes a   15
necessity, if only for relief. Anything else is a violation.

Sue ran away to escape physical connection with Phillotson, only to
find herself in the arms of Jude. But Jude wanted of her more than
Phillotson wanted. This was what terrified her to the bottom of her
nature. Whereas Phillotson always only wanted sexual relief of her,   20
Jude wanted the consummation of marriage. He wanted that deepest
experience, that penetrating far into the unknown and undiscovered
which lies in the body and blood of man and woman, during life. He
wanted to receive from her the quickening, the primitive seed and
impulse which should start him to a new birth. And for this he must go 25
back deep into the primal, unshown, unknown life of the blood, the
thick, source-stream of life in her.

And she was terrified lest he should find her out, that it was wanting
in her. This was her deepest dread, to see him inevitably disappointed
in her. She could not bear to be put into the balance, wherein she knew   30
she would be found wanting.

For she knew in herself that she was cut off from the source and
origin of life. For her, the way back was lost irrevocably. And when
Jude came to her, wanting to retrace with her the course right back to
the springs and the welling-out, she was more afraid than of death. For   35
she could not. She was like a flower broken off from the tree, that lives
a while in water, and even puts forth. So Sue lived sustained and
nourished by the rarefied life of books and art, and by the inflow from
the man. But, owing to centuries and centuries of weaning away from
the body of life, centuries of insisting upon the supremacy and   40

bodilessness of Love, centuries of striving to escape the conditions of
being and of striving to attain the condition of Knowledge, centuries
of pure Christianity, she had gone too far. She had climbed and
climbed and climbed to be near the stars. And now at last, on the
5   topmost pinnacle, exposed to all the horrors and the magnificence of
space, she could not go back. Her strength had fallen from her. Up at
that great height, with scarcely any foothold, but only space, space all
round her, rising up to her from beneath, she was like a thing
suspended, supported almost at the point of extinction by the density
10 of the medium. Her body was lost to her, fallen away, gone. She
existed there as a point of consciousness, no more, like one swooned
at a great height, held up at the tip of a fine pinnacle, that drove
upwards into nothingness.

Jude rose to that height with her. But he did not die as she died.
15 Beneath him the foothold was more, he did not swoon. There came a
time when he wanted to go back, down to earth. But she was fastened
like Andromeda.*

Perhaps, if Jude had not known Arabella, Sue might have per-
suaded him that he too was bodiless, only a point of consciousness.
20 But she was too late, another had been before her, and given her the
lie.

Arabella was never so jealous of Sue as Sue of Arabella. How shall
the saint that tips the pinnacle, Saint Simeon Stylites* thrust on
the highest needle that pricks the heavens, be envied by the man who
25 walks the horizontal earth? But Sue was cruelly anguished with
jealousy of Arabella. It was only this, this knowledge that Jude wanted
Arabella, which made Sue give him access to her own body.

When she did that, she died. The Sue that had been till then, the
glimmering, pale, star-like Sue, died and was revoked on the night
30 when Arabella called at their house* at Aldbrickham and Jude
went out in his slippers to look for her, and did not find her, but came
back to Sue, who in her anguish gave him then the access to her body.
Till that day, Sue had been, in her will and in her very self, true to
one motion, to Love, to Knowledge, to the Light, to the upward
35 motion. Phillotson had not altered this. When she had suffered him,
she had said: "He does not touch me, I am beyond him."

But now she must give her body to Jude. At that moment her light
began to go out, all she had lived for and by began to turn into a
falseness, Sue began to nullify herself.

40 She could never become physical. She could never return down to

earth. But there, lying bound at the pinnacle-tip, she had to pretend she was lying on the horizontal earth, prostrate with a man.

It was a profanation and a pollution, worse than the pollution of Cassandra or of the Vestals.* Sue had her own form: to [break] this form was to destroy her. Her destruction began only when she said 5
to Jude "I give in."

As for Jude, he dragged his body after his consciousness. His instinct could never have made him actually desire physical connection with Sue. He was roused by an appeal made through his consciousness. This appeal automatically roused his senses. His consciousness desired 10
Sue. So his senses were forced to follow his consciousness.

But he must have felt, in knowing her, the "frisson" of sacrilege, something like the Frenchman who lay with a corpse.* Her body, the body of a Vestal, was swooned into that state of bloodless ecstasy wherein it was dead to the senses. Or it was the body of an insane 15
woman, whose senses are directed from the disordered mind, whose mind is not subjected to the senses.

But Jude was physically undeveloped. Altogether he was mediaeval. His senses were vigorous but not delicate. He never realised what it meant to *him*, his taking Sue. He thought he was satisfied. 20

But if it was death to her, or profanation, or pollution, or breaking, it was unnatural to him, blasphemy. How could he, a living, loving man, warm and productive, take with his body the moonlit cold body of a woman who did not live to him, and did not want him. It was monstrous, and it sent him mad. 25

She knew it was wrong, she knew it should never be. But what else could she do? Jude loved her now with his will. To have left him to Arabella would have been to destroy him. To have shared him with Arabella would have been possible to Sue, but impossible to him, for he had the strong, purist idea, that a man's body should follow and be 30
subordinate to his spirit, his senses should be subordinate to and subsequent to his mind. Which idea is utterly false.

So Jude and Sue are damned, partly by their very being, but chiefly by their incapacity to accept the conditions of their own and each other's being. If Jude could have known that he did not want Sue, 35
physically, and then have made his choice, they might not have wasted their lives. But he could not know.

If he could have known, after a while, after he had taken her many times, that it was wrong, still they might have made a life. He must have known that, after taking Sue, he was depressed as she was depressed. 40

He must have known worse than that. He must have felt the devastating sense of the unlivingness of life, things must have ceased to exist for him, when he rose from taking Sue, and he must have felt that he walked in a ghastly blank, confronted just by space, void.

5 But he would acknowledge [nothing] of what he felt. He must feel according to his idea and his will. Nevertheless, they were too truthful ever to marry. A man as real and personal as Jude cannot, from his deeper religious sense, marry a woman unless indeed he can marry her, unless with her he can find or approach the real consummation of
10 marriage. And Sue and Jude could not lie to themselves, in their last and deepest feelings. They knew it was no marriage: they knew it was wrong, all along: they knew they were sinning against life, in forcing a physical marriage between themselves.

How many people, man and woman, live together, in England, and
15 have children, and are never, never asked whether they have been through the marriage ceremony together! Why then should Jude and Sue have been brought to task? Only because of their own uneasy sense of wrong, of sin, which they communicated to other people. And this wrong or sin was not against the community, but against their own
20 being, against life. Which is why they were, the pair of them, instinctively disliked.*

They never knew of happiness, actual, sure-footed happiness, not for a moment. That was incompatible with Sue's nature. But what [they] knew was a very delightful but poignant and unhealthy
25 condition of lightened consciousness. They reacted on each other to stimulate the consciousness. So that, when they went to the flower-show, her sense of the roses, and Jude's sense of the roses, would be most, most poignant. There is always this pathos, this poignancy, this trembling on the verge of pain and tears, in their
30 happiness.

"Happy?" he murmured. She nodded.*

The roses, how the roses glowed for them! The flowers had more being than either he or she. But as their ecstasy over things sank a little, they felt, the pair of them, [as] if they themselves were wanting in real
35 body, as if they were too unsubstantial, too thin and evanescent in substance, as if the other solid people might jostle right through them, two wandering shades as they were.

This they felt themselves. Hence their uncertainty in contact with other people, hence their abnormal sensitiveness. But they had their
40 own form of happiness nevertheless, this trembling on the verge of

ecstasy, when, the senses strongly roused to the service of the consciousness, the things they contemplated took flaming being, became flaming symbols of their own emotions to them.

So that the real marriage of Jude and Sue was in the roses. Then, in the third state, in the spirit, [their]* two beings met upon the roses 5 and in the roses were symbolised in consummation. The rose is the symbol of marriage-consummation in its beauty. To them, it is more than a symbol, it is a fact, a flaming experience.

They went home tremblingly glad. And then the horror when, because of Jude's unsatisfaction, he must take Sue sexually. The 10 flaming experience becomes a falsity, or an ignis fatuus leading them on.

They exhausted their lives, he in the consciousness, she in the body. She was glad to have children, to prove she was a woman. But in her it was a perversity to wish to prove she was a woman. She was no woman. 15 And her children, the proof thereof, vanished like hoar-frost from her.

It was not the stone-masonry that exhausted him and weakened him and made him ill. It was this continuous feeding of his consciousness from his senses, this continuous state of incandescence of the consciousness, when his body, his vital tissue, the very protoplasm in him, 20 was being slowly consumed away. For he had no life in the body. Every time he went to Sue, physically, his inner experience must have been a shock back from life and from this form of outgoing, like that of a man who lies with a corpse. He had no life in the senses: he had no inflow from the source to make up for the enormous wastage. So he gradually 25 became exhausted, burned more and more away, till he was frail as an ember.

And she, her body also suffered. But it was in the mind that she had had her being, and it was in the mind she paid her price. She tried and tried to receive and to satisfy Jude physically. She bore him children, 30 she gave herself to the life of the body.

But as she was formed she was formed, and there was no altering it. She needed all the life that belonged to her, and more, for the supplying of her mind. Since such a mind as hers is found only, healthily, in a person of powerful vitality. For the mind, in a common 35 person, is created out of the surplus vitality, or out of the remainder after all the sensuous life has been fulfilled.

Sue needed all the life that belonged to her, for her mind. It was her form. To disturb that arrangement was to make her into somebody else, not herself. Therefore, when she became a physical wife and a 40 mother, she forswore her own being. She abjured her own mind, she denied it, took her faith, her belief, her very living away from it.

It is most probable she lived chiefly in her children. They were her guarantee as a physical woman, the being to which she now laid claim.
5   She had forsaken the ideal of an independent mind.

She would love her children with anguish, afraid always for their safety, never certain of their stable existence, never assured of their real reality. When they were out of her sight, she would be uneasy, uneasy almost as if they did not exist. There would be a gnawing at her till they
10   came back. She would not be satisfied till she had them crushed on her breast. And even then, she would not be sure, she would not be sure. She could not be sure, in life, of anything. She could only be sure, in the old days, of what she saw with her mind. Of that she was absolutely sure.

15   Meanwhile Jude became exhausted in vitality, bewildered, aimless, lost, pathetically unproductive.

Again one can see what instinct, what feeling it was which made Arabella's boy° bring about the death of the children and of himself. He, sensitive, so bodiless, so self-less as to be a sort of
20   automaton, is very badly suggested, exaggerated, but one can see what is meant. And he feels, as any child will feel, as many children feel to-day, that they are really anachronisms, accidents, fatal accidents, unreal, false notes in their mothers' lives, that, according to her, they have no being: that, if they have being, then she has not. So he takes
25   away all the children.

And then Sue ceases to be: she strikes the line through her own existence, cancels herself. There exists no more Sue Fawley. She cancels herself. She wishes to cease to exist, as a person, she wishes to be absorbed away, so that she is no longer self-responsible.

30   For she denied and forsook and broke her own real form, her own independent, cool-lighted mind-life. And now her children are not only dead, but self-slain, these pledges of the physical life for which she abandoned the other.

She has a passion to expiate, to expiate, to expiate. Her children
35   should never have been born: her instinct always knew this. Now their dead bodies drive her mad with a sense of blasphemy. And she blasphemed the Holy Spirit which told her she is guilty of their birth and their death, of the horrible [nullity], nothing, which they are. She is even guilty of their little, palpitating sufferings and joys of mortal life,
40   now made nothing. She cannot bear it—who could? And she wants to

expiate, doubly expiate. Her mind which she set up in her conceit, and
then forswore, she must stamp it out of existence, as one stamps out
fire. She would never again think or decide for herself. The world, the
past, should have written every decision for her. The last act of her
intellect was the utter renunciation of her mind and the embracing of   5
utter orthodoxy, where every belief, every thought, every decision was
made ready for her, so that she did not exist self-responsible. And then
her loathed body, which had committed the crime of bearing dead
children, which had come to life only to spread nihilism like a
pestilence, that too should be scourged out of existence. She chose the   10
bitterest penalty in going back to Phillotson.

There was no more Sue. Body, soul, and spirit, she annihilated
herself. All that remained of her was the will by which she annihilated
herself. That remained fixed, a locked centre of self-hatred, life-hatred
so utter that it had no hope of death. It knew that life is life, and there is   15
no death for life.

Jude was too exhausted himself to save her. He says of her she was
not worth a man's love.* But that was not the point. It was not a
question of her worth. It was a question of her being. If he had said she
was not capable of receiving a man's love as he wished to bestow it, he   20
might have spoken nearer the truth. But she practically told him this.
She made it plain to him what she wanted, what she could take. But he
overrode her. She tried hard to abide by her own form. But he forced
her. He had no case against her, unless that she made the great appeal
for him, that he should flow to her, whilst at the same time she could   25
not take him completely, body and spirit both.

She asked for what he could not give—what perhaps no man can
give: passionate love without physical desire. She had no blame for
him: she had no love for him. Self-love triumphed in her when she first
knew him. She almost deliberately asked for more, far more, than she   30
intended to give. Self-hatred triumphed in the end. So it had to be.

As for Jude, he had been dying slowly, but much quicker than she,
since the first night she took him. It was best to get it done quickly in
the end.

And this tragedy is the result of overdevelopment of one principle of   35
human life at the expense of the other; an overbalancing; a laying of all
the stress on the Male, the Love, the Spirit, the Mind, the Consciousness, a denying, a blaspheming against the Female, the Law, the Soul,
the Senses, the Feelings. But she is developed to the very extreme, she
scarcely lives in the body at all. Being of the feminine gender, she is yet   40

no woman at all, nor male, she is almost neuter. He is nearer the balance, nearer the centre, nearer the wholeness. But the whole human effort, towards pure life in the spirit, towards becoming pure Sue, drags him along, he identifies himself with this effort, destroys himself and
5 her in his adherence to this identification.

But why, in casting off one or another form of religion, has man ceased to be religious altogether? Why will he not recognise Sue and Jude, as Cassandra was recognised long ago, and Achilles,* and the Vestals, and the nuns, and the monks. Why must being be denied
10 altogether.

Sue had a being, special and beautiful. Why must not Jude recognise it in all its speciality? Why must man be so utterly irreverent, that he approaches each being as if it were no-being? Why must it be assumed that Sue is an "ordinary" woman—as if such a thing existed. Why must
15 she feel ashamed if she is special? And why must Jude, owing to the conception he is brought up in, force her to act as if she were his "ordinary" abstraction, a woman.

She was not a woman. She was Sue Bridehead, something very particular. Why was there no place for her? Cassandra had the temple
20 of Apollo. Why are we so foul, that we have no reverence for that which we are and for that which is amongst us. If we had reverence for our life, our life would take at once religious form. But as it is, in our filthy irreverence, it remains a disgusting slough, where each one of us goes so thoroughly disguised in dirt that we are all alike and indistinguish-
25 able.

If we had reverence for what we are, our life would take real form, and Sue would have a place, as Cassandra had a place, she would have a place which does not yet exist, because we are all so vulgar, we have nothing.

Chapter X.*

It seems as if the history of humanity were divided into two epochs: the Epoch of the Law and the Epoch of Love. It seems as though humanity, during the time of its activity on earth, has made two great efforts: the effort to appreciate the Law and the effort to overcome the Law in Love. And in both efforts it has succeeded. It has reached and proved the Two Complementary Absolutes, the Absolute of the Father, of the Law, of Nature, and the Absolute of the Son, of Love, of Knowledge. What remains is to reconcile the two.

In the beginning, Man said "What am I, and whence is this world around me, and why is it as it is?" Then he proceeded to explore and to personify and to deify the Natural Law, which he called Father. And having reached the point where he conceived of the Natural Law in its purity, he had finished his journey, and was arrested.

But he found that he could not remain at rest. He must still go on. Then there was to discover by what principle he must proceed further than the Law. And he received an inkling of Love. All over the world the same, the second great epoch started with the incipient conception of Love, and continued until the principle of Love was conceived in all its purity. Then man was again at an end, in a cul de sac.

The Law it is by which we exist. It was the Father, the Law-Maker, who said "Let there be light":* it was He who breathed life into the handful of dust and made man. "Thus have I made man, in mine own image. I have ordered his outgoing and his incoming, and have cast the line whereby he shall walk." So said the Father. And man went out and came in according to the ordering of the Lord, he walked by the line of the Lord and did not deviate. Till the path was worn barren, and man knew all the way, and the end seemed to have drawn nigh.

Then he said "I will leave the path. I will go out as the Lord hath not ordained, and come in when my hour is fulfilled. For it is written, a man shall eat and drink with the Lord: but I will neither eat nor drink, I will go hungry, yet I will not die. It is written, a man shall take himself a wife and beget him seed unto the glory of God. But I will not take me a wife, nor beget seed, but I will know no woman. Yet will I not die. And

it is written, a man shall save his body from harm, and preserve his flesh
from hurt, for he is made in the image and likeness of the Father. But I
will deliver up my body to hurt, and give my flesh unto the dust, yet will
I not die, but live. For man does not live by bread alone, nor by the
5   common law of the Father. Beyond this common law, I am I. When my
body is destroyed and my bones have perished, then I am I. Yea, not
until my body is consumed and my bones have mingled with the dust,
not until then am I whole, not until then do I live. But I die in Christ,
and rise again. And when I am risen again, I live in the spirit. Neither
10 hunger nor cold can lay hold on me, nor desire lay hands on me. When
I am risen again, then I shall *know*. Then I shall live in the ineffable
bliss of knowledge. When the sun goes forth in the morning, I shall
know the glory of God, who passes the sun from His left hand to His
right, in the peace of His Understanding. As the night comes in her
15 divers shadows, I know the peace that passeth all understanding. For
God knoweth. Neither does he Will nor Command nor desire nor act,
but exists perfect in the peace of knowledge."

If a man must live still and act in the body, then let his action be to
the recognising of the life in other bodies. Each man is to himself the
20 Natural Law. He can only conceive of the Natural Law as he knows it
in himself. The hardest thing for any man to do is for him to recognise
and to know that the natural law of his neighbour is other than, and
maybe even hostile to, his own natural law, and yet is true. This hard
lesson Christ tried to instil in the doctrine of the other cheek.*
25 Orestes could not conceive that it was the natural law of Clytemnestra's
nature, that she should murder Agamemnon for sacrificing her daughter, and for leaving herself abandoned in the pride of her womanhood,
unmated because he wanted the pleasure of war, and for his unfaithful-
ness to her with other women. Clytemnestra could not understand that
30 Orestes should want to kill her for fulfilling the law of her own nature.
The law of the mother's nature was other than the law of the son's
nature. This they could neither of them see, hence the killing. This
Christianity would teach them: to recognise and to admit the law of the
other person, outside and different from the law of one's own being. It
35 is the hardest lesson of love. And the lesson of love learnt, there must
be learned the next lesson, of reconciliation between different, maybe
hostile things. That is the final lesson. Christianity ends in submission,
in recognising and submitting to the law of the other person: "Thou
shalt love thy enemy."*[   ]
40 Therefore, since by the law man must act or move, let his motion be the

utterance of the God of Peace, of the perfect, unutterable Peace of Knowledge.

And man has striven this way, to utter the Universal Peace of God. And striving on, he has passed beyond the limits of utterance, and has reached once more the silence of the beginning.

After Sue, after Dostoievsky's *Idiot*, after Turner's latest pictures, after the symbolist poetry of Mallarmé and the others, after the music of Debussy,* there is no further possible utterance of the peace that passeth all understanding, the peace of God which is Perfect Knowledge. There is only silence beyond this.

Just as after Plato, after Dante, after Raphael, there was no further utterance of the Absoluteness of the Law, of the Immutability of the Divine Conception.

So that, as the great pause came over Greece, and over Italy after the Renaissance, when the Law had been uttered in its absoluteness, so there comes over us now, over England and Russia and France, the pause of finality, now we have seen the purity of Knowledge, the great, white, uninterrupted Light, infinite and eternal.

But that is not the end. The two great conceptions, of Law and of Knowledge or Love, are not diverse and accidental, but complementary. They are, in a way, contradictions each of the other. But they are complementary. They are the Fixed Absolute, the Geometric Absolute, and they are the radiant Absolute, the Unthinkable Absolute of pure, free motion. They are the perfect Stability, and they are the perfect Mobility. They are the fixed condition of our being, and they are the transcendent condition of knowledge in us. They are our Soul, and our Spirit. They are our Feelings, and our Mind. They are our Body and our Brain. They are Two-in-One.

And everything that has ever been produced, has been produced by the combined activity of the two, in humanity, by the combined activity of soul and spirit. When the two are acting together, then Life is produced, then Life, or Utterance, Something, is *created*. And nothing is or can be created save by combined effort of the two principles, Law and Love.

All through the mediaeval times, Law and Love were striving together to give the perfect expression to the Law, to arrive at the perfect conception of the Law. All through the rise of the Greek nation, to its culmination, the Law and Love were working in that nation to attain the perfect expression of the Law. They were driven by the Unknown Desire, the Holy Spirit, the Unknown and Unexpressed. But the Holy Spirit is the Reconciler, and the Originator. Him we do not know.

The greatest of all Utterance of the Law, has given expression to the Law as it is in relation to Love, both ruled by the Holy Spirit. Such is the Book of Job, such Aeschylus, in the Trilogy, such, more or less, is Dante, such is Botticelli. Those who gave expression to the Law after these, suppressed the contact, and achieved an abstraction—Plato, Raphael.

The greatest utterance of Love has given expression to Love as it is in relation to the Law: so Rembrandt, Shakespeare, Shelley, Wordsworth, Goethe, Tolstoi. But beyond these, there has been Turner, who suppressed the context of the Law. Also there have been Dostoievsky, Hardy, Flaubert. These have shown Love in conflict with the Law, and only Death the resultant, no Reconciliation. So that humanity does not continue for long to accept the conclusions of these writers, nor even of Euripides, and Shakespeare always. These great tragic writers endure by reason of the truth of the conflict they describe, because of its completeness, Law, Love, and Reconciliation all active. But with regard to their conclusions, they leave the soul finally unsatisfied, unbelieving.

Now the aim of man remains to recognise and seek out the Holy Spirit, the Reconciler, the Originator, He who drives the twin principles of Law and of Love across the ages.

Now it remains for us to know the Law and to know the Love, and further to seek out the Reconciliation. It is time for us to build our temples to the Holy Spirit, and to raise our altars to the Holy Ghost, the Supreme, Who is beyond us but is with us.

We know of the Law, and we know of Love, and to that little we know of each of these we have given our full expression. But have not completed one perfect utterance, not one. Small as is the circle of our knowledge, we are not able to cast it complete. In Aeschylus' "Eumenides", Apollo is foolish, Athena mechanical. In Shakespeare's "Hamlet", the conclusion is all foolish. If we had conceived each party in his proper force, if Apollo had been equally potent with the Furies, and no Pallas had appeared to settle the question merely by dropping a pebble, how would Aeschylus [have] solved his riddle.* He could not work out the solution he knew must come, so he forced it.

And so it has always been, always: either a wrong conclusion, or one forced by the artist, as if he put his thumb in the scale to equalise a balance which he could not make level. Now it remains for us to seek the true balance, to give each party, Apollo and the Furies, Love and the Law, his due, and so to seek the Reconciler.

Now the principle of the Law is found strongest in Woman, and the principle of Love in Man. In every creature, the mobility, the law of change, is found exemplified in the male, the stability, the conservatism 5 is found in the female. In woman, man finds his root and establishment. In man, woman finds her exfoliation° and florescence. The woman grows downwards, like a root, towards the centre and the darkness and the origin. The man grows upwards, like the stalk, towards discovery and light and utterance. 10

Man and Woman are, roughly, the embodiment of Love and the Law: they are the two complementary parts. In the body they are most alike, in genitals they are almost one. Starting from the connection, almost unification, of the genitals, and travelling towards the feelings and the mind, there becomes ever a greater difference and a finer distinction 15 between the two, male and female, till at last, at the other closing in the circle, in pure utterance, the two are really one again, so that any pure utterance is a perfect unity, the two as one, united by the Holy Spirit.

We start from one side or the other, from the female side or the male, but what we want is always the perfect union of the two. That is the Law 20 of the Holy Spirit, the law of Consummate Marriage. That every living thing seeks, individually and collectively. Every man starts with his deepest desire, a desire for consummation of marriage between himself and the female, a desire for completeness, that completeness of being which will give completeness of satisfaction and completeness of 25 utterance. No man can as yet find perfect consummation of marriage between himself and the Bride, be the bride either Woman or an Idea, but he can approximate to it, and every generation can get a little nearer.

But it needs that a man shall first know in reverence and submit to the Natural Law of his own individual being: that he shall also know that he 30 is but contained within the great Natural Law, that he is but a Child of God, and not God himself: that he shall then poignantly and personally recognise that the law of another man's nature is different from the law of his own nature, that it may be even hostile to him, and yet is part of the great Law of God, to be admitted: this is the Christian action of "loving 35 thy neighbour", and of dying to be born again: lastly, that a man shall know that between his law and the law of his neighbour, there is an affinity, that all is contained in one, through the Holy Spirit.

It needs that a man shall know the natural law of his own being, then that he shall seek out the law of the female, with which to join himself as 40 complement. He must know that he is half, and the woman is the other half: that they are two, but that they are two-in-one.

He must with reverence submit to the law of himself: and he must with suffering and joy know and submit to the law of the woman: and
5 he must know that they two together are one within the Great Law, reconciled within the Great Peace. Out of this final knowledge shall come his supreme art. There shall be the art which recognises and utters his own law; there shall be the art which recognises his own and also the law of the woman, his neighbour, utters the glad embrace and
10 the struggle between them, and the submission of one; there shall be the art which knows the struggle between the two conflicting laws, and knows the final reconciliation, where both are equal, two-in-one, complete. This is the supreme art, which yet remains to be done. Some men have attempted it, and left us the results of efforts. But it remains
15 to be fully done.

But when the two [clasp] hands, a moment, male and female, [clasp]° hands and are one, the poppy, the gay poppy flies into flower again; and when the two fling their arms about each other, the moonlight runs and clashes against the shadow, and when the two toss
20 back their hair, all the larks break out singing, and when they kiss on the mouth, a lovely human utterance is heard again—and so it is.

LITERARY ESSAYS, 1908–27

Note on the texts

The base-texts for the essays in this volume are as follows:

'Art and the Individual': photocopy of the autograph manuscript, 9 pp. (MS); formerly in the collection of the late John E. Baker Jr, its current location is unknown.

'Rachel Annand Taylor': autograph manuscript, 8 pp. (MS), in the collection of Mr W. H. Clarke; collated with *Young Lorenzo*, by Ada Lawrence and G. Stuart Gelder (Florence, 1932) (O1).

'The Future of the Novel': autograph manuscript, 11 pp. (MS), in ColU; collated with the corrected ribbon copy typescript, 6 pp. (TS), in ColU, and the corrected carbon copy typescript, 6 pp. (TCC), UTul; *Literary Digest International Book Review*, i (April 1923), 5–6, 63 (Per); and *Phoenix* (A1).

'A Britisher Has a Word With an Editor': *Palms*, i (Christmas 1923), 153–4 (Per); collated with DHL's autograph manuscript, 1 p. (MS), UT. Since DHL worked closely with Idella Purnell, editor of *Palms*, on some numbers of the periodical, it has been assumed that he authorised the changes to the text, even though he left Guadalajara, Mexico, before this issue appeared.

'Art and Morality': autograph manuscript, 10 pp. (MS), UT, emended from the corrected carbon copy typescript, 11 pp. (TCC), UCB; collated with *Calendar of Modern Letters*, ii (November 1925), 171–7 (Per) and *Phoenix* (A1).

'Morality and the Novel': autograph manuscript, 10 pp. (MS), UT, emended from the corrected carbon copy typescript, 10 pp. (TCC), UCB; collated with *Calendar of Modern Letters*, ii (December 1925), 269–74 (Per) and *Phoenix* (A1).

'The Novel': corrected typescript, 14 pp. (TS), in UTul; collated with *Reflections on the Death of a Porcupine* (A1).

'Why the Novel Matters': autograph manuscript, 14 pp. (MS), UT; collated with *Phoenix* (A1).

'The Novel and the Feelings': autograph manuscript, 12 pp. (MS), UT; collated with *Phoenix* (A1).

'John Galsworthy': autograph manuscript, 16 pp. (MS), UT, emended from the first English edition in *Scrutinies by Various Writers*, Edgell Rickword, ed. (1928) (E1); collated with *Phoenix* (A1).

The apparatus records all textual variants, except for the following silent emendations:

1 Clearly accidental spelling mistakes by DHL or his typists and obvious typesetter's errors have been corrected.
2 DHL often wrote colloquial contractions without joining them up (e.g. 'does n't') and wrote '&', and these have been normalised ('doesn't', 'and').
3 Apostrophes in contractions and possessives and full stops omitted at the end of sentences where no other punctuation exists, have been supplied.
4 DHL usually wrote 'Mr' and 'Mrs' (O1 and A1 supplied the full stop, as did TS and Per in 'The Future of the Novel' and TS in 'The Novel'); he wrote 'realise', 'recognise', 'civilisation', etc. (A1 altered to '-ize/ -iz-', as did TCC in 'Art and

Morality'); DHL wrote 'for ever' and 'forever' (A1 printed all as 'for ever'); DHL's practices have been adopted throughout.

5 Though DHL frequently placed commas or other stops with quotation marks ambiguously (i.e. directly under the closing marks: ", or ".), he usually placed them inside the closing marks (," or ."), which is the convention followed in all the printings of the essays in periodicals and books, except 'The Novel' in A1. In that volume, as in some typescripts ('The Novel', 'Art and Morality', 'Morality and the Novel') the commas and other stops are placed outside the closing marks (", or ".), except in conversation or full sentence quotation. In all cases, DHL's unambiguous practice has been followed.

6 DHL often followed a full stop, question mark or exclamation mark with a dash before beginning the next sentence (e.g. beings.—And at 210:16). His typists occasionally and the typesetters consistently omitted these dashes; they have been restored in this edition.

Supplementary points to the Note on the texts have been supplied preceding each essay as needed.

ART AND THE INDIVIDUAL
A PAPER FOR SOCIALISTS

Art and the Individual
A Paper for Socialists*

This paragraph from a Socialist Member of Parliament is fairly well known: "The present aim of socialists is to find work for the unemployed, food for the hungry, and clothes for the naked. After that it will make the conquest of the intellectual and artistic world."* We who are readers of the "New Age," also remember the critic's comment: "Men, women and children want food and raiment now; we also need our Beauty—in our streets, in our crafts, in our paintings. Let that obsessed socialist go mend his ways; too many think as he does. In the meantime we starve, and our cities starve, for beauty—while politicians prate of the large sums of money diverted to philanthropy." If the only duty of Socialism is to fight the battle of the hungry and naked, then is it for the Ironsides of Snowden* to wage war; we, who are not hungry and thirsty for material things, and who have not the tough spirit or the single purpose of a political fighter, we will stay at home, and in wicked sloth forget the din that rages round the platform, such time as in our own fields the lark is high. Have we not been seized, we who love the lotus buds,* and thrust into some horrid meeting where voices jangled like weapons?; was it not hideous?; did we not determine to martyr ourselves also for the cause, to clap on the morion and with a double-edged sword go smite the lofty from their seats?;* and the next day, when the sunflowers began to colour the morning mists, did we not recant? We, who had rather sing the melodies of Schubert than the Marseillaise, and who love the lyrics and the Sensitive Plant far better than Queen Mab,* do we not also dread that fierce socialist friend of ours who scans us with pitying regret, since he knows we are limbs dead, hopelessly dead?; and do we not hate a Civil War?; and do we not detest utterly the thought of the Commonwealth and the Rule by Zealots.*

Ours is not, moreover, a weak, selfish cowering that shrinks from the brunt. We are as right as are those who yell for Rights down a trumpet; we believe we are more right, for we are more silent. But we are teachers, and we call upon those unanswerable oracles, the authorities on Education, to defend us; we are victors. Listen! "The ultimate goal

of Education is to produce an individual of high moral character."*
Socialists bow assent, and we mutter "a bit more verbiage." What on
earth is a "high moral character"?—Well, since everybody knows, there
is no need to explain. We will just remark that a moral person must be
5 well cultivated; must be able to reckon on the great influences which
move men, and to estimate the results of such; must, also, have a good
sense of proportion, a quality strangely lacking in most highly moral
persons. Sense of proportion precludes a well-balanced soul—or
mind, if you like. You Ironsides, where is your balance? Have you not
10 plumped down one scale with the great weight of human miseries? You
say a state of balance is inert and ineffectual, well, perhaps I have sunk
down on the side Beauty, and so we make a social equipoise, which is
delightful, is it not? But my muttons, my muttons!*—We must
have a balance somewhere, admit it,—either in the individual soul or in
15 the social. Well then, all the great forces that influence human action
must be directed to the present life we live with as little confusion as
possible. And the great forces! Will you accept the great Interests,
classified by Herbart,* whom we revere, as Six, but to which we
will humbly add a seventh, since the moderns have decreed it so? Here
20 is the table:

	1. Knowledge (Intellectual)		1. Empirical 2. Speculative 3. Aesthetic
Interests arise from	2. Sympathy (Emotional)		1. Sympathetic 2. Social 3. Religious
	3. (Action)		

Here is the explanation:*

30 [I] 1. Empirical:—   Interest in concrete individual things and instances.
     2. Speculative:—   Interest in deeper connections and causes of phe-
                        nomena etc.—these interests become philosophic
                        and scientific studies.
     3. Aesthetic:—   Interest aroused neither by phenomena or causes as
35   such, but by the approval which their harmony and
                        adaptability to an end win from me. (this is Herbart,
                        not me)
     [II] 1. Sympathetic:— personal sympathy

2. Social:— growing comprehension of the incorporation of the individual in the great social body whose interests are large beyond his personal feelings. (Socialists —enlarge)

3. Religious:— when this extended sympathy is directed to the history (origin) and destiny of mankind, when it reverentially recognises the vast scope of the laws of nature, and discovers something of intelligible and consistent purpose working through the whole natural world and human consciousness, religious interest is developed. Then the sense of a man's own importance, and that of his day, is merged in some wonder and reverence—a fruitful condition.

III Lastly comes the wonderful interest in action—doing something. Cricketers and tennis-players need no enlargement.

May I offer you an example.* You are sitting by a sunlit lakelet, and a swan steers proudly up to you. "Look," you cry "there's a swan. Come on, come on! I wish I had something to throw him. Doesn't he arch his wings! And there's his mate coming peeping in every bend!" (Empirical). "I wonder why he puts his wings up like that? The other one is quite slim. Is she the female? And he does it to attract her? He really seems to be showing off to us." (Speculative). "But aren't they handsome! She is like a slim boat gliding through the water, and he's a haughty vessel. Look how their long necks are supple—they wave like shadows under the water when they're looking for food. Isn't there strength in those great hard curves of his wing; they say he could break your leg; I guess he needs strong wings, though.Oh, tell him to go into the water again; what hideous black legs against that plumage; and the way he balances, and his ridiculous gait. Get into the water, you poor fool, you are absurd on shore!" (This is aesthetic interest, appreciation of adaptability of swans to water, and harmony between them and their surroundings. I don't say that there is not another feeling mingled with this.)

Example number 2.* Evening primroses and the tobacco plant we grow in our gardens are exceedingly beautiful by night. Their pure white or sulphur yellow flowers unfold so magically when the sun goes down, and gleam so exquisitely in the moonlight; those clumps of red phlox are black, and their scent is coarse; but the primroses are painted specially for moonlight, and their scent is like the serenade, prepared for night time when the moth will come to minister to the wakeful flowers, and will take back their sweet love-honey and their pollen

kisses; for evening primroses have tubes so deep that only the moth
with his long whip of a tongue can sip up the nectar, so these night
preparations are for the satisfying lover. Moreover, flowers and insects
have developed thus side by side; if the nicotiana and the evening
5   primrose have deepened their tubes and waited till evening to unfold to
hide their treasures from crawling flies and to ensure cross-pollination,
the moth for his part has developed his tongue to touch the deeps of his
beloved. Unconsciously, I think, we appreciate some of the harmony of
this mutual adaptability, and that is how aesthetics come to be allied to
10 religion, for they are a recognition, one of those recognitions which
move unknown, having no revealing cloak of words and word ideas, of
the great underlying purpose which is made visible in this instance, and
which it is, perhaps, the artist's duty to seek. This universal Purpose is
the germ of the God-Idea.* It may be that as the plant develops
15 from the germ, it is twisted and clipped into some fantastic Jehovah-
shape, but—:
        Remark how the scale of Interests rises. The Aesthetic and the
Religious are the highest in their two groups. Remark again that you
are conscious of the activity of the Interests Empiric, Speculative,
20 Sympathetic, Social, and Religious; but which of us has done other
than let his aesthetic interest lead him into a blundering "like and
dislike" for which he can give no reason? You like a thing, and there's
an end of it; no matter how many overlaying material influences thwart
your poor aesthetic soul, and pervert its action, you never question your
25 likings; if some superior artistic person has a slight contempt for the
objects of your taste, it is like his impudence; even if you weary of a
thing you once loved, and paste over the picture you framed with your
own hands with gusto a lustre ago, you regret your inconstancy of soul,
and fear you have fallen away from the old enthusiastic appreciation.
30 You ought to rejoice, and say "the soul of an artist is developing in me,"
just as you would when you found that Rider Haggard was not a prince
of entertainers, but even that distant voice of Sir Thos. More*
could beat him.
        Consider "Aesthetic Interest" and its definition more closely. It is
35 not satisfactory to us as it stands; it is too intellectual. Beauty comes
under the shelter of Aesthetics, and our appreciation of Beauty is very
often not appreciation, but a strong mingled emotion. Indeed the whole
aim of Art seems to be to rouse a certain emotion; this emotion may
have some expression in words or thoughts, or it may not; and as for
40 thought, it depends entirely on language, and so is limited, and leaves

untouched even the majority of our feelings. There have always been two schools of aesthetic thought. The first is the intellectual and mystic:

I. Art—"Beauty is the expression of the perfect and divine *Idea*,"*—considering the Idea in the Platonic sense as of some pure unborn soul or idea forever struggling to find perfect expression through matter, just as one of the Erewhonian Unborns* might pester two unfortunate humans to give him an existence during which he might perfect some art—say that of making impeccable soup. The Hegelian school propounds that "Beauty is the shining of the Idea through matter";* the making of beautiful things, according to Goethe, is the "weaving for God the garment we see him by."*

The opposing emotional and material school is divided:

II. 1. "Art is an activity arising even in the animal kingdom, and springing from sexual desire and propensity to play—and it is accompanied by pleasurable excitement"—Darwin. In this class come Schiller, Spencer and others as well as Darwin.* They explain the dandy, who decks himself as he wins toward maturity, and flirts from a propensity to play. Pray, ladies in short skirts, recognise the dandy as a natural and admirable object, as you did the swan.

2. "Art is the external manifestation by lines, color, words, sounds, movements, of emotions felt by man."*

3. "Art is the production of some permanent object or passing action fitted to convey pleasurable impressions quite apart from personal advantage"—which is, I think, the definition of Grant Allen.*

The first school bases its Beauty on Herbart's "Adaptation"—perfect adaptation shows clearly the fundamental idea and purpose.

Harmony is the name we give to a certain emotional state roused by certain blended components. So Herbart proceeded somewhat towards the second school in his definition, if not very far.

Now let us take a few exceptions and try to prove the rules of our schoolmen. Consider the writings of Poe, De Maupassant, Ibsen, Maxim Gorky; consider the Laocoon, some of the French Realistic paintings, even the "Outcasts" of Luke Fildes, or Watts' "Mammon,"* if this last be Art. These show no divine idea; these are no garments of God; nor are they activities arising from sense of play or sex; nor do they convey pleasure, in the ordinary sense of the word. Their sole object is to set vibrating in the second person the

emotion which moved the producer; and this seems to be the mission of Art. It must be, as Tolstoi says, the second great means of communication between men, and, he insists, the language of Art must be intelligible.* But since "being intelligible" means "able to be
5 thought of," and since thought takes place in language more or less precise, Art has no very great value, since the same effect, or somewhat the same, might have been obtained without recourse to any other form than simple prose. True, as Tolstoi says, if a lad tells a tale to his sister which brings tears to her eyes, then he is an artist;* and Carlyle's
10 Heroes were artists, for they could not speak but in song, for a vigorous emotion moulded all their speech.* But when the lad told the tale, the words were only as the simple melody running clear through the piece; the art was more likely to be in the tones, the gestures; and the value of song is its music, and its power to call up new pictures; and the
15 value, the beauty of the tale or the song lies in the emotion which follows the music of the tones, the harmony of looks and gesture, the quivering feelings for which there are no words, and the pictures which were never on the retina, and never will be. True, some words are themselves artistic, some few rare words such as *wonder*; it is a
20 beautiful, wonderful word; French has no equivalent; see how much gathers round it; and how will you express it? Then words like laughter, chatter, and flash are expressive. But words can rarely describe, call up in another, the feeling that was mother and father to them. They have to "pair like lovers, and chime in the ear"; they must "progress in
25 cosmic fellowship"*—they must, in short, have form, style.

> "Words were nothing if words could say all: ever behind our singing is the silence out of which it broke.
> So too, behind this little book with its words of franchise, my enfranchisement remains untold.
> 30 The trees swing in the gale and make music in it; but in the Earth abiding they keep silence.
> So for you, beloved, abiding in your love, my heart keeps silence while I sing."

It is Art which opens to us the silences, the primordial silences which hold the secret of things, the great purposes, which are themselves
35 silent; there are no words to speak of them with, and no thoughts to think of them in, so we struggle to touch them through art; and the eager, unsatisfied world seeks to put them all into a religious phrase.

Tolstoi defeated his own ends, then, when he demanded that art should be intelligible. It seems to be human fate to strive to know to the uttermost, and men in general cannot bear to touch the Mystery nakedly, without a garment of words. The deepest secrets of all are hidden in human experience, in human feeling, and the human heart is never satisfied till it can command the secret, dress the unutterable experience in the livery of an idea, and prison it with fetters of words. The music of some of the great Germans is too vague, confusing, unintelligible; the poetry of Verlaine, Maeterlinck, and Baudelaire; the pictures of George Clausen* and others are too sketchy; we cannot feel the outline; it is as if we were in a mist. People complain continually, along with Tolstoi, in such terms. They should know that they are purposely led to the edge of the great darkness, where no word-lights twinkle. They had rather listen to a great din of a battle-piece* and exclaim "There, the trumpet sounds charge!, hark, you can tell it's horses galloping!—do you hear the rumble of cannon? —isn't it fine!" The true battle-piece would call up the fury and fear in the hearts of a mass of soldiers, the pain and the primeval lust, without tin-pan clash-of-swords imitation. So Chopin's Funeral March seems far superior to the March in Saul;* it has no drum thumping and artifice and extravagance.

Having discussed at some length what Art may do, we can more easily proclaim what it may not do. It may not call up harmful emotions; if it does it is bad art. Conclusion, French novels are bad art, Marie Corelli* is not. I leave it to you to continue making syllogisms on the limitations of Art.

Everyone sets out, in his own opinion, ready equipped to pass judgment on things of beauty and taste. Unfortunately, his opinion is peculiarly his own; he is condemned for bad taste. "It is a matter of opinion," he says. It is not. If a thing is in bad taste it is so absolutely, just as a sum in mathematics is either wrong or right. If the obnoxious thing appears good to the owner, it is because he has a number of harmful influences perverting his judgment, or because he is so woefully undeveloped that there is no appeal to him save through the primary colours, or because a shallow emotion evokes a similar one in him.

Example: That popular picture, "Wedded," by Lord Leighton.* The emotion conveyed is weak and shallow. A bare-legged, leopard-skin-clad, black haired lad kisses the fingers of a girl in a manner impossible unless he were standing on a little balcony specially erected by an artist for public exhibition. Contrast the passion in Maurice Greiffenhagen's "Idyll."* But Leighton's picture is beautiful—the

technique—. The delight of form in art is said to be largely physical. The movement of the eye is grateful and pleasing along certain curves, certain combinations such as the rhythmic folds of drapery in Leighton's pictures.* Exactly, but the form, the artistic form is purely
5   sensuous, it is beautiful, but not so highly profitable. Look at Watts' "Mammon"; it is hideous and hateful; it does not help us one jot to have a ghastly idol with beastly eyes set up in warning to us not to worship it; the emotion of the artist did not find satisfactory expression. So we condemn one artist because, although he has a sumptuous
10   manner, his feeling is shallow and unprofitable, and another because in the violence of his feeling he outrages art and offends us. The third group that displeases us is that of the English sentimentalists, who wallow in emotion:—little girls about to be mown down by the hand of Time, he who cuts off the fairest flowers—all this written by somebody
15   who thought it a good subject. Sentimentality is by far the most grievous disease that an artist can contract; it renders Art despicable. Let us condemn it severely, if we can.

The triumph of Art? "The chief triumph of Art" says Hume, "is to insensibly refine the temper, and to point out to us those dispositions
20   which we should endeavour to attain by constant bent of mind and by repeated habit"*—"By constant bent of mind and repeated habit"— that is, by carefully educating yourself. You are not a born judge of Beauty—you must learn, by studying the best examples, and by searching your own soul carefully. Then, when your temper is refined,
25   you will undergo a thousand experiences to which you were before dead; you will never find time long, or an hour dreary; a life- long holiday would not be long enough to make you wish you had something to do, for a new charm will be always inviting your soul, and you can remain in delightful possession of yourself, needing no-one to cheer
30   you and fill in the blanks.

RACHEL ANNAND TAYLOR

Supplementary note on the text

See Note on the texts, pp. 130:1. Additional silent emendations are the following:

O1 has the essay in double quotation marks; its quotation marks at the beginning of each paragraph and single quotation marks for quotations and titles of poems have not been recorded.

In the list of poem titles (146:1–7), DHL did not set off the titles with quotation marks and sometimes separated titles with a dash; O1 treated the classifications as titles and ran all the 'titles' together, with single quotation marks separated by commas (which followed the closing quotation marks); the titles have been standardised with no quotation marks and separated by commas. All other titles have been placed in quotation marks following DHL's usual practice at this period.

Rachel Annand Taylor

Mrs Rachel Annand Taylor is not ripe yet to be gathered as fruit for lectures and papers. She is young, not more than thirty; she has been married and her husband has left her: she lives in Chelsea, visits Professor Gilbert Murray* in Oxford, and says strange, ironic 5 things of many literary people, in a plaintive, peculiar fashion. This, then, is raw green fruit to offer you, to be received with suspicion, to be tasted charily and spat out without much revolving and tasting. It is impossible to appreciate the verse of a green fresh poet. He must be sun-dried by time and sunshine of favorable criticism, like muscatels 10 and prunes: you must remove the crude sap of living: then the flavour of his eternal poetry comes out unobscured and unpolluted by what is temporal in him. Is it not so?

Mrs Taylor is, however, personally, all that could be desired of a poetess: in appearance, purely Rossettian:* slim, svelte; big, 15 beautiful bushes of reddish hair hanging over her eyes, which peer from the warm shadow; delicate colouring, scarlet, small, shut mouth; a dark, plain dress with a big boss of a brooch on her bosom, a curious, carven witch's brooch;* then long white languorous hands of the correct subtle radiance. All that a poetess should be. 20

She is a Scotch-woman. Brought up lonelily as a child, she lived on the bible, on the Arabian Nights, and later, on Malory's King Arthur. Her up-bringing was not Calvinistic.* Left to herself, she developed as a choice romanticist. She lived apart from life, and still she cherishes a yew-darkened garden in her soul where she can remain 25 withdrawn, sublimating experience into odours.

This is her value, then: that to a world almost satisfied with the excitement of Realism's Reign of Terror, she hangs out the flags of Romance, and sounds the music of citherns and violes. She is mediaeval; she is as pagan and as romantic as the old minstrels. She 30 belongs to the company of Aucassin and Nicolette,* and to no other.

The first volume of poems* was published in 1904. Listen to the titles of the poems:

Romances—   The Bride, A Song of Gold, The Queen, The Daughter of
                     Herodias, Arthurian Songs, The Knights at Ringstead.

Devotional—   Flagellants, An Early Christian, Rosa Mundi, An Art-lover
                     to Christ.

5   Chant D'Amour—Love's Fool to His Lady, Saint Mary of the Flowers', The
                     Immortal Hour.

Reveries—   The Hostel of Sleep.

I will read you four of the love songs. Against the first, in the book
Mrs Taylor gave me,* I found a dried lily of the valley, that the
10 authoress had evidently overlooked. She would have dropped it in the
fire, being an ironical romanticist. However, here is the poem, stained
yellow with a lily: it is called "Desire."* (p. 73)

That is the first of the love songs. The second is called
"Surrender"* (p. 80)—
15 the third, which is retrospective, is "Unrealised"*
and the fourth is "Renunciation."*

There is the story of Mrs Taylor's married life, that those who run may
read.*

Needless to say, the poetess' heart was broken.
20 "There is nothing more tormenting" I said to her, "than to be loved
overmuch."

"Yes, one thing more tormenting" she replied.

"And what's that?" I asked her.

"To love," she said, very quietly.
25 However, it is rather useful to a poetess or poet to have a broken heart.
Then the rare fine liquor from the fragile vial is spilled in little splashes
of verse most interesting to the reader, most consoling to the writer. A
broken heart does give colour to life.

Mrs Taylor, in her second volume, "Rose and Vine" published last
30 year, makes the splashes of verse from her spilled treasure of love. But
they are not crude startling bloody drops. They are vermeil and gold
and beryl green. Mrs Taylor takes the "pageant of her bleeding
heart,"* first marches it ironically by the brutal daylight, then
lovingly she draws it away into her magic, obscure place apart, where
35 she breathes spells upon it, filters upon it delicate lights, tricks it with
dreams and fancy, and then re-issues the pageant.

"Rose and Vine" is much superior to the "Poems" of 1904. It is
gorgeous, sumptuous. All the full, luscious buds of promise are full
blown here, till heavy, crimson petals seem to brush one's hips in

passing, and in front, white blooms seem leaning to meet one's breasts. There is a great deal of sensuous colour, but it is all abstract, impersonal in feeling, not the least sensual. One tires of it in the same way that one tires of some of Strauss's music—"Electra,"* for instance. It is emotionally insufficient, though splendid in craftman-   5
ship.

Mrs Taylor is, indeed, an exquisite craftsman of verse. Moreover, in her metres and rhythms she is orthodox. She allows herself none of the modern looseness but retains the same stanza form to the end of a lyric. I should like more time to criticise the form of this verse.   10

However, to turn to "Rose and Vine". There is not much recognis-able biography here. Most of the verses are transformed from the experience beyond recognition. A really new note is the note of motherhood. I often wonder why, when a woman artist comes, she never reveals the meaning of maternity, but either paints horses or   15
Venuses or sweet children, as we see them in the Tate Gallery, or deals with courtship and affairs, like Charlotte Brontë and George Eliot. Mrs Taylor has a touch of the mother note. I read you "Four Crimson Violers."*

And now "Song of Fruition (For an October Mother)".*—   20
What my mother would have said to that, when she had me an autumn baby, I don't know.

A fine piece of thoughtful writing is "Music of Resurrection," which, significantly, opens the "Rose and Vine" volume.

That was last year. This year, came the "Hours of Fiammetta"—a   25
sonnet sequence. There are 61 sonnets in the Shakespeare form, and, besides these, a Prologue of Dreaming Women, an Epilogue of Dreaming Women, and an Introduction.* In the Introduction Mrs Taylor says there are two traditions of women—the Madonna, and the Dreaming Woman. The latter is always, the former never, the   30
artist.—Which explains, I suppose, why women-artists do not sing maternity. Mrs Taylor represents the Dreaming Woman of Today, and she is almost unique in her position, when all the women who are not exclusively mothers are suffragists or reformers. Unfortunately, Mrs Taylor has begun to dream of her past life and of herself very   35
absorbedly, and to tell her dreams in symbols which are not always illuminating. She is esoteric. Her symbols do not show what they stand for of themselves: they are cousins of that Celtic and French form of symbolism* which says "Let x = the winds of passion and y = the yearning of the soul for love: 40

> Now the dim, white petalled y
> Draws dimly over the pallid atmosphere
> The scalded kisses of x."

Mrs Taylor has begun the same dodge.

5

> "Since from the subtle silk of agony
> Our lamentable veils of flesh are spun."*

Subtle silk of agony may claim to sound well, but to me it is meaningless.

But I read you the "Prologue of the Dreaming Women,"* which
10 surely is haunting.

How dare a woman, a woman, sister of Suffragists and lady doctors, how dare she breathe such a thing.

But Mrs Taylor is bolder still. Listen to the "Epilogue of the Dreaming Women."*

15 It is, I think, a very significant poem, to think over, and to think of again when one reads "Mrs Bull."*

But these are not Fiammetta. They are her creed. Her idiosyncrasies are in the sonnets, which, upon close acquaintance, are as interesting, more interesting far to trace, than a psychological novel. I read you only
20 one, number XVIII.*

Some of these sonnets are very fine: they stand apart in an age of "Open road" and Empire thumping verse.*

THE FUTURE OF THE NOVEL
[SURGERY FOR THE NOVEL—OR A BOMB]

Supplementary note on the text

See Note on the texts, pp. 130:1. Additional silent emendations are the following:
'*Babbitt*' has been corrected from DHL's '*Babbit*'.

TS and Per put book titles in double quotation marks; but DHL wrote (and A1 printed) in italics.

The Future of the Novel
[Surgery for the Novel—Or a Bomb]*

You talk about the future of the baby, little cherub, when he's in his cradle cooing: and it's a romantic, glamorous subject. You also talk, with the parson, about the future of the wicked old grandfather who is at last lying on his death-bed. And there again you have a subject for much vague emotion, chiefly of fear this time.

How do we feel about the novel? Do we bounce with joy thinking of the wonderful novelistic days ahead? Or do we grimly shake our heads and hope the wicked creature will be spared a little longer?

Is the novel on his death-bed, old sinner? Or is he just toddling round his cradle, sweet little thing?

Let us have another look at him, before we decide.*

There he is, the monster with many faces, many branches to him like a tree: the modern novel. And he is almost dual like a Siamese twin. On the one hand, the pale-faced, high-browed, earnest novel which you have to take seriously: on the other, that smirking, rather plausible hussy, the popular novel.

Let us just for the moment feel the pulses of *Ulysses* and of Miss Dorothy Richardson and Monsieur Marcel Proust, on the earnest side of Briareus; on the other, the throb of *The Sheik* and Mr Zane Grey, and, if you will, Mr Robert Chambers* and the rest.

Is *Ulysses* in his cradle? Oh dear, what a grey face! And *Pointed Roofs*, are they a gay little toy for nice little girls? And M. Proust?

Alas, you can hear the death-rattle in their throats. They can hear it themselves. They are listening to it with acute interest, trying to discover whether the intervals are minor thirds or major fourths. Which is rather infantile, really.

So there you have the "serious" novel, dying in a very long-drawn-out fourteen-volume death-agony, and absorbedly, childishly interested in the phenomenon. "Did I feel a twinge in my little toe, or didn't I?" asks every character in Mr Joyce or Miss Richardson or Monsieur Proust. "Is the odour of my perspiration a blend of frankincense and orange pekoe and boot-blacking, or is it myrrh and bacon-fat and Shetland tweed?"

The audience round the death-bed gapes for the answer. And when, in a sepulchral tone, the answer comes at length, after hundreds of pages: "It is none of these, it is abysmal chloro-coryambasis,"* the audience quivers all over, and murmurs: "That's just how I feel myself."

5   Which is the dismal, long-drawn-out comedy of the death-bed of the serious novel. It is self-consciousness picked into such fine bits that the bits are most of them invisible, and you have to go by smell. Through thousands and thousands of pages Mr Joyce and Miss Richardson tear themselves to pieces, strip their smallest emotions to the finest threads, 10 till you feel you are sewed inside a wool mattress that is being slowly shaken up, and you are turning to wool along with the rest of the woollyness.

It's awful. And it's childish. It really is childish, after a certain age, to be absorbedly self-conscious. One has to be self-conscious at seventeen: 15 still a little self-conscious at twenty-seven; but if we are going it strong at thirty-seven, then it is a sign of arrested development, nothing else. And if it is still continuing at forty-seven, it is obvious senile precocity.

And there's the serious novel: senile precocious. Absorbedly, chil-dishly concerned with *What I am*. "I am this, I am that, I am the other. My 20 reactions are such, and such, and such. And oh Lord, if I liked to watch myself closely enough, if I liked to analyse my feelings, minutely, as I unbutton my pants, instead of saying crudely I unbuttoned them, then I could go on to a million pages, instead of a thousand. In fact, the more I come to think of it, it is gross, it is uncivilised bluntly to say: I unbuttoned 25 my pants. After all, the absorbing adventure of it! Which button did I begin with?—?" etc. etc.

The people in the serious novels so absorbedly concerned with themselves and what they feel and don't feel, and how they react to every mortal trouser-button; and their audience as frenziedly absorbed in the 30 application of the author's discoveries to their own reactions; "that's me! that's exactly it! I'm just *finding* myself in this book!"—why, this is more than death-bed, it is almost *post mortem* behaviour.

Some convulsion or cataclysm will have to get the serious novel out of its self-consciousness. The last great war made it worse. What's to be 35 done?

Because, poor thing, it is really young yet. The novel has never become fully adult. It has never quite grown to years of discretion. It has always youthfully hoped for the best, and felt rather sorry for itself on the last page. Which is just childish.

40 The childishness has become very long-drawn-out. So very many

adolescents who drag their adolescence on into their forties and their fifties and their sixties.

There needs some sort of a surgical operation, somewhere.

Then the popular novels—the *Sheiks* and *Babbitts*° and Zane Greys. They are just as self-conscious, only they do have more illusions 5 about themselves. The heroines do think they are lovelier, and more fascinating, and purer. The heroes do see themselves more heroic, braver, more chivalrous, more fetching. The mass of the populace "find themselves" in the popular novels.

But nowadays it's a funny sort of self they find. A Sheik with a whip 10 up his sleeve, and a heroine with weals on some part of her anatomy: but adored in the end, adored, the whip out of sight, but the weals still faintly visible on the unmentionable part of her anatomy.°

It's a funny sort of self they discover in the popular novels. And the essential moral, of *If Winter Comes*° for example, is so shaky. "The 15 gooder you are, the worse it is for you, poor you, oh poor you. Don't you be so blimey good, it's not good enough." Or *Babbitt*: "Go on, you make your pile, and then pretend you're too good for it. Put it over the rest of the dirty grabbers that way. They're only pleased with themselves when they've made their pile. You go one better." 20

Always the same sort of baking-powder gas to make you rise: the soda counteracting the cream of tartar, and the tartar counteracted by the soda. Sheik heroines with whipped posteriors, wildly adored. Babbitts with solid fortunes, weeping from self-pity. Winter-Comes heroes as good as pie, hauled off to gaol. *Moral*: Don't be too good 25 because you'll go to gaol for it. *Moral*: Don't feel sorry for yourself till you've made your pile and don't need to feel sorry for yourself. *Moral*: Don't let him adore you till he's whipped you into it. Then you'll be partners in mild crime as well as in holy matrimony.

Which again is childish. Adolescence which *can't* grow up. Got into 30 the self-conscious rut and going crazy, quite crazy in it. Carrying on their adolescence into middle age and old age, like the loony Cleopatra in *Dombey and Son*, murmuring "Rose-coloured curtains—"° with her dying breath, old hag.

The Future of the Novel. Poor old novel, it's in a rather dirty, messy 35 tight corner. And it's either got to get over the wall, or knock a hole through it.

In other words, it's got to grow up. Put away childish things° like: "Do I love the girl or don't I?"—"Am I pure and sweet or aren't I?"—"Do I unbutton my pants from the left or from the right?"—"Did 40

my mother ruin my life by refusing to drink the cocoa which my bride had boiled for her?" These questions, and their answers, don't really interest *me* any more, though the world still goes sawing them over. I simply don't care whether I love the girl or not, whether I'm pure or
5   impure, according to government standards, whether I unbutton my pants with my left hand or my right, or what my mother feels about me. I don't give a damn for any of these things any more: though I used to.

In short, the purely emotional and self-analytical stunts are played out in me. I'm finished. I'm deaf to the whole band. I'm blind to the
10   whole blooming circus.

But I'm neither blasé nor cynical, for all that. I'm just interested in something else.

Supposing a bomb were put under this whole scheme of things, what would we be after? What feelings do we want to carry through, into the
15   next epoch? What feelings will carry us through? What is the underlying impulse in us that will provide the motive-power for a new state of things, when this democratic-industrial-lovey-dovey-darling-take-me-to-mammy state of things is bust?

What next? That's what interests me. *What now!* is no fun any more.
20   If you like to look in the past for *What-next?* books, you can find the little early novels by Saint Matthew, Saint Mark, Saint Luke and Saint John, called the Gospels. But these are novels with a clue for the future, a new impulse, a new motive, a new inspiration. They don't care about how it *is* just now, or how it *was* in the past: indifferent entirely to
25   *Main Street* and *Winter Coming* and *Sheiks* and *Scarlet Pimpernels.*° What they want is to put a new impulse into the world.

And they are little novels, in the highest sense. You can't deny it.°

Plato's Dialogues,° too, are queer little novels.
30   It seems to me it was the greatest pity in the world, when philosophy and fiction got split. They used to be one, right from the days of myth. Then they went and parted, like a nagging married couple, with Aristotle and Thomas Aquinas and that beastly Kant.° So the novel went sloppy, and philosophy went abstract-dry. The two should
35   come together again, in the novel. And we get modern kind of gospels, and modern myths, and a new way of understanding.

You've got to find a new impulse for new things, in mankind. And it's really fatal to find it through abstraction. Even in the Gospels there is rather too much sermon. Blessed are X, Y, and Z.°—I don't care
40   about X, Y, and Z. Let me see Tom, Dick, and Harry, each *in propria*

*persona,** being blessed. Let me see if Tom is blessed when he's being meek, or whether he's more blessed when he's being haughty. Those X's in the Beatitudes won't do. X may be all right when he's poor in spirit, but Jack is detestable in the same shoes.

No no, philosophy, and religion, they've both gone too far on the algebraical tack; let X stand for sheep and Y for goats: then X − Y = Heaven and X + Y = Earth and Y − X = Hell.

Thank you! But what coloured shirt does X have on?

And novels have gone too far on the emotional tack. In novels people always sit down and suffer their feelings, or sit down and enjoy 'em. They never say: "Let's get up and change 'em."

No, it's only the novels like the four Gospels, or the picaresque Acts of the Apostles, or Augustine's Confessions, or Religio Medici* that really try to make a great change in feeling, to get on into something really new. And these do stumble a bit among X's, Y's, and Z's.

The novel has got a future. Its future is to take the place of gospels, philosophies, and the present-day novel as we know it. It's got to have the courage to tackle new propositions without using abstractions; it's got to present us with new, really new feelings, a whole new line of emotion, which will get us out of the old emotional rut. Instead of snivelling about what is and has been, or inventing new sensations in the old line, it's got to break a way through, like a hole in a wall. And the public will scream and say it is sacrilege: because, of course, when you've been jammed for a long time in a tight corner, you get really used to its stuffiness and its tightness, till you find it absolutely stinkingly cosy; and then, of course you're horrified when you see a new glaring hole in what was your cosy wall. You're horrified. You back away from the cold stream of fresh air as if it was killing you.

But gradually first one and then another of the sheep filters through the gap, and finds a new world outside.

A BRITISHER HAS A WORD WITH AN EDITOR

A Britisher Has a Word With an Editor

In October's POETRY,* the Editor tells what a real tea-party she had in Britain, among the poets: not a Bostonian one,* either.

But she, alas, has to throw the dregs of her tea-cup in the faces of her hosts. She wonders whether British poets will have anything very 5 essential to say, as long as the King remains, and the "oligarchic social system" continues. The poor King, casting a damper on poetry! And this about oligarchies is good, from an American.

"In England I found no such evidence of athletic sincerity in artistic experiment, of vitality and variety and—yes!—(YES!!) beauty, in 10 artistic achievement, as I get from the poets of our own land."

YANKEE DOODLE, KEEP IT UP.

As for that "worthless dude" George IV, what poet* could possibly have flourished under his contemptible régime? Harriet, look in the history book, and see. 15

Oh what might not Milton have been, if he'd written under Calvin Coolidge!*

ART AND MORALITY

Supplementary note on the text

See Note on the texts, pp. 130–1. Additional silent emendations are the following:

Some details of DHL's hand were misinterpreted by typists, thus producing inconsistencies in the printed texts: DHL occasionally began 'kodak' with a capital letter or 'God' appears to be written with a lower-case 'g', but his most usual form in both cases ('kodak', 'God') has been used throughout; A1 printed the first as 'Kodak'. A1 printed 'All-Seeing' for DHL's 'All-seeing'.

Art and Morality

It is part of the common clap-trap, that "art is immoral." Behold everywhere artists running to put on jazz underwear, to demoralise themselves; or at least, to débourgeoiser themselves.*

For the bourgeois is supposed to be the fount of morality. Myself, I have found artists far more morally finicky.

Anyhow, what has a water-pitcher and six insecure apples on a crumpled tablecloth got to do with bourgeois morality? Yet I notice that most people, who have not learnt the trick of being arty, feel a real moral repugnance for a Cézanne* still-life. They think it is not *right*.

For them, it isn't.

Yet how can they feel, as they do, that it is subtly *immoral*?

The very same design, if it was humanised, and the tablecloth was a draped nude and the water-pitcher a nude semi-draped, weeping over the draped one, would instantly become highly moral. Why?

Perhaps from painting better than from any other art we can realise the subtlety of the distinction between what is dumbly *felt* to be moral, and what is felt to be immoral. The moral instinct of* the man in the street.

But instinct is largely habit. The moral instinct of the man in the street is largely an emotional defence of an old habit.

Yet what can there be, in a Cézanne still-life, to rouse the aggressive moral instinct of the man in the street? What ancient habit in man do these six apples and a water-pitcher succeed in hindering?

A water-pitcher that isn't so very much like a water-pitcher, apples that aren't very appley, and a tablecloth that's not particularly much of a tablecloth. I could do better myself!

Probably! But then, why not dismiss the picture as a poor attempt? Whence this anger, this hostility? The derisive resentment?

Six apples, a pitcher, and a tablecloth can't suggest improper *behaviour*. They don't—not even to a Freudian. If they did, the man in the street would feel much more at home with them.

Where, then, does the immorality come in? Because come in it does.

163

Because of a very curious habit that civilised man has been forming
down the whole course of civilisation, and in which he is now hard-
boiled. The slowly-formed habit of seeing just as the photographic
camera sees.

5   You may say, the object reflected on the retina is *always* photographic.
It may be. I doubt it. But whatever the image on the retina may be, it is
rarely, even now, the photographic image of the object which is actually
taken in by the man who sees the object. He does not, even now, see for
himself. He sees what the kodak* has taught him to see. And man,

10 try as he may, is not a kodak.

When a child sees a man, what does the child *take in*, as an impression?
Two eyes, a nose, a mouth of teeth, two straight legs, two straight arms: a
sort of hieroglyph, which the human child has used through all the ages,
to represent man. At least, the old hieroglyph was still in use when I was a

15 child.

Is this what the child actually *sees*?

If you mean by seeing, consciously registering, then this is what the
child actually sees. The photographic image may be there all right, upon
the retina. But there the child leaves it: outside the door, as it were.

20 Through many ages, mankind has been striving to register the image
on the retina *as it is*: no more glyphs and hieroglyphs. We'll have the real
objective reality.

And we have succeeded. As soon as we succeed, the kodak is invented,
to prove our success. Could lies come out of a black box, into which

25 nothing but light had entered? Impossible! It takes life to tell a lie.

Colour also, which primitive man cannot really *see*, is now seen by us,
and fitted to the spectrum.

Eureka! We have seen it, with our own eyes.

When we see a red cow, we see a red cow. We are quite sure of it,

30 because the unimpeachable kodak sees exactly the same.

But supposing we had all of us been born blind, and had to get our
image of a red cow by touching her, and smelling her, hearing her moo,
and "feeling" her. Whatever should we think of her? Whatever sort of
image should we have her, in our dark minds? Something very

35 different, surely!

As vision developed towards the kodak, man's idea of himself
developed towards the snapshot. Primitive man simply didn't know *what*
he was: he was always half in the dark. But we have learned to see, and
each of us has a complete kodak-idea of himself.

40 You take a snap of your sweetheart, in the field among the buttercups,

smiling tenderly at the red cow with a calf, and dauntlessly offering a cabbage-leaf.

Awfully nice, and absolutely "real." There is your sweetheart, complete in herself, enjoying a sort of absolute objective reality: complete, perfect, all her surroundings contributing to her, incontest- 5 able. She is really "a picture."

This is the habit we have formed: of visualising *everything*. Each man to himself is a picture. That is, he is a complete little objective reality, complete in himself, existing by himself, absolutely, in the middle of the picture. All the rest is just setting, background. To every man, to every 10 woman, the universe is just a setting to the absolute little picture of himself, herself.

This has been the development of the conscious ego in man, through several thousand years: since Greece first broke the spell of "darkness." Man has learnt to *see* himself. So now, he *is* what he sees. He 15 makes himself in his own image.

Previously, even in Egypt, men had not learned to *see straight*. They fumbled in the dark, and didn't quite know where they were, or what they were. Like men in a dark room, they only *felt* their own existence surging in the darkness of other existences. 20

We, however, have learned to see ourselves for what we are, as the sun sees us. The kodak bears witness. We see as the All-seeing Eye sees, with the universal vision. And we *are* what is seen: each man to himself an identity, an isolated absolute, corresponding with a universe of isolated absolutes. A picture! A kodak snap, in a universal film of 25 snaps.

We have achieved universal vision. Even God could not see *differently* from what we see: only more extensively, like a telescope, or more intensively, like a microscope. But the same vision. A vision of images which are real, and each one limited to itself. 30

We behave as if we had got to the bottom of the sack, and seen the Platonic Idea with our own eyes, in all its photographically-developed perfection, lying in the bottom of the sack of the universe. Our own ego!

The identifying of ourselves with the visual image of ourselves has 35 become an instinct; the habit is already old. The picture of me, the me that is *seen*, is me.

As soon as we are supremely satisfied about it, somebody starts to upset us. Comes Cézanne with his pitcher and his apples, which not only are not life-like, but are a living lie. The kodak will prove it. 40

The kodak will take all sorts of snaps, misty, atmospheric, sun-dazed, dancing—all quite different. Yet the image is *the* image. There is only more or less sun, more or less vapor, more or less light and shade.

5   The All-seeing Eye sees with every degree of intensity and in every possible kind of mood; Giotto, Titian, El Greco, Turner, all so different, yet all the true image in the All-seeing Eye.

This Cézanne still-life, however, is *contrary* to the All-seeing Eye. Apples, to the eye of God, could not look like that, nor could a

10   tablecloth, nor could a pitcher. So, it is *wrong*.

Because man, since he grew out of a personal God, has taken over to himself all the attributes of the Personal godhead. It is the all-seeing human eye which is now the Eternal Eye.

And if apples don't *look* like that, in any light or circumstance, or

15   under any mood, then they shouldn't be painted like that.

Oh là-là-là! The apples *are* just like that, to me! cries Cézanne. They *are* like that, no matter what they look like.

Apples are always apples! says Vox Populi, Vox Dei.*

Sometimes they're a sin, sometimes they're a knock on the head,

20   sometimes they're a bellyache, sometimes they're part of a pie, sometimes they're sauce for the goose—

And you can't see a bellyache, neither can you see a sin, neither can you see a knock on the head. So paint the apple in these aspects, and you get—probably, or approximately—a Cézanne still-life.

25   What an apple looks like to an urchin, to a thrush, to a browsing cow, to Sir Isaac Newton, to a caterpillar, to a hornet, to a mackerel who finds one bobbing on the sea, I leave you to conjecture. But the All-seeing must have mackerel's eyes, as well as man's.

And this is the immorality in Cézanne: he begins to see more than

30   the All-seeing Eye of humanity can possibly see, kodak-wise. If you can see in the apple a bellyache and a knock on the head, and paint these in the image, among the prettyness, then it is the death of the kodak and the movies, and must be immoral.

It's all very well talking about decoration and illustration, significant

35   form, or tactile values, or plastique, or movement or space-composition or colour-mass relations,* afterwards. You might as well force your guest to eat the menu card, at the end of the dinner.

What art has got to do, and will go on doing, is to reveal things in their different relationships. That is to say, you've got to see in the

40   apple the bellyache, Sir Isaac's knock on the cranium, the vast moist

wall through which the insect bores to lay her eggs in the middle, and the untasted unknown quality which Eve saw hanging on a tree. Add to this the glaucous glimpse that the mackerel gets as he comes to the surface, and Fantin Latour's apples° are no more to you than enamelled rissoles.

The true artist doesn't substitute immorality for morality. On the contrary, he *always* substitutes a finer morality for a grosser. And as soon as you see a finer morality, the grosser becomes relatively immoral.

The universe is like Father Ocean, a stream of all things slowly moving. We move, and the rock of ages° moves. And since we move and move forever, in no discernible direction, there is no centre to the movement, as far as we can see. To us, the centre shifts at every moment. Even the pole-star ceases to sit on the pole. Allons!° there is no road before us!

There is nothing to do, but to maintain a true relationship to the things we move with and amongst and against. The apple, like the moon, has still an unseen side. The movement of Ocean will turn it round to us, or us to it.

There is nothing man can do, but maintain himself in true relationship to his contiguous universe. An ancient Rameses° can sit in stone absolute, absolved from visual contact, deep in the silent ocean of sensual contact. Michael Angelo's Adam can open his eyes for the first time, and see the old man in the skies, objectively. Turner° can tumble into the open mouth of the objective universe of light, till we see nothing but his disappearing heels. As the stream carries him, each in his own relatedness, each one differently, so a man must go through life.

Each thing, living or unliving, streams in its own odd, intertwining flux, and nothing, not even man nor the God of man, nor anything that man has thought or felt or known, is fixed or abiding. All moves. And nothing is true, or good, or right, except in its own living relatedness to its own circumambient universe; to the things that are in the stream with it.

Design, in art, is a recognition of the relation between various things, various elements in the creative flux. You can't *invent* a design. You recognise it, in the fourth dimension.° That is, with your blood and your bones, even more than with your eyes.

Egypt had a wonderful relation to a vast living universe, only dimly visual in its reality. The dim eye-vision and the powerful blood-feeling of the negro African, even today, gives us strange images, which our eyes can hardly see, but which we know are surpassing. The big, silent statue of Rameses is like a drop of water, hanging through the centuries in dark suspense, and never static. The African fetish-statues have no

5   movement, visually represented. Yet one little motionless wooden figure stirs more than all the Parthenon frieze.* It sits in the place where no kodak can snap it.

As for us, we have our kodak-vision, all in bits that group or jig. Like the movies, that jerk but never move.* An endless shifting and

10   rattling together of isolated images, "snaps," miles of them, all of them jigging, but each one utterly incapable of movement or change, in itself. A kaleidoscope of inert images, mechanically shaken.

And this is our vaunted "consciousness," made up, really, of inert visual images and little else: like the cinematograph.

15   Let Cézanne's apples go rolling off the table for ever. They live by their own laws, in their own ambiente,* and not by the law of the kodak—or of man. They are *casually* related to man. But to those apples, man is by no means the absolute.

A new relationship between ourselves and the universe means a new

20   morality. Taste the unsteady apples of Cézanne, and the nailed-down apples of Fantin Latour are apples of Sodom. If the *status quo* were paradise, it would indeed be a sin to taste the new apples. But since the *status quo* is much more prison than paradise, we can go ahead.

MORALITY AND THE NOVEL

Supplementary note on the text

See Note on the texts, pp. 130–1. An additional silent emendation is the following: A1 printed 'van Gogh' for DHL's 'Van Gogh'.

Morality and the Novel

The business of art is to reveal the relation between man and his circumambient universe, at the living moment. As mankind is always struggling in the toils of old relationships, art is always ahead of the "times," which themselves are always far in the rear of the living 5 moment.

When Van Gogh paints sunflowers,* he reveals, or achieves, the vivid relation between himself, as man, and the sunflower, as sunflower, at that quick moment of time. His painting does not represent the sunflower itself. We shall never know what the sunflower itself is. 10 And the camera will *visualise* the sunflower far more perfectly than Van Gogh can.

The vision on the canvas is a third thing, utterly intangible and inexplicable, the offspring of the sunflower itself and Van Gogh himself. The vision on the canvas is forever incommensurable with the 15 canvas, or the paint, or Van Gogh as a human organism, or the sunflower as a botanical organism. You cannot weigh nor measure nor even describe the vision on the canvas. It exists, to tell the truth, only in the much-debated fourth dimension.* In dimensional space it has no existence. 20

It is a revelation of the perfected relation, at a certain moment, between a man and a sunflower. It is neither man-in-the-mirror nor flower-in-the-mirror, neither is it above or below or across anything. It is in-between everything, in the fourth dimension.

And this perfected relation between man and his circumambient 25 universe is life itself, for mankind. It has the fourth-dimensional quality of eternity and perfection. Yet it is momentaneous.

Man and the sunflower both pass away from the moment, in the process of forming a new relationship. The relation between all things changes from day to day, in a subtle stealth of change. Hence art, which 30 reveals or attains to another perfect relationship, will be forever new.

At the same time, that which exists in the non-dimensional space of pure relationship, is deathless, lifeless, and eternal. That is, it gives us the *feeling* of being beyond life or death. We say an Assyrian lion or an

Egyptian hawk's-head* "lives." What we really mean is that it is beyond life, and therefore beyond death. It gives us that feeling. And there is something inside us which must also be beyond life and beyond death, since that "feeling" which we get from an Assyrian lion or an
5   Egyptian hawk's-head is so infinitely precious to us. As the evening star, that spark of pure relation between night and day, has been precious to man since time began.

If we think about it, we find that our life *consists in* this achieving of a pure relationship between ourselves and the living universe about us.
10 This is how I "save my soul," by accomplishing a pure relationship between me and another person, me and other people, me and a nation, me and a race of men, me and the animals, me and the trees or flowers, me and the earth, me and the skies and sun and stars, me and the moon; an infinity of pure relations, big and little, like the stars of the
15 sky: that makes our eternity, for each one of us. Me and the timber I am sawing, the lines of force I follow, me and the dough I knead for bread, me and the very motion with which I write, me and the bit of gold I have got. This, if we knew it, is our life and our eternity: the subtle, perfected relation between me and my whole circumambient universe.

20 And morality is that delicate, forever trembling and changing *balance* between me and my circumambient universe, which precedes and accompanies a true relatedness.

Now here we see the beauty and the great value of the novel. Philosophy, religion, science, they are all of them busy nailing things
25 down, to get a stable equilibrium. Religion, with its nailed down One God, who says *Thou shalt, Thou shan't*, and hammers home every time; philosophy, with its fixed ideas; science, with its "laws": they all of them, all the time, want to nail us on to some tree or other.

But the novel, no. The novel is the highest complex of subtle inter-
30 relatedness that man has discovered. Everything is true in its own time, place, circumstance, and untrue outside of its own place, time, circumstance. If you try to nail anything down, in the novel, either it kills the novel, or the novel gets up and walks away with the nail.

Morality in the novel is the trembling instability of the balance.
35 When the novelist puts his thumb in the scale, to pull down the balance to his own predilection, that is immorality.

The modern novel tends to become more and more immoral, as the novelist tends to press his thumb heavier and heavier in the pan: either on the side of love, pure love: or on the side of licentious "freedom."
40 The novel is not, as a rule, immoral because the novelist has any

dominant *idea*, or *purpose*. The immorality lies in the novelist's helpless, unconscious predilection. Love is a great emotion. But if you set out to write a novel, and you yourself are in the throes of the great predilection for love, love as the supreme, the only emotion worth living for, then you will write an immoral novel.   5

Because *no* emotion is supreme, or exclusively worth living for. *All* emotions go to the achieving of a living relationship between a human being and the other human being or creature or thing he becomes purely related to.

All emotions, including love and hate, and rage and tenderness, go to   10
the adjusting of the oscillating, unestablished balance between two people who amount to anything. If the novelist puts his thumb in the pan, for love, tenderness, sweetness, peace, then he commits an immoral act: he *prevents* the possibility of a pure relationship, a pure relatedness, the only thing that matters: and he makes inevitable the   15
horrible reaction, when he lets his thumb go, towards hate and brutality, cruelty and destruction.

Life is so made, that opposites sway about a trembling centre of balance. The sins of the fathers are visited on the children.* If the fathers drag down the balance on the side of love, peace, and   20
production, then in the third or fourth generation the balance will swing back violently to hate, rage, and destruction. We must balance as we go.

And of all the art forms, the novel most of all demands the trembling and oscillating of the balance. The "sweet" novel is more falsified, and   25
therefore more immoral than the blood and thunder novel.

The same with the smart and smudgily cynical novel, which says it doesn't matter what you do, because one thing is as good as another, anyhow, and prostitution is just as much "life" as anything else.

This misses the point entirely. A thing isn't life, just because   30
somebody does it. This the artist ought to know, perfectly well. The ordinary bank-clerk buying himself a new straw hat isn't "life" at all: it is just existence, quite all right, like everyday dinners: but not "life."

By life, we mean something that gleams, that has the fourth dimensional quality. If the bank-clerk feels really piquant about his hat,   35
if he establishes a lively relation with it, and goes out of the shop with the new straw on his head, a changed man, be-aureoled, then that is life.

The same with the prostitute. If a man establishes a living relation to her, if only for one moment, then it is life. But if he *doesn't*: if it is just 40 money and function, then it is no life, but sordidness, and a betrayal of living.

If a novel reveals true and vivid relationships, it is a moral work, no matter what the relationships may consist in. If the novelist *honours* the relationship in itself, it will be a great novel.

But there are so many relationships which are not real. When the man in *Crime and Punishment** murders the old woman for sixpence, although it is *actual* enough, it is never quite real. The balance between the murderer and the old woman is gone entirely, it is only a mess. It is actuality, but it is not "life," in the living sense.

The popular novel, on the other hand, dishes up a rechauffé of old relationships: *If Winter Comes.** And old relationships dished up are likewise immoral. Even a magnificent painter like Raphael does nothing more than dress up in gorgeous new dresses relationships which have already been experienced. And this gives a gluttonous kind of pleasure to the mass: a voluptuousness, a wallowing. For centuries, men say of their voluptuously ideal woman: "She is a Raphael Madonna." And women are only just learning to take it as an insult.

A new relation, a new relatedness hurts somewhat in the attaining: and will always hurt. So life will always hurt. Because real voluptuousness lies in re-acting old relationships, and at the best, getting an alcoholic sort of pleasure out of it, slightly depraving.

Each time we strive to a new relation, with anyone or anything, it is bound to hurt somewhat. Because it means the struggle with and the displacing of old connections, and this is never pleasant. And moreover, between living things at least, an adjustment means also a fight; for each party, inevitably, must "seek its own" in the other, and be denied. When, in the two parties, each of them seeks his own, her own, absolutely, then it is a fight to the death. And this is true of the thing called "passion." On the other hand, when, of the two parties, one yields utterly to the other, this is called sacrifice, and it also means death. So The Constant Nymph died of her eighteen-months of constancy.*

It isn't the nature of nymphs to be constant. She should have been constant in her nymph-hood. And it is unmanly to accept sacrifices. He should have abided by his own manhood.

There is, however, the third thing, which is neither sacrifice nor fight to the death: when each seeks only the true relatedness to the other. Each must be true to himself, herself, his own manhood, her own womanhood, and let the relationship work out of itself. This means courage above all things: and then discipline. Courage to accept the life-thrust from within oneself, and from the other person. Discipline, not to exceed oneself any more than one can help. Courage, when one has exceeded oneself, to accept the fact and not whine about it.

Obviously, to read a really new novel will *always* hurt, to some extent. There will always be resistance. The same with new pictures, new music. You may judge of their reality by the fact that they do arouse a certain resistance, and compel, at length, a certain acquiescence.

The great relationship, for humanity, will always be the relation between man and woman. The relation between man and man, woman and woman, parent and child, will always be subsidiary.

And the relation between man and woman will change forever, and will forever be the new central clue to human life. It is the *relation itself* which is the quick and the central clue to life, not the man, nor the woman, nor the children that result from the relationship, as a contingency.

It is no use thinking you can put a stamp on the relation between man and woman, to keep it in the *status quo*. You can't. You might as well try to put a stamp on the rainbow of the rain.

As for the bond of love, better put it off when it galls. It is an absurdity, to say that men and women *must love*. Men and women will be forever subtly and changingly related to one another, no need to yoke them with any "bond" at all. The only morality is to have man true to his manhood, woman to her womanhood, and let the relationship form of itself, in all honour. For it is, to each, *life itself*.

If we are going to be moral, let us refrain from driving pegs through anything, either through each other or through the third thing, the relationship, which is forever the Ghost of both of us. Every sacrificial crucifixion needs five pegs, four short ones and a long one, each one an abomination. But when you try to nail down the relationship itself, and write over it *Love* instead of *This is the King of the Jews*, then you can go on putting in nails forever. Even Jesus called it the Holy Ghost,* to show you that you can't lay salt on its tail.

The novel is a perfect medium for revealing to us the changing rainbow of our living relationships. The novel can help us to live, as nothing else can: no didactic Scripture, anyhow. If the novelist keeps his thumb out of the pan.

But when the novelist *has* his thumb in the pan, the novel becomes an unparalleled perverter of men and women. To be compared only, perhaps, to that great mischief of sentimental hymns like *Lead Kindly Light!** which have helped to rot the marrow in the bones of the present generation.

THE NOVEL

The Novel

Somebody says the novel is doomed. Somebody else says it is the green bay tree getting greener. Everybody says something, so why shouldn't I! Mr Santayana° sees the modern novel expiring because it is getting so thin;——which means, Mr Santayana is bored.   5

I am rather bored myself. It becomes harder and harder to read the *whole* of any modern novel. One reads a bit, and knows the rest; or else one doesn't want to know any more.

This is sad. But again, I don't think it's the novel's fault. Rather the novelists'.   10

You can put anything you like in a novel. So why do people *always* go on putting the same thing? Why is the *vol au vent* always chicken! Chicken *vol au vents* may be the rage. But who sickens first shouts first for something else.

The novel is a great discovery: far greater than Galileo's telescope or   15
somebody else's wireless. The novel is the highest form of human expression so far attained. Why? Because it is so incapable of the absolute.

In a novel, everything is relative to everything else, if that novel is art at all. There may be didactic bits, but they aren't the novel. And the author   20
may have a didactic "purpose" up his sleeve. Indeed most great novelists have, as Tolstoi had his Christian-socialism, and Hardy his pessimism, and Flaubert his intellectual desperation. But even a didactic purpose so wicked as Tolstoi's or Flaubert's cannot put to death the novel.

You can tell me, Flaubert had a "philosophy," not a "purpose." But   25
what is a novelist's philosophy but a purpose on a rather higher level? And since every novelist who amounts to anything has a philo-sophy—even Balzac—any novel of importance has a purpose. If only the "purpose" be large enough, and not at outs with the passional inspiration.   30

Vronsky sinned, did he? But also the sinning was a consummation devoutly to be wished.° The novel makes that obvious: in spite of old Leo Tolstoi. And the would-be-pious Prince in *Resurrection* is a muff,° with his piety that nobody wants or believes in.

There you have the greatness of the novel itself. It won't *let* you tell
didactic lies, and put them over. Nobody in the world is anything but
delighted when Vronsky gets Anna Karenin. Then what about the
sin?—Why, when you look at it, all the tragedy comes from Vronsky's
5   and Anna's fear of *society*. The monster was social, not phallic at all.
They couldn't live in the pride of their sincere passion, and spit in
Mother Grundy's eye.* And that, that cowardice, was the real
"sin." The novel makes it obvious, and knocks all old Leo's teeth out.
"As an officer, I am still useful. But as a man, I am a ruin," says
10 Vronsky—or words to that effect. Well what a skunk, collapsing as a
man and a male, and remaining merely as a social instrument; an
"officer," God love us!—merely because people at the opera turn their
backs on him!*—As if people's backs weren't preferable to their
faces, anyhow!
15 And old Leo tries to make out, it was all because of the phallic sin.
Old liar! Because where would any of Leo's books be, without the
phallic splendour? And then to blame the column of blood, which really
gave him all his life riches! The Judas! Cringe to a mingy, bloodless
Society, and try to dress up that dirty old Mother Grundy in a new
20 bonnet and face-powder of Christian-Socialism. Brothers indeed!
Sons of a castrated Father!
The novel itself gives Vronsky a kick in the behind, and knocks old
Leo's teeth out, and leaves us to learn.
It is such a bore that nearly all great novelists have a didactic
25 purpose, otherwise a philosophy, directly opposite to their passional
inspiration. In their passional inspiration, they are all phallic worshippers. From Balzac to Hardy, it is so. Nay, from Apuleius to E. M.
Forster. Yet all of them, when it comes to their philosophy, or what they
think-they-are, they are all crucified Jesuses. What a bore! And what a
30 burden for the novel to carry!
But the novel has carried it. Several thousands of thousands of
lamentable crucifixions of self-heroes and self-heroines. Even the silly
duplicity of *Resurrection*, and the wickeder duplicity of *Salammbô*, with
that flayed phallic Matho, tortured upon the Cross of a gilt
35 Princess.*
You can't fool the novel. Even with man crucified upon a woman: his
"dear cross." The novel will show you how dear she was: dear at any
price. And it will leave you with a bad taste of disgust against these
heroes who *turn* their women into a "dear cross," and *ask* for their own
40 crucifixion.

You can fool pretty nearly every other medium. You can make a poem pietistic, and still it will be a poem. You can write *Hamlet* in drama: if you wrote him in a novel, he'd be half comic, or a trifle suspicious: a suspicious character, like Dostoevsky's Idiot.* Somehow, you sweep the ground a bit too clear in the poem or the drama, and you let the human Word fly a bit too freely. Now in a novel there's always a tom-cat, a black tom-cat that pounces on the white dove of the Word, if the dove doesn't watch it; and there is a banana-skin to trip on; and you know there is a water-closet on the premises. All these things help to keep the balance.

If, in Plato's Dialogues, somebody had suddenly stood on his head and given smooth Plato a kick in the wind, and set the whole school in an uproar, then Plato would have been put into a much truer relation to the universe. Or if, in the midst of the Timaeus, Plato had only paused to say: "And now, my dear Cleon*—(or whoever it was)—I have a belly-ache, and must retreat to the privy: this too is part of the Eternal Idea of man," then we never need have fallen so low as Freud.

And if, when Jesus told the rich man to take all he had and give it to the poor,* the rich man had replied: *"All right, old sport! You are poor, aren't you? Come on, I'll give you a fortune. Come on!"*—Then a great deal of snivelling and mistakenness would have been spared us all, and we might never have produced a Marx and a Lenin. If only Jesus had *accepted* the fortune!

Yes, it's a pity of pities that Matthew, Mark, Luke, and John didn't write straight novels. They did write novels; but a bit crooked. The Evangels are wonderful novels, by authors "with a purpose." Pity there's so much Sermon-on-the-Mounting.

> "Matthew, Mark, Luke, and John
> Went to bed with their breeches on!"—*

as every child knows. Ah, if only they'd taken them off!

Greater novels, to my mind, are the books of the Old Testament, Genesis, Exodus, Samuel, Kings, by authors whose purpose was so big, it didn't quarrel with their passional inspiration.* The purpose and the inspiration were almost one. Why, in the name of everything bad, the two ever should have got separated, is a mystery! But in the modern novel they are hopelessly divorced. When there *is* any inspiration there: to be divorced from.

This, then, is what is the matter with the modern novel. The modern

novelist is possessed, hag-ridden, by such a stale old "purpose," or
idea-of-himself, that his inspiration succumbs. Of course he denies
having any didactic purpose at all: because a purpose is supposed to be
like catarrh, something to be ashamed of. But he's got it.—They've all
5 got it: the same snivelling purpose.
   They're all little Jesuses in their own eyes, and their "purpose" is to
prove it. Oh Lord!—*Lord Jim! Sylvestre Bonnard! If Winter Comes! Main
Street! Ulysses! Pan!*—They are all pathetic or sympathetic or
antipathetic little Jesuses *accomplis* or *manqués*. And there is a
10 heroine who is always "pure," usually, nowadays, on the muck-heap!
Like the Green Hatted Woman. She is all the time at the feet of
Jesus, though her behaviour there may be misleading. Heaven knows
what the Saviour really makes of it: whether she's a Green Hat or a
Constant Nymph (eighteen months of constancy, and her heart
15 failed), or any of the rest of 'em. They are all, heroes and heroines,
novelists and she-novelists, little Jesuses or Jesusesses. They may be
wallowing in the mire: but then didn't Jesus harrow Hell! *A la bonne
heure!*
   Oh, they are all novelists with an idea of themselves! Which is a
20 "purpose," with a vengeance! For what a weary, false, sickening idea it
is nowadays! The novel gives them away. They can't fool the novel.
   Now really, it's time we left off insulting the novel any further. If
your purpose is to prove your own Jesus qualifications, and the thin
stream of your inspiration is "sin," then dry up, for the interest is dead.
25 *Life as it is!* What's the good of pretending that the lives of a set of
tuppenny Green Hats and Constant Nymphs is Life-as-it-is, when the
novel itself proves that all it amounts to is life as it is isn't life, but a sort
of everlasting and intricate and boring habit: of Jesus peccant and
Jesusa peccante.
30   These wearisome sickening little personal novels! After all, they
aren't novels at all. In every great novel, who is the hero all the time?
Not any of the characters, but some unnamed and nameless flame
behind them all. Just as God is the pivotal interest in the books of the
Old Testament. But just a trifle too intimate, too *frère et cochon,*
35 there. In the great novel, the felt but unknown flame stands behind all
the characters, and in their words and gestures there is a flicker of the
presence. If you are too *personal, too* human, the flicker fades out,
leaving you with something awfully lifelike, and as lifeless as most
people are.
40   We have to choose between the quick and the dead. The quick is

God-flame, in everything. And the dead is dead. In this room where I write, there is a little table that is dead: it doesn't even weakly exist. And there is a ridiculous little iron stove, which for some unknown reason is quick. And there is an iron wardrobe trunk, which for some still more mysterious reason is quick. And there are several books, whose mere corpus* is dead, utterly dead and non-existent. And there is a sleeping cat, very quick. And a glass lamp, that, alas, is dead.

What makes the difference? *Quien sabe!** But difference there is. And I *know* it.

And the sum and source of all quickness, we will call God. And the sum and total of all deadness we may call human.

And if one tries to find out, wherein the quickness of the quick lies, it is in a certain weird relationship between that which is quick and—I don't know; perhaps all the rest of things. It seems to consist in an odd sort of fluid, changing, grotesque or beautiful relatedness. That silly iron stove somehow *belongs*. Whereas this thin-shanked table doesn't belong. It is a mere disconnected lump, like a cut-off finger.

And now we see the great, great merits of the novel. It can't exist without being "quick." The ordinary unquick novel, even if it be a best seller, disappears into absolute nothingness, the dead burying their dead with surprising speed. For even the dead like to be tickled. But the next minute, they've forgotten both the tickling and the tickler.

Secondly, the novel contains no didactive absolute. All that is quick, and all that is said and done by the quick, is, in some way, godly. So that Vronsky's taking Anna Karenin we must count godly, since it is quick. And that Prince in *Resurrection*, following the convict girl, we must count dead. The convict train is quick and alive. But that would-be-expiatory Prince is as dead as lumber.

The novel itself lays down these laws for us, and we spend our time evading them. The man in the novel must be "quick." And this means one thing, among a host of unknown meaning: it means he must have a quick relatedness to all the other things in the novel: snow, bed-bugs, sunshine, the phallus, trains, silk-hats, cats, sorrow, people, food, diphtheria, fuchsias, stars, ideas, God, tooth-paste, lightning, and toilet-paper. He must be in quick relation to all these things. What he says and does must be relative to them all.

And this is why Pierre, for example, in *War and Peace,** is more dull and less quick than Prince André. Pierre is quite nicely related to ideas, tooth-paste, God, people, food, trains, silk-hats, sorrow, diphtheria, stars. But his relation to snow and sunshine, cats, lightning and the phallus, fuchsias and toilet-paper, is sluggish and mussy. He's not quick enough.

The really quick, Tolstoi loved to kill them off or muss them over.
5 Like a true Bolshevist. One can't help feeling Natasha is rather mussy and unfresh, married to that Pierre.

Pierre was what we call, "so human." Which means, "so limited." Men clotting together into social masses in order to limit their individual liabilities: this is humanity. And this is Pierre. And this is
10 Tolstoi, the philosopher with a very nauseating Christian-brotherhood idea of himself. Why limit man to a Christian-brotherhood? I myself, I could belong to the sweetest Christian-brotherhood one day, and ride after Attila with a raw beefsteak for my saddle-cloth,° to see the red cock crow in flame over all Christendom, next day.

15 And that is man! That, really, was Tolstoi. That, even, was Lenin, God in the machine of Christian-brotherhood, that hashes men up into social sausage-meat.

Damn all absolutes. Oh damn, damn, damn all absolutes! I tell you, no absolute is going to make the lion lie down with the lamb: unless,
20 like the limerick,° the lamb is inside.

> "They returned from the ride
> With lamb Leo inside
> And a smile on the face of the tiger!
> Sing fol-di-lol-lol!
25 > Fol-di-lol lol!
> Fol-di-lol-ol-di-lol-olly!"

For man, there is neither absolute nor absolution. Such things should be left to monsters like the right-angled triangle, which does only exist in the ideal consciousness. A man can't have a square on his
30 hypotenuse, let him try as he may.

Ay! Ay! Ay!—Man handing out absolutes to man, as if we were all books of geometry with axioms, postulates and definitions in front. God with a pair of compasses! Moses with a set-square! Man a geometric bifurcation, not even a radish!
35 Holy Moses!

"Honour thy father and thy mother!"—That's awfully cute! But supposing they are not honorable? How then, Moses?

Voice of thunder from Sinai:—"*Pretend to honour them!*"

"Love thy neighbour as thyself."°

Alas, my neighbour happens to be mean and detestable.

Voice of the lambent Dove, cooing: *"Put it over him, that you love him."*

Talk about the cunning of serpents!* I never saw even a serpent kissing his instinctive enemy.

Pfui! I wouldn't blacken my mouth, kissing my neighbour, who, I repeat, to me is mean and detestable.

Dove, go home!

The Goat and Compasses,* indeed!

Everything is relative. Every Commandment that ever issued out of the mouth of God or man, is strictly relative: adhering to the particular time, place and circumstance.

And this is the beauty of the novel; everything is true in its own relationship, and no further.

For the relatedness and interrelatedness of all things flows and changes and trembles like a stream, and like a fish in the stream the characters in the novel swim and drift and float and turn belly-up when they're dead.

So, if a character in a novel wants two wives—or three—or thirty: well, that is true of that man, at that time, in that circumstance. It may be true of other men, elsewhere and elsewhen. But to infer that all men at all times want two, three, or thirty wives; or that the novelist himself is advocating furious polygamy;* is just imbecility.

It has been just as imbecile to infer that, because Dante worshipped a remote Beatrice,* every man, all men, should go worshipping remote Beatrices.

And that wouldn't have been so bad, if Dante had put the thing in its true light. Why do we slur over the actual fact that Dante had a cosy bifurcated wife in his bed, and a family of lusty little Dantinos? Petrarch, with his Laura in the distance,* had *twelve* little legitimate Petrarchs of his own, between his knees. Yet all we hear is *Laura! Laura! Beatrice! Beatrice! Distance! Distance!*

What bunk! Why didn't Dante and Petrarch chant in chorus:

> "Oh be my spiritual concubine
>   Beatrice! |
>   Laura! |
> My old girl's got several babies that are mine,
> But *thou* be my spiritual concubine,
>   Beatrice! |
>   Laura! | ″

Then there would have been an honest relation between all the
bunch. Nobody grudges the gents their spiritual concubines. But
keeping a wife and family—twelve children—up one's sleeve, has
always been recognised as a dirty trick.

5   Which reveals how *immoral* the absolute is! Invariably keeping some
vital fact dark! Dishonorable!

Here we come upon the third essential quality of the novel. Unlike
the essay, the poem, the drama, the book of philosophy, or the scientific
treatise: all of which may beg the question, when they don't downright
10   filch it; the novel inherently is and must be:

    1. Quick.
    2. Interrelated in all its parts, vitally, organically.
    3. Honorable.

I call Dante's *Commedia** slightly dishonorable, with never a
15   mention of the cosy bifurcated wife, and the kids. And *War and Peace* I
call downright dishonorable, with that fat, diluted Pierre for a hero,
stuck up as preferable and desirable, when everybody knows that he
wasn't attractive, even to Tolstoi.

Of course Tolstoi, being a great creative artist, was true to his
20   characters. But being a man with a philosophy, he wasn't true to his
own character.

Character is a curious thing. It is the flame of a man, which burns
brighter or dimmer, bluer or yellower or redder, rising or sinking or
flaring according to the draughts of circumstance and the changing air
25   of life, changing itself continually, yet remaining one single, separate
flame, flickering in a strange world: unless it be blown out at last by too
much adversity.

If Tolstoi had looked into the flame of his own belly, he would have
seen that he didn't really like the fat, fuzzy Pierre, who was a poor tool,
30   after all. But Tolstoi was a personality even more than a character. And
a personality is a self-conscious *I am*: being all that is left in us of a
once-almighty Personal God. So being a personality and an almighty *I
am*, Leo proceeded deliberately to lionise that Pierre, who was a
domestic sort of house-dog.

35   Doesn't anybody call that dishonorable on Leo's part? He might just
as well have been true to *himself*! But no! His self-conscious personality
was superior to his own belly and knees, so he thought he'd improve on
himself, by creeping inside the skin of a lamb: the doddering old lion
that he was! Leo! León!*

Secretly, Leo worshipped the human male, man as a column of rapacious and living blood. He could hardly meet three lusty, roisterous young guardsmen in the street, without crying with envy: and ten minutes later, fulminating on them black oblivion and annihilation, utmost moral thunder-bolts.° 5

How boring, in a great man! And how boring, in a great nation like Russia, to let its old-Adam manhood° be so improved upon by these reformers, who all feel themselves short of something, and therefore live by spite, that at last there's nothing left but a lot of shells of men, improving themselves steadily emptier and emptier, till they 10 rattle with words and formulae, as if they'd swallowed the whole encyclopædia of socialism.

But wait! There is life in the Russians. Something new and strange will emerge out of their weird transmogrification into Bolshevists.°

When the lion swallows the lamb, fluff and all, he usually gets a pain, 15 and there's a rumpus. But when the lion tries to force himself down the throat of the huge and popular lamb—a nasty old sheep, really—then it's a phenomenon. Old Leo did it: wedged himself bit by bit down the throat of wooly Russia. And now out of the mouth of the bolshevist lambkin still waves an angry, mistaken, tufted leonine tail, like an 20 agitated exclamation mark.

Meanwhile it's a deadlock.

But what a dishonorable thing for that claw-biting little Leo to do! And in his novels you see him at it. So that the papery lips of *Resurrection* whisper: "*Alas! I would have been a novel. But Leo spoiled me.*" 25

Count Tolstoi had that last weakness of a great man: he wanted the absolute: the absolute of love, if you like to call it that. Talk about the "last infirmity of noble minds"! It's a perfect epidemic of senility.° He wanted to *be* absolute: a universal brother. Leo was too tight for Tolstoi. He wanted to puff, and puff, and puff, till he became Universal 30 Brotherhood itself, the great gooseberry of our globe.

Then pop went Leo! And from the bits sprang up bolshevists.

It's all bunk. No man can be absolute. No man can be absolutely good or absolutely right, nor absolutely lovable, nor absolutely beloved nor absolutely loving. Even Jesus, the paragon, was only relatively good 35 and relatively right. Judas° could take him by the nose.

No god, that men can conceive of, could possibly be absolute or absolutely right. All the gods that men ever discovered are still God: and they contradict one another and fly down one another's throats, marvellously. Yet they are *all* God: the incalculable Pan.° 40

It is rather nice, to know what a lot of gods there are, and have been, and will be, and that they are all of them God all the while. Each of them utters an absolute: which, in the ears of all the rest of them, falls flat. This makes even eternity lively.

5   But man, poor man, bobbing like a cork in the stream of time, must hitch himself to some absolute star of righteousness overhead. So he throws out his line, and hooks on. Only to find, after a while, that his star is slowly falling: till it drops into the stream of time with a fizzle, and there's *another* absolute star gone out.

10   Then we scan the heavens afresh.

As for the babe of love, we're simply tired of changing its napkins. Put the brat down, and let it learn to run about, and manage its own little breeches.

But it's nice to think that all the gods are God all the while. And if a god
15   only genuinely feels to you like God, then it *is* God. But if it doesn't feel quite, quite altogether like God to you, then wait awhile, and you'll hear him fizzle.

The novel knows all this, irrevocably. "My dear," it kindly says, "one God is relative to another god, until he gets into a machine; and then it's a
20   case for the traffic cop!"

"But what am I to do!" cries the despairing novelist. "From Amon and Ra to Mrs Eddy, from Ashtaroth and Jupiter to Annie Besant,* I don't know where I am."

"Oh yes you do, my dear!" replies the novel. "You are where you are,
25   so you needn't hitch yourself on to the skirts either of Ashtaroth or Eddy. If you meet them, say *how-do-you-do!* to them quite courteously. But don't hook on, or I shall turn you down."

Refrain from hooking on! says the novel.

But be honorable among the host! he adds.

30   Honour! Why, the gods are like the rainbow, all colours and shades. Since light itself is invisible, a manifestation has got to be pink or black or blue or white or yellow or vermilion, or "tinted."

You may be a theosophist, and then you will cry: *Avaunt! Thou dark-red aura! Away!!!—Oh come! Thou pale-blue or thou primrose aura, come!*

35   This you may cry if you are a theosophist. And if you put a theosophist in a novel, he or she may cry *avaunt!* to the heart's content.

But a theosophist cannot be a novelist, as a trumpet cannot be a regimental band. A theosophist, or a Christian, or a Holy Roller, may be *contained* in a novelist. But a novelist may not put up a fence. The wind
40   bloweth where it listeth,* and auras will be red when they want to.

As a matter of fact, only the Holy Ghost knows truly what righteousness is. And heaven only knows what the Holy Ghost is! But it sounds all right. So the Holy Ghost hovers among the flames, from the red to the blue and the black to the yellow, putting brand to brand and flame to flame, as the wind changes, and life travels in flame from the unseen to the unseen, men will never know how or why. Only travel it must, and not die down in nasty fumes.

And the honour, which the novel demands of you, is only that you shall be true to the flame that leaps in you. When that Prince in *Resurrection* so cruelly betrayed and abandoned the girl, at the beginning of her life, he betrayed and wetted on° the flame of his own manhood. When, later, he bullied her with his repentant benevolence, he again betrayed and slobbered upon the flame of his waning manhood, till in the end his manhood is extinct, and he's just a lump of half-alive elderly meat.

It's the oldest Pan-mystery. God is the flame-life in all the universe. Multifarious, multifarious flames, all colours and beauties and pains and sombrenesses. Whichever flame flames in your manhood, that is you, for the time being. It is your manhood, don't make water on it, says the novel. A man's manhood is to honour the flames in him, and to know that none of them is absolute. Even°a flame is only relative.

But see old Leo Tolstoi wetting on the flame. As if even his wet were absolute!

Sex is flame, too, the novel announces. Flame burning against every absolute, even against the phallic. For sex is so much more than phallic, and so much deeper than functional desire. The flame of sex singes your absolute, and cruelly scorches your ego. What, will you assert your ego in the universe? Wait till the flames of sex leap at you like striped tigers.

> "They returned from the ride
> With the lady inside,
> And a smile on the face of the tiger."

You will play with sex, will you! You will tickle yourself with sex as with an ice-cold drink from a soda-fountain! You will pet your best girl, will you, and spoon with her, and titillate yourself and her, and do as you like with your sex?

Wait! Only wait till the flame you have dribbled on flies back at you, later! Only wait!

Sex is a life-flame, a dark one, reserved and mostly invisible. It is a
deep reserve in a man, one of the core-flames of his manhood.

What, would you play with it? Would you make it cheap and nasty!
Buy a king-cobra, and try playing with that.

5   Sex is even a majestic reserve in the sun.

Oh, give me the novel! Let me hear what the novel says.

As for the novelist, he is usually a dribbling liar.

WHY THE NOVEL MATTERS

Supplementary note on the text

See Note on the texts, pp. 130–1. An additional silent emendation is the following: A1 omitted the hyphen from 'man-alive'.

Why the Novel Matters

We have curious ideas of ourselves. We think of ourselves as a body with a spirit in it, or a body with a soul in it, or a body with a mind in it. *Mens sana in corpore sano.*° The years drink up the wine, and at last throw the bottle away: the body, of course, being the bottle. 5

It is a funny sort of superstition. Why should I look at my hand, as it so cleverly writes these words, and decide that it is a mere nothing compared to the mind that directs it? Is there really any huge difference between my hand and my brain?—or my mind? My hand is alive, it flickers with a life of its own. It meets all the strange universe, in touch, 10 and learns a vast number of things, and knows a vast number of things. My hand, as it writes these words, slips gaily along, jumps like a grasshopper to dot an i, feels the table rather cold, gets a little bored if I write too long, has its own rudiments of thought, and is just as much *me* as is my brain, my mind, or my soul. Why should I imagine that there is 15 a *me* which is more *me* than my hand is? Since my hand is absolutely alive, me alive.

Whereas, of course, as far as I am concerned, my pen isn't alive at all. My pen *isn't* me alive. Me alive ends at my finger-tips.

Whatever is me alive is me. Every tiny bit of my hands is alive, every 20 little freckle and hair and fold of skin. And whatever is me alive is me. Only my finger-nails, those ten little weapons between me and an inanimate universe, they cross the mysterious Rubicon° between me alive and things like my pen, which are not alive, in my own sense.

So, seeing my hand is all alive, and me alive, wherein is it just a 25 bottle, or a jug, or a tin can, or a vessel of clay, or any of the rest of that nonsense? True, if I cut it it will bleed, like a can of cherries. But then the skin that is cut, and the veins that bleed, and the bones that should never be seen, they are all just as alive as the blood that flows. So the tin can business, or vessel of clay, is just bunk. 30

And that's what you learn, when you're a novelist. And that's what you are very liable *not* to know, if you're a parson, or a philosopher, or a scientist, or a stupid person. If you're a parson, you talk about souls in heaven. If you're a novelist, you know that paradise is in the palm of

your hand, and on the end of your nose: because both are alive; and
alive, and man-alive, which is more than you can say, for certain, of
paradise. Paradise is after life, and I for one am not keen on anything
that is *after* life.—If you are a philosopher, you talk about infinity, and
5   the pure spirit which knows all things. But if you pick up a novel, you
realise immediately that infinity is just a handle to this self-same jug of
a body of mine; while as for knowing, if I put my finger in the fire, I
know that fire burns, with a knowledge so emphatic and vital, it leaves
Nirvana merely a conjecture. Oh yes, my body, me alive, *knows*, and
10 knows intensely. And as for the sum of all knowledge, it can't be
anything more than an accumulation of all the things I know in the
body, and you, dear reader, know in the body.

These damned philosophers, they talk as if they suddenly went off in
steam, and were then much more important than they are when they're
15 in their shirts. It is nonsense. Every man, philosopher included, ends in
his own finger-tips. That's the end of his man alive. As for the words
and thoughts and sighs and aspirations that fly from him, they are so
many tremulations in the ether,* and not alive at all. But if the
tremulations reach another man alive, he may receive them into his life,
20 and his life may take on a new colour, like a chameleon creeping from a
brown rock on to a green leaf. All very well and good. It still doesn't
alter the fact that the so-called spirit, the message or teaching of the
philosopher or the saint, isn't alive at all, but just a tremulation upon
the ether, like a radio message. All this spirit stuff is just tremulations
25 upon the ether. If you, as man alive, quiver from the tremulation of the
ether into new life, that is because you are man alive, and you take
sustenance and stimulation into your alive man in a myriad ways. But to
say that the message, or the spirit which is communicated to you, is
more important than your living body, is nonsense. You might as well
30 say that the potato at dinner was more important.

Nothing is important but life. And for myself, I can absolutely see life
nowhere but in the living. Life with a capital L is only man alive. Even a
cabbage in the rain is cabbage alive. All things that are alive are
amazing. And all things that are dead are subsidiary to the living. Better
35 a live dog than a dead lion. But better a live lion than a live dog. *C'est la
vie.**

It seems impossible to get a saint, or a philosopher, or a scientist, to
stick to this simple truth. They are all, in a sense, renegades. The saint
wishes to offer himself up as spiritual food for the multitude. Even
40 Francis of Assisi turns himself into a sort of angel cake, of which

anyone may take a slice. But an angel cake is rather less than man alive. And poor St. Francis might well apologise to his body, when he was dying. "Oh pardon me, my body, the wrong I did you through the years!"—It was no wafer, for others to eat.* The philosopher on the other hand, because he can think, decides that nothing but thoughts 5 matter. It is as if a rabbit, because he can make little pills, should decide that nothing but little pills matter. As for the scientist, he has absolutely no use for me so long as I am man alive. To the scientist, I am dead. He puts under the microscope a bit of dead me, and calls it me. He takes me to pieces, and says first one piece, and then another piece, is me. 10 My heart, my liver, my stomach have all been scientifically me, according to the scientist; and nowadays I am either a brain, or nerves, or glands, or something more up-to-date in the tissue line.

Now I absolutely flatly deny that I am a soul, or a body, or a mind, or an intelligence, or a brain, or a nervous system, or a bunch of glands, or 15 any of the rest of these bits of me. The whole is greater than the part. And therefore I, who am man alive, am greater than my soul, or spirit, or body, or mind, or consciousness, or anything else that is merely a part of me. I am a man, and alive. I am man alive, and as long as I can, I intend to go on being man alive. 20

For this reason I am a novelist. And being a novelist, I consider myself superior to the saint, the scientist, the philosopher and the poet, who are all great masters of different bits of man-alive, but never get the whole hog.

The novel is the one bright book of life. Books are not life. They are 25 only tremulations on the ether. But the novel as a tremulation *can* make the whole man-alive tremble. Which is more than poetry, philosophy, science or any other book-tremulation can do.

The novel is the book of life. In this sense, the Bible is a great confused novel. You may say, it is about God. But it is really about 30 man-alive. Adam, Eve, Sarai,* Abraham, Isaac, Jacob, Samuel, David, Bathsheba, Ruth, Esther, Solomon, Job, Isaiah, Jesus, Mark, Judas, Paul, Peter; what is it but man-alive, from start to finish? Man-alive, not mere bits. Even the Lord is another man-alive, in a burning bush, throwing the tablets of stone at Moses' head.* 35

I do hope you begin to get my idea, why the novel is supremely important, as a tremulation on the ether. Plato makes the perfect ideal being tremble in me.* But that's only a bit of me. Perfection is only a bit, in the strange make-up of man-alive. The Sermon on the Mount makes the selfless spirit of me quiver. But that too is only a bit of me. 40

The Ten Commandments sets the old Adam* shivering in me, warning me that I am a thief and a murderer, unless I watch it. But even the old Adam is only a bit of me.

I very much like all these bits of me to be set trembling with life and 5 the wisdom of life. But I do ask that the whole of me shall tremble in its wholeness, some time or other.

And this, of course, must happen in my living.

But as far as it can happen from a communication, it can only happen when a whole novel communicates itself to me. The Bible—but *all* the 10 Bible—and Homer, and Shakespeare: these are the supreme old novels. These are all things to all men. Which means that in their wholeness they affect the whole man alive, which is the man himself, beyond any part of him. They set the whole tree trembling with a new access of life, they do not just stimulate growth in one direction.

15 I don't want to grow in any one direction any more. And if I can help it, I don't want to stimulate anybody else into some particular direction. A particular direction ends in a cul de sac. We're in a cul de sac at present.

I don't believe in any dazzling revelation, or in any supreme Word. 20 "The grass withereth, the flower fadeth, but the Word of the Lord shall stand for ever."*—That's the kind of stuff we've drugged ourselves with. As a matter of fact, the grass withereth, but comes up all the greener for that reason, after the rains. The flower fadeth, and therefore the bud opens. But the Word of the Lord, being man-uttered 25 and a mere vibration on the ether, becomes staler and staler, more and more boring, till at last we turn a deaf ear and it ceases to exist, far more finally than any withered grass. It is grass that renews its youth like the eagle,* not any Word.

We should ask for no absolutes, or absolute. Once and for all and 30 forever, let us have done with the ugly imperialism of any absolute. There is no absolute good, there is nothing absolutely right. All things flow and change, and even change is not absolute. The whole is a strange assembly of apparently incongruous parts, slipping past one another.

35 Me, man alive, I am a very curious assembly of incongruous parts. My yea! of today* is oddly different from my yea! of yesterday. My tears of tomorrow will have nothing to do with my tears of a year ago. If the one I love remains unchanged and unchanging, I shall cease to love her. It is only because she changes and startles me into change and 40 defies my inertia,* and is herself staggered in her inertia by my

changing, that I can continue to love her. If she stayed put, I might as well love the pepper pot.

In all this change, I maintain a certain integrity. But woe betide me if I try to put my finger on it. If I say of myself: I am this, I am that!—then, if I stick to it, I turn into a stupid fixed thing like a lamp-post. I shall never know wherein lies my integrity, my individuality, my me. I *can* never know it. It is useless to talk about my ego. That only means that I have made up an *idea* of myself, and that I am trying to cut myself out to pattern. Which is no good. You can cut your cloth to fit your coat,* but you can't clip bits off your living body, to trim it down to your idea. True, you can put yourself into ideal corsets. But even in ideal corsets, fashions change.

Let us learn from the novel. In the novel, the characters can do nothing but *live*. If they keep on being good, according to pattern, or bad, according to pattern, or even volatile, according to pattern, they cease to live, and the novel falls dead. A character in a novel has got to live, or it is nothing.

We, likewise, in life have got to live, or we are nothing.

What we mean by living is, of course, just as indescribable as what we mean by *being*. Men get ideas into their heads, of what they mean by Life, and they proceed to cut life out to pattern. Sometimes they go into the desert to seek God, sometimes they go into the desert to seek cash, sometimes it is wine, woman, and song, and again it is water, political reform, and votes. You never know what it will be next: from killing your neighbour with hideous bombs and gas that tears the lungs, to supporting a Foundlings Home and preaching infinite Love, and being co-respondent in a divorce.

In all this wild welter, we need some sort of guide. It's no good inventing Thou Shalt Nots!

What then? Turn truly, honorably to the novel, and see wherein you are man alive, and wherein you are dead man in life. You may love a woman as man alive, and you may be making love to a woman as sheer dead man in life. You may eat your dinner as man alive, or as a mere masticating corpse. As man alive you may have a shot at your enemy. But as a ghastly simulacrum of life you may be firing bombs into men who are neither your enemies nor your friends, but just things you are dead to. Which is criminal, when the things happen to be live.

To be alive, to be man alive, to be whole man alive: that is the point. And at its best, the novel, and the novel supremely can help you. It can help you not to be dead man in life. So much of a man walks about dead and a carcase in the street and house, today: so much of women is merely dead. Like a pianoforte with half the notes mute.

But in the novel you can see, plainly, when the man goes dead, the woman goes inert. You can develop an instinct for life, if you will,
5   instead of a theory of right and wrong, good and bad.

In life, there is right and wrong, good and bad, all the time. But what is right in one case is wrong in another. And in the novel you see one man becoming a corpse, because of his so-called goodness, another going dead because of his so-called wickedness. Right and wrong is an
10 instinct: but an instinct of the whole consciousness in a man, bodily, mental, spiritual at once. And only in the novel are *all* things given full play; or at least, they may be given full play, when we realise that life itself, and not inert safety, is the reason for living. For out of the full play of all things emerges the only thing that is anything, the wholeness
15 of a man, the wholeness of a woman, man alive, and live woman.

THE NOVEL AND THE FEELINGS

The Novel and the Feelings

We think we are so civilised, so highly educated and civilised. It is
farcical. Because, of course, all our civilisation consists in harping on
one string. Or at most, on two or three strings. Harp, harp, harp,
twingle-twingle-twang! That's our civilisation, always on one note.   5
   The note itself is all right. It's the exclusiveness of it that is awful.
Always the same note, always the same note!—"Ah, how can you run
after other women, when your wife is so delightful, a lovely plump
partridge?"—Then the husband laid his hand on his waistcoat, and a
frightened look came over his face. "Nothing but partridge?" he   10
exclaimed.
   Toujours perdrix!* It was up to that wife to be a goose and a cow,
an oyster and an inedible vixen, at intervals.
   Wherein are we educated? Come now, in what are we educated? In
politics, in geography, in history, in machinery, in soft drinks and in   15
hard, in social economy and social extravagance: ugh, a frightful
universality of knowings.
   But it's all France without Paris, *Hamlet* without the Prince, and
bricks without straw. For we know nothing, or next to nothing, about
ourselves. After hundreds of thousands of years we have learned how to   20
wash our faces and bob our hair, and that is about all we *have* learned,
individually. Collectively, of course, as a species, we have combed the
round earth with a tooth-comb, and pulled down the stars almost
within grasp. And then what? Here sit I, a two-legged individual with a
risky temper, knowing all about—take a pinch of salt—Tierra del   25
Fuego and Relativity and the composition of celluloid, the appearance
of the anthrax bacillus and solar eclipses, and the latest fashion in
shoes; and it don't do me *no* good! as the charlady said of near
beer.* It doesn't leave me feeling no less lonesome inside! as the
old Englishwoman said, long ago, of tea without rum.   30
   Our knowledge, like the prohibition beer, is always near. But it never
gets there. It leaves us feeling just as lonesome inside.
   We are hopelessly uneducated in ourselves. We pretend that when
we know a smattering of the Patagonian idiom we have in-so-far

educated ourselves. What nonsense! The leather of my boots is just as effectual in turning me into a bull, or a young steer. Alas! we wear our education just as externally as we wear our boots, and to far less profit. It is all external education, anyhow.

5   What am I, when I am at home? I'm supposed to be a sensible human being. Yet I carry a whole waste-paper basket of ideas at the top of my head, and in some other part of my anatomy, the dark continent of my self, I have a whole stormy chaos of "feelings." And with these self-same feelings I simply don't get a chance. Some of

10   them roar like lions, some twist like snakes, some bleat like snow-white lambs, some warble like linnets, some are absolutely dumb, but swift as slippery fishes, some are oysters that open on occasion: and lo! here am I, adding another scrap of paper to the ideal accumulation in the waste-paper basket, hoping to settle the matter that way.

15   The lion springs on me! I wave an idea at him. The serpent casts a terrifying glance at me, and I hand him a Moody and Sankey hymn-book.* Matters go from bad to worse.

The wild creatures are coming forth from the darkest Africa inside us. In the night you can hear them bellowing. If you're a big game

20   hunter, like Billy Sunday,* you may shoulder your elephant gun. But since the forest is inside all of us, and in every forest there's a whole assortment of big game and dangerous creatures, it's one against a thousand. We've managed to keep clear of the darkest Africa inside us, for a long time. We've been so busy finding the North Pole

25   and converting the Patagonians, loving our neighbour and devising new means of exterminating him, listening in and shutting out.

But now, my dear, dear reader, Nemesis is blowing his nose. And muffled roarings are heard out of darkest Africa, with stifled shrieks.

I say feelings, not emotions. Emotions are things we more or less

30   recognise. We see love, like a woolly lamb, or like a decorative decadent panther in Paris clothes: according as it is sacred or profane. We see hate, like a dog chained to a kennel. We see fear, like a shivering monkey. We see anger, like a bull with a ring through his nose, and greed, like a pig. Our emotions are our domesticated

35   animals, noble like the horse, timid like the rabbit, but all completely at our service. The rabbit goes into the pot, and the horse into the shafts. For we are creatures of circumstance, and must fill our bellies and our pockets.

Convenience! Convenience! There are convenient emotions, and

40   inconvenient ones. The inconvenient ones we chain up, or put a ring

through their nose. The convenient ones are our pets. Love is our pet favourite.

And that's as far as our education goes, in the direction of feelings. We have no language for the feelings, because our feelings do not even exist for us.

Yet what is a man? Is he really just a little engine that you stoke with potatoes and beef-steak? Does all the strange flow of life in him come out of meat and potatoes, and turn into the so-called physical energy?

Educated! We are not even *born*, as far as our feelings are concerned.

You can eat till you're bloated, and "get ahead" till you're a by-word, and still, inside you, will be the darkest Africa whence come roars and shrieks.

Man is not a little engine of cause and effect. We must put that out of our minds for ever. The *cause* in man is something we shall never fathom. But there it is, a strange dark continent that we do not explore, because we do not even allow that it exists. Yet all the time, it is within us: the *cause* of us, and of our days.

And our feelings are the first manifestations within the aboriginal jungle of us. Till now, in sheer terror of ourselves, we have turned our backs on the jungle, fenced it in with an enormous entanglement of barbed wire, and declared it did not exist.

But alas! We ourselves only exist because of the life that bounds and leaps into our limbs and our consciousness, from out of the original dark forest within us. We may wish to exclude this inbounding, in-leaping life. We may wish to be as our domesticated animals are, tame. But let us remember that even our cats and dogs have, in each generation, to be tamed. They are not now a tame species. Take away the control, and they will cease to be tame. They will not tame *themselves*.

Man is the only creature who has deliberately tried to tame himself. He has succeeded. But alas, it is a process you cannot set a limit to. Tameness, like alcohol, destroys its own creator. Tameness is an effect of control. But the tamed thing loses the power of control, in itself. It must be controlled from without. Man has pretty well tamed himself, and he calls his tameness civilisation. True civilisation would be something very different. But man is now tame. Tameness means the loss of the peculiar power of command. The tame are always commanded by the untame. Man has tamed himself, and so has lost his power for command, the power to give himself direction. He has no choice in himself. He is tamed, like a tame horse waiting for the rein.

Supposing all horses were suddenly rendered masterless, what would they do? They would run wild. But supposing they were left still shut up in their fields, paddocks, corrals, stables, what would they do? They would go insane.

5 And that is precisely man's predicament. He is tamed. There are no untamed to give the command and the direction. Yet he is shut up within all his barb-wire fences. He can only go insane, degenerate.

What is the alternative? It is nonsense to pretend we can un-tame ourselves in five minutes. That, too, is a slow and strange process, that 10 has to be undertaken seriously. It is nonsense to pretend we can break the fences and dash out into the wilds. There are no wilds left, comparatively, and man is a dog that returns to his vomit.°

Yet, unless we proceed to connect ourselves up with our own primeval sources, we shall degenerate. And degenerating, we shall 15 break up into a strange orgy of feelings. They will be decomposition feelings, like the colours of autumn. And they will precede whole storms of death, like leaves in a wind.

There is no help for it. Man cannot tame himself and then stay tame. The moment he tries to stay tame he begins to degenerate, and gets the 20 second sort of wildness, the wildness of destruction, which may be autumnal-beautiful for a while, like yellow leaves. Yet yellow leaves can only fall and rot.

Man tames himself in order to learn to untame himself again. To be civilised, we must not deny and blank out our feelings. Tameness is not 25 civilisation. It is only burning down the brush and ploughing the land. Our civilisation has hardly realised yet the necessity for ploughing the soul. Later, we sow wild seed. But so far, we've only been burning off and rooting out the old wild brush. Our civilisation, as far as our own souls go, has been a destructive process, up to now. The landscape of 30 our souls is a charred wilderness of burnt-off stumps, with a green bit of water here, and a tin shanty with a little iron stove.

Now we have to sow wild seed again. We have to cultivate our feelings. It is no good trying to be popular, to let a whole rank tangle of liberated, degenerate feelings spring up. It will give us no satisfaction.

35 And it is no use doing as the psychoanalysts have done. The psychoanalysts show the greatest fear of all, of the innermost primeval place in man, where God is, if He is anywhere. The old Jewish horror of the true Adam, the mysterious "natural man," rises to a shriek in psychoanalysis. Like the idiot who foams and bites his wrists till they 40 bleed. So great is the Freudian hatred of the oldest, old Adam, from

whom God is not yet separated off, that the psychoanalyst sees this
Adam as nothing but a monster of perversity, a bunch of engendering
adders, horribly clotted.

This vision is the perverted vision of the degenerate tame: tamed
through thousands of shameful years. The old Adam is the forever   5
untamed: he who is of the tame hated, with a horror of fearful hate: but
who is held in innermost respect by the fearless.

In the oldest of the old Adam, was God: behind the dark wall of his
breast, under the seal of the navel. Then man had a revulsion against
himself, and God was separated off, lodged in the outermost space.   10

Now we have to return. Now again the old Adam must lift up his face
and his breast, and untame himself. Not in viciousness nor in
wantonness, but having God within the walls of himself. In the very
darkest continent of the body, there is God. And from Him issues the
first dark rays of our feeling, wordless, and utterly previous to words;   15
the innermost rays, the first messengers, the primeval, honorable beasts
of our being, whose voice echoes wordless and forever wordless down
the darkest avenues of the soul, but full of potent speech. Our own
inner meaning.

Now we have to educate ourselves, not by laying down laws and   20
inscribing tablets of stone, but by listening. Not listening-in to noises
from Chicago or Timbuctoo.* But listening-in to the voices of the
honorable beasts that call in the dark paths of the veins of our body,
from the God in the heart. Listening inwards, inwards, not for words
nor for inspiration, but to the lowing of the innermost beasts, the   25
feelings, that roam in the forest of the blood, from the feet of God
within the red, dark heart.

And how? How? How shall we even begin to educate ourselves in the
feelings?

Not by laying down laws, or commandments, or axioms and   30
postulates. Not even by making assertions that such and such is
blessed. Not by words at all.

If we can't hear the cries far down in our own forests of dark veins,
we can look in the real novels, and there listen in. Not listen to the
didactic statements of the author, but to the low, calling cries of the   35
characters, as they wander in the dark woods of their destiny.

JOHN GALSWORTHY

Supplementary note on the text

See Note on the texts, pp. 130–1. Additional silent emendations are the following:

For DHL's 'aesthetic' and 'Phaedra' Eɪ and Aɪ used a ligature, and this is not recorded.

John Galsworthy*

Literary Criticism can be no more than a reasoned account of the
feeling produced upon the critic by the book he is criticising. Criticism
can never be a science: it is, in the first place, much too personal, and in
the second, it is concerned with values that science ignores. The   5
touch-stone is emotion, not reason. We judge a work of art by its effect
on our sincere and vital emotion,* and nothing else. All the critical
twiddle-twaddle about style, and form, all this pseudo-scientific clas-
sifying and analysing of books in an imitation-botanical fashion, is mere
impertinence, and mostly dull jargon.   10
A critic must be able to *feel* the impact of a work of art in all its
complexity and its force. To do so, he must be a man of force and
complexity* himself, which few critics are. A man with a paltry,
impudent nature will never write anything but paltry, impudent
criticism. And a man who is *emotionally* educated is rare as a phœnix. 15
The more scholastically educated a man is, generally, the more he is an
emotional boor.
More than this, even an artistically and emotionally educated man
must be a man of good faith. He must have the courage to admit what
he feels, as well as the flexibility to *know* what he feels. So Sainte Beuve 20
remains, to me, a great critic. And a man like Macaulay,* brilliant
as he is, is unsatisfactory, because he is not honest. He is emotionally
very alive, but he juggles his feelings. He prefers a fine effect to the
sincere statement of his aesthetic and emotional reaction. He is quite
intellectually capable of giving us a true account of what he feels. But 25
not morally. A critic must be emotionally alive in every fibre, intellectually capable and skilful in essential logic, and then morally very
honest.
Then it seems to me, a good critic should give his reader a few
standards to go by/ He can change the standards for every new critical 30
attempt, so long as he keeps good faith. But it is just as well to say:
This, and this, is the standard we judge by.
Sainte Beuve, on the whole, set up the standard of the "good man."
He sincerely believed that the great man was essentially the good man,

in the widest range of human sympathy. This remained his universal
standard. Pater's standard° was the lonely philosopher of pure
thought and pure aesthetic truth. Macaulay's standard was tainted by a
political or democratic bias: he must be on the side of the weak. Gibbon
5 tried a purely moral standard,° individual morality.

Reading Galsworthy again—or most of him, for all is too
much—one feels oneself in need of a standard, some conception of a
real man and a real woman, by which to judge all these Forsytes°
and their contemporaries. One cannot judge them by the standard of
10 the good man, nor of the man of pure thought, nor of the treasured
humble nor the moral individual. One would like to judge them by the
standard of the human being, but what, after all, is that? This is the
trouble with the Forsytes. They are human enough, since anything in
humanity is human, just as anything in nature is natural. Yet not one of
15 them seems to be a really vivid human being. They are social
beings.—And what do we mean by that?

It remains to define, just for the purposes of this criticism, what we
mean by a social being as distinct from a human being.° The
necessity arises from the sense of dissatisfaction which these Forsytes
20 give us. Why can't we admit them as human beings? Why can't we have
them in the same category as Sairey Gamp, for example, who is
satirically conceived, or of Jane Austen's people, who are social
enough? We can accept Mrs Gamp or Jane Austen's characters or even
George Meredith's Egoist° as human beings, in the same category
25 as ourselves. Whence arises this repulsion from the Forsytes, this
refusal, this emotional refusal, to have them identified with our
common humanity? Why do we feel so instinctively that they are
inferiors?

It is because they seem to us to have lost caste, as human beings, and
30 to have sunk to the level of the social being, that peculiar creature that
takes the place, in our civilisation, of the slave in the old civilisations.
The human individual is a queer animal, always changing. But the fatal
change, today, is the collapse from the psychology of the free human
individual into the psychology of the social being: just as the fatal
35 change in the past was a collapse from the free-man's psyche to the
psyche of the slave. The free moral and the slave moral:° the
human moral and the social moral: these are the abiding antitheses.

While a man remains a man, a true human individual, there is at the
core of him a certain innocence or naïveté which defies all analysis, and
40 which you cannot bargain with, you can only deal with it, in good faith,

from your own corresponding innocence or naïveté. This does not mean that the human being is nothing but naïve or innocent. He is Mr Worldly Wiseman* also, to his own degree. But in his essential core he is naïve, and money does not touch him. Money, of course, with every man living, goes a long way. With the alive human being it may go as far as his penultimate feeling. But in the last, naked him it does not enter.

With the social being, it goes right through the centre, and is the controlling principle, no matter how much he may pretend, nor how much bluff he may put up. He may give away all he has to the poor,* and still reveal himself as a social being swayed finally and helplessly by the money-sway, and by the social moral, which is inhuman.

It seems to me, that when the human being becomes too much divided between his subjective and objective consciousness, at last something splits in him, and he becomes a social being. When he becomes too much aware of objective reality, and of his own isolation in the face of a universe of objective reality, the core of his identity splits, his nucleus collapses, his innocence or his naïveté perishes, and he becomes only a subjective-objective reality, a divided thing hinged together but not strictly individual.

While a man remains a man, before he falls and becomes a social individual, he innocently feels himself altogether within the great continuum of the universe. He is not divided nor cut off. Men may be against him, the tide of affairs may be rising to sweep him away. But he is one with the living continuum of the universe. From this he cannot be swept away. Hamlet and Lear feel it, as does Œdipus or Phaedra.* It is the last and deepest feeling that is in a man, while he remains a man. It is there the same as in a deist like Voltaire or a scientist like Darwin: it is there, imperishable, in every great man: in Napoleon the same, till material things piled too much on him, and he lost it, and was doomed. It is the essential innocence and naïveté of the human being, the sense of being at one with the great universe-continuum of space-time-life, which is vivid in a great man, and a pure nuclear spark in every man who is still free.

But if man loses his mysterious naïve assurance, which is his innocence; if he gives *too* much importance to the external objective reality, and so collapses in his natural innocent pride; then he becomes obsessed with the idea of objective or material assurance; he wants to *insure* himself, and perhaps everybody else: universal insurance. The

impulse rests on fear. Once the individual loses his naïve at-oneness
with the living universe, he falls into a state of fear, and tries to insure
himself with wealth. If he is an altruist, he wants to insure everybody,
and feels it is the tragedy of tragedies if this can't be done. But the
5   whole necessity for thus materially insuring oneself with wealth, money,
arises from the state of fear into which a man falls who has lost his at-
oneness with the living universe, lost his peculiar nuclear innocence,
and fallen into fragmentariness. Money, material salvation is the only
salvation. What is salvation is God. Hence money is God. The social
10 being may rebel even against this god, as do many of Galsworthy's
characters. But that does not give them back their innocence. They are
only anti-materialists instead of positive materialists. And the anti-
materialist is a social being just the same as the materialist: neither
more nor less. He is castrated just the same, made a neuter by having
15 lost his innocence, the bright little individual spark of his at-oneness.
    When one reads Mr Galsworthy's books, it seems as if there were
not on earth one single human individual. They are all these social
beings, positive and negative. There is not a free soul among them: not
even Mrs Pendyce,* or June Forsyte. If money does not actively
20 determine their being, it does negatively. Money, or property: which is
the same thing. Mrs Pendyce, lovable as she is, is utterly circumscribed
by property. Ultimately, she is not lovable at all, she is part of the fraud:
she is prostituted to property. And there is nobody else. Old Jolyon is
merely a sentimental materialist.—Only for one moment do we see a
25 man: and that is the road-sweeper in *Fraternity*, after he comes out of
prison, and covers his face. But even *his* manhood has to be explained
away by a wound in the head:* an abnormality.
    Now it looks as if Mr Galsworthy set out to make that very point: to
show that the Forsytes were not full human individuals, but social
30 beings, fallen to a lower level of life. They have lost that bit of free
manhood and free womanhood which makes men and women. *The
Man of Property* has the elements of a very great novel, a very great
satire. It sets out to reveal the social being in all his strength and
inferiority. But the author has not the courage to carry it through. The
35 greatness of the book rests in its new and sincere and amazingly
profound satire. It is the ultimate satire on modern humanity, and done
from the inside, with really consummate skill and sincere creative
passion, something quite new. It seems to be a real effort to show up
the social being in all his weirdness. And then it fizzles out.
40   Then, in the love-affair of Irene and Bosinney, and in the sen-

timentalising of old Jolyon Forsyte, the thing is fatally blemished.
Galsworthy had not quite enough of the superb courage of his satire.
He faltered, and gave in to the Forsytes. It is a thousand pities. He
might have been the surgeon the modern soul needs so badly to cut
away the proud flesh of our Forsytes from the living body of men who   5
are fully alive. Instead, he put down the knife and laid on a soft
sentimental poultice, and helped to make the corruption worse.

Satire exists for the very purpose of killing the social being, of
showing him what an inferior he is, and, with all his parade of social
honesty, how subtly and corruptly debased. Dishonest to life, dishonest   10
to the living universe on which he is parasitic as a louse. By ridiculing
the social being, the satirist helps the true individual, the real human
being, to rise to his feet again and go on with the battle. For it is always
a battle, and always will be.

Not that the majority are necessarily social beings. But the majority is   15
only *conscious* socially: humanly, mankind is helpless and unconscious,
unaware even of the thing most precious to any human being, that core
of manhood or womanhood, naïve, innocent at-oneness with the living
universe-continuum, which alone makes a man individual, and as an
individual, essentially happy, even if he be driven mad like Lear. Lear   20
was *essentially* happy, even in his greatest misery. A happiness from
which Goneril and Regan were excluded as lice and bugs are excluded
from happiness; being social beings, and as such, parasites, fallen from
true freedom and independence.

But the tragedy today is that men are only materially and socially   25
conscious. They are unconscious of their own manhood, and so they let
it be destroyed. Out of free men we produce social beings by the
thousand, every week.

The Forsytes are all parasites, and Mr Galsworthy set out, in a really
magnificent attempt, to let us see it. They are parasites upon the   30
thought, the feelings, the whole body of life of really living individuals
who have gone before them and who exist alongside with them. All they
can do, having no individual life of their own, is out of fear to rake
together property, and to feed upon the life that has been given by
living men to mankind. They have no life, and so they live forever, in   35
perpetual fear of death, accumulating property to ward off death. They
can keep up conventions: but they cannot carry on a tradition. There is
a tremendous difference between the two things. To carry on a
tradition, you must add something to the tradition. But to keep up a
convention needs only the monotonous persistency of a parasite, the   40

endless endurance of the craven, those who fear life because they are
not alive, and who cannot die because they cannot live. The social
beings.

As far as I can see, there is nothing but Forsyte in Galsworthy's
books: Forsyte positive, or Forsyte negative: Forsyte successful, or
Forsyte *manqué*. That is, every single character is determined by
money: either the getting it, or the having it, or the wanting it, or the
utter lacking it. Getting it are the Forsytes as such: having it are the
Pendyces and patricians and Hilarys and Biancas* and all that lot:
wanting it are the Irenes and Bosinneys and young Jolyons; and
utterly lacking it are all the charwomen and squalid poor who form
the background: the shadows of the "having" ones, as old Mr Stone
says.* This is the whole Galsworthy gamut, all absolutely
determined by money, and not an individual soul among them. They
are all fallen, all social beings, a castrated lot.

Perhaps the overwhelming numerousness of the Forsytes frightened Mr Galsworthy from utterly damning them. Or perhaps it was
something else, something more serious in him. Perhaps it was his
utter failure to see what you were when you *weren't* a Forsyte. What
was there *besides* Forsytes in all the wide human world? Mr Galsworthy looked, and found nothing. Strictly and truly, after his frightened search, he had found nothing. But he came back with Irene and
Bosinney, and offered us that. Here! he seems to say. Here is the
anti-Forsyte! Here! Here you have it! Love! Pa-assion! PASSION.

We look at this love, this PASSION, and we see nothing but a
doggish amorousness* and a sort of anti-Forsytism. They are the
anti half of the show. Runaway dogs of these Forsytes, running in the
back garden and furtively and ignominiously copulating —this is the
effect, on me, of Mr Galsworthy's grand love affairs, Dark Flowers or
Bosinneys or Apple Trees, or George Pendyce*—whatever they
be. About every one of them, something ignominious and doggish,
like dogs copulating in the street, and looking round to see if the
Forsytes are watching.

Alas! this is the Forsyte trying to be freely sensual. He can't do it;
he's lost it. He can only be doggishly messy. Bosinney is not only a
Forsyte, but an anti-Forsyte, with a vast grudge against property. And
the thing a man has a vast grudge against is the man's determinant.
Bosinney is a property-hound, but he has run away from the kennels,
or been born outside the kennels, so he is a rebel. So he goes sniffing
round the property-bitches, to get even with the successful property-

hounds that way.—One cannot help preferring Soames Forsyte, in a choice of evils.

Just as one prefers June or any of the old aunts, to Irene. Irene seems to me a sneaking, creeping, spiteful sort of bitch, an anti-Forsyte, absolutely living off the Forsytes—yes, to the very end; absolutely living off their money, and trying to do them dirt. She is like Bosinney, a property-mongrel doing dirt in the property kennels. But she is a real property-prostitute, like the little model in *Fraternity.* Only she is *anti*! It is a type recurring again and again in Galsworthy: the parasite upon the parasites. "Big fleas have little fleas etc." And Bosinney and Irene, as well as the vagabond in *The Island Pharisees,* are among the little fleas. And as a tramp loves his own vermin, so the Forsytes and the Hilarys love these, their own particular body-parasites, their *antis*.

It is when he comes to sex, that Mr Galsworthy collapses finally. He becomes nastily sentimental. He wants to make sex important, and he only makes it repulsive. Sentimentalism is the working off on yourself of feelings you haven't really got. We all *want* to have certain feelings: feelings of love, of passionate sex, of kindliness, and so forth. Very few people really feel love, or sex passion, or kindliness, or anything else that goes at all deep. So the mass just fake these feelings inside themselves. Faked feelings! The world is all gummy with them. They are better than real feelings, because you can spit them out when you brush your teeth; and then tomorrow you can fake them afresh.

Shelton, in *The Island Pharisees*, is the first of Mr Galsworthy's lovers, and he might as well be the last. He is almost comical. All we know of his passion for Antonia is that he feels, at the beginning, a "hunger" for her:* as if she were a beefsteak. And towards the end he once kisses her, and expects her, no doubt, to fall instantly at his feet, overwhelmed. He never, for a second, feels a moment of gentle sympathy with her. She is class-bound, but she doesn't seem to have been inhuman. The inhuman one was the lover. He can gloat over her in the distance, as if she were a dish of pig's trotters, *pieds truffés:** she can be an angelic *vision* to him, a little way off. But when the poor thing has to be just a rather ordinary middle-class girl to him, quite near, he hates her with a comical, rancorous hate. It is most queer. He is helplessly *anti*. He hates her for even existing as a woman of her own class, for even having her own existence. Apparently, she should just be a floating female sex-organ, hovering round to satisfy his little "hungers," and then *basta.** Anything of the real meaning of sex, which

involves the whole of a human being, never occurs to him. It is a
function, and the female is a sort of sexual appliance: no more.

And so we have it again and again, on this low and bastard level, all
the human correspondence lacking. The sexual level is extraordinarily
5 low, like dogs. The Galsworthy heroes are all weirdly in love with
themselves, when we know them better; afflicted with chronic narciss-
ism. They know just three types of women: the Pendyce mother,
prostitute to property; the Irene, the essential *anti* prostitute, the
floating, flaunting female organ; and the social woman, the mere lady.
10 All three are loved and hated in turn, by the recurrent heroes. But it is
all on the debased level of property, positive or *anti*. It is all a doggy
form of prostitution. Be quick and have done.

One of the funniest stories is *The Apple Tree*. The young man finds, at
a lonely Devon farm, a little Welsh farm-girl who, being a Celt and not
15 a Saxon, at once falls for the Galsworthian hero. This young gentleman, in the throes of narcissistic love for his marvellous self, falls for
the maid because she has fallen so utterly and abjectly for him. She
doesn't call him "My King," not being Wellsian. She only says: "I can't
live away from you. Do what you like with me. Only let me come with
20 you!"* The proper prostitutional announcement!

For this, of course, a narcissistic young gentleman just down from
Oxford falls at once. Ensues a grand pa-assion. He goes to buy her a
proper frock to be carried away in: meets a college friend with a young
lady sister: has jam for tea and stays the night: and the grand pa-assion
25 has died a natural death by the time he spreads the marmalade on his
bread. He has returned to his own class, and nothing else exists. He
marries the young lady. True to his class. But to fill the cup of his
vanity, the maid drowns herself. It is funny that maids only seem to do it
for these narcissistic young gentlemen who, looking in the pool for their
30 own image, desire the added satisfaction of seeing the face of drowned
Ophelia* there as well; saving them the necessity of taking the
narcissus plunge in person. We have gone one better than the myth.
Narcissus in Mr Galsworthy doesn't drown himself. He asks Ophelia,
or Megan, kindly to drown herself instead. And, in this fiction, she
35 actually does. And he feels so *wonderful* about it!!*

Mr Galsworthy's treatment of passion is really rather shameful. The
whole thing is doggy to a degree. The man has a temporary "hunger";
he is "on the heat" as they say of dogs. The heat passes. It's done. Trot
away, if you're not tangled. Trot off, looking shamefacedly over your
40 shoulder. People have been watching! Damn them! But never mind,

it'll blow over. Thank God the bitch is trotting in the other direction. She'll soon have another trail of dogs after her. That'll wipe out my traces. Good for that! Next time, I'll get properly married, and do my doggishness in my own house.

With the fall of the individual, sex falls into a dog's heat. Oh, if only Mr Galsworthy had had the strength to satirise this too, instead of pouring a sauce of sentimental savouriness over it. Of course, if he had done so, he would never have been a popular writer. But he would have been a great one.

However, he chose to sentimentalise and glorify the most doggy sort of sex. Setting out to satirise the Forsyte, he glorifies the *anti*, who is one worse. While the individual remains real and unfallen, sex remains a vital and supremely important thing. But once you have the fall into social beings, sex becomes disgusting, like dogs on the heat. Dogs are social beings, with no true canine individuality. Wolves and foxes don't copulate on the pavement. Their sex is wild, and in act, utterly private. Howls you may hear. But you will never see anything.—But the dog is tame. And he makes excrement and he copulates on the pavement, as if to spite you. He is the Forsyte *anti*.

The same with human beings. Once they become tame, they become, in a measure, exhibitionists, as if to spite everything. They have no real feelings of their own. Unless somebody "catches them at it," they don't really feel they've felt anything at all. And this is how the mob is today. It is Forsyte *anti*. It is the social being spiting society.

Oh, if only Mr Galsworthy had satirised *this* side of Forsytism, the anti-Forsyte posturing of the "rebel," the narcissus and the exhibitionist, the dogs copulating on the pavement! Instead of that, he glorified it, to the eternal shame of English literature.

The satire, which in *The Man of Property* really had a certain noble touch, soon fizzles out, and we get that series of Galsworthian "rebels" who are like all the rest of the modern middle-class rebels, not in rebellion at all. They are merely social beings behaving in an anti-social manner. They worship their own class, but they pretend to go one better, and sneer at it. They are Forsyte *antis*, feeling snobbish about snobbery. Nevertheless, they want to attract attention and make money. That's why they are *anti*. It is the vicious circle of Forsytism. Money means more to them than it does to a Soames Forsyte, so they pretend to go one better, and despise it, but they will do anything, anything to have it: things which Soames Forsyte would not have done.

If there is one thing more repulsive than the social being positive, it is the social being negative, the mere *anti*. In the great débâcle of decency, this gentleman is the most indecent. In a subtle way, Bosinney and Irene are more dishonest and more indecent than Soames and Winifred. But they are *anti*, so they are glorified. It is pretty sickening.

5 The introduction to *The Island Pharisees* explains the whole show.—"Each man born into the world is born to go a journey, and for the most part he is born on the high road————As soon as he can toddle, he moves, by the queer instinct we call the love of life, along this road:——his fathers went this way before him, they made this road for

10 him to tread, and, when they bred him, passed into his fibre the love of doing things as they themselves had done them. So he walks on and on.——Suddenly one day, without intending to, he notices a path or opening in the hedge, leading to right or left, and he stands looking at the undiscovered. After that, he stops at all the openings in the hedge;

15 one day, with a beating heart, he tries one. And this is where the fun begins."————Nine out of ten get back to the broad road again, and side-track no more. They snuggle down comfortably in the next inn, and think where they might have been.—"But the poor silly tenth is faring on. Nine times out of ten he goes down in a bog; the

20 undiscovered has engulfed him."—But the tenth time, he gets across, and a new road is opened to mankind.—

It is a class-bound consciousness, or at least a hopeless social consciousness which sees life as a high-road between two hedges. And the only way out is gaps in the hedge, and excursions into naughtiness!

25 These little *anti* excursions. From which the wayfarer slinks back to solid comfort, nine times out of ten: an odd one goes down in a bog: and a very rare one finds a way across and opens out a new road.

In Mr Galsworthy's novels we see the nine, the ninety-nine, the nine hundred and ninety-nine slinking back to solid comfort; we see an odd

30 Bosinney go under a bus, because he hadn't guts enough to do something else, the poor *anti*; but that rare figure sidetracking into the unknown we do *not* see.

Because as a matter of fact, the whole figure is faulty at that point. If life is a great high-way, then it must forge on ahead into the unknown.

35 Sidetracking gets nowhere. That is mere *anti*. The tip of the road is always unfinished, in the wilderness. If it comes to a precipice and a canyon—well, then there is need for some exploring.

But we see Mr Galsworthy, after *The Country House*, very safe on the old high-way, very secure in comfort, wealth, and renown. He at least

40 has gone down in no bog, nor lost himself striking new paths. The

hedges nowadays are ragged with gaps, anybody who likes strays out on the little trips of "unconvention." But the Forsyte road has not moved on at all. It has only become dishevelled and sordid with excursionists doing the *anti* tricks and being "unconventional," and leaving tin cans behind. 5

In the three early novels, *The Island Pharisees, The Man of Property, Fraternity*, it looked as if Mr Galsworthy might break through the blind end of the high-way, with the dynamite of satire, and help us out on to a new lap. But the sex ingredient of his dynamite was damp and muzzy, the explosions gradually fizzled off in sentimentality, and we are left in 10 a worse state than before.

The later novels are purely commercial, and, if it had not been for the early novels,* of no importance. They are popular, they sell well, and there's the end of them. They contain the explosive powder of the first books, in minute quantities, fizzling as silly squibs. When you 15 arrive at *To Let*, and the end, at least the *promised* end of the Forsytes,* what have you? Just money! Money, money, money, and a certain snobbish silliness, and many more *anti* tricks and poses. Nothing else. The story is feeble, the characters have no blood and bones, the emotions are faked, faked, faked. It is one great fake. Not 20 necessarily of Mr Galsworthy's. The characters fake their own emotions. But that doesn't help us. And if you look closely at the characters, the meanness and low-level vulgarity are very distasteful. You have all the Forsyte meanness, with none of the energy. Jolyon and Irene are meaner and more treacherous to their son than the older Forsytes were 25 to theirs. The young ones are of a limited, mechanical vulgar egoism far surpassing that of Swithin or James, their ancestors. There is in it all a vulgar sense of being rich, and therefore we do as we like: an utter incapacity for anything like *true* feeling, especially in the women, Fleur, Irene, Annette, June: a glib crassness, a youthful spontaneity which is 30 just impertinence and lack of feeling; and all the time, a creeping, "having" sort of vulgarity of money and self-will, money and self-will:—so that we wonder, sometimes, if Mr Galsworthy is not treating his public in real bad faith, and being cynical and rancorous under his rainbow sentimentalism. 35

Fleur he destroys in one word: she is "having."** It is perfectly true. We don't blame the young Jon for clearing out.—Irene he destroys in a phrase out of Fleur's mouth to June: "Didn't she spoil your life too?"*—And it is precisely what she did. Sneaking and mean, Irene prevented June from getting her lover. Sneaking and 40

mean, she prevents Fleur. She is the bitch in the manger. She is the sneaking *anti*. Irene, the most beautiful woman on earth!—And Mr Galsworthy, with the cynicism of a successful old sentimentalist, turns it off by making June say: "Nobody can spoil a life, my dear. That's
5 nonsense. Things happen, but we bob up."

This is the final philosophy of it all. "Things happen, but we bob up." Very well, then write the book in that key, the keynote of a frank old cynic. There's no point in sentimentalising it and being a sneaking old cynic. Why pour out masses of feelings that pretend to be genuine,
10 and then turn it all off with: "Things happen, but we bob up."

It is quite true, things happen, and we bob up. If we are vulgar sentimentalists, we bob up just the same, so nothing has happened, and nothing can happen. All is vulgarity. But it pays. There is money in it.

Vulgarity pays, and cheap cynicism smothered in sentimentalism
15 pays better than anything else. Because nothing *can* happen to the degraded social being. So let's pretend it does, and then bob up!

It is time somebody began to spit out the jam of sentimentalism, at least, which smothers the "bobbing-up" philosophy. It is time we turned a straight light on this horde of rats, these younger Forsyte
20 sentimentalists whose name is legion. It is sentimentalism which is stifling us. Let the social beings keep on bobbing up while ever they can. But it is time an effort was made to turn a hose-pipe on the sentimentalism they ooze over everything. The world is one sticky mess, in which the little Forsytes indeed may keep on bobbing still, but
25 in which an honest feeling can't breathe.

But if the sticky mess gets much deeper, even the little Forsytes won't be able to bob up any more. They'll be smothered in their own slime, along with everything else. Which is a comfort.

APPENDIX I

'*ART AND THE INDIVIDUAL*', FIRST VERSION

Note on the text

The text is taken from DHL's autograph manuscript, 6pp. (MS), in the collection of Mr W. H. Clarke, which appears to be the copy DHL used when delivering the paper in Eastwood on 19 March 1908. It has been collated with *Young Lorenzo* (O1).

For silent emendations, see the list on pp. 130–1, points 1–3; in addition: O1 has the essay in double quotation marks, and the quotation marks at the beginning of each paragraph have not been recorded; O1 expanded the abbreviated words (these are expanded in square brackets in this edition); and in the list of Herbartian interests, full stops are added after each entry in O1.

'Art and The Individual', First version

These Thursday night meetings are for discussing social problems with a view to advancing a more perfect social state and to our fitting ourselves to be perfect citizens—communists—what not. Is that it? I guess in time we shall become expert sociologists. If we would live a life above the common ruck we must be experts at something, must we not! Besides, we have peculiar qualities which adapt us for particular parts of the social machine. Some of us make good cranks, doubtless each of us would make a good Hub of the Universe. They have advanced the question in Education "Where in the school shall we begin to specialise." Specialise, that's the word! This boy has a strong supple wrist; let him practise pulling pegs out of a board like a Jap dentist's apprentice, then he'll be an expert tooth-puller. Under socialism, every man with the spirit of a flea will become a specialist—with such advantages it were disgraceful not to cultivate that proverbial 'one talent,'* and thus become a shining light on some tiny spot. It will take some four hundred specialists to make a normal family of four. However!

Now listen to the text which describes the ultimate goal of Education. "The ultimate goal of Education is to produce an individual of high moral character."—Take that on the authority of the great experts. Moral character consists, I suppose, in a good sense of proportion, a knowledge of the relative effects of certain acts or influences, and desire to use that knowledge for the promoting of happiness. The desire you may easily possess. We are all altruists. But what about the knowledge, the sense of proportion? How can you have an idea of proportional values unless you have an extensive knowledge of, or at least acquaintance with, the great influences which result in action. Here is the immediate goal of education—and our real purpose in meeting here, after that of making ourselves heard, is to educate ourselves—the immediate goal of education is to gain a wide sympathy; in other words, a *many sided interest*.

Let us look at Herbart's classification of interests, adding one that he overlooked:—

223

	Knowledge intellectual	1. Empirical 2. Speculative 3. Aesthetic
5 Interest arising from	Sympathy emotional	4. Sympathetic 5. Social 6. Religious
	Action	

Empirical:— Int[erest] in concrete individ[ual] things (I see a swan—
it sails up to me and attracts my attention. I notice how it
10   shows itself off to me—it pecks under the water—it
swims nearer—I observe its wings magnificently arched)—(evening flowers) x

Speculative— int[erest] that in deeper connections and causes of
events—scientific and philosophic int[erest]s. (It is
15   remarkable that the swan should raise its wings so
proudly—why can it be—evening flowers)

Aesthetic— Int[erest] aroused neither by phenomena or causes as
such, but by the approval which their harmony and
adaptability to an end win from me. (The swan is very
20   beautiful—the moonlight on the flowers is lovely—why
does it move me so?)

Sympathetic.

Social— growing comprehension of the incorporation of the
indiv[idual] in the great social body whose interests are
25   large beyond his personal feelings. He is a unit, working
with others for a common welfare, like a cell in a
complex body.

Religious— when this extended sympathy is directed to the history
(origin) and destiny of mankind, when it reverentially
30   recognises the vast scope of the laws of nature, and
discovers something of intelligibility and consistent purpose working through the whole natural world and
human consciousness, the religious interest is
developed, and the individual loses for a time the sense
35   of his own and his day's importance, feels the wonder
and terror of eternity with its incomprehensible purposes. This, I hold it, is still a most useful and fruitful
state.

Note parallelism of 1, 2, 3—4, 5, 6—increasing height of planes and examples.

Which of these forms of interest are we most likely to neglect? (Consider)—The aesthetic is our present consideration. Since we have accepted the Herbartian broad interpretation, we must take a broad   5
view of Art to fit it, since Aestheticism embraces all art. Examine the definition; "The Approval which the Harmony and Adaptability (of phenomena) to an end win from us."

It is vague and unsatisfactory. Look closely. "Approval of Harmony."—That is a pleasurable experience. We see or hear something   10
that gives us pleasure—we call it harmony—invert it—we hear or see harmonious blendings—we feel pleasure. We are not much further, except that we recognise that the ultimate test of all harmony, beauty, whatever you call it, is in *personal feeling*. This would place Aesthetic interest under the emotional group. Look at it again. "Approval of   15
Adaptability of things to an end." Here is harmony again—but it is more comprehensible, hence intellectual. We see a good purpose in sure and perhaps uninterrupted process of accomplishment. It is gratifying—we are glad. Why? Because, I believe, we are ourselves almost unconscious agents in a great inscrutable purpose, and it gives   20
us relief and pleasure to consciously recognise that power working out in things beyond and apart from us. But that is aside.

There have been two schools of aesthetic thought since the beginning of such thought.

(1)   Art—Beauty, is the expression of the perfect and divine *Idea* (discuss   25
       Platonic 'Idea'). This is the mystic idea, held by Hegel "Beauty is the
       shining of the Idea thro[ugh] matter."
(2)   a.   Art is an activity arising even in the animal kingdom, and springing
             from sexual desire and propensity to play (Darwin, Schiller, Spencer)
             Introd[uce] the idea of the fop   30
             —and it is accompanied by pleasurable excitement.
       b.   Art is the external manifestation by lines, color, words, sound,
             movements of emotions felt by man.
       c.   Art is the production of some permanent object or passing action
             fitted to convey pleasurable impressions quite apart from personal   35
             advantage.

In the interpretation we have accepted, these two, the mystical and the sensual ideas of Art are blended. Approval of Harmony—that is

sensual—Approval of Adaptation—that is mystic—of course none of
this is rigid. Now apply the case to our swan.

I.   Approval of Harmony—(Beauty we will say)—there is the silken
     whiteness, the satisfying curve of line and mass. Why do these
5   charm us. I cannot answer. Turn to

Adaptation:—Now we might say that we love the silken whiteness and
the grandly raised wings because they are the expression of the great
purpose which leads the swan to raise itself as far as possible to attract a
mate, the mate choosing the finest male that the species may be
10 reproduced in its most advantageous form. That you must sift for
yourselves. But there is a sense (perhaps unconscious) of exquisite
harmony and adaptation to an end when we feel the boat-like build of
the bird, the strength of those arched wings, the suppleness of the long
neck which we have seen waving shadowily under the water in search of
15 food. Contrast the quaint, gobbling, diving ducks. Think too of our
positive pain in seeing the great unwieldy body of the bird standing on
the bank supported by ugly black legs. Why is it ugly. Because a
structure like that could *not* walk with ease or grace—it is unfitted to its
surroundings. The legs are hateful because, being black, they are too
20 violent a contrast to the body which is so white—they are clammy
looking too—and what sense is 'clammy' applied to. Think of evening
primroses in the moonlight and in the noonday. Flowers and insects
have evolved side by side.

     This is Beauty in Nature—but does the same hold good when we
25 turn to the human productions of Art? Often, it does. But think of the
works of Poe, of Zola, de Maupassant, Maxim Gorky, Hood's 'Song of
the Shirt'—think of Watts' 'Mammon' (if that is art), of the 'Laocoon,'
the 'Outcasts' of Luke Fildes. Do you experience any 'pleasure' in
these. Do they excite 'pleasurable' feeling. Do they show Divine
30 purpose? Yet they are Art. Why? Somebody would say "They are so
true." But they are not necessarily true, in the strict sense of the word.
Not true, except that they have been felt, experienced as if they were
true. They express—as well, perhaps, as is possible—the real *feelings* of
the artist. Something more, then, must be added to our idea of Art—it
35 is the medium through which men express their deep, real feelings. By
ordinary words, common speech, we transmit thoughts, ideas, judg-
ments one to another. But when we express a true emotion, it is
through the medium of Art. When Carlyle said that a Hero could
hardly express himself otherwise than through song, he meant that the
40 vigorous emotion so moulded the speech of his hero—Mahommet,

Dante, Burns—that this speech became Art. So Art is the second great means of communication between man and man, as Tolstoi says. Intellectual art, which has no emotion, but only wit, has a cold barren effect. Think of Pope and the great Encyclopedists. This means of communication of emotion is in three ways—by form and colour (as in all painting, sculpture, weaving, building)—by sound (music) by ideas through words—all literature down to the graphic, moving tale told by a boy to his mates. The picture words, the thrilling voice, the animated face and lively gestures, all go to make up the art of story-telling. The English, whatever is said of them, are a truly poetic people, if reserved. Look at our words, words like "flash!" *"laughter"* "wonder". Compare Latin and French 'rideo' and 'rire'.

The essence, then, of true human art is that it should convey the emotions of one man to his fellows. It is a form of sympathy, and sympathy is in some measure harmony and unity, and in harmony and unity there is the idea of consistent purpose, is there not? So it works back to the old definitions. But, you will say, there are emotions desirable and undesirable—and Art may transmit the undesirable. Exactly—then it is bad art. According as the feeling that originated it, art may be bad, weak, good—in all shades. So Tolstoi says that all nude study is bad art. Honi soit qui mal y pense.

This might lead you to reflect that anyone who feels deeply must be an artist. But there you must consider that not one person in a thousand can express his emotions. We are most of us dumb, there, or we can only talk to a few who understand our mute signs, and the peculiar meanings we give to the words we use. The same sentence, in ten different mouths has ten different meanings. We can feel, but we cannot transmit our feelings—we can't express ourselves. When you have tried, when you have felt compelled to write to somebody, for you could not contain yourself, what sort of a letter has it appeared when written? Weak, maudlin, ridiculous. Why? You didn't feel ridiculous. But you did not understand what effect certain words have on readers. You didn't find the picture word, you didn't use a quick, spirited, vigorous style, so your letter is *not* art, for it does *not* express anything adequately. Tolstoi and his simple art—his tales.

This brings us to the technique of art. This again seems to be mostly a question of pleasurable feeling. Take these examples—of drawing—the physiological aspect—of music—of colour—the common basis. Now we are in a position to attempt criticism. Take Leighton's 'Wedded' and Watts' 'Mammon.' We can excellently well

criticise what we call the 'spirit' of the thing—Look—! (*Suggestion)
But we are not so well able to understand, or even to appreciate the
technique. That needs study. "The chief triumph of Art" says Hume
"is to insensibly refine the temper, and to point out to us those
5 dispositions which we should endeavour to attain by constant *bent* of
mind and by repeated *habit*." If we bend our minds, not so much to
things beautiful, as to the beautiful aspect of things, then we gain this
refinement of temper which can *feel* at once a beautiful thing. We are
too gross—a crude emotion carries us away—we cannot feel the
10 beauty of things. It is so in socialism as in everything. You must train
yourself to appreciate beauty or art—refine yourself, or become
refined, as Hume puts it. And what is refinement? It is really delicate
sympathy. What then is the mission of Art? To bring us into a sympathy
with as many men, as many objects, as many phenomena as possible.
15 To be in sympathy with things is to some extent to recognise, to
acquiesce in their purpose, to help on that purpose. We want, we are
forever trying to unite ourselves with the whole universe to carry out
some ultimate purpose—evolution, we call one phase of the carrying
out. The passion of human beings to be brought into sympathetic
20 understanding of one another is stupendous; witness it in the eagerness
with which biographies, novels, personal and subjective writings are
read.
Emotion tends to issue in action—drawing etc.
In socialism you have the effort to take what is general in the human
25 character and build a social state to fit it. In Art is revealed the
individual character. After all, the part of a man's nature which is
roughly common to all his fellows is only a small part of his nature. He
must be more than that—more refined, to understand the hosts of
particular qualities which go to make up the human character, and are
30 influences in the progress of things. So, though Art is general, it is also
particular. Socialism is general. Think. We can still feel the arms of
Ruth round the neck of Naomi; we can feel the tears in the women's
eyes. We, too, can love and suffer at parting. We still count the story of
David and Jonathan° one of the finest in the world. But there are
35 other tales incomprehensible to us; and only a few can recognise the
ideal, the noble emotion which many Mediaeval artists expressed so
perfectly in their Madonnas—moon-faced Madonnas, we say, and turn
aside. But with a little thought and study you might feel a sympathy
grow up for those Madonnas, and understand. So through Art we may
40 be brought to live many lives, taking a common-place life as a unit, and

each may have so many fields of life to wander in as never to feel wretched and empty. These things are not obvious and immediate, so we are apt to despise them. But above all things we must understand much if we would do much.

In conclusion, I would like to suggest that whatever be the subject for 5 discussion, everyone should try and make some study of it, think about it, and, if there is anything they feel inclined to say, say it. It would be a good idea, too, to take a book—socialistic essays, an Essay of Mill or Spencer or anybody, something that costs little, and study it for full discussion one evening, someone presiding. We might, at rare intervals, 10 take a poet, a painting, or a novel, or a play.

APPENDIX II

'ART AND MORALITY',
FIRST VERSION

Note on the text

The text is taken from DHL's autograph manuscript, 9 pp., UT; it has not been published previously.

The original and second readings cancelled by DHL are shown within angle brackets ($\langle$ $\rangle$ and $\langle\langle$ $\rangle\rangle$).

'Art and Morality', First version

"Art is immoral!" they say. And artists run quickly to put on jazz underwear, to demoralise, or at least to débourgeoiser themselves.

But ⟨after all,⟩ yet, there are all sorts and sizes of morality. Why over-exaggerate the bourgeois sort?

What has a water-pitcher, and six insecure apples on a crumpled table-cloth, got to do with bourgeois morality? Yet nearly everybody feels that there ⟨is indeed⟩ sure is an immoral, or at least ⟨an anarchistic⟩ a destructive element, in a Cézanne still-life.

Why? The very same design, if it was *humanised*, and the table-cloth was a draped nude and the pitcher a semi-nude, something you could *identify* yourself with, and feel sympathetic about, would instantly cease to be immoral:

⟨⟨It is perhaps easier to see in painting ⟨than in any other art to see the⟩ the subtle⟩⟩ Perhaps from painting sooner than from any other art can we realise the subtle distinction between what is *felt* to be immoral, and what is *felt* to be moral, instinctively. Instinct is largely habit. And that which goes against an old habit, in mankind, is at once pronounced immoral.

But against what instinct, against what old human habit does a Cézanne still-life militate? Merely a water-pitcher that isn't very much like a water-pitcher, and apples which aren't very appley, and a table-cloth that isn't *my* idea of a table cloth! All right! It mayn't be life-like—lots of bad paintings aren't. But where does the "immoral" touch come in? Because there it is.

The picture rouses a *definite* feeling of hostility: not merely a negative condemnation as a poor piece of work. It arouses anger, and a certain hate. It is a violation of some deep old instinct.

Being merely apples, pitcher, and table-cloth, it can't suggest improper behaviour. It *doesn't* suggest improper behaviour—even to a Freudian. If it did, everybody would feel much more at home with it.

Yet is is immoral.

Then why?

Because of a very peculiar, but very deep-seated habit in mankind.

233

The slowly-formed habit of seeing just as the photographic camera sees, as far as line and mass are concerned. We have been working for centuries to make the "ideal" fit the "real." And visually, by the time of the advent of the kodak, we had succeeded.

5 Colour also we have learned to see "as it is": that is to say, according to the spectrum. We have formed the habit.

When the ordinary child sees a man, he sees he knows not what. But he registers two eyes, a nose, a mouth of teeth, two straight legs, two straight arms: a sort of hieroglyph, with which we are all acquainted.

10 For centuries men have been improving on this hieroglyph, and bringing it up to the kodak mark.

And as vision developed consciously towards the kodak, man's idea of himself developed towards the snap-shot image. At every instant, he was a complete thing, complete in himself, enjoying a sort of absolute-

15 ness and a sort of perfection. The rest of the world contributed to his absoluteness and his perfection. ⟨He was his own picture."⟩

This agrees entirely with a kodak "snap." You take a snap of your sweetheart, in the field among the buttercups, stroking a mare and smiling tenderly at the foal.

20 Awfully nice, and absolutely "real." There is your sweetheart, absolute in herself, complete, perfect, all her surroundings contributing to her, incontestable. She is "a picture."

And this is the habit we have formed: the habit of being, each man to himself, a picture. With the rest of the universe for his "setting." Each

25 woman to herself, a superlative "picture," with man for her immediate setting.

This has been the development of the conscious ego in man, according to visual reality, through three thousand years. Painting, the visual art, achieved the highest development among the arts. Nothing

30 can be imagined, more *complete* than a Velasquez portrait, or a Titian portrait, or a Rembrandt: nothing more "life-like" than a Reynolds, or, in another sort of life, a Manet, or in still another degree of life, a Sargent portrait.

The visual world seen through the eye of man. Which eye, having

35 been brought to a kodak perfection, becomes universal, as the eye of God. Instead of being my own pair of eyes, part of limited *me*, it becomes The Human Eye in me, through which I see everything. And I, in my own ego, am the seer and the clue to all things.

Nothing is real until it is visualised, in our modern intelligence. So

40 we have achieved a vision of the universe which is a real satisfactto

us. We feel as if we had got to the bottom of the sack, and seen the Platonic Idea with our own eyes, in all its scientific absoluteness, lying there in the bottom of the sack of the universe.

This is the vast habit mankind has formed. The habit is now an instinct. And to thwart this instinct of accepting the universe as real 5 because it is seen, and ourselves as central in the picture—the eternal picture—this is immorality.

And this is the immoral element in a Cézanne still-life. The picture repudiates the kodak: and repudiates, therefore, the Eternal Eye. It contains a great deal that is *not seen*, and never to be seen, in ⟨a⟩ the 10 photographic sense. The apples are not apples according to the visual ideal, the tablecloth is not right according to the ⟨accepted idea⟩ proper look of a tablecloth, and a carpenter would disown the table itself. It isn't human. Man, that ineffable ego, with his all-seeing eye, is elbowed out.

⟨Because, since man⟩ As for man, since he dispensed with a Personal 15 God, he has assumed unto himself, in his own ego, ⟨all the attributes of [his?]⟩ every single qualification for the Personal ⟨God:⟩ Godhead: above all, the Eternal Eye. ⟨attribute.⟩ ⟨⟨qualification.⟩⟩

And now, the visual art itself comes to thwart him! Monstrous!

But if apples don't *look* like that, why should they be painted like that? 20 Why paint a *lie*!

Oh là-là-là! The apples *are* like that, just now, says Mr Cézanne.

Apples are always apples, says Vox Populi, Vox Dei.

Sometimes they're a sin, sometimes they're a bellyache, sometimes they're part of a pie, and sometimes they're Cézanne, comes the 25 unrecorded answer.

In fact, the apple fulfils the injunction to be all things to all men, and goes a bit farther. It is all things to all things.

What an apple ⟨is⟩ looks like to a caterpillar, to an urchin, to a thrush, to a browsing cow, to Sir Isaac Newton, to the tree it hangs on and the 30 earth it rots in, I leave you to consider. But they are all concerned.

And the immorality of Cézanne is probably the morality of the urchin, the tree, the earth, ⟨the⟩ and Sir Isaac. The caterpillar, the browsing cow would probably repudiate the immoral monstrosity with rage, their bellies being contrary. Just as pictorial little man repudiates the 35 monstrosity, seeing himself shoved out of the centre of the ⟨stage,⟩ canvas, his all-seeing eye blackened and puffing up.

If you're really an artist, you don't substitute immorality for morality. On the contrary: you usually substitute morality for immorality.

Take the prince of pseudo-artists, Raphael. His art is "perfect." 40

Which means, man, egoistic man occupies the plumb centre of the canvas, and his aura, or extended ego, spreads right into the picture-frame, with not so much as the whistle of a grasshopper to obstruct it, like a pebble in a stream.

5 All this stuff that they talk about art, of decoration and illustration, and significant form, and movement, and tactile values, and space-composition, and colour quality, and all that, is ⟨all⟩ all very well, afterwards. But you might as well ⟨eat⟩ force your guests to eat the menu card, ⟨instead⟩ at the end of the dinner.

10 Art is *always* moral, and pseudo-art is *always* immoral. Raphael is immoral. Art had diabetes for a long time, owing to his sugar diet. Our civilisation still has diabetes, from excess of sugar.

The business of all art, from A to Zee, as the Americans say, is to show things in their true relationships. The universe is like Father 15 Ocean, a stream of all things slowly moving. We move, and the rock of ages moves. There is no centre to the picture. Even the pole-star ceases to sit on the pole. Art must live for ever, because the relationship between all things will for ever change, and must forever be shown anew, because ⟨they are⟩ it is new.

20 An ancient Rameses can sit in stone absolute, without contact: beautiful and eternal. That was *his* eternality. And Michael Angelo's Adam can sit sentient and vulnerable in the universal heavens, to which he has just awakened. That is *his* eternality. And Turner can dissolve out into air and light and wind and earth, as a mood among the 25 elements. That is his eternality.

But every time, even in Corot and Turner, *man* covers the canvas, and the universe is only the moods of man.

Now the time has come for a new relationship. Man swims in the stream along with all things, and is relative to all things. The human 30 consciousness is no longer a nail driven through the centre of creation. Each thing streams in its own odd, intertwining flux, and nothing, not even man nor the God of man, is absolute, or fixed, or abiding. And nothing is true, or good, or right, except in its living relation to the other things that form its context.

35 And what is design, in art, but the recognition of the living—and therefore eternal—relation between the various elements of any creative composition. The strange, wonderful things the Egyptians did, in their worship of Life in all its manifestations. That is, in their accepting the subtle, vast flux of relationship between man and the 40 living universe, in all its forms and appearances. The strange relation-

ship which negro Africa has with the alive world, and which it reveals in marvellous little idols! And then our tiresome, dead, kodak vision, which sees all things static and grouped. Our very movement, like our movies, is only an endless shifting of static groups. The ⟨great⟩ big silent statue of Rameses is like a ⟨great dark⟩ ⟨⟨dark⟩⟩ drop of water 5 which hangs motionless, in ⟨perfect⟩ dark suspense. But a Sargent portrait is an artificial combination of lines and masses and lights, absolved from the stream of life, cut off from all context, existing as an assertion of human smartness, jigging without changing.

Let Cézanne's apples go rolling off the table for ever. They live by 10 their own laws, in their own ambiente, and not by the law of man. They are *casually* related to man. But to those apples, man is no absolute.

It is the vision of a new relationship. And this implies a new morality. As soon as a new morality comes into being, persisting in the old morality becomes immoral. Therefore, for one who has once tasted the 15 apple of Cézanne, the apples of Fantin Latour are apples of Sodom. They are out of keeping. ⟨with the life-flow.⟩

Art is moral because it has no absolutes; ⟨and because,⟩ it moves, and therefore, if you ⟨are⟩ want to catch up with real morality, ⟨it keeps you moving.⟩ you've got to move⟨, [on,?]⟩ also, and keep 20 moving.

APPENDIX III

'MORALITY AND THE NOVEL', FIRST VERSION

Note on the text

The text is taken from DHL's autograph manuscript, 9 pp., UT; it is previously unpublished.

The original readings cancelled by DHL are shown within angle brackets (⟨ ⟩). The editorial emendation is given in square brackets.

'Morality and the Novel', First version

The business of art is to ⟨show⟩ reveal the true relation ⟨existing⟩
attainable between man and ⟨the⟩ his circumambient universe, at a
particular momentary epoch. If Van Gogh paints sunflowers, he
⟨reveals the⟩ achieves a relation between himself, as man, and the   5
yellow sunflower. His painting does not represent the sunflower itself.
Heaven only knows what the sunflower itself is. And the camera will
give you the most unexceptional, universal picture of it. But Van
Gogh's painting is, as it were, the offspring of himself and the flower
itself. It is a third thing: the human soul, or spirit, or consciousness ⟨,⟩   10
(using this to mean the unrealised consciousness) fused and consummated with some object that is not itself. So that a painting of
sunflowers—by Van Gogh at least—is neither man-in-the-mirror, nor
sunflowers-in-the-mirror, but a reality in the fourth dimension, the
creative dimension, which is neither up nor down nor across, but in-   15
between. It is a revelation of a perfected relationship between man and
the circumambient universe.

And this relationship changes. In fact, it is this change in the
relationship between man and the universe which makes human time.

Therefore, art and life must change forever. From day to day the   20
relation between all things changes, in a subtle stealth of change.

And every new relationship formed between a man and the universe
hurts somewhat in the forming. So that living must always hurt, to a
certain extent, in the process. Even the real *seeing* of a new picture must
hurt at first. Because it means the forming of a new relation between   25
ourselves and—say sunflowers.

Pseudo-art, even such magnificent art as Raphael's, dresses up and
gorgeously presents again an already experienced relationship. Hence
it is a source of *pure* pleasure: a sort of voluptuousness or wallowing.
Actual art will always rouse resistance. It roused resistance in the artist   30
even before he brought forth his presentation.

If we look into it, life itself consists essentially in the forming of a true
relationship—which means, in every case, a more or less new
one—between the self and the circumambient universe. It is not the *self*

241

which is all in all: a man cannot save his own soul. And it is not the *object*, even the beloved, which is the all in all. The all in all is the third thing, the Ghost of religion, the relationship itself, which is beyond either of the parties.

5   And a relationship changes all the time: you can't drive a nail through it, and nail it down. A perfect relationship is a moment of eternity, and no one moment is like any other moment. There is an infinity of different Nirvanas, and each man in his one life-time may pass through a strange cycle of them. Or he may fail to realise one

10 single moment: he may fail to make even one sheer relationship, with anything, be it a sunflower or a woman or a dog or a stone or a harvest of maize, or even a piece of gold.

Now the novel obviously concerns itself solely and simply with the relationships established between man and the universe that surrounds

15 him. The central relation is between man and woman: but there is an infinite host of others: man and man, woman and woman, other people, children, creatures, cities, skies, trees, flowers, mud, microbes, motor-cars, guns, sewers—everything.

The business of the novel is the true relationship existing between

20 man and all the things that can move him. The *morality* of the novel is to discriminate between genuine relationships—which are always *new*—and fake relationships, which are always a rechauffé of old ones, with varying ingredients.

Take the central theme of most important novels: the relation

25 between man and woman. You can get a James Joyce or a Marcel Proust to say as many last words as they like—and they like to say a legion—yet they never say anything except the innumerable last words about their own specific case. The relation between man and woman will change forever, and will forever be new, and will forever be the

30 central clue to human life, even more central than eating and drinking and reproducing. It is the *relation itself* which is the quick and the central clue to life, not any accompanying contingency like children, family, home.

The old novel—the old European novel—ended with marriage.

35 Marriage put the stamp on, and finished the relationship. It was supposed to remain henceforth *in statu quo*, the relationship between the man and the woman. There was some mysterious *bond*, called love, which was even eternal.

Of course, the oldest novels were not like that: ⟨neither⟩ not even

40 *Daphnis and Chloe*, ⟨not⟩ and certainly not *The Golden Ass*, nor the

Satiricon.* *The Golden Ass* and the *Satiricon* are full of the woe of
changing relationships that will not stay where they're put. ⟨And⟩ Even
if you *eat* the rose of all roses, it only acts as a purge.

The modern novel has not advanced a step, it seems to me, beyond
The Golden Ass or the *Satiricon*. Of course, in one sense, the novel is   5
always the novel, and can neither advance nor recede. Once it succeeds
in being a novel, it is there, in that place of the fourth dimension, where
there is no forwards nor backwards nor higher nor lower, nor even
better nor worse.

The highest quality in man is pure courage, the courage to meet life,   10
and establish the new relationship. Meeting death is not so very
important, since we ⟨shall⟩ have all to meet it, willy nilly. But about
meeting life itself, we have a choice. And the choice depends on our
courage.

And I can find no purer courage in *Madame Bovary** than in the   15
fragmentary *Satiricon*: perhaps not so pure. And no purer courage in
The Idiot than in *The Golden Ass*: not so robust.

They call the relation between man and woman, "sex." But sex is
such a silly, mechanical little word. The Freudians have made it worse:
a mere ⟨phallic⟩ Jack-in-the-box with one gesture and one squeak. It   20
is both ludicrous and bathetic.

The relation between man and woman has been, and will be, the
quick of all human life. But it changes all the time. For a long time,
woman was supposed to be a mere sacrifice to man. Then the tables
were turned, and man was supposed to be a devoted self-sacrificer,   25
sacrificing himself to the woman and the child. First mankind tried to
nail down woman, as subservient to man. Then it tries to nail down
man, as subservient to the mother-and-child, the reproducing and
conservation of life.

And the novel shows you, that neither will do. Woman bound down   30
to inferiority gives you the woe and the disaster of the *Satiricon* and the
Golden Ass. Man tied down to paternity and productive domesticity
give[s] you the bathos of *War and Peace* and ⟨are⟩ lies at the root of the
horrors of *The Brothers Karamazov*.*

It won't do. Just as power, glorious power, would not do, in Greek   35
and Roman days, so love, boundless love, will not do in ours. But since
we have fallen sick with love, the novels do nothing but go on
prescribing more love, carrying the homoeopathic treatment to weird
lengths.

The men and women kill each other off, with love, in every other   40 novel you open. The Constant Nymph herself dies of heart failure, after eighteen months of love-constancy. She couldn't keep it up, constant as she might be, and however much of a nymph, for longer than that.

5 Yet the novelist would prescribe "more love," instead of "less love." And that I call immoral.

The relation between men and women is supposed to be pure love. When the pure love finishes off one or other, or both of the parties, we are supposed to feel luscious about it. Because the ideal is, that both 10 parties *shall* sacrifice themselves to the perfect relationship, called love.

This is almost more trying, and certainly more deadly, than the sacrificing of woman to man, or man to woman. Love is a relationship between things, as intangible as the rainbow; which itself is the bridge between sun and rain, the Holy Ghost in all its colours. Now, that we 15 should proceed to sacrifice both the sun and the rain to the rainbow, is just nonsense. Yet men and women are supposed actually to sacrifice themselves to this "livelier iris" of love. Which begets pure nonsense in us all.

The novel, however, pounds away at the theme.

20 Now if it is futile and disastrous to nail down woman or to nail down man, either one on the cross of the other, how much more futile and disastrous is it to try and nail down the relation between them. You might just as well try to pin the rainbow on the clouds with safety pins.

But we have committed the absurdity. We have said that men and 25 women *must love*. Love is a definite, specific emotion, and they must go on feeling it: because, presumably, they like the feel of it, when they get it.

Men and women will go on being livingly related to each other for ever. But that you can suddenly peg down the relationship, and make 30 man and woman gyrate round it like a couple of tethered asses, treading the eternal round of "love," is ridiculous and monstrous.

And this is the ridiculousness and the monstrosity of the modern novel: the immorality. ⟨too.⟩

The relation between man and woman will last forever, but it will 35 change forever. You can call it love, if you like, so long as you never attempt to define love. If a nymph wants to be constant, let her be constant to her nymph-hood; and a man to his manhood, and a woman to her womanhood. If you set any of them being constant to ⟨some⟩ one another, or to some iridescent abstraction whose very nature is 40 change, you make fools of them all round.

If we are going to be moral, let us refrain from driving pegs through ourselves, or through another person, or through the third thing, the relationship, the Holy Ghost itself. It is monstrous to crucify or to be crucified. But to crucify a relationship on the upright of man and the horizontal of woman, is a madness pure and simple.   5

The novel is the one perfect medium for revealing to us the changing glimmer of our living relationships. The novel can help us to live as no other utterance can help us. It can also pervert us as no other can.

APPENDIX IV

'JOHN GALSWORTHY',
FRAGMENT OF AN EARLY DRAFT

Note on the text

The text is taken from DHL's autograph manuscript, 6pp. (MS), UT: collated with *Phoenix* (A1), where it appeared under the title '[The Individual Consciousness v. the Social Consciousness]' (see Introduction, p. lii).

'John Galsworthy', Fragment of an early draft

The more one reads of modern novels, the more one realises that, in
this individualistic age, there are no individuals left. People, men,
women and children, are *not* thinking their own thoughts, they are *not*
feeling their own feelings, they are *not* living their own lives. 5
The moment the human being becomes conscious of himself, he
ceases to be himself. The reason is obvious. The moment any
individual creature becomes aware of its own individual isolation, it
becomes instantaneously aware of that which is outside itself, and
forms its limitation. That is, the psyche splits in two, into subjective and 10
objective reality. The moment this happens, the primal integral *I*,
which is for the most part a living continuum of all the rest of things,
collapses, and we get the I which is staring out of the window at the
reality which is not itself. And this is the condition of the modern
consciousness, from early childhood. 15
In the past, children were supposed to be "innocent." Which means
that they were like the animals, not split into subjective and objective
consciousness. They were one living continuum with all the universe.
This is the essential state of innocence or of naïveté, and it is the
persistence of this state all through life, as the *basic* state of conscious- 20
ness, which preserves the human being all his life fresh and alive, a true
individual. Paradoxical as it may sound, the individual is only truly
himself when he is unconscious of his own individuality, when he is
unaware of his own isolation, when he is not split into subjective and
objective, when there is no *me or you*, no *me or it* in his consciousness, 25
but the *me and you*, the *me and it* is a living continuum, as if all were
connected by a living membrane.
As soon as the conception *me or you, me or it* enters the human
consciousness, then the individual consciousness is supplanted by the
social consciousness. The social consciousness means the cleaving of 30
the true individual consciousness into two halves, subjective and
objective, me on the one hand, you or it on the other. The awareness of
"you" or of "it" as something definitely limiting "me," this is the social
consciousness. The awareness of "you" or of "it" as a continuum of

"me"—different, but not separate: different as the eye is different from the nose—this is the primal or pristine or basic consciousness of the individual, the state of "innocence" or of "naïveté."

5 This consciousness collapses, and the real individual lapses out, leaving only the social individual, a creature of subjective and objective consciousness, but of no innocent or genuinely individual consciousness. The innocent or radical individual consciousness alone is unanalysable and mysterious, it is the queer nuclear spark in the protoplasm, which is life itself, in its individual manifestation. The

10 moment you split into subjective and objective consciousness, then the whole thing becomes analysable, and, in the last issue, dead.

Of course, it takes a long time to destroy the naïve individual, the old Adam, entirely, and to produce creatures which are completely social in consciousness, that is, always aware of the "you" set over against the

15 "me," always conscious of the "it" which the "I" is up against. But it has happened now in even tiny children. A child nowadays can say: *Mummy!*—and his fatal consciousness of the cleft between him and Mummy is already obvious. The cleavage has happened to him. He is no longer one with things: worse, he is no longer *at one* with his mother

20 even. He is a tiny, forlorn little social individual, a subjective-objective little consciousness.

The subjective-objective consciousness is never truly individual. It is a product. The social individual, the me-or-you, me-or-it individual, is denied all naïve or innocent or really individual feelings. He is capable

25 only of the feelings, which are really sensations, produced by the reaction between the "me" and the "you," the "I" and the "it." Innocent or individual feeling is only capable when there is a continuum, when the me and the you and the it are a continuum.

Man lapses from true innocence, from the at-oneness, in two ways.

30 The first is the old way of greed or selfishness, when the "me" wants to swallow the "you" and put an end to the continuum that way. The other is the way of negation, when the "I" wants to lapse out into the "you" or the "it," and so end all responsibility of keeping up one's own bright nuclear cell alive in the tissue of the universe. In either way, there is a

35 lapse from innocence and a fall into the state of vanity, ugly vanity. It is a vanity of positive tyranny, or a vanity of negative tyranny. The old villains-in-the-piece fell into the vanity of positive tyranny, the new villains-in-the-piece, who are still called saints and holy persons, or at worst, god's fools, are squirming in the vanity of negative tyranny. They

40 won't leave the continuum alone. They insist on passing out into it.

Which is as bad as if the eye should insist on merging itself into a oneness with the nose. For we are none of us more than a cell in the eye-tissue, or a cell in the nose-tissue or the heart-tissue of the macrocosm, the universe.

And, of course, the moment you cause a break-down in living tissue, 5 you get inert Matter. So, the moment you break the continuum, the naïveté, the innocence, the at-oneness, you get materialism and nothing but materialism.

Of course, inert Matter exists, as distinct from living tissue: dead protoplasm as distinct from living, nuclear protoplasm. But the living 10 tissue is able to deal with the dead tissue. Whereas the reverse is not true. Dead tissue cannot do anything to living tissue, except try to corrupt it and make it dead too. Which is the main point concerning Materialism, whether it be the spiritual or the carnal Materialism.

The continuum which is alive can handle the dead tissue. That is, 15 the individual who still retains his individuality, his basic at-oneness or innocence or naïveté, can deal with the material world successfully. He can be analytical and critical upon necessity. But at the core, he is always naïve or innocent or at one.

The contrary is not true. The social consciousness can only be 20 analytical, critical, constructive but not creative, sensational but not passionate, emotional but without true feeling. It can know, but it cannot be. It is always made up of a duality, to which there is no clue. And the one half of the duality neutralises, in the long run, the other half. So that, whether it is Nebuchadnezzar or Francis of Assisi,* 25 you arrive at the same thing, nothingness.

You can't make art out of nothingness. Ex nihilo nihil fit!* But you can make art out of the collapse towards nothingness: the collapse of the true individual into the social individual.

Which brings us to John Galsworthy with a bump. Because, in all his 30 books, I have not been able to discover one real individual—nothing but social individuals. Ex nihilo nihil fit. You can't make art, which is the revelation of the continuum itself, the very nuclear glimmer of the naïve individual, when there is no continuum and no naïve individual. As far as I have gone, I have found in Galsworthy nothing but social 35 individuals.

Thinking you are naïve doesn't make you naïve, and thinking you are passionate doesn't make you passionate. Again, being stupid or limited is not a mark of naïveté, and being doggishly amorous is not a sign of passion. In each case, the very reverse. Again, a peasant is by no means 40 necessarily more naïve, or innocent or individual than a stockbroker, nor a sailor than an educationalist. The reverse may be the case. Peasants are often as greedy as cancer, and sailors as soft corrupt as a rotten apple.

[End of manuscript]

EXPLANATORY NOTES

EXPLANATORY NOTES

Study of Thomas Hardy

7:2 **Study of . . . Gai Savaire]** For the probable origin of the editorial title 'Study of Thomas Hardy' see Introduction, p. xxxvi.

DHL' version of 'le gai savoir' (French) or 'lo gai saber' (Provençal) – the gay science or skill – a term invented by the medieval troubadour poets for their poetic craft. While he may have heard it from Ezra Pound (*Letters*, ii. 295 n. 1), the use of it as a title seems more likely to have come through Nietzsche's title *Die fröhliche Wissenschaft* (1882–7). In *Beyond Good and Evil*, which DHL read in Oscar Levy's English edition (1909) while at Croydon, Nietzsche pours scorn on 'The *unmanliness* of that which is called "sympathy"' which he sees throughout Europe (section 293): 'I wish people to put the good amulet, "gai saber" ("gay science", in ordinary language), on heart and neck, as a protection against it.' It is likely but not certain that DHL also read *The Case of Wagner*, trans. Oscar Levy (1888), in which Nietzsche further defined 'la gaya scienza' (Italian) as 'light feet, wit, fire, grace; the great logic; the dance of the stars; the exuberant spirituality; the southern shivers of light; the *smooth* sea – perfection' (section 10). (In 1915 DHL was searching for 'a nice title – like Morgenrot in German', *Letters*, ii. 317, for his revised philosophy, clearly with Nietzsche's *Die Morgenröte*, 'The Dawn', in mind.)

7:6 **- 1 -** Only the second section (10:1) is numbered in TS; it may represent an earlier chapter division. There is a similar omission in chap. ix. See Introduction, p. xxxiii–xxxiv.

7:18 **systole of its heart-beat,** DHL had used the systole–diastole (7:18–20) opposition in 'Foreword to *Sons and Lovers*' (see Introduction, p. xxiv–xxv). Several of the polarities in 'Hardy' were probably first discovered in Ralph Waldo Emerson's 'Compensation' (1841). The relevant passage reads: 'Polarity, or action and reaction, we meet in every part of nature; in darkness and light; in heat and cold; in the ebb and flow of water; in male and female; in the inspiration and expiration of plants and animals; in the systole and diastole of the heart; in the undulations of fluids and of sound; in the centrifugal and centripetal gravity . . .' (The essay was reprinted in *The International Library of Famous Literature*, 20 vols, 1899, ed. Richard Garnett, xv, pp. 7105–22, which the Lawrence family owned.)

7:22 **self-preservation.** A term in wide circulation. DHL had read as a student, for instance, Herbert Spencer's *Education* (1861) which began with a distinction between living 'in the mere material sense only' and 'in the widest sense'. Spencer classified kinds of activities which constitute human life, the first being 'activities which minister to self-preservation'. (See also note on 98:7.)

7:24 **huge barns of plenty.** Probably an allusion to Luke xii. 15–21. If DHL had this parable in mind he is more likely to have written 'barns' than 'a barn', as suggested by Edward McDonald. The references to 'walls of brass' and the 'rage' of self-preservation may echo Shakespeare's Sonnet lxv and *Julius Caesar* I. iii. 93ff.

7:33   **considering the ruddy lily.**   See Matthew vi. 28; DHL's argument recalls vi. 25–34. Cf. Song of Solomon v. 10, 13. DHL notes 'The red lilies are dead, and the white Madonna lilies hold their place' *Letters*, i. 63

8:8   **the ant and the grasshopper;**   'The Ant and the Grasshopper' in William R. Titterton's *Studies in Solitary Life* (1908) depicts the ant as a wealthy industrialist and the grasshopper as a 'chirruping' poet who dies of starvation at his door. Titterton was a contributor to the *New Age*. See note on 135:2 and *Letters*, i. 100.

8:14   **[physics]**   A conjectural reading to fill the gap in TS; cf. *The Rainbow* chap. xv, where Dr Frankstone, a physicist, suggests to Ursula 'May it not be that life consists in a complexity of physical and chemical activities . . . ?' Later Ursula asks herself 'For what purpose were the incalculable physical and chemical activities nodalized in this shadowy, moving speck under her microscope? . . . She only knew that it was not limited mechanical energy, nor mere purpose of self-preservation and self-assertion.'

8:17   **the place . . . no more.**   Psalm ciii. 16.

8:24   **a phoenix.**   A mythical bird, also a traditional Christian symbol of resurrection, was adopted by DHL as a personal emblem in late 1914 (see *Letters*, ii. 252 and n. 5), and this parable is his first extended use of it. See James C. Cowan, 'Lawrence's Phoenix: An Introduction' in *DHL Review*, v (1972), 187–99.

8:36   **old [man] knew . . . in his innermost heart**   The reading in TCC of 'The old know this' probably derived from the blurred 'e' in 'knew' in TS . . . McDonald marked the transposition of the phrase in TCC (see Textual apparatus).

9:8   *always*   To indicate italics in print TS uses either underlining or double spacing of letters as here; the Textual apparatus records the double spacing.

10:10   **flaunting vanity,"**   Cf. 10:33. See Ecclesiastes i. 2ff. Behind the old man's utterances may also lie the essay 'On the Vanity of Existence' by Arthur Schopenhauer (1788–1860); see Delavenay, i. 78.

10:31   **unprovided**   'Improvided' in TS is an archaic form; however Koteliansky occasionally misread DHL's 'un-' as 'im-' (cf. 120:16).

10:33   **[transience]**   'Transium' in TS is not a word, nor is 'transitation' at 103:24; in both cases Kot misread the manuscript. TCC's solution here is the obvious one. See also 103:24 and note.

11:2   **Où sont . . . de l'antan?**   'Ballade des Dames du Temps jadis' by François Villon (b. 1431) ['Mais où . . . d'antan?']. DHL then recalls the translation 'The Ballad of Dead Ladies' (1870) by Dante Gabriel Rossetti (1828–82):
Where's Hipparchia, and where is Thais
Neither of them the fairer woman? . . .
But where are the snows of yesteryear? (lines 3–4, 8)

11:7   **Dido . . . Aeneas**   Tragic queen of Carthage . . . heroic scion of the Trojan royal family; see Virgil's *Aeneid*, Books i–iv. For Aeneas's greeting of Dido in the Underworld, see *Aeneid* vi. 456ff.

11:10 **"Didon dina ... dindon",** A tongue-twister used in classroom drill by students of French.

11:17 **pillar of fire,** Phrase derived from Exodus xiii. 21–2.

12:9 **regulation cabbage ... value.** DHL refers to the practice of binding the outer leaves round the heart of the cabbage to discourage 'bolting', i. e. going to seed. Seeding cabbages have no market value.

12:33 **[incontrovertible],** 'Introvertible' in TS is meaningless. For DHL's use of 'incontrovertible' see 68:24, 77:10, 95:34.

12:35 **"to them ... be given."** Cf. 13:25. DHL's adaptation of Matthew xiii. 12, xxv. 29 *et al.*

14:2 **Women's Suffrage,** For DHL's early contact with the women's suffrage movement through Alice Dax and Blanche Jennings, see Introduction to 'Art and the Individual'. For a graphic account of a suffragist rally (and his reactions to it), see *Letters*, i. 123–4 and 277. See also Helen Corke, *In Our Infancy* (Cambridge, 1975), p. 163.

15:19 **"Physician, heal thyself."** Luke iv. 23.

15:29 **a malaria** I.e. in the original sense of 'bad, unwholesome air' from 'mala aria' (Italian).

16:4 **under the bushel,** See Matthew v. 15.

16:7 **tip-cat** A game in which a short piece of wood is 'tipped' at one end with a stick so as to spring up, and then knocked to a distance.

16:24 **[not]** Clearly a word has been omitted in TS (A1 added 'also' after 'against ourselves'): the 'not' makes this phrase parallel to the similar thought in the following sentence.

16:33 **[be]** In TS Kot left a space for three letters. For 'be' cf. 16:6, 17:5ff; however, cf. also 17:20–2 for McDonald's reading 'risk' in A1.

17:3 **"world disaster":** Like the 'just and righteous war' and 'the Prussian yoke' (16:24–7), from patriotic propaganda of the First World War.

17:17 **We must [17:12] ... fear or brutality.** DHL returned to this theme, with a graphic account of a wounded soldier, in 'The Crown', chap. v (*Phoenix II* 400–2).

17:27 **Christ's Commandment:** Matthew xix. 19; see also 43:23 and note, 63:37ff.

18:17 **horrific space of the void,** Cf. 'Le silence éternel de ces espaces infinis m'effraie' ['The eternal silence of these infinite spaces terrifies me'] in *Pensées* (1670), iii. 206 by Blaise Pascal (1623–62). See also note on 98:7.

19:11 **save his ... the waters.** Allusions to Matthew xvi. 25 ['whosoever would ... life shall lose it', (RV)] (see also 77:29) and Ecclesiastes xi. 1.

20:5 **the Judgement Book.** See Revelation xx. 12.

22:4 **must be taken chronologically,** Abercrombie argued against a chronological treatment of Hardy's novels and in favour of arranging them 'according to their own interrelationships'. He nevertheless provided a chronological list against which DHL ticked the major novels in his copy (Abercrombie 60–2).

The novels discussed by DHL are: *Desperate Remedies* (1871), *Under the Greenwood Tree* (1872), *A Pair of Blue Eyes* (1873), **Far from the Madding Crowd* (1874), *The Hand of Ethelberta* (1876, serially 1875), **The Return of the Native* (1878), *The Trumpet-Major* (1880), *A Laodicean* (1881), **Two on a Tower* (1882), **The Mayor of Casterbridge* (1886), **The Woodlanders* (1887), **Wessex Tales* (1888), **Tess of the d'Urbervilles* (1891), **Jude the Obscure* (1896, serially 1894–5), **The Well-beloved* (1897, serially 1892). (* denotes those ticked by DHL.)

23:1 time. [Sergeant] Troy This solution to a crux in TS appears in TCC where there is evidence of erasure and change. The TS reading 'time, subject', suggests that a further phrase about Gabriel Oak should have followed and that the next sentence should begin with 'Troy', the form used in 22:39 and 23:3.

25:5 It is the Heath. Abercrombie praised Hardy's art for exceeding 'the mere delight in taking part in existence' to reach an acceptance of, and delight in, 'the tragic ground-bass which keenly civilized consciousness always hears accompanying the tune of the world'. In a footnote he added 'See the famous description of Egdon Heath with which *The Return of the Native* opens . . .' (p. 22).

25:9 [earth] The TS reading 'hearth' is clearly an error. Kot may have picked up the 'h' of the next word ('heaved'), but he made the same typing mistake at 40:14. The absence of a capital 'H' (see the six other occurrences of the name between 25:1 and 25:30), together with the emphasis on soil rather than Egdon Heath in this sentence, which is a restatement of 25:6, make 'earth' preferable to A1's 'heath'.

25:13 What matter Since the sentence repeats the formula one line later, DHL probably intended a parallelism (see Textual apparatus).

26:27 "An inner [26:16] . . . itself here." *The Return of the Native*, Book II, chap. VI ['. . . preying upon an outer . . . thought-worn he . . . even though there is . . .'].

26:37 He should . . . his being, From Acts xvii. 28.

26:39 "he was . . . was expected", DHL is recalling *Return of the Native*, Book III, chap. I rather than quoting: 'He had been a lad of whom something was expected. Beyond this all had been chaos. That he would be successful in an original way, or that he would go to the dogs in an original way, seemed equally probable.'

27:6 And his emotions The 'hid' of TS was probably an uncancelled mistyping of 'his', which follows it correctly, rather than a part of DHL's text (as A1 printed it). There is no question of Clym's emotions being hidden; they are simply undeveloped.

27:11 "As is . . . a ray." *Return of the Native*, Book III, chap. VI.

27:21 "to preach . . . enriching themselves." *Return of the Native*, Book III, chap. II ['Yeobright preaching to the . . .'].

29:6 [confined] This editorial conjecture fills the space in TS 33:9 for a word of this length. It may be, however, that no word was omitted or intended as the passage makes adequate sense.

29:19 deliberate ironies, little tales of widows Reference to Hardy's short story collections: *Life's Little Ironies* (1894), *Wessex Tales* (1888) and *A Group of Noble Dames* (1891). Abercrombie also made a distinction between the 'principal novels' and the short stories with which he included *The Trumpet-Major*, *Under the Greenwood Tree* and *Two on a Tower* (chap. IV).

29:38 **Anna Karenin,** Tolstoy's eponymous heroine; DHL had read the novel (1878) enthusiastically in his early years (*Letters*, i. 127) and alluded to it frequently, e.g. 'The Novel', 179:31ff.

31:4 **IV . . . always excess, the biologists say,** On chapter misnumbering in TS, see Introduction, pp. xxxiii–xxxiv . . . for instance, Charles Darwin in *The Origin of the Species* (1859), chap. III.

32:13 **Weltschmerz** World-weariness, Romantic pessimism (German).

32:19 **Mary of Bethany.** See Luke x. 38–42. For DHL's use of Mary as a type see 114:32.

32:26 **the poor have ye always with you.** Matthew xxvi. 11 ['ye have the poor always . . .'].

32:34 **beat** The pencilled alteration to 'bent' in TS has no authority; see Introduction, p. xxxiv. (The change at 34:7 likewise has no authority.)

32:36 **Carlyle . . . it is all,** Thomas Carlyle (1795–1881) in, e.g. *Past and Present* (1843), Book III, chap. XI, 'Labour'.

32:39 **the tail . . . this serpent.** DHL frequently used the traditional image of the snake with its tail in its mouth to describe circular arguments, e.g. his essay 'Him with his Tail in his Mouth' (*Reflections on the Death of a Porcupine*, Philadelphia, 1925).

33:7 **the lesson book.** While at Nottingham High School DHL studied Emil Otto's *German Conversation-Grammar* (1887 *et seq.*) which contains proverbs, e.g. 'Wer nicht arbeitet, soll nicht essen' ('Who works not, should not eat'), but not those DHL quoted. If he is referring to a beginner's textbook, it has not been identified. See D. J. Peters, 'Young Bert Lawrence as pupil at city High School' in *Nottingham Guardian Journal* (22 March 1972).

33:10 **[proverb]** The TS reading 'problem' was probably Kot's error, unless DHL were thinking of examples in his German textbook as 'problems'; A1's emendation is adopted.

37:27 **[not]** [37:21] **. . .[owning].** Both 'not' and the 'n' in 'owning' have been added in ink to TS. All later states of the text read 'owing', but Frieda, in quoting the passage – one of her favourites – in *Frieda Lawrence: The Memoirs and Correspondence*, ed. E. W. Tedlock (1961), p. 107, has 'owning'. Since her memoir (1935–?) is later than TCC (1930), it is likely that she made the corrections to TS when transcribing the passage.

39:11 **As for me** [39:4] **. . . heal himself."** See Introduction, p. xxx for DHL's plan for his ideal community: 'away from this world of war and squalor . . . It is to be a colony built up on the real decency which is in each member of the Community – a community which is established upon the assumption of goodness in the members, instead of the assumption of badness' (*Letters*, ii. 259).

40:2 **the Angel** DHL's meaning is seen in context at 43:8; cf. 'my Angels and Devils are old-fashioned symbols for the flower into which we strive to burst . . . I am just in love with mediaeval terms, that is all –' (*Letters*, ii. 275).

40:9 **as a habit,** DHL marked the following passage in his copy of Abercrombie: All the innumerable processes whereby this Immanent Will of Hardy's utters and articulates existence, it has long since got by heart; it is concerned with nothing but this habit of multitudinously existing . . . as things are now, the habit is grown to such perfect precision that is has lulled the Will into a drowse, wherein nothing is active but the habit itself . . . the mere habit of causing existence is everything. (p. 209)

(For DHL's note on this passage, see Introduction, fn. 43.) Abercrombie's reference is to the utterances of the Spirit of the Years in *The Dynasts*, e.g. in the Fore Scene.

40:35 **[repeats]** The simplest resolution of the muddle in TS 'repents' makes no sense here; it is possible that Kot misread 'a' as 'n', and 'repeats' picks up the references to repetition.

41:33 **unacquaint,** Unaware (archaic).

42:27 **[me]** The editorial insertion is suggested by the style of the context.

43:23 **help my neighbour,** Cf. 17:27 and note. DHL's interpretation of this commandment (see also Luke x. 27ff.) underlies his quarrel with Christianity and his castigation of charitable love or benevolence in 'Hardy', chap. II. He returns to this theme later. See 63:37ff.

44:4 **"Ye must be born again,"** John iii. 7 (AV); see also 65:4–6.

44:31 **the Tree.** See 34:22–36 for the development of this image, pervasive in DHL's philosophy. See also 'Education of the People' (*Phoenix* 610) and 'Epilogue' to *Movements in European History* (Oxford, 1971).

45:30 **the while [   ]** The break in the text is due to a missing page (57) in TS. McDonald deleted the phrase 'who is all the while' in TCC and replaced it with a full stop; 'In' (in A1) was added later. About 320 words are missing in which DHL may have discussed another early Hardy novel.

45:31 **a "prédilection d'artiste"** 'An artist's preference' (French). Paula in *A Laodicean* uses this phrase; see 46:23.

45:35 **[ever]** This conjectural reading in TCC makes better sense than 'even' for 'evee' in TS; 'e' and 'r' are adjacent letters on a typewriter keyboard.

46:27 **The heroine [46:18]** . . . **"animal pedigree".** DHL transposes and summarises two scenes from *A Laodicean* (Book I, chap. XIV; Book III, chap. v) (proper names are identified in Macmillan edn, 1975, pp. 445, 448).

46:37 **a prédilection de savant . . . a prédilection d'economiste.** A scientist's (or scholar's) preference . . . an economist's preference (French); the terms are DHL's.

47:25 **[communal] morality,** While the reading of TS makes sense, DHL uses 'communal morality' at 47:20 and 48:2 so that 'commune' is more likely to have been Kot's mistyping.

47:29 **[condemned],** DHL's use of 'condemnation' in the next sentence makes it probable that 'contemned' is a typing error. However, see 102:19 and note for DHL's use of 'contemn'.

48:3 **a leprosy, a white sickness:** A reference to the characteristic whitening of the skin in leprosy. .

49:11 **communist** An adherent to communist or socialist principles; not a reference to membership of a Communist party; see also an early version of 'Art and the Individual', 223:4.

49:36 **Hence the pessimism.** DHL appears to be countering Abercrombie (pp. 28–30), who barely admitted pessimism in Hardy.

49:38 **oldness of temper,** There is no clear reason to emend to 'coldness' as in TCC. DHL's context emphasises the 'old adhesion', the old communal influence.

50:5 **pathetic rather than tragic figures.** Of Tess and Jude, Abercrombie wrote that their condition was 'more pathetic, because more natural, than any tragic interference from the outside' (p. 31).

50:14 **Agamemnon sacrifices . . . pledged wife [50:12] . . . the Erinyes of his father** A brief plot summary of the *Oresteia* trilogy (458 B.C.) by the Greek dramatist Aeschylus (525–456 B.C.). The plays are *Agamemnon, The Choephori* and *The Eumenides* . . . an identification of the Ghost of King Hamlet in Shakespeare's *Hamlet* with one of the avenging Furies in Greek mythology who, for instance, pursued Orestes; see also 94:25.

50:20 **"Thou shalt not kill."** Exodus xx. 13.

50:38 **the rank of pure tragedy.** In this claim, DHL is expressing his disagreement with Abercrombie's central argument; see chap. II.

53:5 **like Sappho into the sea.** Greek poetess from Lesbos (*c.* 600 B.C.). Her unrequited love for Phaon and her suicide, by leaping off a cliff into the sea from the rock of Leucas, are legendary.

53:12 **[dips]** An emendation of the reading in TS 'drips'. DHL had already used 'dips' in a similar passage at 52:19.

53:17 **[wave]** TS's reading 'wake' is possible but scarcely gives an appropriate sense. Cf. the passage which follows, where 'wave' is used five times, to suggest a leading rather than a following motion of water.

53:30 **[clashed]** The imagery of clashing and seething which follows suggests that TS's 'clasped' is an error, possibly induced by eye-skip from the 'sp' of 'spill' in the line above it.

53:38 **dogs-mercury . . . the oak-tree,** *Mercuriatis Perennis*, a poisonous yellow-flowered herb having separate male and female plants . . . separate male and female catkins are carried on the same oak-tree.

56:2 **Of Being and Not-Being.** A keynote of DHL's philosophy in 1913–14: 'We are Hamlet without the Prince of Denmark. We cannot *be*. "To be or not to be" – it is the question with us now, by Jove. And nearly every Englishman says "Not to be."' (*Letters*, i. 504). Cf. 'Foreword to *Sons and Lovers*' (*The Letters of D. H. Lawrence*, ed. Aldous Huxley, 1932, pp. 95–102), and chaps. I and II of 'Hardy'.

57:20 **[big]** To replace TS reading ('try') which is nonsensical; cf. 57:12.

58:22 **[these]** This correction of 'there' is necessary since DHL shows that the attributes of God and the qualities of woman are identical; cf. 61:16–19.

59:7 **[a] race,** The emendation seems to be required by the remainder of the sentence: 'that race's . . . the race'.

59:14   **the religious effort of Man.**   For an early anticipation of this view see 'Art and the Individual', e.g. 140:33–7.

61:10   **[eventually]**   An emendation on the assumption that the reading of TS ('even') at the end of one line was not completed on the next; also the context requires some emendation be made.

61:28   **David,**   King David (d. *c.* 970 B.C.) whose history is found in 1 and 2 Samuel and 1 Kings. It is as the traditional author of the Psalms that DHL considers him here, not just in his relations with his several wives and concubines.

61:36   **Solomon . . . Shulamite,**   King Solomon (reigned 970–930 B.C.), son and successor of David, and supposed author of the Song of Solomon which begins 'The song of songs, which is Solomon's' . . . the woman extravagantly praised in the Song is addressed as the Shulamite in vi. 13. (See also *Letters*, i. 227.)

63:6   **"For I . . . that love me."**   Exodus xx. 5–6 ['. . . I the . . . God am . . . iniquity . . . me; And shewing . . .', (AV)].

63:26   **Monism**   The philosophical doctrine that 'there is but One Being' as opposed to dualism. See *Letters*, i. 147.

63:38   **"Who is my mother?"**   Matthew xii. 48.

64:18   **"In the . . . New Testament.**   John i. 1. For the allusion to the Annunciation see Luke i. 26–38.

64:39   **Job remained . . . true to it.**   See Job ii. 9–10.

66:5   **All the little figures . . . the Absolute,**   For DHL's use of this view of the medieval cathedral with its jeering imps, see *The Rainbow*, chap. VII.

66:8   **Dürer,**   Albrecht Dürer (1471–1528), German artist. DHL mentioned the 'genuine Dürer engravings' in the house of Frieda's brother-in-law, Edgar Jaffe, where he and Frieda stayed twice in 1913 (*Letters*, ii. 63), but his references suggest acquaintance with Dürer's paintings and drawings.

66:11   **[contained],**   The emendation provides the sense needed; cf. *The Rainbow*, chap. VII, where the cathedral 'contains' the movement of birth and death, etc. Koteliansky's error can be explained by the number of surrounding words ending in '-ent'.

66:32   **Botticelli . . . National Gallery.**   DHL is referring to the *Mystic Nativity* by the Florentine Alessandro Botticelli (1444–1510) in the National Gallery which he frequented during his years in Croydon. Presumably the discussion of this painting and Raphael's *Nativity* (also in the National Gallery) was based on recently renewed experience of the two works; see *Letters*, ii. 233.

67:6   **Aphrodite issued exposed to the clear elements,**   DHL refers to Botticelli's *Birth of Venus* (*c.* 1487; Uffizi, Florence), in which the goddess is depicted emerging from the sea and exposed to the elements. Aphrodite was the Greek goddess of beauty, love and reproduction (Roman Venus). In one legend she is born of the sea-foam and washed ashore at Paphos. See also 114:6 and 114:31.

67:15   **deified separately, as a bull . . . Correggio.**   Probably a reference to Dionysos. DHL had for many years been interested in Egyptian mythology (see *Letters*, i. 86) in which Osiris was identified with Apis the sacred bull. However, he had more recently read Jane Harrison's *Ancient Art and Ritual* (1913), in which she discussed the emergence of a Greek Bull-God and linked it with Dionysos (pp. 98–104); see *Letters*, ii. 90 . . . Antonio Allegri da Correggio (1494–1534), Italian painter from Parma.

68:18   **the Parthenon Frieze**   The frieze from the 'cella' of the Parthenon of Athens (now in the British Museum) was designed by Phidias and depicts the procession at the festival of Athena. It was discussed at length by Jane Harrison in chap. VI of her book (see note above), which may also have prompted DHL's comparison of it with the art of Babylon and Egypt.

68:36   **Andrea del Sarto . . . Rembrandt . . . the Impressionists,**   Florentine painter (1486–1531) . . . Rembrandt van Rijn (1606–69), Dutch painter noted for his handling of light and shade, especially in his portraits; see also 83:33 and note . . . the Impressionists were French painters of the late nineteenth century (Monet, Renoir, Pissarro, Sisley, etc.) who wanted to record experience by a system of fleeting impressions, especially of natural light effects. DHL later placed Cézanne among the post-impressionists and described him as the 'most interesting figure in modern art' in 'Introduction to These Paintings' (reprinted in *Phoenix* 571); see also *Phoenix* 563–5.

68:40   **"Madonna degli Ansidei" . . . [motionless,]**   Altarpiece on wood painted by the Perugian painter Raphael (Raffaelo Sanzio) (1483–1520). The painting, commissioned by the Ansidei family in 1506 (now in the National Gallery), depicts the Madonna and Child with St John the Baptist and St Nicholas of Bari. The semicircular arch which encloses the composition is dramatically bisected by the dark perpendicular of the Madonna's throne; see 72:6–11 . . . there is a hiatus in TS. DHL implies a contrast with the child of Botticelli's *Nativity* who is 'a radiating spark of movement' (66:34); cf. 74:7 where Michelangelo's Madonna is 'motionless'.

69:13   **Fra Angelico . . . [bore] us**   Fra Angelico (1387–1455), Italian fresco painter and Dominican friar, whose *Last Judgement* is in the Museo di San Marco, Florence . . . 'bore' is McDonald's marginal suggestion in TCC for TS's 'love'; cf. *The Rainbow*, chap. X where Ursula suddenly becomes bored with the 'architectural conception' of Fra Angelico's *Last Judgement*.

69:19   **Primavera**   'Spring' (Italian), an allegory of spring (Uffizi, Florence) painted by Botticelli about 1487. It depicts Venus attended by Mercury, the three Graces, Cupid, Flora and two Zephyrs.

70:40   **The Greek sculptors . . . [Myron],**   The space in TS suggests a short name like Myron (fifth century B.C.). However, with Phidias (*c.* 490–*c.* 415 B.C.), sculptors of the great age would have to include not only Myron (famed for his Discobolus, the discus-thrower) but Polyclitus and Praxiteles. Myron's work survives only in later copies.

71:12   **"Hail to . . . wert—"**   Shelley's ode 'To A Skylark' (1820), line 1; see also 90:35–9 and note.

72:16   **in living [when]**   While no space was left in TS 'when' is required in the sentence. McDonald suggested inserting 'when' after 'living' in TCC, but it was placed before 'in living' in A1 (see Textual apparatus).

72:35   **Ewige Wiederkehr.**   'Eternal return or recurrence' (German). Nietzsche uses the phrase particularly in *Thus Spake Zarathustra* (1883–5), e.g. 'Souls are as mortal as bodies. But the complex of causes in which I am entangled will recur – it will create me again! I myself am part of these causes of the eternal recurrence' (Part III: 'The Convalescent', section ii).

74:15 **Thus he [73:40] ... Michael Angelo's pictures.** Although DHL refers to 'pictures' of Michelangelo Buonarroti (1475–1564), the figures he cites are done in marble sculpture, marble relief or fresco: *Moses* (1513–16) for the tomb of Pope Julius II (Giuliano de' Medici), San Pietro in Vincoli, Rome; *David* (1501–4), Accademia, Florence; *The Slaves* (1513–16), begun for the tomb of Pope Julius, but unfinished, consists of two statues – *The Dying Slave* and *The Rebellious Slave*, Musée du Louvre, Paris; *Madonna* (there are at least six representations of the Madonna; the depiction of a 'motionless' figure suggests the *Bruges Madonna*, *c.* 1501, a marble sculpture in the Church of Notre Dame, Bruges); *Adam* (1508–12), fresco of the Creation of Man, Sistine Chapel, Vatican.

75:6 **sceptical, in the Russian sense.** DHL may have had in mind here the quality which Tolstoy describes as a 'vague and exclusively Russian feeling of contempt for everything conventional, artificial, human, for everything that is regarded by the majority of men as the highest good in the world' in *War and Peace*, trans. Constance Garnett, Part XI, chap. XVII. Scepticism of this kind is in sharp contrast to the 'indifference' and 'fatalism' which DHL attributes to 'the Italian race'.

75:23 **the Futurist Boccioni ... Space",** For Futurism associated with Marinetti, Giacomo Balla (1871–1958) and Gino Severini (1883–1966), and its influence on DHL in 1914, see Introduction, p. xxvi; see also *Letters*, ii. 180–4. Umberto Boccioni (1882–1916), Italian painter and sculptor, was one of its theorists. His bronze *Development of a Bottle through Space* dates from 1912–13. He did three versions of it: the one usually cited is now in the New York Museum of Modern Art. DHL knew it only from the photograph of one casting in Soffici's *Cubismo e Futurismo*, and hence mistakenly refers to its medium as 'stone' at 76:4.

77:2 **"The Light of the World."** John viii. 12. In DHL's dualism, light is the equivalent of spirit as against body. This antinomy is the key to his continuing discussion of post-Renaissance art. Cf. 'Introduction to These Paintings' (*Phoenix* 563).

    TS has this title spaced as if to indicate italics (see Textual apparatus). DHL might have intended it as a quotation of Christ's words or a reference (perhaps ironical) to the famous painting of that name by Holman Hunt (1827–1910) now in St Paul's Cathedral – or both. To conform to the treatment of titles in this work, the words are placed in quotation marks.

77:8 **those other supreme three,** I.e. Botticelli, Raphael and Michelangelo.

78:15 **"Think not ... fulfilled."** Matthew v. 17–18 ['. . . not that I am come . . . law, or . . . I am not come to . . . fulfil. For . . . Till . . . law . . .', (AV)].

78:25 **"Know thyself."** The saying was inscribed in the Greek temple at Delphi.

79:12 **"This is . . . communion,** Matthew xxvi. 26 ['Take, eat; this is my body.']

79:14 **"Come unto me all . . . rest."** Matthew xi. 28 ['. . . me, all . . .'].

79:22 **says Christ,** DHL's version of Christ's message: cf. Philippians ii. 5–8. The other 'quotations' in this paragraph are similarly DHL's paraphrases. Also "Ye are . . . of you," (lines 38–9), but see John xiv. 14–20.

80:4 **the Unforgivable Sin . . . no forgiveness.** See Matthew xii. 31–2.

80:16 **we see . . . glass, darkly.** See 1 Corinthians xiii. 12 (AV); also lines 24–5 ['shall I know even as also I . . .', (AV)].

80:27 **"Thou shalt . . . jealous God?** Exodus xx. 3, 5 ['. . . other gods . . .', (AV)].

81:40 **"Light is . . . the world."** John iii. 19.

82:4 **light of life.** This emendation is based on the context – 'this light of life' immediately follows – and on the fact that Kot typed 'the/ spirit', cancelled 'spirit' and added 'life', but neglected to cancel 'the'.

82:8 **"It is the spirit . . . life."** John vi. 63 ['. . . nothing: the words that I . . . are spirit . . .', (AV)]. The emendation 'profiteth' replaces TS's 'forgeteth' which suggests that Kot misread the manuscript. It is unlikely that DHL would substitute a word so meaningless in such a well-known quotation.

82:16 **"And it came . . . keep it.'"** Luke xi. 27–8 ['. . . voice, and . . . paps which thou . . . Yea rather . . .', (AV)].

82:23 **"And there . . . receive it."** Matthew xix. 12 ['For there are some eunuchs, which were so born from their mother's womb: and there are some eunuchs, which were made eunuchs of men: and . . . eunuchs, which . . .', (AV)].

83:2 **"Hail, holy Light!" of Milton.** *Paradise Lost* III. 1.

83:33 **Rembrandt paints . . . and again,** Rembrandt painted more than ninety self-portraits over forty years. DHL might recently have seen the *Self-Portrait Aged 63* (1669) in the National Gallery.

84:10 **[inexhaustible]** Kot left blank space for a word of eleven or twelve letters. McDonald marked the hiatus for closure in TCC but queried it in the margin. For the source of this conjectural reading see 84:32.

85:10 **the great northern confusion.** DHL developed his distinction between northern and southern Europe after 'Hardy' as can be seen in his additions to *Twilight in Italy* (1915); see particularly 'The Lemon Gardens' section.

85:23 **[consummate.]** Kot did not complete the sentence; for the source cf. 85:19.

85:40 **the voice, or the Wind.** These identifications are probably based on Biblical references to God making himself known through the 'still small voice' (1 Kings xix. 12) or as the 'rushing mighty wind' at Pentecost (Acts ii. 2, AV). The women alluded to are presumably the medieval mystics or recluses like Juliana of Norwich or St Teresa; see also 122:8–9 and note.

86:14 **Turner.** Joseph Mallord William Turner (1775–1851), landscape painter and master of water-colours. 'Some of Turner's landscape compositions are, to my feelings, among the finest that exist', 'Introduction to These Paintings' (*Phoenix* 561).

86:32 **"Norham Castle, Sunrise",** DHL presumably means the oil painting (*c.* 1840–5) in the Tate Gallery. Turner's earlier water-colour version is less well-known.

87:1 **Corot . . . with life.** Jean Baptiste Camille Corot (1796–1875), French landscape painter. In 1911, DHL attempted to copy 'a nice big Corot, half did it, spoiled it, and tore it in thirty pieces' (*Letters*, i. 282); DHL's '"Landscape" (after Corot)' is reproduced in *Young Lorenzo*, by Ada Lawrence and G. Stuart Gelder (Florence, 1932). His poem 'Corot', probably written at about the same time, speaks of 'the trailing, leisurely rapture of life' which 'Drifts dimly forward easily hidden' (lines 9–10) in a Corot painting (*The Complete Poems of D. H. Lawrence*, ed. Vivian de Sola Pinto and Warren Roberts, 1964, ii. 468).

88:9   **And in some men ... blasphemy.**   DHL had given substance to these examples in Mr Massey in 'Daughters of the Vicar' and the captain in 'The Prussian Officer' in *The Prussian Officer and Other Stories*, ed. John Worthen (Cambridge, 1983).

89:2   **A nos Moutons.**   I.e. 'to the matter in hand' (French). Cf. 'Art and the Individual', 136:13 where DHL uses the English 'my muttons!'

89:23   **Euripides ... Base Closer of Doom,**   Probably an allusion to Euripides' questioning of current mythologies in his plays: 'He really seems to feel that if there are conscious gods ruling the world, they are cruel or "inhuman" beings' (*The Trojan Women*, trans. Gilbert Murray, 1905, Notes p. 82). See also *Electra* (trans. Gilbert Murray, 1905): in his introduction, Murray discusses the problem of the god enjoining 'mother-murder'. (Murray's translations had 'a fearful fascination' for DHL, *Letters*, i. 525.)

90:39   **"Hail to ... lay."**   See 71:12 and note ['. . . Pourest thy full heart/ In profuse strains of unpremeditated art']. The quotation was corrected in A1.

91:21   **Spinoza's "Amor ... externae",**   'Love is a pleasurable excitement coupled with an awareness of its external cause' (Latin), from the *Ethics* (Book III, Definition vi) of Baruch Spinoza (1632–77), the Dutch philosopher. Six years before 'Hardy', DHL had mistranslated this definition as 'Love is a tickling, therefore accompanied by some external influence' (Emile Delavenay, 'Notes sur une exemplaire de Schopenhauer' in *Revue Anglo-Américaine*, February 1936, 235; reprinted Nehls, i. 67).

91:34   **in**   In TS the typed 'is' is overwritten to read 'in'. There are two other such careful corrections in ink to chap. IX ('so' is inserted at 93:9 and 'out' is added to make 'outstretched' at 104:34). Since they are distinct from other 'corrections' in TS (see Introduction, p. xxiv) and since they passed on without hesitation to TCC, they are taken as Koteliansky's, and thus probably represent DHL's manuscript readings.

92:21   **Peter when he denied ... repented.**   Mark xiv. 66–72.

92:26   **the reminiscences of Tolstoi** [92:18] **... in it."**   *Reminiscences of Tolstoy* by Count Ilya Tolstoi, trans. George Calderon (New York, 1914), pp. 144–5. DHL's general claim that Tolstoy 'degraded himself infinitely' could derive from any of a number of sources: e.g. in *My Confession* (1884), 'I cannot now think of those years without horror, loathing, and heartache. I ... lived loosely, and deceived people. Lying, robbery, adultery of all kinds, drunkenness, violence, murder ... there was no crime that I did not commit . . .'

92:30   **the Parable of the Sower,**   Matthew xiii. 3–9.

93:4   **[fleshly] ... [that]**   An emendation of 'fleshy' in TS since clearly a moral not a physical quality is intended; cf. 22:9 ... the addition of 'that' seems necessary to avoid ambiguity; cf. Textual apparatus. It was probably a simple omission in TS.

93:13   **But it** [93:8] **... the extreme.**   Abercrombie had argued the opposite case; see Introduction, pp. xxvii–xxviii.

93:36   **"Dost thou know [93:24] . . . unto them."** Job xxxvii. 16–18 ['. . . strong,', (AV)] . . . Job xxxvii. 22 (AV) . . . Job xxxix. 1–4 ['. . . forth? or . . . fulfil? or . . . are in good liking . . .', (AV)]. 'They grow forth' in TS for 'they go forth' (line 36) is probably Kot's mistyping since the rest of the quotation is correct.

93:38   **conceipt**   The use of this archaic form here and at 95:7, 10 suggests that it was DHL's manuscript with the meaning 'conceit' or 'self-conceit' intended.

94:3   **"Therefore have . . . and ashes."** Job xlii. 3, 5–6 ['. . . by the hearing . . . ear: but . . .', (AV)].

94:6   **But Jude ends . . . the womb."**   See *Jude the Obscure*, Part VI. chap. XI, where Jude quotes from Job. DHL is quoting neither Jude nor Job, who says: 'Why died I not from the womb?' (Job iii. 11).

95:31   **girl in *The Woodlanders*,**   I.e. Marty South, with reference to her frustrated devotion to Giles Winterbourne.

96:30   **Troy**   I.e. Sergeant Troy in *Far from the Madding Crowd*. See 22:34ff.

97:14   **[hard] labour**   The reading 'take to hand, labour' in all states of the text is meaningless. It is assumed that DHL had in mind passages such as that in chap. XLI of *Tess* where Angel Clare's sufferings and hardship in Brazil are recounted. A misreading of 'r' as 'n' is frequent in TS.

98:7   **Darwin and Spencer and Huxley . . . Space, which so frightened** Charles Darwin (1809–82), who formulated the theory of evolution by natural selection. Herbert Spencer (1820–1903), philosopher who applied evolutionary theory to the study of society. Thomas Henry Huxley (1825–95), leading British exponent of Darwin's theory of evolution . . . DHL was probably recalling Hardy's Preface to the 1912 Wessex Edition: the 'universe concerning which Spencer owns to the "paralyzing thought" that possibly there exists no comprehension of it anywhere'. The same thought may underlie 18:15–17.

99:31   **the famous Russian nobles,**   This may refer historically to liberal reformers in Russia from the Napoleonic era on. It is more likely that DHL is thinking of such fictional noblemen as Pierre and Prince Andrei in *War and Peace*, and Levin in *Anna Karenin*, as well as their creator Count Leo Tolstoy. Cf. 'The Novel', pp. 179–80, where DHL discusses Tolstoy's 'Christian Socialism'.

101:3   **a better salvation.**   Presumably DHL's reflection is sarcastic, but it is possible that he wrote 'bitter' and that Kot misread it.

102:5   **"fools rush in".**   From Pope's 'Essay on Criticism' (1711), line 625 ['For Fools rush in where Angels fear to tread'].

102:19   **contemn**   DHL's use of this word may have been prompted by Hardy's use of it: '[Jude] pitied her [Arabella] while he contemned her' (Part III, chap. IX). Cf. note on 47:29.

102:32   **His attitude was . . . good man."**   These qualities are indirectly attributed to Job (Job i. 1–5); he does not claim them himself.

103:21   **"Wille zur Macht".**   'The Will to Power' (German) is Nietzsche's term. In *The Will to Power* (1906) Nietzsche discusses the 'will to power' in art; *inter alia* he refers to the 'state of intoxication' of a man in love: 'he seems to himself transfigured, stronger, richer, more perfect . . .' (ed. Oscar Levy, section 808). DHL had a broader understanding of this elusive term: 'The great serpent to destroy, is the Will to Power: the desire for one man to have some dominion over his fellow man', but closer to the present context is: 'That which we call passion is a very one-sided thing, based chiefly on hatred and Wille zur Macht. There is no Will to Power here ... in these [Ajanta] frescoes' in which DHL found 'the perfect perfect intimate relation between the men and women ... a very perfection of passion, a fulness, a whole blossom' (*Letters*, ii. 272, 489). See John B. Humma, 'D. H. Lawrence as Friedrich Nietzsche' in *Philological Quarterly*, liii (1974), 110–20.

103:24 **[transition]**   TCC's conjecture is taken for Kot's obvious misreading of the manuscript; see Textual apparatus. Cf. 103:15–16 and *Letters*, ii. 143.

103:36 **roué,**   When DHL revised the proofs of his *Prussian Officer* stories in October 1914, in 'The White Stocking' he wrote that Sam Adams possessed 'some of the automatic irony of the *roué*' (ed. Worthen, p. 151).

103:38 **unfortunately**   This word is heavily cancelled in pencil in TS. Although it is omitted from TCC which may suggest that it is an early deletion, the pencil is indistinguishable from that used elsewhere in TS by Angelo Ravagli much later. There is no clear reason to omit the word. Cf. 104:10.

104:34 **outstretched,**   See note to 91:34.

105:21 **"there are ... daughters of men"**   Behind this quotation there is probably an allusion to Genesis vi. 2. Cf. *The Rainbow*, chap. x where Ursula is 'stirred as by a call from far off' by this passage in Genesis.

105:24 **Fielding's "Amelia" ... Dickens' "Agnes",**   In *Amelia* (1751) by Henry Fielding (1707–54) ... Agnes Wickfield in *David Copperfield* (1849–50) by Charles Dickens.

106:2 **Reynolds**   Sir Joshua Reynolds (1723–92), portrait painter and first president of the Royal Academy.

108:13 **kinsman to Tess.**   DHL may appear to be misleading here, but see 99:2. Jude and Sue were cousins, while Alec Stoke-d'Urberville was the son of Mr Simon Stoke who had only annexed 'd'Urberville' to his own name 'for himself and his heirs eternally' (*Tess of the d'Urbervilles*, Book I, chap. v).

108:19 **Cassandra,**   Daughter of King Priam of Troy, priestess of Apollo with eloquent prophetic gifts; see also note on 117:4. Her description here, along with Sue and Tess, as the witch or prophetess type (108:24) suggests that DHL was familiar with contemporary accounts of the connection between homosexual temperaments and unusual psychic and prophetic powers. See, for instance, Emile Delavenay, *D. H. Lawrence and Edward Carpenter* (1971), pp. 212–15, and cf. *Letters*, ii. 297–8.

109:5 **the Gretchens ... Turgenev heroines,**   Gretchen, the heroine of *Faust* by Johann Wolfgang von Goethe (1749–1832) ... Ivan Sergeevich Turgenev (1818–83), Russian novelist of whose work DHL had read *Fathers and Sons* (1862), *Rudin* (1856) and *The Torrents of Spring* (1872) by 1914.

109:24 **Aspasia [109:9] ... the Greeks,**   Mistress of the Athenian statesman Pericles (fifth century B.C.) famed for her intellectual attainments. Jude associated Sue with Aspasia (*Jude*, Part V, chap. III) ... probably a reference to Part II, chap. III in which Sue actually purchases Greek statuettes of Venus and Apollo.

110:37 **receive this drainage,** Unless there is an error in TS, the meaning of 'receive' must be 'experience, suffer'.

110:39 **One man had died.** An undergraduate at Christminster with whom Sue was friendly (Part III, chap. IV).

111:9 **[hunted]** The 'haunted' of TS is probably a mistyping in TS; cf. the use of 'hunted' at 111:25.

113:29 **The Widow Edlin said . . . one of them.** DHL confused Widow Edlin with Sue's Aunt Drusilla who said: 'And Phillotson the schoolmaster, of all men! . . . there be certain men here and there that no woman of any niceness can stomach. I should have said he was one' (*Jude*, Part III, chap. IX).

113:35 **"Thou hast . . . thy breath."** The two-line form of the quotation suggests that DHL was quoting from Hardy (*Jude*, Part II, chap. III) rather than directly from Swinburne's 'Hymn to Proserpine' (1866), line 35. Hence the colon is from Hardy's quotation (see Textual apparatus).

114:7 **She turned to look . . . Pallas and Christ.** The contrasts here are mostly derived from *Jude* (Part II, chap. III), but DHL adds the allusion to Pallas, the Athenian goddess of wisdom.

114:19 **Why does a snake . . . newt corresponds?** Richard Jefferies had explored similar reactions – to a toad and a snake, for instance – in *The Story of My Heart*: the 'shock to the mind' these creatures offered, derived from their 'anti-human character': they point to 'designless, formless chaos . . .' (chap. IV). DHL had referred to this book when writing 'Hardy': see Introduction, p. xxiv and footnote 30.

114:35 **She might . . . Venus Urania** Venus Urania is the goddess of sacred rather than profane love. In *Jude* Sue tells Jude that the people around them recognise only relations between the sexes 'based on animal desire', and she continues: 'The wide field of strong attachment where desire plays, at least, only a secondary part, is ignored by them – the part of – who is it? – Venus Urania' (Part III, chap. VI). Cf. note on 108:19.

116:17 **fastened like Andromeda.** Andromeda angered Poseidon (Greek god of the sea) by boasting that her daughter was more beautiful than the nereids. In punishment, he sent a sea-monster which could be placated only by the sacrifice of Andromeda. She was chained to a rock in the sea (but rescued by Perseus). DHL may be suggesting some element of punishment for Sue in her immobility.

116:23 **Saint Simeon Stylites** From 423 he lived on a pillar near Antioch, where he spent the remaining years of his life (*c.* 390–459) preaching to and instructing those who came to consult him.

116:30 **the night when Arabella called at their house** *Jude*, Part V, chap. II.

117:4 **pollution of Cassandra or of the Vestals.** Cassandra is abducted by Agamemnon (in Euripides' *The Trojan Women*) and subsequently murdered by Clytemnestra (in Aeschylus' *Oresteia*). The Vestals, virgin priestesses of the Roman domestic goddess Vesta, were regarded as untouchable in their purity.

117:13 **the Frenchman . . . a corpse.** Allusion to *La légende de St Julien l'hospitalier* (1877) by Gustav Flaubert (1821–80) in which St Julien's ultimate act of mortification is to lie with a dying leper; the leper is miraculously transformed into

Christ who carries St Julien to heaven; see also 119:24. Cf. *The Trespasser*, ed. Mansfield, p. 111.

118:21 instinctively disliked. See *Jude*, Part v, chap. vi, but the move from social censoriousness to instinctive dislike by the townspeople is DHL's.

118:31 "Happy?" ... **She nodded.** *Jude*, Part v, chap. v. DHL proceeds in the next four paragraphs to extrapolate from Hardy ('They went ... Sue sexually', 119:9–10, is not in Hardy).

119:5 [their] TCC amends to 'these', but 'their' better accounts for Kot's misreading as 'then'.

120:18 Arabella's boy Arabella and Jude's son is called 'little Jude' or 'Little Father Time' (*Jude*, Part v, chap. iiiff.).

121:18 she was not worth a man's love. Jude says this to Sue (*Jude*, Part vi, chap. viii).

122:8 Achilles, The hero of Homer's *Iliad*. His inclusion here among priestesses and other religious may be explained either by traditions that he was marked by the gods as a hero, or by the suggestions of his 'Uranian' nature in his love of Patroclus; see note on 108:19.

123:1 Chapter X. For 'XII' in TS see Introduction, p. xxxiii. There is no title in TS, though a space appears to have been left for one.

123:22 "Let there be light": Genesis i. 3.

124:24 doctrine of the other cheek. See Matthew v. 39, Luke vi. 29.

124:39 "Thou shalt love thy enemy." Matthew v. 44 ['But I say unto you, Love your enemies, bless them that curse you ...', (AV)]. Immediately following this quotation five lines were left blank, and the next word ('Therefore') was not indented in TS. The context suggests that a paragraph or more is lacking; presumably Kot recognised the manuscript was defective.

125:8 after Dostoievsky's *Idiot* ... Mallarmé ... Debussy, DHL's first references to his reading *The Idiot* (1868) by Fyodor Mikhailovitch Dostoievsky (1821–81) date from 1915 (*Letters*, ii. 311), presumably he was then re-reading it ... Stéphane Mallarmé (1842–98), French symbolist poet ... Claude Debussy (1862–1918), French composer and critic. DHL expresses 'love' of Debussy's piano and chamber music (*Letters*, i. 205, 308–9), but is disapproving of his 'averted face' in, presumably, his opera *Pelléas et Mélisande* (1902) (*Letters*, i. 247); cf. *The Trespasser*, ed. Mansfield, p. 52 and n.

126:36 by dropping a pebble ... solved his riddle. In Aeschylus' *Eumenides*, Pallas Athena orders the Judges to pass judgement on Orestes by casting sea-stones in one of two urns to signify guilt or innocence ... the 'riddle' is: if Orestes slew his mother by the will of Zeus (who also wills that he be freed), he has nevertheless broken the Law and is deserving of punishment. Athena herself casts the pebble which acquits Orestes.

127:7 exfoliation DHL's use of this word is probably fortuitous. Much of the philosophy of 'Hardy', however, with its insistence on the full flowering of the self, suggests his acquaintance with Edward Carpenter's theory of Exfoliation. ('Exfoliation' in *Civilization Its Cause and Cure*, 1889 et seq.). Carpenter says, for instance, that 'there is a force at work throughout creation, ever urging each type onward into newer and newer forms.' This force is, at first, desire; ultimately in man it is love. See also Delavenay, *Lawrence and Edward Carpenter*, pp. 70–6.

128:17 [clasp] ... [clasp] TCC's reading is adopted as giving the preferable reading in context; cf. 62:8, 66:30, 68:33, 34. However both occurrences are clearly 'clap' in TS; cf. 'Foreword to *Sons and Lovers*', where the moment of 'the Holy Ghost' is 'a Clapping of Hands'.

Literary Essays, 1908–27
Art and the Individual

135:2 A Paper for Socialists The subtitle was added when DHL revised the paper, but cf. 223:2–5. Both the titles and the opening paragraph reflect DHL's interest in the Socialist paper *The New Age: A Weekly Review of Politics, Literature and Art*, edited (1907–22) by A. R. Orage (1873–1934). Orage had been an advocate of Guild Socialism and of the protection of the individuality of workmanship in the arts and crafts. A three-part article entitled 'The Restoration of Beauty to Life' by A. J. Penty which appeared in the *New Age*, i (May 1907), 5, 21, 37 may have influenced DHL. Jessie Chambers, recalling the Eastwood circle into whom DHL read this paper, wrote: 'a Socialist and a Suffragette ... first showed us A. R. Orage's *New Age* which Lawrence took regularly for a time. He liked it far more for its literature than its politics' (E. T. 120).

135:6 This paragraph ... artistic world." In the *New Age* for 8 August 1908, pp. 295–6, there appeared an unsigned review (probably by Orage himself) of *Fifty Years of Modern Painting: Corot to Sargent* by J. E. Phythian (1908). DHL has adapted the opening paragraph of the review: 'Mr Phythian quotes, apparently with approval, the Socialist Member of Parliament who said: "The present aim of Socialists ... artistic world." (The quotation is from p. 176 of Phythian's book.) The statement is a socialist commonplace of the period. The M. P. is not identified, but Phythian states that it 'was said in a public speech'.
DHL also quotes from the review at 135:8–13 ['... we need now Beauty ... crafts, and in our ... Socialist ... starve for beauty ...'].

135:14 the Ironsides of Snowden I.e. those who fought for social justice through organised political parties (as the Ironsides fought for Cromwell in the Civil War). Philip Snowden, later 1st Viscount Snowden of Ickornshaw (1864–1937), M.P. for Blackburn, was at this time a member of the Independent Labour Party and one of its most forthright spokesmen, particularly on economic matters. Enid Hilton states that DHL met him at the Hopkins' house (Nehls, i. 135).

135:19 love the lotus buds, I.e. who are aesthetically rather than politically motivated.

135:23 morion ... go smite the lofty from their seats?; A sixteenth-seventeenth century war helmet; see note to 135:14 ... Cf. Luke i. 52 ['He hath put down the mighty from their seats, and exalted them of low degree', (AV)].

135:26 the lyrics ... Queen Mab, Lyric poems, 'The Sensitive Plant' (1820) and 'Queen Mab' (*c.* 1812), by Percy Bysshe Shelley (1792–1822). DHL contrasts lyrical and romantic verse with Shelley's early crude didactic poem in which the fairy Queen Mab rails against the viciousness and 'imbecility' of human institutions.

135:30   **the Commonwealth ... Zealots.**   A reference to the Commonwealth under Cromwell, 1649–60, and to the puritan fanatics.

136:1   **"The ultimate goal ... moral character."**   This definition is a conflation of two Herbartian ideas: 'the one and the whole work of education may be summed up in the concept – Morality', and 'The teacher ought to make it a point of honour to leave the individuality [of pupils] as untouched as possible . . .' (*Science of Education*, pp. 17, 35). 'The building up of a firmly established self-contained moral character through the operation of enlightened will was . . . the goal of all Herbart's educational efforts', wrote his translators in their Introduction (p. 5). For Herbart see note on 136:18.

136:13   **my muttons!**   See note on 89:2.

136:18   **the great Interests, classified by Herbart,**   Johan Friedrich Herbart (1776–1841), German philosopher, psychologist and educationist, who became influential in educational circles in England and America from the 1890s through the work of Henry and Emmie Felkin whose translation of his *Science of Education* appeared in 1897. During his teacher-training DHL was acquainted with this book, and in the table which follows, he draws on its translators' introduction (p. 50) rather than on Herbart's own extensive presentation. The idea of the development of a many-sided interest was fundamental to Herbart's psychology and pedagogy. For DHL's knowledge of Herbart at this time, see 'The Collected Letters of Jessie Chambers', ed. George Zytaruk, *DHL Review*, xii (1979), 98.

136:29   **Here is the explanation:**   In his explanation of the six interests, DHL is quoting and paraphrasing from an earlier work by the Felkins, *Introduction to Herbart's Science and Practice of Education* (1895), pp. 96–7 (not from Herbart himself):

Many-sided interest he divides into interest arising from knowledge, and interest arising from sympathy.

Interest arising from knowledge is of three kinds: –

First, empirical interest, which grows from knowledge gained by experience and observation of manifold phenomena. This knowledge excites pleasure in the mind by the strength, change, and novelty of the impressions produced; and the desire to progress in it is the result of an empirical interest.

Second, speculative interest, aroused by the consciousness of the mysterious and the obscure, excites a desire to pass from mere empirical observation to the investigation of the origin of, and causal relations between phenomena.

Third, aesthetic interest is aroused neither by phenomena nor their causes, but by "the approval which their harmony and adaptability to an end win from us." It is synonymous with interest in the naturally, artistically, or morally beautiful.

These three classes of interest arising from knowledge may be illustrated from biology. The various characteristics of individual animals would appeal to *empirical interest*; the theory of evolution of species by natural selection would appeal to *speculative interest*; the adaptation of animals to their circumstances and mode of life (*e.g.*, protective colouring) would appeal to *aesthetic interest.*

Interest arising from sympathy is also of three kinds. First, sympathetic interest is personal, and springs from intercourse. It is aroused by the reproduction in the

individual of the feelings of others in their varieties of joy and sorrow, pleasure and pain.
Second, social interest. When to the former feeling are added a comprehension of the larger relationships of society, and a participation in that which makes the weal or woe of the many, that general interest in the progress of humanity arises which Herbart calls social interest.
Third, religious interest is developed, when this enlarged sympathy is directed to the history and destiny of the entire human race. When understanding and feeling become clear, that the guidance of humanity and the direction of the individual lot are alike withdrawn from human power, then the heart is filled with fear and hope. "Belief springs out of need," and religious interest is awakened.

137:16 **an example.** No doubt suggested by the Felkins' illustration in *Introduction to Herbart's Science*: the characteristics of animals.

137:34 **Example number 2.** On the back of the preceding page of MS opposite these words is the aside 'Pardon me if I am a schoolteacher'. In a letter to Blanche Jennings enclosing MS, DHL wrote: 'I send you the long promised paper on Art. Don't let the tone offend you; I confess I am a school teacher' (*Letters*, i. 72).

138:14 **God-Idea.** DHL used this compound fairly frequently at this time; for his views see *Letters*, i. 39–41. In MS, DHL appears to have deleted 'Idea' leaving the text to read 'the germ of the God- ', but restoring the second element is probably the only way to retain the sense.

138:32 **Rider Haggard ... Sir Thos. More** Sir Henry Rider Haggard (1856–1925), author of romantic adventure stories, including *King Solomon's Mines* (1885) and *She* (1887). DHL and Jessie Chambers read his books about 1905–6 (E. T. 94) ... Sir Thomas More (1478–1535), Chancellor to Henry VIII, statesman and author of *Utopia*.

139:4 **"Beauty is ... divine *Idea*,"** Probably DHL's own summary formulation of the characteristic thought of Schelling and Hegel, for instance. See the summaries Tolstoy gives in *What is Art?*, trans. Aylmer Maude (World's Classics, 1930), pp. 90–100. This is the translation (1898) which DHL used.

139:7 **the Erewhonian Unborns** See chaps. XVIII and XIX of *Erewhon* (1872) by Samuel Butler (1835–1902).

139:10 **The Hegelian school ... through matter";** Quoted by Tolstoy, *What is Art?*, p. 100.

139:12 **Goethe ... we see him by."** In Goethe's *Faust* (Part I, i) the hero summons the Spirit of Earth who works in 'endless motion': "Tis thus at the roaring Loom of Time I ply,/ And weave for God the Garment thou seest Him by.' This section is translated in *Sartor Resartus* (1834) by Thomas Carlyle (1795–1881), Book I, chap. VIII. But, as Carlyle's Professor Teufelsdröckh states, the Garment which the Spirit weaves is Nature, not Art as DHL states.

139:18 **"Art is an activity ... as well as Darwin.** The quotation is Tolstoy's summary of the views of Schiller, Darwin and Spencer (*What is Art?*, p. 119).

139:23 **"Art is ... felt by man."** Tolstoy's summary of the view of Eugène Véron, author of *L'Esthétique* (1878) (*What is Art?*, p. 119) ['... manifestation, by means of lines, colours, movements, sounds, or words, of ...'].

139:27   **"Art is ... the definition of Grant Allen.** The definition is from James Sully, *Sensation and Intuition* (1874); Tolstoy quotes it and gives the correct author (*What is Art?*, p. 119) ['. . . action which is fitted not only to supply an active enjoyment to the producer, but to convey a pleasurable impression to a number of spectators or listeners, quite apart from any . . .'].

139:37   **the Laocoon ... the French Realistic paintings ... the "Outcasts" of Luke Fildes ... Watts' "Mammon,"**   Group of statues (Rhodes, *c.* 25 B.C.) portraying Laocoon, a Trojan priest of Apollo, and his two sons wrestling with the sea-serpents which killed them. For DHL's knowledge of it see *Apocalypse and the Writings on Revelation*, ed. Mara Kalnins (Cambridge, 1980) note on 126:16 and *Letters*, i. 5, 122–3 . . . French Realism, a movement associated with Gustave Courbet (1819–77) and others . . . Sir Luke Fildes (1844–1927), painter and illustrator. By the 'Outcasts' DHL probably meant his drawing *Houseless and Hungry* from the *Graphic* (December 1869) . . *Mammon (Dedicated to his Worshippers)* (1885), an allegorical painting by George Frederic Watts (1817–1904), now in the Tate Gallery. DHL later referred to it as 'vulgar bestial *Mammon*, with long teeth . . .' (*Letters*, i. 107).

140:4   **It must be ... intelligible.** 'Art like speech is a means of communication and therefore of progress . . .' (*What is Art?*, p. 231). Tolstoy earlier addressed the question of intelligibility: 'When a universal artist . . . composed his work he naturally strove to say what he had to say so that it should be intelligible to all men' (p. 156).

140:9   **as Tolstoi says ... he is an artist;** *What is Art?*, p. 122. DHL's 'sister' is 'hearers' in Tolstoy. Aylmer Maude, in in his introduction, makes the hearers the boy's parents. In his earlier version DHL makes them the boy's mates; see 227:8.

140:11   **Carlyle's Heroes ... their speech.** DHL had read *On Heroes, Hero-Worship and the Heroic in History* (1841) by Carlyle in the spring of 1906 (see E. T. 102). DHL recalls a passage from Lecture III:

> It is only when the heart of him is rapt into true passion of melody, and the very tones of him, according to Coleridge's remark, become musical by the greatness, depth and music of his thoughts, that we can give him right to rhyme and sing; that we call him a Poet, and listen to him as the Heroic of Speakers, – whose speech *is* Song.

Cf. the reference at 226:38–227:1 where he apparently conflates memories of Lectures II and III.

140:25   **"pair like lovers ... cosmic fellowship"** In the *New Age* (15 August 1908), 312–13, F. S. Flint reviewed a volume of prose poems *The Great Companions* (1908) by Henry Bryan Binns. He quoted from Binns' 'Introductory':

> 'The verse-makers . . . contrive how they may pair together most admirably, as they were lovers, certain words whose chime is pleasant to the ear: they set between them the due intervals: they weave them thus into their theme . . .
>
>   'But every poet hears, flowing amid the silence, the living intricate rhythm of the immortal song; its words progress together in a cosmic fellowship, inseparable, moving forward in the liberty of a living thing.'

It is not known whether DHL read Binns' volume.

DHL then quotes from 'Envoi' by Binns, which was quoted by Flint in his review ['Words were worth nothing . . .']. Flint pronounced this poem: 'Perfect! It enters the brain like a drench of perfume'.

141:8 **some of the great Germans . . . George Clausen** MS originally read 'Wagner' (p. 6). DHL is probably drawing on Tolstoy, *What is Art?*, chap. x, etc. rather than on his own experience of this music; see *Letters*, i. 99 . . . Sir George Clausen (1852–1944), painter; cf. *The White Peacock*, ed. Andrew Robertson (Cambridge, 1983) 28:11 and note.

141:13 **a battle-piece** A piece of music descriptive of a battle.

141:18 **Chopin's Funeral March . . . the March in Saul;** Funeral March in B♭ Minor by Frederic Chopin (1810–49) which, in 1839, he incorporated into the B♭ Minor Sonata, op. 35 . . . Dead March in *Saul*, an oratorio by George Frederick Handel (1685–1759) first performed in London in 1739.

141:23 **Marie Corelli** (1854–1924), popular novelist; author of *A Romance of Two Worlds* (1886), *Barabbas* (1893), *The Sorrows of Satan* (1895), etc.

141:35 **"Wedded," by Lord Leighton.** Painting (*c.* 1881–2) by Frederic Lord Leighton (1830–96), now in the Art Gallery of New South Wales, Sydney. It was frequently reproduced at the time.

141:40 **Maurice Greiffenhagen's "Idyll."** Maurice Greiffenhagen (1862–1931), an English artist of Danish origin, whose painting *An Idyll* was first exhibited in the Royal Academy in 1891 (now in Walker Art Gallery, Liverpool). Blanche Jennings may have given DHL a reproduction of it in 1908: it is not mentioned in the first version of the paper. For its considerable impact on DHL see *Letters*, i. 103 and n. 3 and Jeffrey Meyers, *Painting and the Novel* (1975), p. 46ff.

142:4 **The delight . . . Leighton's pictures.** These two sentences were added on the verso of p. 6 of MS, but although DHL keyed them to the text on p. 7, there is some doubt about their exact location.

There is yet another sentence underneath the addition, apparently in pencil: 'In this diagram, notice the effects of following the left hand and then the right.' This seems to be more of a note than an addition to the text. (The diagram is unlocated.) If the sentence refers to *Wedded*, it is hard to see what DHL meant; if to *An Idyll*, there is some point but the text is severely disrupted, and thus it is excluded from the main text.

142:21 **"The chief triumph . . . habit"** David Hume (1711–76), Scottish philosopher, in *Essays Moral, Political and Literary* (1741–2), Essay XVIII 'The Sceptic'.

Rachel Annand Taylor

145:5 **her husband has left her . . . Chelsea . . . Professor Gilbert Murray** Rachel Annand Taylor was thirty-four when DHL met her. In MS(p. l) DHL first wrote 'she has left her husband'. The correction is probably closer to the truth; they separated because of his mental illness . . . inner suburb of London then associated with artists and literati . . . Sir George Gilbert Aimé Murray (1866–1957), classical scholar noted for verse translations of Greek dramatists (see also note on 89:23). Rachel Annand Taylor corresponded with Murray who reviewed her poems, praising her 'intense emotion and exquisite craftsmanship'.

145:15 **purely Rossettian:** I.e. in the style of the paintings of Dante Gabriel Rossetti (1828–82), one of the founders of the Pre-Raphaelite Brotherhood. Lizzy

Siddal, his favourite model, and later his wife, had abundant red hair. There is a photograph of Rachel Annand Taylor in *Letters*, i. following p. 216.

145:19 witch's brooch; In Scotland, a brooch which used to be worn as a charm against witches; properly a 'witch-brooch'.

145:23 Brought up . . . not Calvinistic. A member of a large family, she was not lonely as a child. Her father was a 'radical', and the family was not narrowly 'Calvinistic'. Her fondness for the Bible grew from her own reading rather than from instruction. *The Arabian Nights* or *The Thousand and One Nights*, a collection of Arabic tales trans. by Edward Wilson (1840).

145:31 Aucassin and Nicolette, Eponymous hero and heroine of a thirteenth century Provençal legend in prose with interspersed lyrics. DHL gave the English translation (Everyman, 1910) to Arthur McLeod at Christmas 1910; see *Letters*, i. 213.

145:33 The first volume of poems DHL quotes the titles from the contents pages of *Poems* (1904) where they are grouped under the four headings he gives.

146:9 Mrs Taylor gave me, See Introduction, p. xliii.

146:12 "Desire." As the Darkness calls to the day, so the lover's soul is 'yearning, tyrannous and tender'. The second and final stanza continues:

> Why do I love thee? – Hearken Death desiring
> All the yellow roses, loth to die,
> All the lovely lovers and their loves untiring,
> All the days of lapis lazuli,
> All the chiming rondels. – Hearken Death desiring
> So in silver samite like a bride to fold thee,
> So to hush thee, hide thee, so to have and hold thee. –
> It is I. (p. 73)

146:14 "Surrender"

> I strove, and strove with Fate. I leave my throne
> Of proud virginity, pearl-pale, apart,
> Where I have loved to sit and hark alone
> The dim pure pulses of my dreaming heart.
> Behold! most impotent kisses must I rain
> From lips for Death kept sweet
> On thine indifferent feet
> That yearn away to some strange laurelled goal.
> Oh! She is fallen, yea, and fallen in vain, –
> My once-imperial Soul! (p. 80)

146:15 "Unrealised" In this little poem the Beloved is asked to forget 'That Love has aught desirable but this, –/ The wistful lilies, the long sigh, the kiss.' (p. 84).

146:16 "Renunciation." In this poem the soul is crucified:

> Now change thee the love-stars in thine eyes,
> And thy roses twined in vain,
> For the upward stare of agony,
> And the aubéspine of pain . . . (p. 94)

146:18 that those who run may read. Hymn by John Keble (1792–1866) in *The Christian Year* (1827), line 1 ['There is a book, who runs may read'].

146:33 "pageant of her bleeding heart," Cf. 'The Grande Chartreuse' by Matthew Arnold (1822–88), lines 133–6:
> What helps it now, that Byron bore,
> With haughty scorn which mock'd the smart,
> Through Europe to the Aetolian shore
> The pageant of his bleeding heart?

DHL's remark probably offended Rachel Annand Taylor; see Introduction, p. xliv.

147:4 Strauss's music—"Electra," Richard Strauss (1864–1949), whose opera *Elektra* (1909) DHL saw with Alice Dax in the famous Beecham series at Covent Garden in March 1910; see *Letters*, i. 157.

147:19 "Four Crimson Violers." A 'Pre-Raphaelite' ballad for which the title is a refrain:
> *Four crimson Violers,*
> Two at the foot and two at the head,
> They made sweet sound by the Duchess' bed . . . (p. 5)

147:20 "Song of Fruition (For an October Mother)". The third and fourth stanzas of this five-stanza poem read:
> Oh! dear, most dear the tender Spring,
> The thrilled strange days of flowering!
> 'Mid lilies, songs, and violing
> The bridal-path I trod,
> But now amid the autumn-peace
> With vines and wheat I yield increase,
> I yield amid the autumn-peace,
> Oblation to my God.

> When from the world serene and sweet
> Is gathered in the golden wheat,
> A vintager with pure still feet
> I to the Temple-gate
> With all the harvesters will go,
> My delicate love-sheaf to show,
> My little Cup of Wine aglow,
> My secret Pomegranate. (p. 38)

147:28 a Prologue ... an Epilogue ... an Introduction. 'The Prologue of the Dreaming Women' and 'The Epilogue of the Dreaming Women' are the first and last poems in *The Hours of Fiammetta* (1910). They are not sonnets but in stanzas. The 'Introduction' is the prose Preface. For DHL's use of the idea of the 'Dreaming Women' see *The Trespasser*, ed. Elizabeth Mansfield (Cambridge, 1981), p. 64.

147:39 Celtic and French form of symbolism Among the French symbolist poets DHL had read Baudelaire, Verlaine, Rimbaud and Mallarmé; the 'Celtic' probably alludes to the Irish poet William Butler Yeats.

148:6 "Since from ... are spun." *The Hours of Fiammetta*, II 'Perils', lines 1–2.

148:9 "Prologue of the Dreaming Women,"
We carry spices to the gods.
  For this we are wrought curiously,
  All vain-desire and reverie,
To carry spices to the gods.

We carry spices to the gods.
  Sacred and soft as lotos-flowers
  Are those long languorous hands of ours
That carry spices to the gods.

We know their roses and their rods,
  Having in pale spring-orchards seen
  Their cruel eyes, and in the green
Strange twilights having met the gods.

Sometimes we tire. Upon the sods
  We set the great enamels by,
  Wherein the occult odours lie,
And play with children on the sods.

Yet soon we take, O jealous gods,
  Those gracious caskets once again,
  Storied with oracles of pain,
That keep the spices for the gods.

We carry spices to the gods.
  Like sumptuous cold chalcedony
  Our weary breasts and hands must be
To carry spices to the gods. (pp. 11–12)

148:14 "Epilogue of the Dreaming Women."
Take back this armour. Give us broideries.
  Against the Five sad Wounds inveterate
In our dim sense, can that defend, or these?
  In veils mysterious and delicate
Clothe us again, in beautiful broideries.

Take back this justice. Give us thuribles.
  While ye do loudly in the battle-dust,
We feed the gods with spice and canticles.
  To our strange hearts, as theirs, just and unjust
Are idle words. Give graven thuribles.

Keep orb and sceptre. Give us up your souls
  That our long fingers wake them verily
Like dulcimers and citherns and violes;
  Or at the burning disk of ecstasy
Impose rare sigils on your gem-like souls.

Give mercies, cruelties, and exultations,
  Give the long trances of the breaking heart;

And we shall bring you great imaginations
To urge you through the agony of Art.
Give cloud and flame, give trances, exultations. (pp. 74–5)

148:16   **"Mrs Bull."** The pseudonym of the author of 'John Bull's Womenfolk', a column in Horatio Bottomley's weekly *John Bull*, which discussed fashion, diet and affairs of interest to the middle-class woman in her home. On 29 October 1910 the first issue of *Mrs Bull* appeared; this was a separate forty-page weekly expanded from the now disbanded column but under the editorship of 'Mary Bull'. Either would fit DHL's allusion.

148:20   **number XVIII.** 'The Doubt'
> I am pure, because of great illuminations
>   Of dreamy doctrine caught from poets of old,
> Because of delicate imaginations,
>   Because I am proud, or subtle, or merely cold.
> Natheless my soul's bright passions interchange
>   As the red flames in opal drowse and speak:
> In beautiful twilight paths the elusive strange
>   Phantoms of personality I seek.
> If better than the last embraces I
>   Love the lit riddles of the eyes, the faint
> Appeal of merely courteous fingers, – why,
>   Though 'tis a quest of souls, and I acquaint
> My heart with spiritual vanities, –
> Is there indeed no bridge twixt me and these? (p. 30)

148:22   **"Open road" and Empire thumping verse.** Presumably DHL had in mind poems like 'Tewkesbury Road' by John Masefield (1878–1967), 'The Open Road' collection by E. V. Lucas (1868–1938), 'Recessional' by Rudyard Kipling (1865–1936) and 'Land of Hope and Glory' by A. C. Benson (1862–1925). The Lucas collection is listed in the course of study for the Teacher's Certificate examination which DHL took in 1908; see Delavenay 659.

The Future of the Novel

151:2   **[Surgery for the Novel—Or a Bomb]** The editorial title supplied by the *Literary Digest International*; see Introduction, p. xlvi.

151:13   **we decide.** 'This rather serious case' (see Textual apparatus) was added by the *Literary Digest* apparently to restore the full double-column format after an indentation to accommodate the accompanying illustration.

151:22   **Ulysses ... Mr Robert Chambers,** The novel *Ulysses* (Paris, 1922) by James Joyce was the subject of controversy and legal action; see Introduction, p. xlv ... Dorothy Richardson (1882–1957) published a sequence of twelve novels *Pilgrimage* (1915–38) of which *Pointed Roofs* (1915) was the first ... Marcel Proust, author of *À la recherche du temps perdu* (1913–27). DHL's aversion to Proust appears to have been life-long: see Carswell 41, for an opinion in 1916, and letter to Aldous and Maria Huxley, 15? July 1927: 'too much water-jelly' ... in Greek mythology, Briareus was a monster who helped Zeus in his battle against the Titans; Homer and Virgil give him a hundred hands . . . *The Sheik*, best-selling popular novel (1919) by Edith Maude Hull (see also note on 153:13) . . . Zane Grey, popular American author (1875–1939) of westerns like *Riders of the Purple Sage* (1912). In *Kangaroo*, chap. x, Somers and Harriet find Zane Grey novels in the School of Arts Library in Murrumbimby . . . Robert William Chambers (1865–1933), prolific American novelist and illustrator.

152:3   **abysmal chloro-coryambasis,"**   A meaningless term of DHL's invention.

153:4   ***Babbitts*** *Babbitt* (1922) was, with *Main Street* (1920), among the most popular novels of the American writer Sinclair Lewis (1885–1951).

153:13   **A Sheik** [153:10] . . . **anatomy.**   The Sheik's cruelty is demonstrated on horses and disobedient servants: there is no mention in the novel of his taking a whip to the heroine, Diana Mayo, but the novel is far from explicit.

153:15   ***If Winter Comes***   Popular novel (1921) by the American author A. S. M. Hutchinson (1879–1971); the hero, Mark Sabre, is subjected to disgrace and suffering for his belief in 'Justice'.

153:33   **loony Cleopatra in *Dombey and Son* . . . "Rose-coloured curtains—"**   In Dickens' *Dombey and Son* (1847–8), Mrs Skewton, the second wife of Mr Dombey, is known as 'Cleopatra' from her resemblance in her barouche to Queen Cleopatra in her galley . . . see chaps. XXVII and XLI.

153:38   **Put away childish things**   See 1 Corinthians xiii. 11.

154:25   ***Scarlet Pimpernels.***   *The Scarlet Pimpernel* (1905), the best-selling novel by Baroness Emmuska Orczy (1865–1947).

154:28   **find the** [154:20] . . . **can't deny it.**   This passage is the first of five cuts made to the text in Per; see Textual apparatus entries for 154:20; 154:35; 154:38; 155:9; 155:17. All contain references to the gospels and presumably were made because some readers might have construed them as sacrilegious; see Introduction, p. xlvi.

154:29   **Plato's Dialogues,**   Twenty-five dialogues by the Athenian philosopher (*c.* 429–347 B.C.) in most of which Socrates takes part and teaches that 'Virtue is Knowledge' – to be good, one has to know what is meant by 'good'.

154:33   **that beastly Kant.**   In a letter to Aldous Huxley, 27 March 1928, DHL includes the German philosopher Immanuel Kant (1724–1804) in a list of 'grand perverts'. He condemns them for their 'ineffable conceit' in that they 'tried to . . . intellectualize and so utterly falsify the phallic consciousness'.

154:39   **Blessed are X, Y, and Z.**   The formulaic expression of the Beatitudes (see 155:3) in Matthew v. 1–11, the opening of 'The Sermon on the Mount'. See also 181:27 and 195:39.

155:1   *in propria persona,*   'In his own person' (Latin).

155:13   **Augustine's Confessions . . . Religio Medici**   The spiritual autobiography of St Augustine (354–430 A.D.) . . . the spiritual apologia (1642) of Sir Thomas Browne (1605–82), medical doctor and antiquary ['The Religion of a Physician', Latin].

A Britisher Has a Word With an Editor

159:2   **October's POETRY,**   *Poetry: A Magazine of Verse* (Chicago), edited since 1912 by its founder, Harriet Monroe (1860–1936). She was the first to publish DHL's poems in America; see *Letters*, ii. 167, 170. For the October 1923 issue (Vol. xxiii) Miss Monroe wrote an editorial 'Comment' in the form of a letter recording her recent visit to Britain: 'The Editor In England' (pp. 32–45). The concluding remarks of this letter prompted DHL's reply. Recalling a statue of George IV (Prince Regent 1811– 20, King 1820–30) in Edinburgh, she wrote:

> No keener satire upon the whole monarchical system could be desired than this operatic effigy of the worthless dude who for some years encumbered the British throne. But the British king will probably be the last to go, and the oligarchic social system which he typifies, though somewhat shaken by the Great War, still stands intact, the cracks in it scarcely visible.
>
> One wonders whether British poets will have anything very essential to say so long as it endures – ... in England I found no such evidence of athletic sincerity in artistic experiment, of vitality and variety and – yes – beauty, in artistic achievement, as I get from the poets of our own land.

159:3   **not a Bostonian one,**   A reference to the so-called Boston Tea Party in 1773, when three British ships in Boston harbour were raided by the citizens and chests of tea were dumped overboard as a protest against taxes on tea.

159:13   **what poet**   Among those who wrote during the reign of George IV were, of course, Wordsworth, Coleridge, Byron, Shelley and Keats.

159:17   **Coolidge!**   John Calvin Coolidge (1872–1933), thirtieth President of the USA (1923–9) and a man of simple puritan upbringing. In this context the irony of his nickname 'Silent Cal' would not have been lost on DHL.

Art and Morality

163:4   **jazz ... débourgeoiser themselves.**   The adjectival sense, popular in the 1920s, was 'vividly coloured, unconventional, sensational' ... consciously to separate themselves from the bourgeoisie or middle-class (French).

163:10   **Cézanne**   Paul Cézanne (1839–1906), French artist, generally associated with Post-Impressionism.

163:19   **of**   See Textual apparatus. This is DHL's correction to TS; see Introduction, p. xlviii.

164:9   **kodak**   The proprietary name of a range of cameras produced by Kodak Ltd but popularly applied to any snapshot camera.

166:18   **Vox Populi, Vox Dei.**   'The voice of the people (public opinion) is the voice of God' (Latin).

166:36   **decoration ... colour-mass relations,**   DHL is playing with the jargon of art criticism. For DHL's antipathy to such jargon see his letter to Koteliansky of 21 December 1928 where he refers to 'all that significant form piffle'. 'Significant form' was coined by Clive Bell (1881–1964) in *Art* (1914), chap. 1; 'tactile values' derives from Bernard Berenson (1865–1959) and refers to 'an illusion of tangibility' in painting; and 'plastique' (French) is a clay-like composition material for use in modelling.

167:4 Fantin Latour's apples Ignace Henri Jean Théodore Fantin-Latour (1836–1904), French painter. In England he was popular for his meticulous still-life and flower paintings.

167:11 rock of ages From the hymn 'Rock of ages cleft for me ...' by Augustus Montague Toplady (1740–78).

167:14 Allons! Let's go! (French).

167:21 An ancient Rameses Of the twelve Ancient Egyptian kings of that name between ?1315–?1090 B.C., DHL probably means Rameses II, who was noted for the construction of colossal monuments, including statues of himself, especially those in the rock temple at Abu Simbel.

167:24 Michael Angelo's Adam ... Turner See notes on 74:15 and 86:14.

167:37 the fourth dimension. The dimension of time, in addition to the three spatial dimensions. For DHL's belief in the metaphysical nature of the fourth dimension see Richard O. Young, '"Where Even the Trees Come and Go": D. H. Lawrence and the Fourth Dimension', *DHL Review*, xiii (1980), 30–44. See also 171:19.

168:6 The African fetish-statues ... the Parthenon frieze. For DHL's interest in these statues cf. *Women in Love*, chap. VII, and see Jack F. Stewart, 'Primitivism in *Women in Love*', *DHL Review*, xiii (1980), 45 ... see note on 68:18.

168:9 movies, that jerk but never move. An allusion to the technical crudity of some motion pictures of DHL.'s time. Cf. *The Lost Girl*, ed. John Worthen (Cambridge, 1981), where a film is described as a 'dithering eye-ache' (86:26 and see also note).

168:16 ambiente, 'Ambience' (Italian).

Morality and the Novel

171:7 When Van Gogh paints sunflowers, Vincent Van Gogh (1853–90), Dutch Post-Impressionist painter. *Sunflowers* (August 1888) was painted at Arles, but he made many sunflower studies as decorations for his rooms.

171:19 much-debated fourth dimension. See note on 167:37.

172:1 an Assyrian lion or an Egyptian hawk's-head The Assyrian statue 'The Lion of Babylon' (first millennium B.C.) still stands in the ruined city of Babylon. The Egyptian hawk's-head may refer to Horus, the falcon-headed god, son of Isis and Osiris; the Pharaohs associated themselves with Horus.

173:19 The sins of the fathers ... children. Cf. Exodus xx. 5.

174:7 the man in *Crime and Punishment* Raskolnikov in the novel (1866) by Dostoievsky.

174:12 If Winter Comes. See note on 153:15.

174:33 The Constant Nymph ... constancy. In the popular novel *The Constant Nymph* (1924) by Margaret Kennedy (1896–1967), the heroine, Teresa Sanger is unwavering in her love for Lewis Dodd with whom she finally elopes. The 'eighteen-months' is roughly the period of the story.

175:35 **This is the ... Holy Ghost,** Luke xxiii. 28 ... DHL's interpretation of the Trinity can be seen more fully in the 'Foreword to *Sons and Lovers*' (Huxley, *Letters of D. H. Lawrence*, pp. 95–102), and 'Hardy', chaps. VII, VIII, X.

176:3 **Lead Kindly Light!** Hymn (1833) by John Henry, Cardinal Newman (1801–90). See also 'Hymns in a Man's Life' (*Phoenix II* 597–601).

The Novel

179:4 **Mr Santayana** George Santayana, American philosopher, poet and critic (1863–1952). The comment DHL attributes to him here has not been located, but cf. his 'Penitent Art' in the *Dial* (July 1922).

179:32 **Vronsky ... a consummation devoutly to be wished.** Count Alexei Kirillovich Vronsky, Anna's lover in *Anna Karenin*; see note on 29:38 ... *Hamlet* III. i. 63–4.

179:34 **Prince in *Resurrection* is a muff,** I.e. weak, foolish. The hero of Tolstoy's *Resurrection* (1899–1900) is Prince Dmitri Ivanovich Nekhlyudov who by chance is on the jury at the murder trial of Katerina 'Katusha' Maslova, brought up by the Prince's aunts as 'half-servant, half young-lady', seduced by him and left pregnant, and is overcome by remorse (chap. XXVIII). In his essay 'Resurrection' (?January 1925) DHL wrote: 'I have just read, for the first time, Tolstoy's *Resurrection* ...' (*Phoenix* 737).

180:7 **spit in Mother Grundy's eye.** Mrs Grundy is the figure of conventional prudery from *Speed the Plough* (1798) by Thomas Morton (*c.* 1764–1838).

180:13 **"As an officer ... backs on him!** *Anna Karenin*, Part VIII, chap. V. It is not known which translation DHL read, but the only word he seems to misremember is 'officer' ... Part V, chap. XXXIII, but it is Anna who is insulted at the opera.

180:35 **Salammbô ... Matho ... gilt Princess.** *Salammbô* (1862), an historical novel set in Carthage by Gustav Flaubert (1821–80). Salammbô is priestess of the goddess Tanit, Matho the commander of mercenaries who are besieging Carthage. He is defeated and tortured to death by flaying; she, who had been forced to give herself to him, dies of grief. It is clear from the underlining of Salammbô in MS that DHL intended the title, not the character.

181:4 **Dostoevsky's Idiot.** Prince Leo Nikolayevich Myshkin and see note on 125:8.

181:15 **Plato's Dialogues ... Timaeus ... my dear Cleon** See note on 154:29 ... *Timaeus* is a dialogue with four speakers – Socrates, Timaeus, Critias and Hermocrates ... Cleon, an Athenian politician (d. 422 B.C.) was satirised by Aristophanes in his early plays. DHL seems to have confused him with Critias.

181:19 **when Jesus told the rich man ... poor,** See Matthew xix. 21.

181:29 **Sermon-on-the-Mounting ... breeches on!"—** See Matthew v. and note on 154:39 ... a popular parody of 'Matthew, Mark, Luke, and John,/ The Bed be blest that I lie on . . .' It was added when DHL was revising TS, perhaps because Dorothy Brett reminded him of it; see Nehls, ii. 406–7.

181:33 **passional inspiration.** In his manuscript DHL wrote 'passionate inspiration' (p. 3) : to the first typescript carbon copy (p.2) he added a passage using 'passional' and then twice corrected 'passionate' to 'passional' later in the same copy (2:5 and 3:11.) He did not, however, correct the present instance in either the first or second typescript, but since there is a clear distinction in meaning between the two words, it has been treated as an oversight and corrected editorially.

182:8 *Lord Jim*! . . . *Pan*! *Lord Jim* (1900), novel by Joseph Conrad (1857–1924) . . . *Le Crime de Sylvestre Bonnard* (1881), novel by Anatole France (1844–1924) . . . *If Winter Comes*, see note on 153:15 . . . *Main Street*, see note on 153:4 . . . *Ulysses*, see note on 151:22 . . . *Pan* (1894), novel by Knut Hamsun (1859–1952).

182:9 **Jesuses** *accomplis* or *manqués.* 'Perfect (complete) or deficient Jesuses' (French).

182:11 **the Green Hatted Woman.** *The Green Hat* (1924), a popular novel by Michael Arlen (Dikran Kouyoumdjian, 1895–1956). DHL found Arlen 'a bit blatant and pushing' (*Letters*, ii. 473).

182:14 **misleading . . . a Constant Nymph** DHL had trouble with the lady's behaviour from manuscript to final TS. First it was 'more than startling' – to which he added 'But always to be pitied, the dear!' Next it was 'extremely questionable' (MS, Roberts E280a p. 6) then 'distasteful' (E280b p. 4), then 'undiscriminating' (E280c p. 4) and finally 'misleading' (E340.6 p. 4). See note on 174:33.

182:18 **didn't Jesus harrow Hell . . . A la bonne heure!** According to legend Jesus delivered worthies of earlier days from their imprisonment in Hell at his resurrection. See also 'Resurrection' (*Phoenix* 737–9) . . . 'Well and good' (French).

182:29 **life as it is isn't life . . . peccante.** DHL's manuscript and all typescripts omit 'is': it was added to the text in A1. Both the context and the grammar require it . . . 'sinning' (Italian).

182:34 *frère et cochon,* 'Brother and pig' (French); the phrase suggests an unwarranted and unpleasant intimacy.

183:6 **corpus** 'Body' (Latin), i.e. the mere physical presence of the books.

183:8 *Quien sabe!* 'Who knows' (Spanish).

183:38 **War and Peace,** Count Pierre Bezuhov, Prince Andrei Bolkonsky and Natasha Rostova are principal characters in Tolstoy's novel.

184:13 **Attila . . . saddle-cloth,** Attila, king of the Huns (d. 453), known as the 'Scourge of God'. In *Movements in European History* (1921), chap. vi, DHL wrote of the Huns: 'For food, they cut some slices of raw meat, and these, placed like a saddle, cooked a little between the heat of the horse's body and the warrior's thigh.'

184:20 **the lion lie down with the lamb ... like the limerick,** Cf. Isaiah, xi. 6
... DHL parodies a popular limerick (see 189:30–2), of which one version reads:

> There was a young lady of Riga,
> Who rode with a smile on a tiger;
> They returned from the ride
> With the lady inside,
> And the smile on the face of the tiger.

The Limerick Book, ed. Langford Reed (1925).

184:39 **"Honour thy father ... neighbour as thyself."** Exodus xx. 12 ...
Matthew xix. 19.

185:4 **the cunning of serpents!** Cf. Matthew x. 16: 'Be ye therefore wise as
serpents, and harmless as doves.'

185:9 **The Goat and Compasses,** Popularly believed to be a euphemistic form of
'God encompasses' (cf. 184:33) and frequently used as an inn name. See also
Introduction, p. xxxi.

185:23 **if a character** [185:19] ... **furious polygamy;** Perhaps inspired by
reviews of *The Boy in the Bush* in 1924 critical of the hero's polygamous desires, e.g. L.
P. Hartley in *D. H. Lawrence: The Critical Heritage*, ed. R. P. Draper (1970), pp. 233–4.

185:25 **a remote Beatrice,** The *Vita Nuova* (1292) of Dante Alighieri
(1265–1321), a series of lyrics with prose links, tells of his love for Beatrice, whom he
first saw at the age of nine, and again at the age of eighteen. He married Gemma
Donati, who bore him at least three children.

185:30 **Petrarch, with his Laura in the distance,** Francesco Petrarca
(1304–74), Italian poet, author of the series of love poems addressed to Laura which
make up the *Canzoniere* or *Rime in Vita e Morte di Madonna Laura*. Laura is thought to
have been Laure de Noves, wife of Count Hugues de Sade to whom she bore eleven
children. There is no record of Petrarch's marrying, although he had at least two
illegitimate children.

186:14 **Dante's *Commedia*** In the third part of the *Divina Commedia*, Beatrice,
transfigured, acts as the poet's guide to Paradise.

186:39 **inside the skin of a lamb ... León!** Cf. Matthew vii. 15 ... DHL used
and carefully corrected in the final TS the Spanish form 'León'; either the Centaur
editor or the printer substituted the French 'Léon' in A1.

187:5 **moral thunder-bolts.** DHL slightly modifies the episode recalled by
Maxim Gorky in *Reminiscences of Leo Nicolayevitch Tolstoy*, trans. S. S. Koteliansky and
Leonard Woolf (1920), section 36. See DHL's letter to Kot, 24 December 1920:
'Gorki *Reminiscences* just come – what a charming little book!' (*Letters*, iii. 640).

187:7 **its old-Adam manhood** Manhood unredeemed by the 'new Adam',
Christ; see 1 Corinthians xv. 22, 45.

187:14 **But wait ... Bolshevists.** Inserted by DHL in the final TS.

187:28 **the absolute of love ... of senility.** Added to the final TS. For the
quotation see Milton, *Lycidas*, line 71 ['that last ... mind'].

187:36 **Judas** In the final TS DHL substituted 'Judas'; 'Trajan' appears in all
earlier versions.

187:40 **the incalculable Pan.** The Greek fertility god, son of Hermes, who is often represented with goat's horns, ears and hooves. He was likely to be dangerous if disturbed and to effect terror – whence 'panic'. See DHL's story 'The Overtone' (*St. Mawr and Other Stories*, ed. Brian Finney, Cambridge, 1983, pp. 3–17) and his essay 'Pan in America' (*Phoenix* 22–31); E. M. Forster's 'The Story of a Panic' (1911); and *Letters*, ii. 275.

188:22 **Amon ... Annie Besant,** Amon, Egyptian god Amun or Ammon ... Ra, Egyptian sun-god ... Mary Baker Eddy (1821–1910), American founder of Christian Science ... Ashtaroth, ancient Semitic fertility goddess ... Jupiter, Olympian Father of the Gods ... Annie Besant (1847–1933), follower of Mme Blavatsky; President of the Theosophical Society, 1907.

188:40 **a Holy Roller ... The wind bloweth where it listeth,** A member of a sect that expresses its religious ecstasy by rolling or writhing on the floor ... John iii. 8.

189:11 **wetted on** In the final TS, DHL substituted these words for 'pissed upon' and also 'wetting' for 'pissing', 'his wet' for 'the piss' (line 22) and 'dribbling' for 'masturbating' (190:7); see Introduction, p. xlix.

189:21 **absolute. Even** See Textual apparatus. The typist of TS misread DHL's manuscript, but the apparent upper point in the colon is a clear slip of DHL's pen.

Why the Novel Matters

193:4 *Mens sana in corpore sano.* 'A sound mind in a healthy body' (Latin), from Juvenal, *Satires* x. 356.

193:23 **the mysterious Rubicon** 'To cross the Rubicon', a proverb meaning to take a decisive step. Caesar's crossing of this stream in Northern Italy marked the beginning of war with Pompey.

194:18 **tremulations in the ether,** The ether was thought to be the medium through which radio waves and electromagnetic radiations are propagated. Oliver Lodge in *Ether and Reality* (1925) wrote of 'fearfully rapid tremors or ether vibrations which can be excited electrically in a form which we know as X-rays'.

194:36 **than a dead lion ... C'est la vie.** See Ecclesiastes ix. 4: 'a living dog is better than a dead lion' ... 'That's life' (French).

195:4 **no wafer, for others to eat.** I.e. like Christ's body in the Mass.

195:31 **Sarai,** The original name of Abraham's wife Sarah; see Genesis xvii. 15.

195:35 **a burning bush ... tablets of stone at Moses' head.** See Exodus iii. 2–6 and xxxii. 15–19.

195:38 **Plato makes ... tremble in me.** Cf. DHL's references in 'Hardy' 70–1; 125–6 and note on 154:29.

196:1 **The Sermon on the Mount ... the Old Adam** See Matthew v. and note on 154:39 ... see note on 187:7.

196:21 **"The grass withereth ... for ever."** Isaiah xl. 8 ['... fadeth: but ... word of our God ...', (AV)].

196:28 **renews its youth like the eagle,** See Psalm ciii. 5.

196:36 **My yea! of today** Cf. Matthew v. 37: 'But let your communication be, Yea, yea; Nay, nay: for whatsoever is more than these cometh of evil', (AV).

196:40 **my inertia,** Cf. 'Hardy' 59:3–61:12.

197:10 **cut your cloth to fit your coat,** Cf. the proverb: 'Cut your coat according to your cloth'.

The Novel and the Feelings

201:12 *Toujours perdrix!* Literally 'Always partridge!' (French).

201:29 **near beer.** A malt beverage of high nutritive value and very low or no alcohol content: common in the Prohibition Era.

202:17 **Moody and Sankey hymn-book.** *Sacred Songs and Solos* by Dwight Lyman Moody (1837–99) and Ira David Sankey (1840–1908), American evangelists and hymnodists, noted for revivalist campaigns in Britain and USA.

202:20 **Billy Sunday,** Popular name for William Ashley Sunday (1862–1935), American evangelist who characteristically preached divine wrath in vivid terms: hence the 'elephant gun' he took to the feelings of his listeners.

204:12 **a dog that returns to his vomit.** See Proverbs xxvi. 11: 'As a dog returneth to his vomit, so a fool returneth to his folly', (AV).

205:22 **listening-in ... Timbuctoo.** I.e. to a radio. Cf. Connie's attitude to Clifford's radio in *Lady Chatterley's Lover* (1928), chap. x ... Timbuktu, a town in central Mali; popularly, any distant or outlandish place.

John Galsworthy

209:1 **John Galsworthy** Novelist and playwright (1867–1933); O. M., 1929; Nobel Prize for Literature, 1932. DHL refers to Galsworthy's novels: *The Island Pharisees* (1904), *The Country House* (1907), *Fraternity* (1909), *The Patrician* (1911), *The Dark Flower* (1913), *The Apple Tree* (1918), and *The Forsyte Saga* (1922). The latter comprises *The Man of Property* (1906), *Indian Summer of a Forsyte* (1918), *In Chancery* (1920), *Awakening* (1920), and *To Let* (1921). For Galsworthy's criticism of *The Rainbow* in a letter to Pinker, see Keith Sagar, *The Art of D. H. Lawrence* (Cambridge, 1966), p. 69.

209:7 **our sincere and vital emotion,** DHL's view of art as the communication of emotion goes back to his earliest writing, see an early version of 'Art and the Individual', 227:13ff.

209:13 **a man of force and complexity** Either in typescript or proofs DHL revised the MS reading 'a man of emotional force and complexity'. His view that the 'emotionally educated' man is extremely rare may be compared with one expressed twenty years earlier in an early version of 'Art and the Individual', 227:23–7.

209:21 **Sainte Beuve ... Macaulay,** Charles Augustin Sainte-Beuve (1804–69), French critic and novelist, asserted the necessity for a critic to reach the man behind the work, his nature and his development. He defended his method as a 'natural historian of minds' in his work on Chateaubriand (1862); his comparison of criticism and botany may have prompted DHL's deprecation of 'critical twiddle-twaddle' as analysis 'in an imitation-botanical fashion' (209:7–10) . . . Thomas Babington, 1st Baron Macaulay (1800–59), historian, essayist and statesman. See, for instance, his *Critical and Historical Essays* (1843).

210:2 Pater's standard Walter Horatio Pater (1839–94); see, e.g. his Preface to *The Renaissance* (1873) where he outlines his critical standards.

210:5 Gibbon tried a purely moral standard, Presumably DHL has in mind *An Essay on the Study of Literature* (English trans. 1764) by Edward Gibbon (1737–94). DHL had also read his *Decline and Fall of the Roman Empire* (1776–88).

210:8 all these Forsytes Like Galsworthy DHL intends not just members of the Forsyte family. See e.g. *The Man of Property* Part I, chap. VIII.

The elder generation of ten Forsyte brothers and sisters included Jolyon ('Old Jolyon'), tea merchant (212:23); James, solicitor, and Swithin, land agent (219:27); and the 'old aunts', Ann, Julia and Hester (215:3). James had a daughter, Winifred (218:4), and a son, Soames (215:1), who was married first to Irene Heron (212:40), and later divorced. Soames then married Annette Lamotte and a daughter, Fleur (219:29), was born.

'Young Jolyon' (214:10), Old Jolyon's son, married three times. June Forsyte (212:19), was the child of his first marriage. She was for a time engaged to Philip Bosinney (212:40), an architect; however, he planned to elope with Irene (then married to Soames) but was run over by a bus and killed. Irene eventually became Young Jolyon's third wife; their son was also Jolyon ('Jon') (219:37).

210:18 a social being as distinct from a human being. For DHL's first attempt at this distinction, see pp. 249–50. For the probable influence of the psychoanalyst Trigant Burrow on DHL at this time, see Introduction, p. lii and footnotes 59 and 60. The following passage was deleted in MS at this point: 'The distinction between the social being and the human being is very important today, and it is very necessary to make it. The human individual is a queer animal, always changing. But the supreme and fatal change that takes place when the human individual is converted completely and finally into the social individual is one that our day has to reckon with' (pp. 2–3). Burrow had argued similarly, though in clinical terms, in his paper on the 'Reabsorbed Affect' (p. 214). It is nevertheless a distinction inherent in DHL's philosophy: see, e.g. 'Hardy', pp. 20ff.

210:24 Sairey Gamp . . . George Meredith's Egoist A comic character in Dickens' *Martin Chuzzlewit* (1843–4) . . . Sir Willoughby Patterne, the central figure of George Meredith's novel *The Egoist* (1879).

210:36 The free moral and the slave moral: The phrase recalls Nietzsche's 'noble-morality' and 'slave-morality'; see his *Beyond Good and Evil* (Leipzig, 1886), chap. IX. English edition by Oscar Levy (1909–12).

211:3 Mr Worldly Wiseman Allegorical character in *The Pilgrim's Progress*, Part I, by John Bunyan (1628–88).

211:11 give away . . . to the poor, Cf. 1 Corinthians xiii. 3.

211:28 Œdipus or Phaedra. Presumably the Oedipus of Sophocles' Theban plays and Phaedra in the *Hippolytus* of Euripides. Phaedra, however, may be an allusion to the *Phèdre* of Racine (1639–99). Cf. *The First Lady Chatterley* (New York, 1944) where Clifford reads Racine to his wife and comments: 'I can't help feeling that Hamlet is in bad taste. Orestes or Phèdre are much deeper down to the bedrock of the same sort of feelings, without so much contortion' (p. 37).

212:19   **Mrs Pendyce,**   In this extensively re-written passage in MS, DHL overlooked his cancelling of 'Mrs'. Apart from MS, it is clear that he intended Mrs Pendyce (and not her husband), who was 'averse to any change in the existing order of things . . .' (*The Country House*, Part I, chap. I), and in Part II, chap. I she makes a bid for freedom. See also Part I, chap. V in which she recalls 'a night in her youth'. In his notes on the novel DHL wrote of her: 'Mrs Pendyce is nice, but rather like a tame mouse nervously nibbling the wires. No fire at all, always wet' (Roberts E181.3a; UT).

212:27   **the road-sweeper in *Fraternity* . . . wound in the head:**   DHL conflates several details from the novel. The road-sweeper, Mr Hughs attacks his wife with a bayonet when she is jealously raving at him about his infatuation with a model (see note to 215:8), and he is imprisoned briefly: 'They only give him a month, considerin' of him bein' wounded in the war . . . The man . . . is a poor, violent creature, who has been wounded in the head; he is not quite responsible . . .' (chaps. XXIV, XXXIII). When he emerges from prison, Hughs returns home and lies with his face to the wall (chap. XXXVIII). DHL has apparently confused this with the time when Joshua Creed shouted at Hughs that he ought to be ashamed of attacking his wife: 'Hughs stood silent, the back of his arm covering his eyes' (chap. XXIV).

214:9   **Hilarys and Biancas**   Hilary and Bianca Dallison in *Fraternity* (1909). In his preliminary notes, DHL wrote: 'A trashy bit of social gossip about a stale little model: and a strong defence of class! The chief distinction between the classes seems to be a distinction in smell. Well, upper classes smell often enough of stale violet-powder' (Roberts E181.3a).

214:13   **the shadows of the "having" ones, as old Mr Stone says.**   In *Fraternity*, chap. II: ' "Each of us," [Mr Stone] said, "has a shadow in those places – in those streets." ' The remark is several times repeated, and the idea of the poor and oppressed as 'shadows' of the rich is developed through the book. DHL takes the term 'having' from *The Forsyte Saga*. See also 219:36 and note.

214:26   **doggish amorousness**   DHL picks up Galsworthy's imagery of dogs; e.g. in *Fraternity*, chap. XXIII: 'The mistress of the house [Bianca] was herself returning from her annual visit to the Royal Academy, where she still went, as dogs, from some perverted sense, will go and sniff round other dogs to whom they have long taken a dislike.' Cf. *Lady Chatterley's Lover*, chap. XVI.

214:30   **grand love affairs . . . George Pendyce**   DHL alludes to the grand love affairs of Mark Lennan and several women (*The Dark Flower*), Bosinney and Irene (*The Man of Property*), Frank Ashurst and Megan David (*The Apple Tree*) and George Pendyce and Mrs Jaspar Bellew (*The Country House*).

215:8   **the little model in *Fraternity*.**   'Her name, [Ivy] Barton, and address had been given him by a painter of still life . . .' (chap. IV); she and Hilary Dallison have a 'relationship'.

215:11   **"Big fleas have little fleas . . . the vagabond in *The Island Pharisees*,**   See Swift, 'On Poetry: A Rhapsody', lines 337–40; cf. *Letters*, i. 216 . . . the young foreigner, Louis Ferrand (chap. I).

215:28 a "hunger" for her: See chap. II: '"Antonia," he said, "I love you." She started as if his whisper had intruded on her thoughts; but his face must have expressed his hunger, for the resentment in her eyes vanished.'

215:33 *pieds truffés*: Truffled pig's trotters (French).

**215:40 *basta.* 'Enough' (Italian).

216:20 *The Apple Tree* [216:13] ... with you!" Frank Ashurst and Megan David. The nearest of Megan's exclamations to DHL's quotations are: '"I shall die if I can't be with you."' and '"I only want to be with you!"' Cf. Beatrice in H. G. Wells's *Tono-Bungay* (1909) who says to George Ponderevo 'Of course I will marry you. You are my prince, my king' (Book III, chap. III). DHL's notes read: 'great bunk – hero loving himself – inventing that Megan – And what a very tall passion he must have had for his Megan, if other folks ask him to tea he forgets her!!' (Roberts E181.3a).

216:31 the face of drowned Ophelia See *Hamlet* IV. vii. 167ff.

216:35 Megan, kindly ... about it!! At this point MS reads: 'kindly to ⟨be his substitute⟩ drown herself instead. And in this fiction she actually does. ⟨And young men lap it up. It is pure bathos.⟩ And he feels so *wonderful* about it!!' DHL added a sentence (see Textual apparatus) which he later deleted from the *Scrutinies* text.

219:13 the early novels, DHL probably cancelled the 'four' in MS reading 'the four early novels' (p. 15) when checking the typescript or proofs and noting the preceding paragraph refers to 'the three early novels'. (Presumably the fourth would have been *The Country House*, mentioned in 218:38.)

219:17 the promised end of the Forsytes, DHL appears to have ignored *The White Monkey* (1924) and *The Silver Spoon* (1926), the first two parts of a second Forsyte trilogy: *A Modern Comedy.* He could not have known *Two Forsyte Interludes* (1927) or *Swan Song* (1928) at the time he was writing, and *On Forsyte Change* appeared after his death in 1930.

219:36 she is "having." In attempting to persuade Jon Forsyte to break off his relationship with his cousin Fleur, Holly Dartie says, 'Val and I don't really like her very much ... We think she's got rather a "having" nature' (*To Let*, Part II, chap. X).

219:39 "Didn't she spoil your life too?" For this question and June's answer to it (220:4–5) see *To Let*, Part III, chap. X.

Appendix I: Art and The Individual

223:16 'one talent,' See Matthew XXV. 14–30.

228:34 Ruth ... Naomi ... David and Jonathan See Ruth i–iv ... See I Samuel xviii; 2 Samuel i. 23–7.

Appendix III: Morality and the Novel

243:1 *Daphnis and Chloe ... The Golden Ass ... Satiricon.* A pastoral romance attributed to Longus (fl. 3rd century) ... a Latin novel by Apuleius (c. 123–?) ... a satirical novel by Petronius Arbiter (d. 65).

243:15 *Madame Bovary* Novel (1856) by Gustav Flaubert (1821–80).

243:34 *The Brothers Karamazov.* Novel (1880) by Dostoievsky.

Appendix IV: John Galsworthy

251:25 **Nebuchadnezzar or Francis of Assisi,** King of Babylon – see 2 Kings xxivff. – and St Francis (1181–1226), founder of the Friars Minor.

251:27 **Ex nihilo nihil fit!** Nothing will come of nothing (Latin).

TEXTUAL APPARATUS

TEXTUAL APPARATUS

Study of Thomas Hardy

The following symbols are used to distinguish states of the text:

TS = Typescript of DHL's manuscript
Per = First periodical publication (see Introduction)
TCC = Carbon copy typescript (1930) revised by Edward McDonald
A1 = First American edition

All subsequent impressions reproduce *A1*.

Whenever the *TS* reading is adopted, it appears within the square bracket with no symbol. When a reading from a source later than the *TS* has been preferred, it appears with its source-symbol within the square bracket. Rejected readings follow the square bracket, in chronological sequence, with their first source denoted; *Per* precedes *TCC* for chap. III. (When the *TS* and another reading correspond, both symbols are given within the square bracket.) When the entry itself does not make evident why an accepted reading was chosen, the reader is referred to the notes.

The following symbols are used editorially:
Ed. = Editor
Om. = Omitted
/ = Line or page break resulting in variation in punctuation, hyphenation or word error
= Internal division
~ = Repeated word in recording a punctuation variant
P = Paragraph division
[ ] = Editorially supplied word (see Note on the text, p. 4)

7:1	Study of Thomas Hardy [Le Gai Savaire] *Ed.*] Le Gai Savaire. *TS* Study of Thomas Hardy *TCC* STUDY OF THOMAS HARDY *A1 see notes*	7:23	huge barns *Ed.*] huge barn *TS* a huge barn *TCC see notes*
		7:31	on,] ~ *TCC*
		8:11	children," *TCC*] ~ ", *TS*
		8:14	the [physics] and *Ed.*]
7:6	- 1 - *Ed.*] *Om. TS see notes*		the and *TS* the [?] and *TCC*
7:10	shelter,] ~ ; *TCC*		the *A1 see notes*
7:15	property,] ~ ; *TCC*	8:18	that." *TCC*] ~ ". *TS*
7:21	self-preservation *TCC*] self pre-servation *TS*	8:24	Story] story *A1*
		8:28	into] in to *A1*
7:23	secured] secure *A1*	8:31	Oh] ~ , *TCC*

295

8:34 [man] *Ed.*] *Om. TS* man *A1 see
      notes*
8:34 knew *TS, A1*] know *TCC*
8:35 the red . . . innermost heart] in
      his innermost heart, the red out-
      burst at the top of the poppy,
      TCC in his . . . poppy *A1 see notes*
8:37 were] was *TCC*
9:3   poppy red] poppy-red *TCC*
9:7   door.] ~: *TCC* ~, *A1*
9:8   *always Ed.*] a l w a y s *TS* always
      TCC
9:16 unattractive] ~, *TCC*
9:16 say] ~, *TCC*
9:17 'No *Ed.*] "no *TS* 'No, *TCC*
9:17 you mother:] ~, ~; *TCC*
9:17 rose.' *TCC*] ~? *TS*
9:18 "Wherefore *TCC*] ~ *TS*
9:20 say,] ~ *TCC*
9:23 'Ah!' *TCC*] "~!" *TS*
9:24 'Must *TCC*] "~ *TS*
9:25 wasted!' *TCC*] ~!" *TS*
9:26 said] ~, *TCC*
9:26 'There, *TCC*] "~ *TS*
9:27 creatures] creature *TCC*
9:27 it. '*TCC*] ~".*TS*
9:28 "My *TCC*] ~ *TS*
9:31 five   and   twenty]   five-and-
      twenty *TCC*
9:34 muttering] ~, *TCC*
9:35 Conceit *TCC*] conceit *TS*
9:37 poppy bud] poppy-bud *TCC*
10:1 -2-] 2. *TCC* # *A1*
10:2 such] *Om. TCC*
10:3 rapture] ~, *TCC*
10:3 poppies!"] ~!"—*A1*
10:4 flowers!",—] ~!"— *TCC*
10:7 corn";] ~!" *TCC* ~!"—*A1*
10:8 nosegays:] ~, *TCC*
10:9 sleep," *TCC*] ~", *TS*
10:10 vanity," *A1*] ~ ", *TS* ~ ;" *TCC*
10:11 be] is *TCC*
10:14 virtue] virtues *TCC*
10:14 tumble] crumble *TCC*
10:21 sure:—] ~— *TCC* ~: *A1*
10:30 flame,] ~ *TCC*
10:31 unprovided *TCC*] improvided
      TS see notes

10:33 [transience] *Ed.*] transium *TS*
      transience *TCC see notes*
10:36 death.] ~? *TCC*
11:1 yesteryear] yester-year *TCC*
11:1 Où sont . . . de l'antan?] *Où sont
      les neiges d'antan? TCC*
11:2 Hippolita] Hippolyta *A1*
11:2 Thais] Thaïs *TCC*
11:3 yesteryear.] yester-year? *TCC*
11:7 say] ~, *TCC*
11:10 dindon",] ~," *TCC*
11:11 [a] *Ed.*] *Om. TS* a *TCC*
11:12 half globe] half-globe *TCC*
11:25 breathe.] ~? *TCC*
11:27 bran-new] brand-new *TCC*
11:27 Otherwise,] ~ *TCC*
12:3 so-called *TCC*] so/ called *TS*
12:8 losing] losing a *TCC*
12:14 holds] hold *A1*
12:18 vanity",] ~" *TCC*
12:19 think, that] ~ ~, *TCC*
12:23 *be Ed.*] b e *TS* be *TCC*
12:28 fluttering] ~, *TCC*
12:33 [incontrovertible] *Ed.*] introver-
      tible *TS* incontrovertible *A1 see
      notes*
12:34 said] ~, *TCC*
13:1 consideration; *TCC*] ~ *TS*
13:17 self-preservation,] ~; *A1*
13:20 always *TCC*] alway *TS*
13:24 [if] *Ed.*] *Om. TS* if *TCC*
13:25 To them *TCC*] To them who *TS*
14:2 about] About *TCC*
14:3 some] Some *A1*
14:3 Fancyful] Fanciful *TCC*
14:5 sad,] ~ *TCC*
14:5 to-day] today *TCC*
14:6 women suffragists] woman-suf-
      fragists *TCC*
14:11 what?—a] ~? A *TCC*
14:14 woman] women *TCC*
15:3 And] ~, *TCC*
15:5 many employers,] ~, ~ *TCC*
15:6 you] ~, *TCC*
15:13 you . . . woman . . . you] ~
      . . .woman, . . . ~ *TCC* your . . .
      woman, . . . your *A1*
15:16 Because] ~, *TCC*

15:16   not,—] ~—*A1*
15:16   then] ~, *TCC*
15:21   all the] all *TCC*
15:28   conditions— *TCC*] ~ *TS*
16:6   *be TCC*] b e *TS*
16:7   rush] ~, *TCC*
16:8   Then] ~, *TCC*
16:8   rate] ~, *TCC*
16:8   perhaps",] ~," *A1*
16:11   *be TCC*] b e *TS*
16:12   us] ~, *TCC*
16:17   security.] ~? *TCC*
16:18   time] ~, *TCC*
16:22   ourselves] ~, *TCC*
16:22   all.] ~? *TCC*
16:24   [not] *Ed.*] *Om. TS see notes*
16:25   ourselves,] ourselves also, *A1*
16:25   self-love *TCC*] self love *TS*
16:27   yoke:] ~; *TCC*
16:28   well-being:] ~; *TCC*
16:33   *live TCC*] l i v e *TS*
16:33   to [be] ourselves *Ed.*] to   our-
        selves *TS* to [live?] ourselves
        TCC to [risk] ourselves *A1 see
        notes*
16:35   end then] ~, ~, *TCC*
17:1   poltroons,] ~ *A1*
17:7   *be TCC*] b e *TS*
17:15   course,] ~; *TCC*
17:20   *be TCC*] b e *TS*
17:25   pity,] ~ *TCC*
17:27   Thou *TCC*] thou *TS*
17:29   By *TCC*] by *TS*
17:31   *ourselves TCC*] o u r s e l v e s *TS*
17:31   I then] ~, ~, *TCC*
17:31   [a] *Ed.*] *Om. TS* a *TCC*
17:38   —ah] —Ah *TCC* Ah *A1*
18:3   my own] my-/ self *TCC* myself *A1*
18:6   side-track] side-/ track *TCC*
        sidetrack *A1*
18:6   [vent] *Ed.*] rent *TS* vent *TCC*
18:8   and] ~, *TCC*
18:9   further, *TCC*] ~ *TS*
18:9   Alas *TCC*] alas *TS* Alas, *A1*
18:10   do." *TCC*] ~". *TS*
18:12   neighbour, and] ~; ~ *TCC*
18:14   rich] rich young *TCC*
18:14   crouches] ~, *TCC*

18:19   *truth TCC*] t r u t h *TS*
18:27   crying] ~, *TCC*
18:27   Alas *Ed.*] alas *TS* Alas, *TCC*
18:28   dwindlers.] ~! *TCC*
18:31   imminent] immanent *TCC*
18:32   out-post] outpost *TCC*
18:33   flag,] ~,/ *TCC* ~ *A1*
18:35   the earth] earth *TCC*
19:1   firing line, where] firing-line;
        there, *TCC*
19:1   *is TCC*] i s *TS*
19:18   safety] ~, *TCC*
20:1   Chapter III.] *Om. Per* CHAP-
        TER III: *TCC* CHAPTER III *A1*
20:2   Containing Six Novels and *TS*,
        TCC] Six Novels of Thomas
        Hardy and *Per*
20:3   a book *TS*, *TCC*] *Om. Per*
20:4   to] ~, *TCC*
20:6   care *TS*, *TCC*] cared *Per*
20:9   in, *TS*, *TCC*] ~ *Per*
20:11   by love] ~ ~, *TCC*
20:12   via media] *via media Per*
20:12   love, and *TS*, *TCC*] ~ ~ *Per*
20:18   quite, quite *Per*] ~ ~ *TS*
20:23   state *TS*, *TCC*] ~, *Per*
20:24   licences] licenses *TCC*
20:28   act *TS*, *TCC*] acts *Per*, *A1*
20:35   system] scheme *TCC*
21:1   How] Now *TCC*
21:2   with. And *TS*, *TCC*] ~; and *Per*
21:3   comically-,] ~, *A1*
21:3   insufficiently-, treated *Ed.*]   in-
        sufficiently,-treated *TS* insuf-
        ficiently-treated *Per* insufficiently
        treated *A1*
21:6   self-preservation,] ~ *Per*
21:10   Community] community *TCC*
21:13   remained, remained *TCC*] re-
        mained remained *TS* remained
        Per
21:14   impregnable,] ~; *Per*
21:19   wilderness] ~, *TCC*
21:20   security, *TS*, *TCC*] ~ *Per*
21:21   imprisonment, *TS*, *TCC*] ~ *Per*
21:24   side: *TS*, *A1*] ~; *Per*
21:29   this: *TS*, *A1*] ~; *Per*
21:32   community] ~, *Per*

21:32 second *Per*] Second *TS*
21:35 lands *TS, TCC*] and lands *Per*
21:37 if *Per*] If *TS*
21:38 convention",] ~," *TCC*
21:38 else, *TS,TCC*] ~ *Per*
21:39 oh, *TS, TCC*] ~! *Per*
21:39 die"—] ~', *Per* ~!"— *TCC*
22:7 the convention] convention *TCC*
22:7 dare *TS, TCC*] dares *Per*
22:9 Manston *TS, TCC*] Marston *Per*
22:9 fleshly] fleshily *TCC*
22:12 death] ~, *Per*
22:12 Cytherea and Springrove *Per*] Springrove Cytherea and Springrove *TS* Springrove and Cytherea *TCC*
22:16 Clergyman *TS, TCC*] clergyman *Per*
22:17 school-mistress *TS, TCC*] schoolmistress *Per*
22:23 Elfride *TS, A1*] Elfrida *Per*
22:25 idea] ideas *TCC*
22:26 instinct] ~, *Per*
22:26 Elfride *TS, A1*] Elfrida *Per*
22:33 *from TS, TCC*] From *Per*
22:35 pretendant *TS, TCC*] protendant *Per*
22:40 dog that *TS, TCC*] dog, and *Per*
23:1 time. [Sergeant *Ed.*] time, subject *TS* time. Sergeant *Per see notes*
23:4 Boldwood,] ~; *Per*
23:6 Morgana,] ~; *A1*
23:6 good] ~, *TCC*
23:8 fine] first *TCC*
23:11 Julian] Julius *TCC*
23:14 Mountclere] Mountclerc *A1*
23:14 estates *TS, TCC*] ~, *Per*
23:15 sound] ~, *TCC*
23:16 Moral,] ~: *TCC*
23:16 for a] for the *TCC*
23:17 Lord] lord *Per*
23:21 "Love",] 'love', *Per* "Love" *TCC*
23:22 common-sense] commonsense *Per*
23:23 shoulders] ~, *TCC*
23:25 *The Trumpet-Major Per*] the Trumpet Major *TS The Trumpet Major A1*

23:26 hard] ~, *Per*
23:27 half grinning] half-/ grinning *TCC* half-grinning *A1*
23:29 Elfride *TS, A1*] Elfrida *Per*
23:29 beloved] ~, *TCC*
23:29 killed,] ~; *TCC*
23:35 loves first] ~, ~, *TCC*
23:36 newly returned *TS, A1*] newly-returned *Per*
23:38 self-realisation; *TS, TCC*] self-realization: *Per* self-realization; *A1*
23:39 says] ~, *TCC*
23:40 beau monde] *beau monde Per*
23:40 would stay *Per*] would stayed *TS* would have stayed *TCC*
23:40 unsatisfaction. *TS, TCC*] ~! *Per*
24:1 beau monde] *beau monde Per*
24:1 What then] ~, ~, *Per*
24:2 know,] ~; *TCC*
24:4 school *Per*] School *TS*
24:4 [as] *Ed.*] Om. *TS, TCC* as *Per, A1*
24:7 deep] ~, *Per*
24:12 side-track *TS, TCC*] sidetrack *Per, A1*
24:13 Eustacia] ~, *Per*
24:14 die,] ~; *TCC*
24:14 Clym] ~, *Per*
24:19 sentiment,] ~; *TCC*
24:21 feelings *TCC*] feeling/ *TS* feeling *Per*
24:24 self:] ~; *A1*
24:30 or] nor *A1*
24:33 crashing down] crashing-down *TCC*
24:34 old, *TS, TCC*] ~ *Per*
24:35 non-conventional,] ~; *TCC*
24:38 reduced,] ~; *TCC*
25:1 great, *TS, TCC*] ~ *Per*
25:2 book?—it] ~? It *TCC*
25:3 Heath?—first] ~? First, *TCC*
25:9 [earth] *Ed.*] hearth *TS* earth *Per* heath *TCC see notes*
25:10 instinct,] ~. *TCC*
25:10 Egdon] ~, *Per*
25:13 matter *Ed.*] matters *TS see notes*
25:14 married: *TS, TCC*] ~; *Per*
25:15 heath *TS, TCC*] heather *Per*

25:15 furze] ~, *A1*
25:16 Egdon.] ~? *TCC*
25:18 happen] happens *A1*
25:22 come, *TS, A1*] ~; *Per*
25:23 matter!] ~? *TCC*
25:24 Heath,] ~; *TCC*
25:30 earth,] ~ *Per*
25:34 heavy, *TS, TCC*] ~ *Per*
26:17 singular— — — *Ed.*] ~ —— *TS*
    ~. *Per* ~… *TCC* ~…. *A1*
26:18 thought-worn *TCC*] thought-/
    worn *TS* thoughtworn *Per*
26:20 unfrequently] infrequently *TCC*
26:20 men] man *TCC*
26:22 flesh] the flesh *TCC*
26:26 need] seed *A1*
26:29 un-ease] ~, *TCC*
26:30 thought. *Ed.*] ~.. *TS* ~? *Per*
26:32 disease,] ~ *TCC*
26:32 than *TS, TCC*] then *Per*
26:39 expected",] ~," *TCC*
27:3 [Far] *Ed.*] For *TS* For, *Per* Far
    TCC
27:5 developed. And his *Ed.*]
    developed. And hid his *TS*
    developed, and his *Per*
    developed. And, hid, his *TCC see*
    notes
27:11 carcase] carcass *TCC*
27:12 carcase] carcass *TCC*
27:16 prison.] ~? *TCC*
27:19 No— *TS, TCC*] ~: *Per*
27:21 themselves." *TS, TCC*] ~'. *Per*
27:23 root.] ~! *A1*
27:24 [they] *Ed.*] *Om. TS* they *Per*
27:26 expression.] ~? *TCC*
27:27 not] no *TCC*
27:31 in *TS, TCC*] into *Per*
27:36 him] his *TCC*
28:4 on *TS, TCC*] ~, *Per*
28:11 forth.] ~? *TCC*
28:12 talking.] ~? *TCC*
28:15 out] ~, *Per*
28:17 being.] ~? *TCC*
28:22 preached] ~, *Per*
28:23 blindness indeed *TS, A1*] ~, ~,
    Per
28:24 died: *TS, TCC*] ~; *Per*

28:26 regrettable,] ~; *A1*
28:26 body] ~, *Per*
28:30 then] ~, *TCC*
28:31 enact *TS, TCC*] exact *Per*
28:40 morality *TS, TCC*] ~, *Per*
29:2 pathetic] ~, *Per*
29:4 nature] ~, *Per*
29:5 die [confined] in *Ed.*] die in
    TS, TCC die in *Per, A1*
29:13 chance] chances *A1*
29:24 nature,] Nature; *Per* nature;
    TCC
29:26 consciousness *TS, TCC*] ~, *Per*
29:27 nature *TS, TCC*] Nature *Per*
29:31 system *TS, TCC*] ~, *Per*
29:32 holds, *TS, TCC*] ~ *Per*
29:35 connection] connexion *A1*
29:36 against the] ~, ~ *TCC*
29:38 Karenin] Karenina *Per*
29:38 Sue *TS, TCC*] ~, *Per, A1*
30:2 Karenin] Karenina *Per*
30:4 society; *TS, TCC*] ~: *Per*
30:12 tragedy:] ~; *TCC*
30:13 compromised] comprehended
    TCC
30:15 But, being] ~ ~, *Per*
30:16 [find] *Ed.*] fixd *TS* fixed *Per* find
    TCC
30:16 themselves] ~, *TCC*
30:16 drawn] ~, *TCC*
30:21 tragic? *Per*] ~. *TS*
30:24 man] men *TCC*
30:25 souls,] ~ *TCC*
30:25 eternal] Eternal *TCC*
30:29 Short sighted] Shortsighted *Per*,
    A1 Short-/ sighted *TCC*
30:29 [pore] *Ed.*] bore *TS* pore *Per*
30:30 journeys] ~, *A1*
31:1 IV. … *Ed.*] III. *TS* IV *TCC see*
    notes
31:4 brimming over] brimming-/
    over *TCC* brimming-over *A1*
31:9 excess, *TCC*] ~ *TS*
31:9 briimming over] brimming-over
    TCC
31:10 glow worm] glow-worm *TCC*
31:11 errand boy] errand-boy *TCC*
31:13 it] It *TCC*

31:14 glow worm ... glow worm]
       glow-worm ... glow-worm *TCC*
31:19 man,] ~ *TCC*
31:27 spring-time *TCC*] spring time *TS*
32:5   overfull *Ed.*] overful *TS* over-full
       TCC
32:13 Weltschmerz] *Weltschmerz TCC*
32:13 pains] ~, *TCC*
32:17 decree *Ed.*] decr ee *TS* door *TCC*
32:18 foremost,—] ~— *TCC*
32:20 largely] ~, *TCC*
32:21 eat,—] ~— *TCC*
32:28 —You must,— *Ed.*] —~ ~⊤
       TS ~ ~, *TCC*
32:29 —Yet] ~ *TCC*
32:30 must,—] ~— *TCC*
32:31 —Let] ~ *TCC*
32:33 Oh] ~, *TCC*
32:34 amusement,] ~ *TCC*
32:34 beat] bent *TCC see notes*
32:34 this then] ~, ~, *TCC*
32:36 it] It *TCC*
33:2   —what?" *TCC*] ——~? *TS*
33:2   work",] ~," *A1*
33:4   Nottingham,] ~ *TCC*
33:5   man] Man *TCC*
33:6   essen",] ~," *TCC*
33:7   eat a] ~." A *TCC*
33:7   lesson book] lesson-book *TCC*
33:8   written "one] ~, "One *TCC*
33:9   work".] ~. " *TCC*
33:10 [proverb] *Ed.*] problem *TS*
       proverb *A1 see notes*
33:10 says "one] ~, "One *TCC*
33:10 live". *Ed.*] ~." *TS*
33:11 live",] ~," *TCC*
33:12 living".] ~." *A1*
33:30 necessity] ~, *TCC*
33:35 accurately,] ~ *TCC*
34:1   mechanism,] ~ *A1*
34:3   farm-labourer *TCC*] farm-
       laborer *TS* farm labourer *A1*
34:4   perfectly] ~, *TCC*
34:7   node] mode *TCC see note on*
       32:34
34:16 man,] ~ *TCC*
34:17 man, is] ~ ~, *TCC*
34:35 perfect,] ~ *TCC*

34:38 life, *Ed.*] ~/ *TS* ~; *TCC*
34:40 passage,] ~; *TCC*
35:6   been.] ~? *TCC*
35:6   fighting line] fighting-line *TCC*
35:8   been.] ~? *TCC*
35:9   being.] ~? *TCC*
35:10 is.] ~? *TCC*
35:15 [is] *Ed.*] Om. *TS* is *TCC*
35:16 reason,] ~ *TCC*
35:18 in] is *TCC*
35:24 old, *TCC*] ~ *TS*
35:28 own,] ~ *TCC*
36:5   tip] ~, *TCC*
36:8   life] ~, *TCC*
36:10 labour saving] labour-saving
       TCC
36:27 green-glass *TCC*] greeng-/ glass
       TS
36:28 smelling salts] smelling-salts
       TCC
36:28 machine turned] machine- turned
       TCC
36:29 machine carving] machine-carv-
       ing *TCC*
36:36 put! *TCC*] ~? *TS*
36:38 effort] ~, *TCC*
37:7   working man] working-man *TCC*
37:9   man *TCC*] men *TS*
37:21 [not] *Ed.*] Om. *TS* not *TCC see*
       note on 37:27
37:27 [owning] *Ed.*] owing *TS see notes*
37:28 weak,] ~ *TCC*
37:34 belly," *TCC*] ~", *TS*
37:35 breeches," *TCC*] ~", *TS*
38:1   self-respecting *TCC*] self re-
       specting *TS*
38:3   food.] ~? *TCC*
38:6   leave the] ~, ~ *TCC*
38:17 take] ~, *TCC*
38:24 circumscribed, *TCC*] ~/ *TS*
38:26 pot-bound.] ~? *TCC*
39:2   These states and nations] Those
       State educations *TCC*
39:5   Come *TCC*] come *TS*
39:11 come,] ~; *TCC*
39:14 furnace] ~, *TCC*
40:6   re-discovers] rediscovers *A1*
40:14 [earth] *Ed.*] hearth *TS* earth *TCC*

40:28 Long] ∼, *TCC*
40:35 [repeats] *Ed.*] repe-/ ents *TS*
represents *TCC see notes*
41:5 re-discovered] re-/ discovered
TCC rediscovered *A1*
41:8 on to] onto *A1*
41:9 is and] ∼, ∼ *TCC*
41:25 struggle *TCC*] struggled *TS*
41:39 later developed] later-developed
TCC
42:3 *knowing*] knowing *TCC*
42:3 a now] now an *A1*
42:4 late,] ∼; *TCC*
42:14 loosened, *TCC*] ∼/ *TS*
42:16 knowing] knowledge *TCC*
42:16 grosser] greater *TCC*
42:22 cell wall] cell-wall *TCC*
42:26 mass,] mess *TCC* mass *A1*
42:27 [me] *Ed.*] *Om. TS see notes*
42:32 origin] ∼, *TCC*
42:32 great] ∼, *TCC*
42:40 intensified,] ∼; *TCC*
43:1 parts,] ∼; *TCC*
43:2 neutrality] ∼, *TCC*
43:10 How] Now *TCC*
43:13 road,] ∼; *TCC*
43:13 neighbour] ∼, *TCC*
43:15 I] ∼, *TCC*
43:23 neighbour,] ∼ *TCC*
43:29 others,] ∼; *TCC*
43:30 purity,] ∼ *TCC*
43:33 a *TCC*] an *TS*
44:13 twenty three] twenty-three *TCC*
44:16 [spermatazoon] *Ed.*] spermazoon
TS spermatazoon *TCC*
44:20 I then] ∼, ∼, *TCC*
44:27 not. *TCC*] ∼, *TS*
44:33 maybe *TCC*] may be *TS*
44:35 some] *Om. TCC*
44:37 [not] *Ed.*] *Om. TS* not *TCC*
45:15 all, *TCC*] ∼ *TS*
45:17 morality-play] morality play *TCC*
45:21 obtains *A1*] obtain *TS*
45:23 Murderer, *TCC*] Murderer/ *TS*
45:24 descends *TCC*] descend/ *TS*
45:25 receives *TCC*] receive *TS*
45:27 morality-play] morality play *A1*
45:28 between whiles] between-whiles
TCC

45:29 girl, who ... while [ ]/ *A
Ed.*] girl ... while/ "The *TS*
girl./ *The TCC* girl. P In *The A1
see notes*
45:31 "prédilection d'artiste"] *prédilection d'artiste A1*
45:33 lower class] lower-class *TCC*
45:35 [ever] *Ed.*] evee *TS* ever *TCC see notes*
45:36 *The TCC*] the *TS*
45:37 same, *TCC*] ∼/ *TS*
45:40 Manston *TCC*] Maneton *TS*
46:1 *A Ed.*] the *TS* The *TCC*
46:3 *The TCC*] the *TS*
46:4 and Jude ... [46:10] Alec d'Urberville,] *Om. TCC*
46:17 *A Ed.*] the *TS* The *TCC*
46:22 Newcomen *TCC*] New Comen
TS
46:22 Telford *Ed.*] Tylford *TS*
46:23 prédilection d'artiste] *prédilection d'artiste TCC*
46:24 sort," *TCC*] ∼", *TS*
46:25 Pheidias] Phidias *TCC*
46:27 pedigree".] ∼." *A1*
46:28 pedigree"? If *TCC*] ∼", If *TS*
46:29 working men] working-men *TCC*
46:30 Hers *TCC*] Her *TS*
46:30 prédilection d'artiste] *prédilection d'artiste TCC*
46:35 prédilection d'artiste] *prédilection d'artiste TCC*
46:36 prédilection de savant] *prédilection de savant TCC*
46:37 prédilection d'economiste] *prédilection d'economiste TCC*
46:38 prédilection d'artiste] *prédilection d'artiste TCC*
47:1 nor] not *TCC*
47:2 law abiding] law-abiding *TCC*
47:3 or] *Om. TCC*
47:5 Why] ∼, *TCC*
47:8 [not] *TCC*] *Om. TS* not *A1*
47:15 exceptional *TCC*] exception/ *TS*
47:16 faults. *TCC*] fault/ *TS*
47:18 *Native, Ed.*] Native, *TS Native
TCC*
47:19 civic,] ∼ *TCC*

47:20   *A Ed.*] A *TS The TCC*
47:22   Eustacia] ~, *TCC*
47:24   [communal] *Ed.*] commune *TS*
      see notes
47:26   *The TCC*] the *TS*
47:27   *Casterbridge, Ed.*] Casterbridge,
      TS Casterbridge TCC
47:29   [condemned] *Ed.*] contemned
      TS condemned *TCC see notes*
47:29   unlikeable] unlikable *TCC*
47:32   blond *A1*] blonde *TS*
47:34   dark *Ed.*] darl *TS* a dark *TCC*
47:35   villainess] villain *TCC*
47:38   loved; *TCC*] ~,/ *TS*
47:40   shift over] shift-over *TCC*
47:40   volte-face] *volte-face A1*
48:3   anti-social *TCC*] anti/ social *TS*
48:5   *Was*] Was *TCC*
48:9   Jude,] ~ *A1*
48:9   tragedy.] ~? *TCC*
48:16   *The TCC*] the *TS*
48:22   are:] ~ *TCC*
48:28   rather *TCC*] ~, *TS*
48:39   *The TCC*] the *TS*
49:1   are,] ~: *TCC*
49:3   Sue. *TCC*] ~, *TS*
49:4   novels:/ 1.] ~: *P* 1. *TCC*
49:5   individualist] individual *TCC*
49:6   Henchard] ~, *TCC*
49:6   etc./ 2.] ~. *P* 2. *TCC*
49:9   Constantine./ 3.] ~. *P* 3. *TCC*
49:12   physically:] ~. *A1*
49:14   community./ 4.] ~. *P* 4. *TCC*
49:19   person] ~, *TCC*
49:31   individual,] ~ *TCC*
49:32   every] the *TCC*
49:37   oldness] coldness *TCC see notes*
50:1   individuality,] ~ *TCC*
50:10   Iphigenia *TCC*] Ipheginia *TS*
50:13   Erinyes *A1*] Erinnys *TS*
50:16   Goddess or God] goddess or god
      TCC
50:23   he.] ~? *TCC*
50:30   Why?—] ~? *A1*
50:30   irrevocably] ~, *TCC*
52:1   VI. *Ed.*]. V *TS* VI *TCC see note on*
      31:4
52:17   on] ~, *TCC*

52:19   red] rest *TCC*
52:24   and] ~, *TCC*
52:25   love] live *TCC* life *A1*
52:26   on,] ~ *TCC*
52:31   procreation.] ~? *TCC*
53:2   unknown,] ~ *TCC*
53:3   of] of the *TCC*
53:4   Sappho *A1*] Sapho *TS*
53:6   my poppy] the poppy *TCC*
53:8   [reaches] *Ed.*] reacts *TS* reaches
      TCC
53:12   [dips] *Ed.*] drips *TS see notes*
53:17   [wave] *Ed.*] wake *TS* wave *TCC see*
      notes
53:23   is *A1*] Is *TS*
53:30   [clashed] *Ed.*] clasped *TS see notes*
53:34   there] ~, *TCC*
53:38   dogs-mercury] dog's mercury *A1*
53:38   oak-tree] oak tree *A1*
54:2   overflowing, there] ~: ~, *TCC*
54:8   motion travels *Ed.*] motions
      travels *TS* motions travel *TCC*
54:11   earth. *P* And] ~. And *A1*
54:12   need] seed *TCC*
54:14   need] seed *TCC*
54:16   full] ~, *TCC*
54:21   stream, ... stream,] ~ ... ~
      TCC
54:22   flesh: it] ~? It *TCC*
54:33   [is] *Ed.*] *Om. TS* is *TCC*
55:9   [is] *Ed.*] in *TS* is *TCC*
55:11   completed] complete *TCC*
56:1   VII. *Ed.*] IV *TS* VII *TCC see note on*
      31:4
56:8   close clasping] close-clasping
      TCC
56:11   form, *A1*] ~ *TS*
56:12   pivot] ~, *A1*
56:12   sex life] sex-life *A1*
56:13   in] is *TCC*
57:10   trembles] troubles *TCC*
57:20   [big] *Ed.*] try *TS see notes*
57:29   woman,] ~ *TCC*
58:4   Gods] gods *TCC*
58:11   man] Man *TCC*
58:20   living. And *TCC*] ~, And *TS*
58:22   [these] *Ed.*] there *TS* these *A1 see*
      notes

58:26 against,] ~: *TCC* ~; *A1*
58:27 of him] of himself *TCC*
58:31 [change] *Ed.*] charge *TS* change *TCC*
58:35 [his] *Ed.*] is *TS* his *TCC*
59:1 centre,] ~; *TCC*
59:7 predominates *TCC*] predominate *TS*
59:7 [a] *Ed.*] *Om. TS see notes*
59:19 which *TCC*] for which *TS*
59:27 interacted] intersected *TCC*
60:8 [and] *Ed.*] *Om. TS* and *TCC*
60:17 standing ground] standing-ground *TCC*
60:20 or,] *Om. TCC*
60:28 Will-to-Inertia] ~, *TCC*
60:29 motion.] ~? *TCC*
60:29 yet] ~, *TCC*
60:36 speed. And . . . rest of] *Om. TCC*
61:4 and of] and *TCC*
61:10 [eventually] *Ed.*] even/ *TS* even *TCC see notes*
61:25 became] becomes *TCC*
61:36 Shulamite,] ~ *TCC*
61:37 moment] ~, *TCC*
62:6 God.] ~; *TCC*
62:7 him . . . him] Him . . . Him *TCC*
62:9 moment,] ~ *TCC*
62:15 him . . . him] Him . . . Him *TCC*
62:19 God,] ~; *TCC*
62:21 passive;] ~, *TCC*
62:32 Its] The *TCC*
62:33 ego] age *TCC*
62:35 ego] age *TCC*
62:39 ten commandments] Ten Commandments *A1*
63:7 woman.] ~? *TCC*
63:8 own.] ~? *TCC*
63:9 her,] ~ *TCC*
63:14 he] He *TCC*
63:15 woman] ~, *TCC*
63:17 one-ness] oneness *A1*
63:31 Woman,] ~ *TCC*
63:33 race] ~, *A1*
63:37 thou] Thou *TCC*
63:38 woman] Woman *TCC*
64:2 Thou *TCC*] thou *TS*
64:2 thyself",] ~," *TCC*

64:3 Thou *TCC*] thou *TS*
64:8 maybe] ~, *TCC*
64:17 woman] Woman *TCC*
64:17 body] ~, *TCC*
64:18 Word," *TCC*] ~ ", *TS*
64:19 Male,] ~ *TCC*
64:22 he] He *TCC*
64:25 him] Him *TCC*
64:26 he was Spirit] He ~ ~ *TCC*
64:26 he was Male] He ~ ~ *A1*
64:26 he] He *TCC*
64:31 flesh, *A1*] ~/ *TS* ~; *TCC*
65:2 persisted] ~, *TCC*
65:4 his] His *TCC*
65:4 that] That *TCC*
65:6 [Ye] *Ed.*] Yet *TS* Ye *TCC*
65:17 exists,] ~ *TCC*
65:20 he] He *TCC*
65:21 Separator,] ~; *TCC*
65:21 and he] ~ He *TCC*
65:27 her hands out] out her hands *TCC*
65:32 period] ~, *TCC*
65:34 stupendous] ~, *TCC*
65:40 sum,] ~ *TCC*
66:11 [contained] *Ed.*] content *TS see notes*
66:12 moments,] ~ *TCC*
66:16 Mediaeval] mediaeval *TCC* medieval *A1*
66:16 Art] art *A1*
66:17 Union] union *TCC*
66:20 Virgin,] ~ *TCC*
66:30 clasped] ~, *TCC*
66:32 Saviour"] *Saviour, TCC*
66:39 Mother,] ~ *TCC*
67:2 is] which is *TCC*
67:8 unwilling] ~, *TCC*
67:22 naive] naïve *A1*
67:22 stage,] ~ *TCC*
67:25 art,] ~; *TCC*
67:28 Basket"] *Basket, TCC*
67:32 artist *TCC*] Artist *TS*
67:33 with,] ~ *TCC*
67:39 experience,] ~ *TCC*
68:19 exist,] ~; *TCC*
68:23 his] him *TCC*
68:25 and] ~, *TCC*

68:26 and] ~, *TCC*
68:28 starting point] starting-point *TCC*
68:30 discover,] ~; *TCC*
68:36 Botticelli] ~, *TCC*
68:37 hand] ~, *TCC*
68:37 becomes *TCC*] become *TS*
68:40 drooping [motionless,] the *Ed.*] drooping the *TS* drooping, the *TCC* drooping, the *A1 see notes*
69:13 [bore] *A1*] love *TS see notes*
69:17 joyous] ~, *TCC*
69:38 all,] ~ *TCC*
69:39 Plato's *Ed.*] the Plato's *TS* the Plato *TCC*
70:4 stability, *TCC*] ~ / *TS*
70:8 becomes *TCC*] become *TS*
70:9 [the] *Ed.*] *Om. TS*
70:9 almost,] ~ *TCC*
70:11 geometric-idea] geometric idea *TCC*
70:17 woman,] ~ *TCC*
70:27 Turgenev] Turgeniev *A1*
70:27 and perhaps, ... and perhaps,] ~, ~, ... ~, ~ *TCC* ~, ~, ... ~, ~, *A1*
70:34 contented,] ~ *TCC*
70:37 man,] ~ *TCC*
70:40 and [Myron], then *Ed.*] and , then *TS* and then *TCC* and then *A1 see notes*
71:6 bodyless] bodiless *A1*
71:13 spirit,] Spirit!— *A1*
71:13 wert—" *P* Why] ~—"? ~ *TCC* ~!—"? ~ *A1*
71:15 bodylessness *Ed.*] bodylesness *TS* bodilessness *TCC*
71:16 beauty.] ~? *TCC*
71:30 is] ~, *TCC*
71:36 out, out *Ed.*] out out *TS* out *TCC*
71:38 Botticelli] ~, *TCC*
72:16 in living [when] *Ed.*] in living *TS* in living ?when *TCC* when in living *A1*
72:34 Ewige Wiederkehr] *Ewige Wiederkehr TCC*
72:38 is] this is *TCC*

73:8 one. To *Ed.*] ~: To *TS* ~; to *TCC* ~: to *A1*
73:16 re-acting] reacting *TCC*
73:19 incandescence, a *TCC*] incandescencea *TS*
73:27 Man,] ~ *TCC*
73:29 female—] ~ *TCC*
73:31 re-acted] reacted *TCC*
73:32 stability,] ~ *TCC*
73:39 re-acting] reacting *TCC*
74:6 Slaves] slaves *A1*
74:6 bondage,] ~ *A1*
74:7 Virgin,] ~ *TCC*
74:26 the effects ... are full of] *Om. TCC*
74:29 him,] ~; *TCC*
75:7 idea, *TCC*] ~ / *TS*
75:10 Marriage] marriage *A1*
75:22 sculpture] ~, *TCC*
75:33 male,] ~ *A1*
75:33 as *TCC*] as it *TS*
75:36 timeless,] ~ *A1*
76:3 abstraction,] ~ *TCC*
77:2 "The Light of the World." *Ed.*] The Light of the World. *TS* The Light ... World *TCC* The Light of the World *A1 see notes*
77:10 [reacted] *Ed.*] reached *TS* reacted *TCC*
77:11 characterisation, *TCC*] ~ / *TS* characterization, *A1*
77:23 Geometric] Geometrical *TCC*
77:26 [Non]-Consummation *Ed.*] No-/ Consummation *TS*
78:13 prophets] Prophets *TCC*
78:14 fulfil!] ~. *TCC*
78:16 Christ,] ~ *TCC*
78:23 commandment] ~, *TCC* ~: *A1*
78:25 thyself." *TCC*] ~". *TS*
78:37 through *TCC*] though *TS*
78:40 *BE Ed.*] B E *TS* BE *TCC*
79:6 in] *Om. TCC*
79:10 Law,] ~; *TCC*
79:10 Old] old *TCC*
79:12 body] Body *TCC*
79:12 communion] Communion *TCC*
79:13 me] Me *TCC*

79:14   heavy laden] heavy-laden *TCC*
79:15   man,] ~ *TCC*
79:19   say] ~, *TCC*
79:20   Christ." Each *Ed.*] ~." each *TS*
        ~;" each *TCC* ~ each *A1*
79:20   saying] ~, *TCC*
79:24   says "In *Ed.*] ~ "in *TS* ~, "In *TCC*
79:24   Father." *TCC*] ~. *TS*
79:29   Spirit," *TCC*] ~, *TS*
79:31   but] ~, *TCC*
79:34   he] He *TCC*
79:35   Father,] ~; *TCC*
79:35   he] He *TCC*
79:35   said,] ~ *TCC*
79:37   Father *TCC*] father *TS*
79:38   My] my *TCC*
80:5   himself] Himself *TCC*
80:6   other,] ~: *TCC*
80:14   female,] ~; *TCC*
80:17   is she] ~ ~, *TCC*
80:20   us,] ~ *TCC*
80:27   me] Me *TCC*
80:27   Our] our *TCC*
80:28   It . . . It] it . . . it *TCC*
80:30   Absolute? *TCC*] ~. *TS*
81:4   he] He *TCC*
81:6   say,] ~ *TCC*
81:7   The *TCC*] the *TS*
81:9   be,] ~ *TCC*
81:12   via media] *via media TCC*
81:14   say] ~, *TCC*
81:14   body", *Ed.*] ~," *TS*
81:15   say] ~, *TCC*
81:15   spirit", *Ed.*] ~," *TS*
81:19   race] ~, *TCC*
81:19   reason] ~, *TCC*
81:19   hollow] ~, *TCC*
81:23   unworthy." *TCC*] ~". *TS*
81:30   Spirit,] ~; *TCC*
81:30   myself",] ~," *TCC*
81:39   God",] ~," *A1*
81:40   annunciation] ~, *TCC*
81:40   world." *TCC*] ~". *TS*
82:1   again,] ~; *TCC*
82:4   of *Ed.*] of the *TS see notes*
82:7   [profiteth] *Ed.*] forgeteth *TS*
        forgetteth *TCC see notes*

82:10   him] Him *TCC*
82:10   he] He *TCC*
82:12   he] He *TCC*
82:13   him,] Him: *TCC*
82:13   'Blessed . . . sucked.' *TCC*] "~
        . . . ~" *TS*
82:15   he] He *TCC*
82:15   'Yea . . . it.'" *Ed.*] "yea . . . ~."
        TS Yea . . . ~." *TCC*
82:17   this,] ~ *TCC*
82:20   he] He *TCC*
82:20   eunuchs;] ~, *TCC*
82:27   John,] ~ *A1*
82:32   there *TCC*] then *TS*
82:36   day] ~, *TCC*
83:4   *are TCC*] a r e *TS*
83:4   meet,] ~ *TCC*
83:9   stability, *TCC*] ~ / *TS*
83:14   who] Who *TCC*
83:14   whom . . . whom] Whom . . .
        Whom *TCC*
83:20   Spirit *TCC*] spirit *TS*
83:24   manyfold] manifold *A1*
84:4   Spirit *Ed.*] spirit *TS*
84:5   The] In the *TCC*
84:10   offering [inexhaustible] satisfac-
        tion *Ed.*] offering   satisfac-
        tion *TS* offering satisfaction *A1*
        see notes
84:13   Rembrandt,] ~ *TCC*
84:13   re-act] react *A1*
84:20   woman,] ~; *TCC*
84:28   hope,] ~; *TCC*
85:4   and,] ~ *TCC*
85:5   consummation,] *Om. TCC*
85:7   my] My *TCC*
85:8   eat",] ~," *TCC*
85:18   So in Rembrandt] ~, ~ ~, *TCC*
85:20   Raphael] ~, *TCC*
85:21   two,] ~; *TCC*
85:22   Rembrandt,] ~ *TCC*
85:23   never [consummate.] *Ed.*] never
        TS never. *A1 see notes*
85:27   in one . . . take place] *Om. TCC*
86:23   One-ness] Oneness *A1*
86:32   [faintest *Ed.*] fainted *TS* faintest
        TCC
86:39   Corot] ~, *TCC*

87:39	art,] ~ *TCC*		93:28	majesty". *Ed.*] ~." *TS*
88:10	fellow man] fellow-man *TCC*		93:32	calve?—] ~? *A1*
89:3	-1- *Ed.*] *Om. TS see note to* 7:6		93:34	forth?—] ~? *A1*
89:4	the Law] Law *TCC*		93:35	sorrows.—] ~. *A1*
89:7	Love,] ~ *TCC*		93:36	go *TCC*] grow *TS*
89:33	have] has *A1*		93:37	Hardy. But *TCC*] ~, ~ *TS*
89:34	Two] ~, *TCC*		93:38	conceipt] concept *TCC see notes*
90:16	overstrong] over-strong *TCC*		93:39	Therefore *TCC*] therefore *TS*
90:25	abstraction,] ~ *TCC*		94:1	"I *TCC*] ~ *TS*
90:30	he, *TCC*] ~/ *TS*		94:1	hearing *TCC*] heaving *TS*
90:35	"Hail ... spirit,] ~ ... Spirit! *A1*		94:3	"Wherefore *TCC*] ~ *TS*
			94:5	who] Who *TCC*
90:36	wert] ~, *TCC*		94:9	passions are *TCC*] passionare *TS*
90:37	heaven] Heaven *A1*		94:14	male,] ~ *TCC*
90:38	forth thy] thy full *A1*		94:19	her body] herself *TCC*
90:39	profusest] profuse *A1*		94:25	Love,] *Om. TCC*
90:39	lay."] art. *A1*		94:25	Erinyes *A1*] Errinyes *TS* Erin-
91:2	wert",] ~" *TCC*			nyes *TCC*
91:3	*is TCC*] i s *TS*		94:36	Spirit] spirit *A1*
91:4	art",] ~," *A1*		94:40	braggard] braggart *TCC*
91:5	it",] ~," *A1*		95:5	his] His *TCC*
91:21	externae",] ~," *TCC*		95:23	her,] ~ *TCC*
91:22	Sea] sea *TCC*		95:30	*The TCC*] the *TS*
91:28	overdeveloped, oversensitive]		96:10	fulfilment:] ~; *TCC*
	over-developed, over-sensitive		96:12	way:] ~; *A1*
	TCC		96:19	Christianity, *TCC*] ~ *TS*
92:21	For] *Om. TCC*		96:20	self-sacrifice *TCC*] self
92:25	Anna Karenin, *Ed.*] Anna			sacrifice *TS*
	Karenin/ *TS* Anna Karenina;		96:38	senses,] ~; *TCC*
	TCC Anna Karenina; A1		97:14	[hard] labour *Ed.*] hand, labour
92:27	Father,] ~ *TCC*			*TS see notes*
92:29	[as] *Ed.*] *Om. TS* as *TCC*		97:31	ultra-Christian *TCC*] ul-
92:30	it] ~, *TCC*			tra-christian *TS*
92:33	Law," *TCC*] ~", *TS*		98:1	bodiless:] ~; *TCC*
92:36	*Native, Ed.*] Native, *TS Native*		98:5	meet, *TCC*] ~ *TS*
	TCC		98:14	aristocrat,—] ~— *TCC*
92:40	[fleshly] *Ed.*] fleshy *TS see note*		98:15	aristocrat,—] ~— *TCC*
	on 93:4		98:17	alone,] ~ *TCC*
93:4	[that] the *Ed.*] the *TS* that *A1 see*		98:17	the "neighbour", *Ed.*] ~ ~",
	notes			*TS* "~ ~", *TCC* "~ ~," *A1*
93:7	the] *The TCC*		98:20	now,] ~ *TCC*
93:8	[as] *Ed.*] *Om. TS* as *TCC*		98:25	sources] source *TCC*
93:15	that perhaps] ~, ~, *TCC*		98:31	him *TCC*] her *TS*
93:25	knowledge?—] ~? *A1*		98:35	elements] element *TCC*
93:26	wind?—] ~? *A1*		98:38	fellows,] ~ *TCC*
93:27	strong?—" *Ed.*] ~—"/ *TS* ~?"		99:30	re-union] reunion *A1*
	TCC		99:36	in to him.] into him? *TCC*
93:28	with] With *TCC*		99:40	democratic] ~, *TCC*

100:8 d'Urberville *Ed.*] D'Urberville
TS d'Urberville, *TCC*
100:14 thou] Thou *TCC*
100:15 thyself",] ~," *TCC*
100:29 Orestes,] ~ *A1*
100:39 wrong,] ~ *TCC*
101:2 Indeed] ~, *TCC*
101:4 -2-] 2. *TCC # A1 see note on* 7:6
101:10 But] ~, *TCC*
101:21 [he] *Ed.*] *Om. TS* he *TCC*
101:25 strict,] ~ *TCC*
101:33 pig-killing:] ~; *TCC*
101:36 pig-sticking] ~, *TCC*
101:36 false hair] false-hair *TCC*
101:37 her,] ~ *TCC*
102:1 so-forth] so forth *TCC*
102:5 in".] ~." *A1*
102:5 [are] *Ed.*] as *TS* are *TCC*
102:9 her hands] hands *TCC*
102:22 wants,] ~ *TCC*
102:26 somewhere] somewhat *TCC*
102:29 existed,] ~ *TCC*
102:32 and also] ~, ~ *TCC*
102:35 complement:] ~; *TCC*
103:6 conscious *TCC*] Conscious *TS*
103:13 Principles] principles *TCC*
103:15 maleness",] ~," *TCC*
103:15 is: "she] ~, "She *TCC*
103:16 myself".] ~." *TCC*
103:17 attitude] ~, *TCC*
103:21 "Wille zur Macht"] *Wille zur Macht TCC*
103:23 this,] ~ *TCC*
103:24 [transition] *Ed.*] transi-/ tation *TS* transition *TCC see notes*
103:26 often.] ~? *TCC*
103:32 of possession] possession of *TCC Om. A1*
103:36 roué] *roué TCC*
103:38 unfortunately] *Om. TCC see notes*
103:39 this *TCC*] his *TS*
104:10 dulness] dullness *A1*
104:11 the many] many *TCC*
104:15 Wille zur Macht] *Wille zur Macht TCC*
104:23 ever yielding] ever-yielding *TCC*
104:25 *is, TCC*] i s., *TS*

104:36 Embrace,] ~ *A1*
104:37 roué] *roué TCC*
105:8 that *A1*] the *TS* tha *TCC*
105:9 wonderful.] ~? *TCC*
105:10 there.] ~? *TCC*
105:14 unknown.] ~? *TCC*
105:16 myself.] ~? *TCC*
105:21 There *TCC*] there *TS*
105:21 women,] ~; *TCC*
105:24 "Amelia"] ~ *TCC*
105:24 Dickens'] Dickens's *A1*
105:24 "Agnes"] ~ *TCC*
106:1 "Amelia",] ~ *TCC* "~ " *A1*
106:1 "Agnes",] ~, *TCC* "~," *A1*
106:8 half criminal] half-criminal *TCC*
106:8 reckless daredevil] ~, dare-devil *TCC*
106:9 her] ~, *TCC*
106:11 Jude? *TCC*] ~. *TS*
106:26 re-inforce] reinforce *TCC*
106:28 because, *TS, A1*] ~ *TCC*
106:28 that] ~, *TCC Om. A1*
106:31 time,] ~ *TCC*
107:2 Don] don *TCC*
107:2 cut and dried] cut-and-dried *TCC*
107:3 connection] connexion *A1*
107:7 academics.] ~? *TCC*
107:8 [pervertedness] *Ed.*] pervertness *TS* perverseness *TCC*
107:14 [he] *Ed.*] the *TS* he *A1*
108:2 senses,] ~. *TCC*
108:9 blasé] *blasé TCC*
108:10 conscious, *TCC*] ~/ *TS*
108:14 desire; like *Ed.*] ~; Like *TS* ~. like *TCC*
108:17 belonged] ~, *TCC*
108:20 effort] effect *TCC*
108:21 Sue,] ~ *TCC*
108:24 Virgin] virgin *TCC*
108:38 that] ~, *TCC*
109:4 Turgenev] Turgeniev *A1*
109:28 natural, that] ~ ~, *TCC*
109:31 self-destruction *TCC*] self des-truction *TS*
109:33 suggesting] suggesting to *A1*
110:5 rousing] roused *A1*
110:15 return.] ~? *A1*

110:19 male.] ~? *TCC*
110:38 again.] ~? *TCC*
111:8   idée fixe] *idée fixe TCC*
111:9   [hunted] *Ed.*] haunted *TS see notes*
111:21 knowledge,] ~ *TCC*
111:21 utterance.] ~? *TCC*
111:21 time,] ~ *TCC*
111:32 Great then] ~, ~, *TCC*
111:33 then] *Om. A1*
111:35 was as himself] ~, ~ ~, *TCC*
112:4   study, was] ~ ~, *TCC*
112:12 state, *TCC*] ~/ *TS*
112:25 virility] vitality *TCC*
112:28 self,] ~ *TCC*
112:30 her,] ~ *TCC*
112:31 step] steps *A1*
112:32 first, necessary] ~ ~ *TCC*
112:33 rudimentary] ~, *TCC*
112:39 Arabella] ~, *TCC*
113:8   Which] ~, *TCC*
113:11 female. Sexually *TCC*] femaleSexually *TS*
113:12 but] ~, *TCC*
113:15 functioning] function *A1*
113:22 mechanical] ~, *TCC*
113:23 "Savant"] *Savant TCC*
113:26 spiritual] ~, *TCC*
113:30 short.] ~? *TCC*
113:35 "Thou] ~ *A1*
113:35 Galilean: *Ed.*] ~ *TS* ~! *TCC see notes*
113:36 thy] Thy *TCC*
113:36 breath." *P* In] ~."/ In *TCC* ~./ In *A1*
113:38 her,] ~ *TCC*
113:39 insentient *TCC*] insensient *TS*
114:3   to her,] in her; *TCC*
114:4   this] this is *TCC*
114:19 decay, *TCC*] ~/ *TS*
114:20 excreta? *TCC*] ~. *TS*
114:21 life,] ~; *TCC*
114:27 But,] ~/ *TCC* ~ *A1*
115:12 balked] baulked *TCC*
115:27 thick,] ~ *TCC*
116:4   climbed and climbed to] climbed to *TCC*
116:4   now] ~, *TCC*

116:12 pinnacle,] ~/ *TCC*
116:20 late,] ~; *TCC*
116:20 her,] ~ *TCC*
116:23 Simeon] Simon *TCC*
116:30 Aldbrickham] ~, *A1*
116:36 me,] ~; *TCC*
117:4   [break] *Ed.*] breath *TS* break *TCC*
117:6   Jude] ~, *TCC*
117:12 "frisson"] *frisson TCC*
117:24 him.] ~? *TCC*
117:30 idea,] ~ *TCC*
117:35 Sue,] ~ *TCC*
118:5   [nothing] *TCC*] *Om. TS*
118:11 marriage:] ~; *TCC*
118:12 along:] ~; *TCC*
118:16 together!] ~? *TCC*
118:22 of] *Om. A1*
118:24 [they] *Ed.*] *Om. TS* they *TCC*
118:34 [as] *Ed.*] *Om. TS* as *TCC*
118:40 happiness] ~, *TCC*
119:5   [their] *Ed.*] then *TS* these *TCC see notes*
119:7   them,] ~ *TCC*
119:11 becomes] became *TCC*
119:11 ignis fatuus] *ignis fatuus TCC*
119:20 tissue] tissues *TCC*
119:23 this] the *TCC*
119:34 mind. Since] ~, since *A1*
119:38 Sue] She *TCC*
120:16 unproductive *Ed.*] improductive *TS* nonproductive *A1*
120:19 self-less] selfless *A1*
120:21 to-day,] today; *TCC* today, *A1*
120:32 these] those *TCC*
120:37 Spirit] ~, *TCC*
120:38 horrible [nullity], nothing, *Ed.*] horrible   , nothing, *TS* horrible nothing *TCC*
120:40 could? *TCC*] ~. *TS*
121:1   mind] ~, *TCC*
121:24 that she] she *A1*
121:35 overdevelopment] over-development *TCC*
121:36 overbalancing] over-/ balancing *TCC* over-balancing *A1*
121:37 Consciousness,] ~; *TCC*
122:1   male,] ~; *TCC*

122:4   along,] ∼; *TCC*
122:9   monks.] ∼? *TCC*
122:10   altogether.] ∼? *TCC*
122:14   existed.] ∼? *TCC*
122:15   special] specialised *TCC*
122:17   woman.] ∼? *TCC*
122:19   temple] Temple *TCC*
122:20   foul,] ∼ *TCC*
122:21   us.] ∼? *TCC*
122:27   place, she] ∼; ∼ *TCC*
123:1   X. *Ed.*] XII. *TS* X *TCC* *see*
         notes
123:10   said] ∼: *TCC*
123:20   cul de sac] *cul de sac TCC* cul-de-
         sac *A1*
123:22   who said] Who ∼: *TCC*
123:22   light] Light *TCC*
123:22   who breathed] Who ∼ *TCC*
123:26   Lord,] ∼; *TCC*
123:29   said] ∼: *TCC*
124:6   Yea] Yes *TCC*
124:16   he] He *TCC*
124:26   nature,] ∼ *TCC*
124:29   women. *Ed.*] ∼ *TS* ∼; *TCC*
124:32   see,] ∼: *TCC*
124:37   hostile] ∼, *TCC*
124:38   person: *Ed.*] ∼ *TS* ∼. *TCC*
124:39   enemy." [   ]/ Therefore]
         ∼." # P Therefore *TCC see notes*
125:4   And] ∼, *TCC*
125:6   *Idiot TCC*] "Idiot" *TS*
125:14   Italy] ∼, *TCC*
125:15   so] *Om. TCC*

125:20   complementary *TCC*] compli-
         mentary *TS*
125:27   Spirit. They *Ed.*] ∼, ∼ *TS* ∼,
         they *TCC*
125:29   produced,] ∼ *TCC*
126:1   Reconciler,] ∼ *TCC*
126:3   Law,] ∼ *TCC*
126:5   Aeschylus,] ∼ *TCC* Æschylus *A1*
126:7   these,] ∼ *TCC*
126:7   abstraction— *Ed.*] ∼/ *TS* ∼:
         TCC ∼. *A1*
126:11   these,] ∼ *TCC*
126:11   has *Ed.*] have *TS*
126:12   Law. Also] ∼; also *TCC*
126:16   Euripides,] ∼ *TCC*
126:18   Reconciliation] ∼, *TCC*
126:31   Aeschylus'] Æschylus's *A1*
126:33   "Hamlet", *Ed.*] ∼, *TS* Hamlet
         TCC
126:34   Furies,] ∼ *TCC*
126:36   [have] *Ed.*] *Om. TS* have *TCC*
126:36   riddle.] ∼? *TCC*
127:5   male,] ∼; *TCC*
127:6   woman,] ∼ *TCC*
127:7   man,] ∼ *TCC*
127:36   neighbour",] ∼," *A1*
127:37   neighbour,] ∼ *TCC*
128:9   embrace] embraces *TCC*
128:16   [clasp] ... [clasp] *Ed.*] clap ...
         clap *TS* clasp ... clasp *TCC see*
         notes
128:19   shadow,] ∼; *TCC*
128:20   singing,] ∼; *TCC*

Literary Essays, 1908–27

The following symbols are used for states of the texts:

MS   = Manuscript (see Note on the texts, p. 130)
TS   = Ribbon copy typescript, corrected by DHL ('The Future of the Novel',
         'The Novel')
TCC = Carbon copy typescript, corrected by DHL ('Art and Morality', 'Morality
         and the Novel')
Per = Periodical (see Note on the texts, p. 130)
E1   = First English edition ('John Galsworthy')
O1   = First publication, *Young Lorenzo* (Florence), 1932 ('Rachel Annand
         Taylor')
A1   = First American edition, *Phoenix* (New York), 1936, or *Reflections on the*
         Death of a Porcupine (Philadelphia), 1925 ('The Novel')

Whenever the base-text reading (*MS*, except for 'A Britisher Has a Word with an Editor' and 'The Novel') is adopted, it appears within the square bracket with no symbol. Corrupt readings follow the square bracket in chronological sequence, with their first source denoted. In the absence of information to the contrary, the reader should assume that a variant recurs in all subsequent states.

The following symbols are used editorially:

Ed.	=	Editor
Om.	=	Omitted
P	=	Paragraph
~	=	Repeated word in recording an accidental variant
/	=	Line or page break resulting in punctuation, hyphenation or spelling error

Art and the Individual

Unless otherwise indicated the reading within the square bracket is editorial.

135:2   Socialists] ~. *MS*
135:7   "New Age,"] ~ ~, *MS*
136:9   Have] have *MS*
136:29 [I]] *Om. MS*
136:31 Interest in] [*MS* has ditto marks]
136:38 [II]]   *Om. MS*
137:29 gait.] ~; *MS*
137:30 shore!"] ~ *MS*
138:14 God-Idea] God- *MS see notes*
138:18 Religious] religious *MS*
139:13 divided:] ~ *MS*

139:29 adaptation] adaption *MS*
139:36 "Outcasts"] '~' *MS*
139:36 Watts'] Watt's *MS*
139:37 "Mammon,"] '~,' *MS*
140:4   "being intelligible"] '~ ~'*MS*
140:4   "able ... of,"] '~ ... ~,' *MS*
141:12 battle-piece] battle piece *MS*
141:40 "Idyll."] '~'. *MS*
142:5   Watts'] Watt's *MS*
142:21 "By ... habit"] '~ ... ~'*MS*

Rachel Annand Taylor

The chronological sequence is *MS, O1*.

145:4   her:] ~, *O1*
145:6   people,] ~ *O1*
145:6   fashion. This,] ~. *P* "This *O1*
145:7   then,] ~ *O1*
145:10 favorable] favourable *O1*
145:11 living:] ~, *O1*
145:13 him. Is] ~—is *O1*
145:15 svelte;] ~, *O1*
145:15 big,] ~ *O1*
145:16 eyes,] ~ *O1*
145:18 on her] in the *O1*
145:18 curious,] ~ *O1*
145:19 witch's *O1*] witches *MS*
145:19 long white] ~, ~, *O1*
145:20 correct] ~, *O1*

145:22 bible] Bible *O1*
145:22 Arabian Nights] '~ ~' *O1*
145:22 King Arthur] '~ ~' *O1*
145:23 up-bringing] upbringing *O1*
145:25 her] the *O1*
145:28 flags] flag *O1*
145:29 citherns] citterns *O1*
145:29 violes] viols *O1*
145:30 as pagan and as] pagan and *O1*
146:1   A *Ed.*] The *MS*
146:2   Ringstead.] Kingstead, *O1*
146:5   D'Amour— *Ed.*] ~: *MS* d'Arm-our', *O1*
146:5   Flowers', *Ed.*] ~— *MS* ~', *O1*
146:7   Reveries— *Ed.*] ~: *MS* '~', *O1*

146:8 four *O1*] a four *MS*
146:10 authoress] author *O1*
146:12 "Desire." *Ed.*] ~ *MS* '~ ". *O1*
146:12 (p. 73)] *Om. O1*
146:14 "Surrender" (p. 80)—] '~'. *O1*
146:15 the] The *O1*
146:15 retrospective, *Ed.*] ~ *MS*
146:15 "Unrealised"] '~', *O1*
146:18 read. *P* Needless] ~. Needless *O1*
146:20 tormenting"] ~, ' *O1*
146:22 tormenting"] ~,' *O1*
146:24 quietly./ However] ~. *P* "However *O1*
146:27 verse] ~, *O1*
146:29 "Rose and Vine" *Ed.*] Rose & Vine / *MS* 'Rose and Vine', *O1*
146:31 crude startling] ~, ~, *O1*
146:32 "pageant ... heart,"*Ed.*] '~ ... ~,' *MS* ~ ... ~ *O1*
146:33 marches it] marches *O1*
146:34 apart,] ~ *O1*
146:37 "Poems" *Ed.*] '~' *MS* ~ *O1*
146:39 hips] lips *O1*
147:1 breasts] breast *O1*
147:4 Strauss's *Ed.*] Straus's *MS* Strauss' *O1*
147:9 looseness] ~, *O1*
147:15 horses] ~, *O1*
147:17 courtship] ~, *O1*
147:17 Brontë *Ed.*] Bronte *MS*, *O1*
147:19 Violers] Violets *O1*
147:20 And *Ed.*] and *MS*
147:20 Song *Ed.*] A Song *MS*
147:20 Fruition *Ed.*] ~" *MS*
147:20 For an] An *O1*
147:20 Mother)" *Ed.*] ~) *MS*
147:21 that,] ~ *O1*
147:21 me] ~, *O1*
147:21 autumn] Autumn *O1*
147:22 know.] ~! *O1*
147:23 A] "~ *O1*
147:24 significantly,] ~ *O1*
147:25 year,] ~ *O1*
147:26 Shakespeare *O1*] Shakespere *MS*
147:26 and,] ~ *O1*

147:27 Prologue ... Women,] '~ ... ~,' *O1*
147:27 Epilogue ... Women,] '~ ... ~' *O1*
147:30 Dreaming Woman. The] dreaming woman. *P* The *O1*
147:31 artist.—Which] ~: which *O1*
147:31 suppose,] ~ *O1*
147:31 women-artists] women artists *O1*
147:32 Dreaming Woman of Today,] dreaming woman of today— *O1*
147:34 reformers. Unfortunately] ~. *P* "Unfortunately *O1*
147:35 herself] ~, *O1*
147:36 absorbedly,] ~; *O1*
147:39 says] ~— *O1*
147:39 x] X *O1*
147:39 passion] ~, *O1*
147:39 y] Y *O1*
147:40 love: *Ed.*] ~ *MS* ~.' *O1*
148:1 Now ... y ... x./ Mrs *Ed.*] "Now ... Mrs *MS* "'*Now* ... Y ...X.' *P* Mrs *O1* [Poetic passage in italics in *O1*]
148:5 "Since ... spun."/ Subtle ... [148:7] agony] "'*Since* ... *spun*.' *P* "'~ ... ~' *O1* [Poetic passage in italics in *O1*]
148:9 "Prologue of the Dreaming Women," *Ed.*] Prologue of Dreaming Women, *MS* 'Prologue of Dreaming Women,' *O1*
148:10 haunting.] ~:— *O1*
148:12 thing. *P* But] ~! But *O1*
148:13 "Epilogue of the Dreaming Women." *P* It] Epilogue of Dreaming Women. *P* It *MS* 'Epilogue of Dreaming Women." It *O1*
148:15 over,] ~ *O1*
148:19 trace,] ~ *O1*
148:20 number XVIII. *P* Some] No. 18. ~ *O1*
148:22 Open] open *O1*

The Future of the Novel [Surgery for the Novel—Or a Bomb]

The chronological sequence is *MS, TS, Per, A1.*

151:1 The Future of the Novel/ [Surgery for the Novel—Or a Bomb] *Ed.*] The Future of the Novel *MS* Surgery for the Novel—Or a Bomb *Per* SURGERY FOR THE NOVEL—OR A BOMB *A1 see notes*

151:3 his] the *Per*

151:4 cooing:] ~ ; *Per*

151:10 longer? *P* Is] ~ ? Is *Per*

151:12 thing? *P* Let] ~ ? Let *Per*

151:13 him,] ~ *Per*

151:13 decide.] decide this rather serious case. *Per see notes*

151:14 him] ~ , *Per*

151:15 dual] ~ , *Per*

151:15 a Siamese twin] Siamese twins *Per*

151:16 novel] ~ , *Per*

151:17 seriously:] ~ ; *Per*

151:20 Monsieur] M. *Per*

151:22 rest. *P* Is] ~ . Is *Per*

151:23 Oh dear, what] ~ , ~ ! What *Per*

151:23 grey *MS, A1*] gray *Per*

151:23 *Roofs, MS, A1*] Roofs", *TS* Roofs," *Per*

151:24 Proust? *P* Alas, you] ~ ? ~ ! You *Per*

151:30 absorbedly, *Per*] ~ / *MS* ~ *TS*

151:32 in Mr] of Mr. *Per*

151:32 Miss] of Miss *Per*

151:32 Monsieur] M. *Per*

151:33 "Is] ~ *Per*

151:33 the odour ... perspiration] my aura *Per*

151:34 tweed?" *P* The] ~ ? The *Per*

152:12 woollyness] woolliness *Per*

152:18 senile precocious] senile-precocious *Per*

152:19 *What*] *what TS*

152:20 And oh] ~ , ~ , *Per*

152:21 analyse] analyze *Per*

152:21 feelings,] ~ *Per*

152:22 pants] gloves *Per*

152:23 pages,] ~ *Per*

152:25 pants] gloves *Per*

152:26 with?—?"] ~ ?" *Per*

152:26 etc. etc. *TS*] etc etc. *MS* etc. *Per*

152:27 novels] novels are *Per*

152:29 trouser-button] button *Per*

152:30 reactions;] ~ : *Per*

152:30 that's ... that's] That's ... That's *Per*

152:31 *finding*] finding *A1*

152:31 —why] —Why *TS* Why *A1*

152:32 *post mortem*] *post-mortem Per* post-mortem *A1*

152:32 behaviour] behavior *Per*

152:33 the] this *TS*

152:35 done? *P* Because] ~ ? Because *Per*

152:36 it is] it's *Per*

152:39 childish. *P* The] ~ . The *Per*

153:2 sixties. *P* There] ~ ! There *Per*

153:3 a] *Om. A1*

153:5 Greys] Grey novels *Per*

153:9 novels. *P* But] ~ . But *Per*

153:11 some part ... anatomy:] her back, *Per*

153:13 on the ... anatomy] *Om. Per*

153:15 moral,] ~ *Per*

153:15 *Comes*] Comes" *TS* Comes," *Per* Comes, *A1*

153:16 oh] ~ , *Per*

153:19 dirty] *Om. Per*

153:23 heroines ... posteriors,] heroines, duly whipt, *Per* heroines, duly whipped, *A1*

153:25 gaol] jail *Per*

153:25 good] ~ , *Per*

153:26 gaol] jail *Per*

153:28 whipped *MS, A1*] whipt *Per*

153:32 loony] looney *Per*

153:33 *Son A1*] Sons *MS* Sons *TS* Son *Per*

153:33 Rose-coloured] Rose-colored *Per*

153:33 curtains—"] ~ " *Per*

153:34 breath, old hag.] breath *Per*
153:35 Future ... Novel.] future ...
        novel? *Per*
153:35 messy *MS, A1*] merry *TS* messy,
        Per
153:36 wall,] ~ *Per*
153:37 it. *P* In] ~. In *Per*
153:39 girl] ~, *Per*
153:39 sweet] ~, *Per*
153:39 aren't I] am I not *Per*
153:40 pants ... right] right glove first,
        or my left *Per*
154:2 questions, ... answers,] ~ ...
        ~ *Per*
154:3 *me*] me *A1*
154:3 though *MS, A1*] tho *Per*
154:4 whether I ... a damn] *Om. Per*
154:7 any more:] now, *Per*
154:7 though *MS, A1*] tho *Per*
154:7 to. *P* In short, the] to. The *Per*
154:9 band. I'm blind ... circus. *P*
        But] band. But *Per*
154:11 blasé] *blasé A1*
154:13 this] the *Per*
154:14 through,] ~ *Per*
154:16 motive-power] motive power *Per*
154:18 -mammy] -mamma *Per*
154:19 *What now!*] "What now?" *Per*
154:20 like] wish *Per*
154:20 in] into *Per*
154:20 *What-next?*] what-next *Per*
154:20 find the ... [154:28] it. *P* Plato's]
        go back to the Greek philoso-
        phers. Plato's *Per see note on* 154:28

154:29 Dialogues, too,] Dialogues *Per*
154:29 novels. *P* It] ~. It *Per*
154:35 again,] ~ — *Per*
154:35 And ... understanding.] *Om. Per*
154:37 things,] ~ *Per*
154:37 mankind. And] ~, and *Per*
154:38 abstraction. Even ... [155:4]
        shoes. *P* No] abstraction. No, *Per*
155:5 no, philosophy,] ~; ~ *Per*
155:6 tack; let] ~; Let *TS* ~: Let *Per*
155:6 − Y =] minus Y equals *Per*
155:7 Heaven] ~, *Per*
155:7 + Y =] plus Y equals *Per*
155:7 Earth] ~, *Per*
155:7 − X =] minus X equals *Per*
155:7 Hell. *P* Thank] ~. Thank *Per*
155:8 coloured] colored *Per*
155:9 And novels ... [155:16] Z's.]
        Om. Per
155:17 got] *Om. Per*
155:17 Its future ... know it.] *Om. Per*
155:20 new line of] line of new *Per*
155:21 old] *Om. A1*
155:23 a wall] the wall *Per*
155:26 absolutely stinkingly] suffocat-
        ingly *Per*
155:27 cosy] cozy *Per*
155:27 and then] then *Per*
155:27 course] ~, *Per*
155:28 cosy] cozy *Per*
155:29 was] were *Per*
155:29 you. *P* But] ~. But *Per*
155:30 gradually] ~. *Per*

A Britisher Has a Word With an Editor

Unless otherwise indicated the reading within the square brackets is *Per*.

159:1 an Editor] Harriett Monroe *MS*
159:2 In October's POETRY, the
        Editor tells] Miss Monroe tells
        (in October's Poetry) *MS*
159:3 one,] ~ *MS*

159:10 variety *MS*] ~, *Per*
159:13 dude" *MS*] ~," *Per*
159:14 régime *MS*] regime *Per*
159:14 Harriet] Harriett *MS*
159:16 been,] ~ *MS*

Art and Morality

The chronological sequence is *MS, TCC, Per, A1*.

163:2   part] a part *A1*
163:2   clap-trap,] ~ *Per* claptrap *A1*
163:2   Behold everywhere] ~, ~, *A1*
163:4   or at least, to] or at least to *TCC*
         or to at least *Per* or, at least, to *A1*
163:4   débourgeoiser] *débourgeoiser A1*
163:19   of *TCC*] in *MS, A1 see notes*
163:23   be,] ~ *A1*
163:23   still-life,] ~ *A1*
163:31   tablecloth *Per*] table-cloth *MS*
163:32   *behaviour MS, A1*] behaviour *Per*
164:3   slowly-formed   *TCC*]   slowly
         formed *MS, A1*
164:9   kodak] Kodak *TCC*
164:12   arms: *MS, A1*] ~; *Per*
164:13   hieroglyph, *TCC*] ~ *MS, Per*
164:13   ages,] ~ *Per*
164:16   *sees*] sees *TCC*
164:19   it: *MS, A1*] ~; *Per*
164:20   ages, *MS, A1*] ~ *Per*
164:25   Impossible! *MS, A1*] ~; *Per*
164:28   Eureka] *Eureka Per*
164:33   her.] ~? *A1*
164:35   surely! *MS, A1*] ~? *Per*
164:39   kodak-idea *Ed.*] kodak idea *MS*
         Kodak idea *A1*
165:1   dauntlessly *MS, A1*] doubtless
         Per
165:6   "a picture] ~ "~ *A1*
165:13   man, *MS, A1*] ~ *Per*
165:17   learned] learnt *A1*
165:20   existences] creatures *A1*
165:23   seen: *MS, A1*] ~; *Per*
165:27   God] god *A1*
165:30   real *MS, A1*] reals *TCC*
165:32   photographically-developed]
         photographically developed *A1*
165:39   not only are *MS, A1*] are not only
         Per
166:3   vapor] vapour *Per*
166:6   mood;] ~: *A1*
166:12   godhead] Godhead *A1*
166:16   Oh] ~, *Per*

166:16   là-là-là] *là-là-là A1*
166:16   me! *MS, A1*] ~, *Per*
166:18   apples! *MS, A1*] ~, *Per*
166:21   goose—] ~.—*TCC* ~. *A1*
166:24   approximately— *MS, A1*] ~, *Per*
166:27   All-seeing]   all-seeing   *Per*
         All-Seeing *A1*
166:32   prettyness] prettiness *Per*
166:32   kodak] Kodak *TCC*
166:35   movement] ~, *A1*
166:35   space-composition] ~, *A1*
166:40   vast] ~, *A1*
167:2   untasted] ~, *Per*
167:4   Fantin Latour's] Fantin-Latour's
         A1
167:10   universe *MS, A1*] Universe *TCC*
167:10   slowly moving *MS, A1*] moving
         slowly *Per*
167:12   forever] for ever *Per*
167:13   as far ... see. *TCC*] to us. *MS,*
         Per
167:14   Allons] *Allons Per*
167:16   do,] ~ *Per*
167:20   do,] ~ *Per*
167:23   Michael   Angelo's]   Michel-
         angelo's *A1*
167:25   light, *MS, A1*] ~ *Per*
167:32   right, *MS, A1*] ~; *Per*
167:38   even more than *TCC*] as well as
         MS, Per
168:1   negro] Negro *A1*
168:1   today *MS, A1*] to-day *Per*
168:2   big,] ~ *A1*
168:3   Rameses *MS, A1*] ~, *Per*
168:8   kodak-vision] Kodak-vision *TCC*
168:14   else: *MS, A1*] ~; *TCC*
168:16   ambiente] *ambiente A1*
168:16   law] laws *A1*
168:17   *casually*] casually *TCC*
168:21   Fantin   Latour]   Fantin-Latour
         A1
168:22   apples. But] ~; but *A1*

Morality and the Novel

The chronological sequence is *MS, TCC, Per, A1*.

171:17 measure *MS, A1*] ~, *Per*
171:24 in-between] in between *TCC*
171:28 sunflower *MS, A1*] Sunflower *TCC*
171:33 relationship,] ~ *Per*
171:33 lifeless, *MS, A1*] ~ *Per*
172:1 hawk's-head] hawk's head *Per*
172:2 and therefore *MS, A1*] ~, ~, *Per*
172:5 hawk's-head *Ed.*] hawk's head *MS*
172:10 soul," *Ed.*] ~" *MS, Per*
172:14 moon;] ~: *A1*
172:15 us. Me] ~, me *A1*
172:16 follow,] ~; *A1*
172:25 nailed down] nailed-down *Per* nailed-/ down *A1*
172:26 who *MS, A1*] Who *Per*
172:27 science,] ~ *A1*
172:27 laws *MS, A1*] ~ *Per*
172:27 they] ~, *Per*
172:29 no. *MS, A1*] ~! *Per*
172:29 complex] example *A1*
172:32 down, *MS, A1*] ~ *Per*
172:39 love:] ~, *Per*
173:1 *idea, MS, A1*] ~ *Per*
173:9 to. P All *TCC*] ~. All *MS, Per*
173:11 unestablished *MS, A1*] inestablished *Per*
173:18 made,] ~ *Per*
173:20 peace, *MS, A1*] ~ *Per*
173:22 rage, *MS, A1*] ~ *Per*
173:26 immoral] ~, *A1*
173:26 blood and thunder] blood-and-thunder *A1*
173:30 life,] ~ *Per*
173:31 know,] ~ *Per*
173:32 bank-clerk] bank clerk *Per*

173:33 dinners: *MS, A1*] ~; *Per*
173:34 fourth dimensional] fourthdimensional *TCC* fourth-dimensional *Per*
173:35 bank-clerk] bank clerk *Per*
173:40 he] it *A1*
174:1 no] not *A1*
174:9 entirely,] ~; *A1*
174:10 life," *MS, A1*] ~" *Per*
174:11 rechauffé] réchauffé *A1*
174:16 centuries, *MS, A1*] ~ *Per*
174:19 relatedness *MS, A1*] ~, *Per*
174:19 attaining:] ~; *A1*
174:21 re-acting *MS A1*] reacting *Per*
174:21 and *MS, A1*] ~, *Per*
174:23 relation, *MS, A1*] ~ *Per*
174:23 anything, *MS, A1*] ~ *Per*
174:25 connections] connexions *A1*
174:25 And *MS, A1*] ~, *Per*
174:26 things *MS, A1*] ~, *Per*
174:27 fight; *TCC*] ~, *MS, Per*
174:28 When, *MS, A1*] ~ *Per*
174:28 parties, *MS, A1*] ~ *Per*
174:32 The] the *Per*
174:32 eighteen-months] eighteen months *A1*
175:1 things: *MS, A1*] ~; *Per*
175:17 relationship, *MS, A1*] ~ *Per*
175:21 of] or *Per*
175:24 another,] ~; *A1*
175:30 Ghost] ghost *TCC*
175:37 live, *MS, A1*] ~ *Per*
176:2 hymns] ~, *A1*
176:2 *Lead Kindly Light!*] ~ ~ ~! *Per* "Lead, Kindly Light," *A1*

The Novel

The chronological sequence is *TS, A1*.

179:5 thin;——] ~; *A1*
180:3 Karenin] Karénina *A1*

180:9 officer,] ~ *A1*
180:12 their backs] backs *A1*

180:18 mingy] mangy *A1*
180:33 *Salammbô Ed.*] Salmmbô *TS*
181:11 Dialogues] *Dialogues A1*
181:24 Matthew *Ed.*] Mathew *TS*
181:26 Evangels] *Evangels A1*
181:28 Matthew *Ed.*] Mathew *TS*
181:33 passional *Ed.*] passionate *TS see notes*
181:36 there:] ~, *A1*
182:22 off] *off A1*
182:27 it is isn't *A1*] it isn't *TS see note on 182:29*
182:29 Jesusa peccante] *Jesusa peccante A1*
182:34 Old Testament] *Old Testament A1*
182:34 frère] *frére A1*
182:37 too] *too A1*

182:37 human] *human A1*
183:25 way,] ~ *A1*
183:26 Karenin] Karénina *A1*
183:35 tooth-paste *A1*] toothpaste *TS*
183:40 food] foods *A1*
184:33 set-square] set square *A1*
184:38 Sinai:—] ~: *A1*
185:34 "Oh] ~ *A1*
185:40 Laura!   "] ~! *A1*
186:38 lamb:] ~; *A1*
186:39 León] Léon *A1 see notes*
187:34 beloved] ~, *A1*
188:28 Refrain . . . on!] "~ . . . ~!" *A1*
188:29 But . . . host!] "~ . . . ~!" *A1*
189:16 universe. Multifarious] ~; multifarious *A1*
189:21 absolute. Even *Ed.*] ~: Even *TS*
          ~: even *A1 see notes*

Why the Novel Matters

The chronological sequence is *MS, A1.*

193:1   Matters *A1*] ~. *MS*
193:5   away: *Ed.*] ~/ *MS* ~, *A1*
193:9   brain?—or] ~? Or *A1*
193:10 universe,] ~ *A1*
193:13 i] *i A1*
193:19 me] *me A1*
194:1   nose:] ~, *A1*
194:7   put] find *A1*
194:9   Oh] ~, *A1*
194:36 vie.] ~! *A1*
194:40 angel cake] angel-cake *A1*
195:1   angel cake] angel-cake *A1*
195:2   was dying.] is dying: *A1*
195:3   Oh] ~, *A1*
195:4   eat. The] ~. *P* The *A1*
195:4   philosopher] ~, *A1*
195:17 therefore] ~, *A1*
195:22 philosopher] ~, *A1*
195:26 *can*] can *A1*

195:28 science] ~, *A1*
195:32 Bathsheba] Bath-Sheba *A1*
195:33 Peter;] ~: *A1*
195:35 Moses'] Moses's *A1*
195:40 that too] ~ , ~, *A1*
196:1   sets] set *A1*
196:7   my] me, *A1*
196:10 Shakespeare *A1*] Shakspeare *MS*
196:15 And] ~, *A1*
196:17 cul de sac.] *cul-de-sac. A1*
196:17 cul de sac] *cul-de-sac A1*
197:2   pepper pot] pepper-pot *A1*
197:4   myself:] ~, *A1*
197:30 honorably] honourably *A1*
197:37 live] alive *A1*
197:39 supremely] ~, *A1*
198:1   carcase] carcass *A1*
198:12 play;] ~, *A1*

The Novel and the Feelings

The chronological sequence is *MS, A1*.

201:4   most,] ~ *A1*
201:5   twingle-twingle-twang] twingle, twingle-twang *A1*
201:8   women,] ~ *A1*
201:16 ugh,] ~! *A1*
201:18 *Hamlet A1*] Hamlet *MS*
201:34 in-so-far] in so far *A1*
202:8   my self,] myself. *A1*
202:19 game hunter] game-hunter *A1*
202:26 listening in] listening-in *A1*
202:26 shutting out] shutting-out *A1*
202:39 emotions,] ~ *A1*
203:22 We] we *A1*
203:24 in-leaping] inleaping *A1*
203:31 alas,] ~! *A1*

204:6   command] commands *A1*
204:7   barb-wire] barbed wire *A1*
204:8   un-tame] un-/ tame *A1*
204:13 Yet,] ~ *A1*
204:16 precede *A1*] proceed *MS*
204:23 untame] un-tame *A1*
205:12 untame] un-tame *A1*
205:14 body,] ~ *A1*
205:14 issues] issue *A1*
205:15 words;] ~ : *A1*
205:16 honorable] honourable *A1*
205:21 tablets] tables *A1*
205:22 Timbuctoo] Timbuktu *A1*
205:23 honorable] honourable *A1*
205:34 listen in] listen-in *A1*

John Galsworthy

The chronological sequence is *MS, E1, A1*.

209:1   John Galsworthy *E1*] A Scrutiny of the Work of John Galsworthy. *MS*
209:2   Criticism] criticism *E1*
209:6   touch-stone] touchstone *E1*
209:8   style,] ~ *E1*
209:10 impertinence,] ~ *E1*
209:12 of force *E1*] of emotional force *MS*
209:16 is,] ~ *E1*
209:20 Sainte Beuve] Sainte-Beuve *A1*
209:24 of his] of the *A1*
209:29 me,] ~ *E1*
209:32 This, and this,] ~ ~ ~ *E1*
209:33 Sainte Beuve] Sainte-Beuve *A1*
209:34 man,] ~ *E1*
210:4   bias:] ~ , *E1*
210:17 purposes] purpose *E1*
210:21 Gamp,] ~ *E1*
210:24 beings,] ~ *E1*
210:29 caste,] ~ *E1*
210:31 place,] ~ *E1*
210:31 civilisation,] ~ *E1* civilization *A1*
210:33 change,] ~ *E1*

210:33 today,] to-day *E1* today *A1*
210:34 being:] ~ , *E1*
210:35 free-man's] freeman's *E1*
210:36 slave moral:] ~ ~ *E1*
210:39 naïveté *MS, A1*] *naïveté E1*
210:40 it,] ~ *E1*
210:40 faith,] ~ *E1*
211:1   naïveté *MS, A1*] *naïveté E1*
211:3   also,] ~ *E1*
211:5   living,] ~ *E1*
211:6   last,] ~ *E1*
211:8   being,] ~ *E1*
211:8   centre,] ~ *E1*
211:9   principle,] ~ *E1*
211:11 poor,] ~ *E1*
211:14 me,] ~ *E1*
211:16 him,] ~ *E1*
211:19 naïveté *MS, A1*] *naïveté E1*
211:28 man,] ~ *E1*
211:31 him,] ~ *E1*
211:32 it,] ~ *E1*
211:32 naïveté *MS, A1*] *naïveté E1*
211:38 reality,] ~ *E1*
211:38 pride;] ~ , *E1*

211:39 objective] objectives *E1*
212:2   universe,] ~ *E1*
212:2   fear,] ~ *E1*
212:3   altruist,] ~ *E1*
212:7   innocence,] ~ *E1*
212:13 materialist:] ~, *E1*
212:16 books,] ~ *E1*
212:18 and *E1*] or *MS*
212:18 them:] ~, *E1*
212:19 Mrs *Ed.*] *Om. MS see notes*
212:20 property:] ~, *E1*
212:22 fraud:] ~, *E1*
212:25 man:] ~, *E1*
212:25 *Fraternity,*] ~ *E1*
212:26 prison,] ~ *E1*
212:30 beings,] ~ *E1*
212:40 love-affair] love affair *E1*
213:4   badly] ~, *E1*
213:6   soft] ~, *E1*
213:8   of showing] showing *E1*
213:9   is,] ~ *E1*
213:16 humanly *E1*] individually *MS*
213:16 unconscious, unaware *E1*] un-
        aware, unconscious. Unaware
        MS
213:19 individual, and] ~ ~, *E1*
213:20 essentially] *essentially A1*
213:21 *essentially*] essentially *A1*
213:23 happiness;] ~, *E1*
213:23 and as] ~, ~ *E1*
213:25 today *MS, A1*] to-day *E1*
213:28 thousand,] ~ *E1*
213:37 conventions:] ~, *E1* convention,
        A1
213:37 but they cannot *E1*] they cannot
        even *MS*
213:39 tradition,] ~ *E1*
214:2   live. The] live—the *E1*
214:5   positive,] ~ *E1*
214:5   negative:] ~, *E1*
214:5   successful,] ~ *E1*
214:8   such:] ~; *E1*
214:9   lot:] ~; *E1*
214:12 background:] ~ — *E1*
214:24 it! *E1*] ~. *MS*
214:30 Bosinneys] ~, *E1*
214:30 Trees,] ~ *E1*
214:31 them,] ~ *E1*

214:38 property-hound] property hound
        E1
214:40 property-bitches]   property
        bitches *E1*
214:40 property-hounds]   property
        hounds *E1*
215:3   aunts,] ~ *E1*
215:6   money,] ~ *E1*
215:7   property-mongrel]   property
        mongrel *E1*
215:8   property-prostitute]   property
        prostitute *E1*
215:8   *Fraternity E1*] Fraternity *MS*
215:10 parasites.] ~, *E1*
215:10 little fleas] ~ ~, *E1*
215:11 *The A1*] *Om. MS*
215:13 body-parasites] body parasites *E1*
215:15 sex,] ~ *E1*
215:16 nastily *E1*] objectionally *MS*
215:24 tomorrow] to-morrow *E1* to-/
        morrow *A1*
215:27 feels,] ~ *E1*
215:27 beginning,] ~ *E1*
215:28 her:] ~, *E1*
215:29 feet,] ~ *E1*
215:30 never,] ~ *E1*
215:30 second,] ~ *E1*
215:34 him,] ~ *E1*
215:34 off. But] ~, but *E1*
215:35 quite near, *E1*] *Om. MS*
215:38 for even having *E1*] having *MS*
215:38 Apparently,] ~ *E1*
216:2   appliance:] ~, *E1*
216:6   better;] ~, *E1*
216:10 turn,] ~ *E1*
216:18 Wellsian. She] ~: she *E1*
216:23 in:] ~, *E1*
216:24 sister:] ~, *E1*
216:24 night:] ~, *E1*
216:27 lady. True] ~, true *E1*
216:33 Narcissus] ~, *A1*
216:33 Galsworthy] ~, *A1*
216:34 And,] ~ *E1*
216:34 fiction,] ~ *E1*
216:35 it!! *Ed.*] it!! *P* It brings readers,
        no doubt, among the little nar-
        cissuses and forget-me-nots of
        today. *MS* it! *E1*

217:1 God] ~, *E1*
217:3 time,] ~ *E1*
217:3 married,] ~ *E1*
217:8 so,] ~ *E1*
217:8 writer. But] ~, but *E1*
217:11 Forsyte] Forsytes *E1*
217:16 wild,] ~ *E1*
217:16 act,] ~ *E1*
217:17 hear. But] ~, but *E1*
217:18 tame. And] ~ —and *E1*
217:20 tame,] ~ *E1*
217:24 today *MS, A1*] to-day *E1*
217:31 are] ~, *E1*
217:34 better,] ~ *E1*
217:34 *antis E1*] antis *MS*
217:36 *anti E1*] anti *MS*
217:38 anything,] *Om. E1*
217:39 it:] ~ — *E1*
218:1 débâcle] debacle *E1*
218:2 decency,] ~ *E1*
218:2 way,] ~ *E1*
218:4 Winifred. But] ~, but *E1*
218:5 *The A1*] *Om. MS*
218:6 show.—] ~: *E1*
218:7 road———] ~ *E1*
218:9 road:——] ~: ... *E1*
218:12 on.——] ~ *E1*
218:12 Suddenly] ~, *E1*
218:14 that,] ~ *E1*
218:16 ———— Nine] ... ~ *E1* —~ *A1*
218:17 side-track *MS*] side-/ track *E1* sidetrack *A1*
218:20 time,] ~ *E1*
218:23 high-road] high road *E1*
218:24 hedge,] ~ *E1*
218:25 *anti E1*] anti *MS*
218:25 excursions. From] ~, from *E1*
218:26 comfort,] ~ *E1*
218:26 ten:] ~; *E1*
218:26 bog:] ~; *E1*
218:30 bus *MS, A1*] '~ *E1*
218:31 *anti; Ed.*] anti; *MS* anti! *E1* anti! *A1*
218:31 sidetracking *MS, A1*] side-tracking *E1*

218:32 see. *P* Because] ~. Because, *E1*
218:34 high-way] highway *E1*
218:35 Sidetracking *MS, A1*] Side-tracking *E1*
218:37 canyon] cañon *A1*
218:37 then] ~, *E1*
218:37 exploring. *P* But] ~. But *E1*
218:39 high-way] highway *E1*
219:2 unconvention] unconventions *E1*
219:4 *anti E1*] anti *MS*
219:4 unconventional,"*E1*] ~." *MS*
219:4 and leaving ... behind. *E1*] *Om. MS*
219:6 *The A1*] *Om. MS*
219:8 high-way,] highway *E1*
219:10 explosions] explosion *E1*
219:10 fizzled *E1*] fizzed *MS*
219:11 before *E1*] we were before *MS*
219:13 early *E1*] four early *MS see notes*
219:15 books,] ~ *E1*
219:16 end of] ~, ~ *E1*
219:17 money, and] ~ ~ *E1*
219:18 *anti E1*] anti *MS*
219:21 Galsworthy's] Galsworthy *E1*
219:24 meanness *E1*] meannesses *MS*
219:25 and more treacherous *E1*] *Om. MS*
219:26 mechanical] ~, *E1*
219:31 just *E1*] mere *MS*
219:33 self-will:—] ~, *E1*
219:33 wonder, sometimes,] ~ ~ *E1*
219:39 And] and *E1*
220:2 *anti E1*] anti *MS*
220:3 the cynicism ... sentimentalist, *E1*] cynicism piled on cynicism, *MS*
220:7 then] ~, *E1*
220:8 it and ... cynic. *E1*] it. *MS*
220:9 genuine,] ~ *E1*
220:10 up."] ~"? *E1*
220:12 happened,] ~ *E1*
220:13 But it ... in it. *E1*] *Om. MS*
220:14 Vulgarity *E1*] But vulgarity *MS*
220:22 hose-pipe] hosepipe *E1*
220:28 slime,] ~ *E1*

Appendix I: Art and The Individual

The chronological sequence is *MS, O1*.

223:6 something,] ~ — *O1*
223:6 not!] ~? *O1*
223:9 Hub] hub *O1*
223:9 Universe] universe *O1*
223:10 Education] education— *O1*
223:11 specialise.] ~? *O1*
223:11 strong] ~, *O1*
223:13 tooth-puller] tooth puller *O1*
223:13 socialism,] Socialism *O1*
223:15 'one talent,'] ~ ~, *O1*
223:19 Education ... Education] education ... education *O1*
223:21 character."— *Ed.*] ~ "— *MS* ~." *O1*
223:22 experts] expert *O1*
223:28 of,] ~ *O1*
223:28 acquaintance with, *Ed.*] ~, ~, *MS* ~ ~ *O1*
223:30 in meeting] of meeting *O1*
223:31 ourselves—the] ~. The *O1*
223:31 sympathy;] ~, *O1*
223:32 words,] ~ *O1*
223:32 *many sided*] *many-sided O1*
223:34 overlooked:—] ~. *O1*
224:4 intellectual] Intellectual *O1*
224:9 emotional] Emotional. *O1*
224:11 Action] Action. *O1*
224:12 Empirical:—Int[erest] *Ed.*] ~: —Int. *MS* EMPIRICAL: *P* Interest *O1*
224:16 flowers)x] ~). *O1*
224:17 Speculative—int[erest] that *Ed.*] ~—int. that *MS* SPECULATIVE: *P* Interest *O1*
224:18 int[erest]s. (It *Ed.*] ints. (It *MS* interests (it *O1*
224:20 flowers)] ~). *O1*
224:21 Aesthetic—Int[erest] *Ed.*] Aesthetic—Int. *MS* AESTHETIC: *P* Interest *O1*
224:21 or] nor *O1*
224:24 moonlight] moon-light *O1*
224:26 Sympathetic.] SYMPATHETIC: *O1*

224:27 Social—growing] ~: Growing *O1*
224:31 complex] complete *O1*
224:32 Religious—when] RELIGIOUS: *P* When *O1*
224:38 developed,] ~ *O1*
225:1 3—...6—] 3,—...6,— *O1*
225:1 planes] ~. *O1*
225:1 and examples *Ed.*] & examples *MS Om. O1*
225:4 (Consider)—The] ~—the *O1*
225:7 definition;] ~, *O1*
225:7 (of phenomena) *Ed.*] (of phenoma) *MS Om. O1*
225:9 Harmony."] ~' *O1*
225:11 hear or see] see or hear *O1*
225:14 Aesthetic] aesthetic *O1*
225:16 Adaptability] adaptability *O1*
225:16 to *O1*] in *MS*
225:17 comprehensible, *O1*] ~ *MS*
225:17 hence] more *O1*
225:19 glad. Why?] ~ —why? *O1*
225:23 aesthetic] Aesthetic *O1*
225:25 Art—Beauty,] ~. ~ *O1*
225:25 *Idea*] Idea *O1*
225:25 (discuss Platonic 'Idea')] *Om. O1*
225:26 idea] Idea *O1*
225:26 Hegel] ~, *O1*
225:28 Art *O1*] "~ *MS*
225:28 kingdom,] ~ *O1*
225:30 *Introd[uce] ... fop*] Introd. the ... *fop MS*
225:31 —and *Ed.*] —& *MS* and *O1*
225:32 color] colour *O1*
225:32 sound] sounds *O1*
225:33 emotions] emotion *O1*
225:35 fitted] filled *O1*
225:35 impressions] imression *O1*
225:36 advantage. / In] ~. *P* "In *O1*
226:1 —Approval] —approval *O1*
226:3 Harmony—] ~ *O1*
226:5 us.] ~? *O1*
226:5 answer. Turn] ~. *P* "Turn *O1*
226:6 *Adaptation*] Adaptation *O1*

226:8   leads] lead *O1*
226:15 quaint,] ~ *O1*
226:16 bird] ~, *O1*
226:17 ugly.] ~? *O1*
226:21 to.] ~? *O1*
226:25 Often,] ~ *O1*
226:26 'Song *O1*] ~ *MS*
226:27 Watts' *O1*] Watt's *MS*
226:27 'Mammon' *Ed.*] ~ *MS*
226:27 art),] Art) *O1*
226:27 'Laocoon,' *Ed.*] ~, *MS*
226:28 'Outcasts' *Ed.*] ~ *MS*
226:28 Fildes *Ed.*] Filde *MS*
226:29 these.] ~? *O1*
226:29 pleasurable' feeling. *Ed.*] ~' ~'.
        MS ~ feelings?' *O1*
226:30 say "They] ~, '~ *O1*
226:31 true." *Ed.*]~" *MS* ~.' *O1*
226:33 well, perhaps,] ~ ~ *O1*
226:34 more,] ~ *O1*
226:37 ideas,] *Om. O1*
226:37 judgments] ~, *O1*
226:38 Art. When] ~. *P* "When *O1*
226:38 Hero] hero *O1*
226:40 Mahommet *O1*] Mahammet *MS*
227:1   Burns—] ~,— *O1*
227:3   art] Art *O1*
227:3   a] *Om. O1*
227:8   words, *O1*] ~ *MS*
227:8   voice, *O1*] ~ *MS*
227:11 words,] ~ — *O1*
227:11 "flash!" "*laughter*" "wonder".]
        '~', 'laughter', '~'. *O1*
227:12 French] ~, *O1*
227:13 essence, then,] ~ ~ *O1*
227:17 definitions] definition *O1*
227:19 art] Art *O1*
227:19 as] to *O1*
227:20 art] Art *O1*
227:20 good—] ~, *O1*
227:20 Tolstoi *O1*] Tolstoy *MS*
227:21 art.] ~ — *O1*
227:26 sentence, in *Ed.*] ~, ~, *MS* ~
        ~ *O1*

227:31 ridiculous. Why] ~ —~ *O1*
227:35 Tolstoi ... tales.] *Om. O1*
227:40 Watts' *O1*] Watt's *MS*
228:1   Look—!] look! *O1*
228:1   (*Suggestion)] *Om. O1*
228:2   appreciate] ~, *O1*
228:3   "The ... Art"] '~ ... art,' *O1*
228:3   Hume "is] ~, '~ *O1*
228:4   temper,] ~ *O1*
228:6   *habit.*" If] ~.' *P* "If *O1*
228:8   at once] *Om. O1*
228:10 socialism] Socialism *O1*
228:11 art] Art *O1*
228:13 a] *Om. O1*
228:15 to recognise,] *Om. O1*
228:17 forever] for ever *O1*
228:17 universe] ~, *O1*
228:22 read. *P* Emotion] ~. Emotion
        O1
228:23 action—drawing etc.] action.
        O1
228:24 socialism] Socialism *O1*
228:26 all,] ~ *O1*
228:26 man's *O1*] Mans *MS*
228:28 hosts of] host of the *O1*
228:29 character,] ~ *O1*
228:30 Art] art *O1*
228:31 general. Think. We] ~. *P*
        "Think, we *O1*
228:32 neck *O1*] Neck *MS*
228:32 Naomi;] ~, *O1*
228:33 We,] ~ *O1*
228:34 Jonathan *O1*] Johnathan *MS*
228:34 But there] There *O1*
228:35 and only *O1*] And only *MS*
228:36 Mediaeval] medieval *O1*
228:37 moon-faced] moon faced *O1*
228:39 those] these *O1*
228:40 common-place] commonplace
        O1
229:8   book—] ~, *O1*
229:8   Essay] essay *O1*
229:10 might,] ~ *O1*
229:11 a painting] painting *O1*

Appendix IV: John Galsworthy

The chronological sequence is *MS, A1*.

249:12 things] living things *A1*
249:32 me ... you ... it] "~" ... "~"
     ... "~" *A1*
250:8 mysterious,] ~; *A1*
250:21 consciousness]   Consciousness
    A1
250:26 you," *A1*] ~", *MS*
250:28 me ... you ... it] *me ... you ...*
    it A1

250:39 god's] God's *A1*
251:27 Ex nihilo nihil fit! *Ed.*] Ex nihil
    nihil fit! *MS Ex nihilo nihil fit! A1*
251:32 Ex nihilo ... fit.] *Ex nihilo ...*
    fit! A1
251:39 doggishly] doggedly *A1*
252:1 innocent] ~, *A1*
252:3 soft] soft and *A1*

Of the compound words which are hyphenated at the end of a line in this edition, only the following hyphenated forms should be retained in quotation:

7:21	self-preservation	164:2	hard-boiled
13:17	self-preservation	166:1	sun-dazed
14:5	second-rate	166:27	All-seeing
14:16	cabbage-patch	172:29	inter-relatedness
15:4	sex-degraded	183:28	would-be-expiatory
15:6	sex-degraded	195:33	Man-alive
18:40	self-preservation	197:5	lamp-post
26:18	thought-worn	202:10	snow-white
47:38	arch-sinner	202:16	hymn-book
59:36	Will-to-Motion	203:24	in-leaping
63:26	self-sufficient	211:33	universe-continuum
70:10	God-idea	212:6	at-oneness
102:17	deep-feeling	212:12	anti-materialist
103:10	Woman-reverence	214:40	property-hounds
108:10	self-conscious	233:22	table-cloth
110:23	ultra-Christian	233:23	life-like
120:21	to-day	236:2	picture-frame
138:15	Jehovah-shape	236:6	space-composition
141:12	battle-piece	241:15	in-between
141:36	leopard-skin-clad	242:17	motor-cars
151:29	long-drawn-out		

Lightning Source UK Ltd.
Milton Keynes UK
21 December 2009

147833UK00001B/29/A